ARE YOU HAPPY NOW

Readers are loving Yun, Emory, Andrew and Fin's story . . .

'A quietly crushing yet devastatingly tender work filled
with insight and emotional intelligence'
★ ★ ★ ★ ★

'Her prose brought to mind Hanya Yanagihara,
Donna Tartt and Scott Spencer'
★ ★ ★ ★ ★

'This book was honestly so incredible and a massive mind f**k . . . a
great social study of the psyche of millennials right now'
★ ★ ★ ★ ★

'Where this book comes alive is the main characters. They are
incredibly real – honest, compelling but deeply flawed like us all'
★ ★ ★ ★ ★

'Literary fiction with just a hint of something almost sci-fi.
The pandemic isn't the focus, the people are, and there's some
great commentary in there about how society treats the afflicted.
This is definitely my number one read of 2023 so far'
★ ★ ★ ★ ★

'I adored this novel just as much as I did Jameson's last novel
The Last. The characters were three-dimensional, and an ever-present
sense of dread kept the story taut with anxiety. So good!'
★ ★ ★ ★ ★

'This book was honestly phenomenal . . . I think
I am going to go away and write a thesis'
★ ★ ★ ★ ★

'I was stunned by thi
★ ★ ★ ★ ★

T0322170

Acclaim for *Are You Happy Now* . . .

'The novel is compared with *Never Let Me Go*, but rather
than the long, achy aftertaste of Ishiguro, there is a
harder edge, more tannin on the tongue'
Irish Times

'This intense, twisty and beautifully written narrative is
especially wonderful on the two couples navigating the beginning
of their relationships against the backdrop of the possible end of
humanity. This book is thought-provoking and unique'
Daily Mail

'Yun, Emory, Andrew and Fin are all searching for their own versions
of happiness in this dark, addictive novel set in New York'
Red

'Mixing nihilism with vulnerability, it'll leave you asking
yourself: if you could give up on life, would you?'
Stylist

'Jameson explores how you live through a crisis caused
by the terrible hand your generation has been dealt'
Grazia

'A conversation-starting exploration of the way we live in the
modern age, bringing an original concept to life with
warmth, empathy and anger in equal measure'
Daily Express

'Timely and astute . . . a gripping, naturalistic and
strangely hopeful read'
Mirror

'Clever and insightful'
Woman's Weekly

ARE YOU HAPPY NOW

HANNA JAMESON

PENGUIN BOOKS

PENGUIN BOOKS

UK | USA | Canada | Ireland | Australia
India | New Zealand | South Africa

Penguin Books is part of the Penguin Random House group of companies
whose addresses can be found at global.penguinrandomhouse.com.

First published by Viking 2023
Published in Penguin Books 2023
003

Copyright © Hanna Jameson, 2023

The moral right of the copyright holders has been asserted

From *All Of Us: The Collected Poems* by Raymond Carver, published by Harvill Press.
Copyright © Raymond Carver 1997. Reprinted by permission of The Random House Group Ltd.

The publisher is grateful to the following for the use of: on page 171, Reddit share button based on
noun-share-4184102; on page 202, Weibo comment based on noun-speech-bubble-1072940; on page 202,
Weibo share based on noun-share-4184102; on page 202, Weibo like by noun-like-button-3182359; on
page 291, Curious cat like by noun-love-4781864; on page 291 Curious cat comment based on
noun-quote-4763644; on page 291, Curious cat share based on noun-home-424780.

Typeset by Jouve (UK), Milton Keynes
Printed and bound in Great Britain by Clays Ltd, Elcograf S.p.A.

The authorized representative in the EEA is Penguin Random House Ireland,
Morrison Chambers, 32 Nassau Street, Dublin D02 YH68

A CIP catalogue record for this book is available from the British Library

ISBN: 978-0-241-99263-0

www.greenpenguin.co.uk

This is dedicated to the countless people who publish stories for free online. Your enthusiasm, talent and support for each other's work is what continues to make me a better writer.

Yun and Emory

'But depression wasn't the word. This was a plunge
encompassing sorrow and revulsion far beyond the personal:
a sick, drenching nausea at all humanity and human
endeavor from the dawn of time.'

– Donna Tartt, *The Goldfinch*

I.

Boy meets girl at a wedding and the world ends. The classic meet-cute.

Yun's memories of the wedding were malleable, different parts of that night in late April shifting into brighter and greater significance, like raking through coloured sand. The DJ wore a red baseball cap and ill-fitting blazer, and started his set with a drinking game to 'Roxanne'. Whenever Sting sang 'Roxanne' all the women took a drink. Whenever he sang 'put on the red light' all the men took a drink. It was an efficient strategy; got everyone the maximum amount of drunk in the minimum amount of time.

Over the DJ's incessant hollering and grainy speakers, Yun caught snatches of conversation at the next table, between three guys he vaguely remembered from NYU.

'Yeah yeah yeah, that's the dream though, isn't it,' one of them said. 'Just take the consultancy money and fuck off to, like, Taiwan for a year.'

'Get tan, teach English for, like, four hours a day and bang foreign girls.'

The only other person Yun knew well at this thing was his best friend, Andrew Zhou, who looked about as immaculate as one would expect from the only son of a wealthy Chinese-Canadian family. He was over by the bar arguing with his wife, both of them adopting the low, strained voices of people who had been together too long.

Yun couldn't blame her for wanting to leave early. The only reason he and Andrew used to get on with Mike Ellison – who was already cataclysmically wasted along with his bride – was because he always had a steady and shareable supply of pot. Mike's friends from Economics had mostly seemed like budding serial killers or, at the very least, flag-waving white nationalists waiting to happen. From what Yun could tell, they mostly spent their studies presenting graphs explaining why the majority of people in the world deserved to starve, actually.

He had a joint in his pocket but he wasn't planning to go outside and smoke it unless the night became truly unbearable. He looked at his phone, then cast his eyes about, noticing some older relatives talking to each other, a few younger women scattered around the room who seemed forlorn. It was ten p.m. and heels were already being taken off on the dance floor.

A lot of the charm of weddings is in their clichés. The house lights were a little too bright, giving the venue a warehouse aesthetic. There was even a chocolate fountain. Yun grimaced as the DJ yelled, 'Ladies, make some noooooise!' But he also acknowledged that people like him – single people conspicuously refusing to enjoy themselves, as well as the couples having quiet altercations – were as much of a cliché as the rest of it.

A microcosm of happy ignorance, like a scene in a snow globe.

Another eruption of obnoxious laughter from the next table. Waiting staff started to clear dessert plates and empty glasses while the DJ messed up a transition, moving from one song to another with halts and gaps, which he tried to cover with a 'We all feeling good tonight?'

Scrolling through the news cycle on his phone, restraining his displeasure to a slight shake of the head, Yun glanced at the dance floor and saw her looking at him. She was wearing a dress the colour of peaches, slow-dancing with Lara – the bride – who was leaning against her shoulder in a delighted drunken haze.

Maybe she hadn't been looking at Yun at all, and they just happened to catch each other's eyes. Maybe he was flattering himself to think about it that way. But the way he remembered it, she was already smiling.

He looked back at his phone, but he wasn't seeing it.

When his gaze flicked back up, she wasn't looking at him any more. Lara was saying something and she laughed. He saw her exchange a look with one of the waiters; a young guy with black, slicked-back hair who was smirking to himself.

The song changed. The Killers. Another terrible transition, and Yun began to think more seriously about leaving. He found himself scrolling through the news again but felt no corresponding emotion.

'You don't like The Killers?'

He turned and there she was, sitting in the chair next to him.

His expression of mild surprise made her laugh. She'd had more to drink than he had but wasn't as far gone as the rest of them. Her eyes were distractingly blue, and her smile was sincere and imperfect in a way he found interesting.

'I don't like *him*.' He inclined his head at the DJ.

She raised her eyebrows. 'And you could do better?'

'I was Mike's first choice to DJ.' He put his phone on the table face down. 'So I could, actually.'

'Prove it.' When she smiled again, he noticed her canines were slightly elongated.

'I don't wanna drag you away,' he said, gesturing at the dance floor.

'I don't mind. I'm Emory Schafer, by the way.' She leaned forward to read the name written on his place card. 'And you're . . . Yun?'

She pronounced it like *sun*.

'*Yun*,' he corrected her, rhyming it with *soon*. 'It's Korean. It's *Dan* Yun, really. Daniel Yun. But . . . who'd remember a DJ called Dan?'

One stolen bottle of bourbon later and they found themselves in the vacated ballroom on the lower floor of the hotel. Yun switched on the lights inside the doorway. It looked like there had been another party earlier, but there hadn't been a chance to clear up yet. Green and pink decorations lay across tables, empty champagne flutes. A grand piano in the far corner.

Emory preceded him inside, holding the bourbon, looking at the high ceilings and festive debris with wide-eyed awe, like someone walking through a forest.

'So they hired the smaller room,' Yun remarked, surprised by how large the space was compared to the one they'd just left. He looked at the crystal doorknobs and estimated that each one was worth a decent percentage of his rent. He added, 'I'm not saying I could afford either . . .'

'Lara hates being around too many people.' She glanced over her shoulder as he made his way to the piano and sat down.

6

He started playing a tune that fell into time with her steps. When she noticed, she laughed in a way that made him laugh too; a nervous laugh that didn't feel like his own.

'You clearly weren't busy tonight,' she said, with another look over her shoulder. 'So why aren't you DJ-ing?'

'I told him I didn't have time to put a playlist together. Though honestly, we just don't have the same taste in music.' He spread his hands, aware he was coming off as a snob. 'I think he felt like he then had to invite me to be polite.'

When Emory came to join him, finally, she had several items collected in her dress, which – she was excited to tell him – also had pockets. The bottle of bourbon *thunked* on the top of the piano, and she shifted on to the stool. The ruffles of her dress were gathered up like some rural, historical woman who'd been collecting berries, and her knee was touching his.

'So you're a musician?'

'Mostly. I produce too. What did you find?'

'Thirty cents.' She placed the coins carefully on top of the piano.

'Amazing.'

'Two lighters.'

'Always useful.'

'A spork.'

'Genius invention.' He was smiling, too much. *Calm down.* 'Great name.'

'And someone left this.' She held up a crucifix on a thin gold chain that caught the light.

'You're not some weird Christian, are you?'

A mock frown as she took a gulp of bourbon. 'I like to think of myself as a *non*-weird Christian, thank you.'

He took the bottle from her and also drank. It was overly sweet. 'I like to think of myself as a *don't know*.'

'You're agnostic.'

'I thought that was more *don't care*.' He played another tune. Something upbeat.

'Can you put this on for me?' She held up the necklace again. 'I've got whiskey-hands.'

He took it from her and she turned on the stool, brushing her long, white-blonde hair over one shoulder before gathering it up in her hands. He was suddenly extremely aware of his breathing. It wasn't always this overwhelming when someone made it clear they wanted something from him. But Emory's attention felt overwhelming.

He encircled her neck with the chain, and after fastening the catch he looked for a long time at the pale, exposed skin at the nape of her neck.

The air between them pulled tight, like a length of rope.

A phone vibrated. The rope slackened. She let her hair fall and took her phone out of her pocket.

Yun pretended to be absorbed with playing something on the piano, but wasn't thinking about the music so much as occupying his hands, masking some mild annoyance.

She said, 'Lara's noticed I'm gone.'

And the moment was over, he thought, as she stood. She looked at his hands, still resting on the keys. 'You're really good at that.'

'Oh, I've only been playing – my whole life.'

It took him a few seconds to follow her, and by the time he caught up she was in the doorway. Voices approached. One of the waiters – the one with the slicked-back hair – followed by a young, delicate-looking man from the wedding upstairs who Yun didn't know.

'Do you often do this at weddings?' the young man asked.

'More than you'd think.' The waiter pushed a rattling, clinking trolley full of empty glasses.

One couple glanced at the other as they passed in the quiet, dimly lit corridor. Yun met the young man's eyes, and no one said anything.

He walked with Emory towards the stairwell. They knocked shoulders briefly, he smiled, and then she stopped so abruptly he had to turn back to meet her exasperated expression.

She said, 'Are you going to kiss me or what?'

He laughed, and immediately wished he hadn't. It wasn't cool.

'Ah,' he said, because it was all he could manage.

First, he stooped to put the bottle of whiskey on the floor. He took a step forward and she took a step back, until she was standing against the wall. Unsure of what to do with his hands, he took another step to lean them on the wall either side of her, and then she closed the space between them.

It was as if he'd fallen into his own body from a huge height. He kissed her gently. She kissed him back less gently. He could taste the bourbon as she pulled him closer, hands under his jacket. He was touching her face, then her hair. Pressed against the wall, he felt her shiver in his arms, let out a sigh against his lips.

A *clunk* from close by made them both jump; the sound of a glass hitting the ground.

Emory laughed. 'We should get back.'

He didn't want to. He wanted to kiss her again and was leaning in when a gasp, or maybe more of a sigh, came from further down the corridor. They took that as their cue to go.

Yun walked a little behind Emory in the stairwell, then she was lost to the onslaught and noise of the wedding party.

Realizing they had left the bottle of whiskey downstairs, Yun went to the bar and found Andrew drinking a lime and soda alone. Looking over his shoulder, he saw Emory talking to Lara, who glanced with pointed interest in his direction.

'Where's Nicola?' Yun asked, though he never wanted to know.

It's not that he disliked her, but her presence had recently started to bring out the worst in her husband, and likewise Andrew brought out the worst in her.

'She called a car.' Andrew waved at the bartender and ordered Yun a beer. 'It's all right, I can still drive you home.'

'I thought you guys were in therapy?'

'We are. The only conclusion we've come to is we're not good at being in the same room.'

Yun wasn't sure what to say, so he put a hand on Andrew's shoulder and drank in solidarity. He searched for Emory, but she was dancing and wasn't looking for him.

At some point later in the night, someone else who Yun didn't know punched his boyfriend in the face. They were separated by a bleary-eyed Mike and a couple of other guys, and Yun was vaguely aware that the young man left clutching his eye was the same man he had seen in the downstairs hallway with the waiter.

The new sound was hard to distinguish at first over the music, the men who were still shouting. But Yun was sure he heard a woman scream, and he craned his neck towards a small group – Emory and Lara among them – gathered in a knot around someone on the floor.

The screaming stopped momentarily. Yun glanced at Andrew, who shrugged but also moved to take a closer look. It didn't strike Yun as anything to worry about, not in the context of expected wedding dramas. But all the same, it was curious. The young woman in the teal dress appeared to have sat down, right in the middle of the dance floor.

Someone waved a hand in front of her face, having to yell over 'I Believe' by Stevie Wonder. 'Rose? Rose!'

'The perils of a free bar,' a man behind Yun remarked.

Andrew had gone, and Yun noticed him talking to the young man with the swollen eye, whose assailant was now nowhere to be seen. Yet another thing that only gained significance with time.

Emory took both of Rose's hands and gently pulled, but as soon as she exerted enough force to threaten to bring her to her feet, Rose snatched herself out of Emory's grasp with what could only be described as a snarl. Her face was contorted, teeth bared. Only when she was free did her expression slacken once again. Her eyes, though, those were blank. Even while her body wrenched itself away, Rose's eyes never focused on anything.

'Rose, snap out of it!' Lara was less patient. It was her wedding, after all. 'Come on, how much have you had to drink?'

'Are you sure she's okay?' Another woman hovered behind Lara, like she didn't want to venture too close. 'She looks . . . weird.'

Everyone was talking over each other, and Yun found it amusing that no one considered telling the DJ to turn the music down.

'Rose! Can you walk?' Lara tried pulling her up, a lot rougher than Emory.

Then came the screaming again. Even in the midst of so much noise, it made Yun take a step back. It was angry and distressed, like an animal caught in a hunting trap, and it made Lara let go immediately.

'She can't get on the subway like this.' Emory touched Lara's arm. 'Shouldn't we try and take her to the ER?'

Lara exclaimed, 'Well I can't, I'm *fucked*.'

'I can drive, if you want?'

Yun was hoping Andrew wouldn't offer. He was Yun's ride home, and leaving now meant leaving without speaking to Emory again. But of course he offered. Andrew, with his pristine haircut, open face and eternal obliviousness to how he made most women lose their minds.

He even carried Rose to his car, and when she was being carried she didn't scream or fight back. The outro to 'I Believe' was still playing while she hung pliant in Andrew's arms. Her gaze didn't land on anyone or anything, but when another of her friends tried to make her drink some water she jerked away as the glass was pressed to her lips.

Yun left his beer on a random table and tried to catch Emory's eyes, but her gaze never found him again. As he left, he wondered why he always seemed destined to be slightly too far ahead or too far behind his own life.

In the car, Yun sat in the front next to Andrew, and tried not to look into the back seat.

Every so often, Rose's friend, Michelle, would try to get her attention. 'Rose! Rose, can you just answer me?' – clicking her fingers in front of her face, clapping her hands – 'Can you drink something? Can you just . . . say *something*?'

As they pulled into the parking lot across from the ER, Michelle started weeping with frustration and didn't stop. Andrew helped her carry Rose into the hospital while Yun waited in the car. When he returned, he took a moment before starting the engine.

'It's strange,' he said softly. 'I don't think I've seen anyone that out of it before.'

'Maybe it was that stupid drinking game.'

'Maybe someone put something in her drink. Nicola said she had her drink spiked once and it just wipes you out. One minute you're fine and the next you don't even know where you are. Total blackout.'

Yun shrugged. He was getting a headache and didn't want to go home. He had looked at the girl in the back of the car and wished he could feel genuine concern, but all he felt was dehydrated. Being driven through New York at night always made him melancholy.

Andrew kept staring unseeingly at the entrance to the ER like someone else trapped by their own relentless trajectory, like he wasn't driving his own car, and Yun realized they were still sitting there because he didn't want to go home either.

2.

Emory woke at two in the afternoon in her tiny Greenpoint apartment, and messaged Rose twice in the time it took a couple of painkillers to dissolve in a glass of water. By the sounds of it her room-mates were, thankfully, all out. When she received no response – the messages unread – she went back to bed and held the phone above her face to message Michelle.

Michelle called back immediately.

Looking at the incoming call like an act of aggression, Emory repressed the urge to ignore it. 'Hey, what's going on?'

Michelle's voice was cracked, like she hadn't slept or had anything to drink. 'I'm still at the hospital.'

'*What?* Is Rose okay?'

'No, she's really not. They don't know what's wrong with her. I found her parents in her emergency contacts and I'm still waiting for them to get here.' A sigh, and Michelle sounded on the verge of tears when she said, 'They live in Columbus. It's going to take them nine hours to drive.'

Emory dragged herself upright. 'Did someone spike her drink or something?'

'That's what the doctors thought. But when that happens you just sleep it off, right? She's still exactly the same. I can't get her to say *anything*, I can't even get her to look at me. It's . . .' Her voice broke. 'It's scary, I don't know what to do.'

'Which hospital are you at? I'll come wait with you. Did you message Lara?'

'No. Do you think I should?'

Emory swung her legs out of bed and willed the pain-killers to kick in. 'Actually, let's not bother her unless we have to.'

'Do you think she took a bad pill?'

'Rose?' It was hard to concentrate on the conversation while struggling to get her legs into a pair of pants. 'I don't think so. Was anyone on anything last night?'

'Honestly, I was too drunk to notice.' Michelle sniffed. 'Maybe I shouldn't have got so out of it, I'd have been able to check on her.'

'We were all out of it, it isn't anyone's fault.' Emory wedged the phone between her shoulder and chin to put on a shirt. 'Unless someone *did* spike her drink, in which case we'll find out who it was. Do you want me to bring you coffee?'

'Oh God, can you? The coffee here *sucks*. Also maybe a spare toothbrush?'

While on the subway Emory searched the side-effects of different date-rape drugs, and realized with a dull, sinking feeling – which may have also been the hangover – that Rose's symptoms were too general to reach any solid conclusions, or start suspecting any specific men who had been in attendance. Most confusingly, she couldn't find any cases of people becoming violent after having their drinks spiked. Those drugs usually removed the capacity to fight back against manhandling; that was the point. But Rose had been able to fight just fine.

She didn't know Rose that well compared to the rest of

Lara's work friends, couldn't remember the last time she had hung out with them. They were all into coke – a finance thing – but it was hard to imagine anyone spiking a drink with it.

Two blocks from the hospital, Emory ducked into a cafe to buy two oat-milk lattes, extra hot, and two grilled breakfast sandwiches.

Michelle was half sitting, half lying across the chairs in the waiting area when Emory arrived. She was still wearing her burgundy wrap dress from the night before, her jacket and a pair of Crocs that were several sizes too big. Her heels were on the floor.

'What are *those*?' Emory gestured at the ridiculous shoes.

'Staff Crocs.' As Michelle stood up to hug her, she muttered, 'I told them you're her sister. I thought they might tell you something.'

'Have you looked through her bag?'

'Yeah, nothing.' Michelle took a long gulp of coffee and scraped at the dried mascara under her eyes with her thumbnail. 'Thank God she had her insurance info on her.'

Emory took the black clutch and sat down to rifle through it. Phone, lipstick, keys, portable charger, wallet. Nothing in the wallet either, aside from some store cards and her emergency information.

'So she's still *exactly* the same?' Emory looked up as Michelle slumped into the chair next to her again. 'Did she sleep?'

'Not that I noticed. I slept a couple of hours so I guess she might have slept at the same time.' She shook her head. 'They said they had to strap her down to get the IV in because she wouldn't drink anything without going crazy.

Like, she's totally unresponsive but freaks out when anyone tries to get her to do *anything*.'

Emory stood up, leaving the sandwiches next to Michelle. 'I'm going to ask them what's going on, see if I can find out anything else. It's Rose *Hailey*, right?'

With another quick scan of Rose's driver's licence, Emory walked up to the desk and asked where her sister's room was. It was another ten minutes before a doctor came – a woman with long braids and a calming tone – and escorted her down the corridor.

'The good news,' the doctor explained as they walked, 'is that she *is* responsive to certain stimuli, even if the outbursts do sound and appear distressing. We were told she was drinking but obviously this isn't a common response to alcohol so I wanted to ask, did you know of your sister ever taking recreational drugs?'

'Nothing heavy, I don't think. Maybe some coke at parties.'

'I've only seen comparable reactions to certain types of methamphetamines. Or synthetic cathinones like bath salts. You may have heard of them?'

Emory almost laughed, and stifled it quickly. 'No. No way. Who takes meth at a wedding?'

'Has Rose ever suffered from depression or any other mental illness?'

'Not that I know of.' She swallowed, beginning to feel uneasy. 'Can I see her now?'

'In a moment.' They had paused outside a door. 'Has Rose ever suffered from blackouts or psychotic episodes?'

'You mean like schizophrenia? I really have no idea.'

'If the blood tests don't offer anything conclusive, I'd like to send her for an MRI as a next step, to see if the problem is neurological. We've given her a sedative to calm her down, so she's been sleeping. You're free to talk to her, but she is restrained for her own safety. Try not to worry, she is comfortable.'

'Has she said anything to you at all?'

The doctor pulled a face that Emory didn't like. 'She hasn't been responding to instructions, and was also unresponsive to a basic cranial nerve examination.'

'What does that mean?'

'Her pupils show signs of light sensitivity, she's capable of blinking, her pupils dilate. She just won't focus on a light or follow it when instructed, which is reminiscent of catatonic states. So if she does have a history of depressive episodes, it would be useful to know.'

When the doctor finally left, Emory took a seat next to Rose's bed. She messaged Michelle so she could update Rose's parents. It was only when several minutes had passed, and Emory was still looking at her phone, that she realized she was delaying looking directly at her.

She reached forward and took her hand. 'Rose?'

Rose didn't open her eyes. Her fingers were bone cold.

Emory tried to remember how she'd ended up sitting in the middle of the dance floor. Emory had come back to the party with that guy, gossiped with Lara, some other guy had punched his boyfriend, and by the time anyone noticed Rose she was already on the floor.

Careful not to let go of Rose's hand, Emory made a note in her phone to check if anyone had been filming or taking photos. Maybe someone had witnessed the moment it happened.

'Rose?' She tried again a little louder, squeezing her hand. Still nothing.

Standing up, Emory brushed some of Rose's hair out of her face and tentatively opened one of her eyes with her thumb. Rose couldn't lash out, but she didn't look at her either. Emory wondered if she would fight back if she tried to make her stand up, even while sedated, but knew it would be too cruel to attempt. She felt Rose's forehead; a little cold, but that was probably normal for someone who was sedated and unmoving.

After a while, Michelle came to join her and sat on the other side of the bed. 'I spoke to her parents again. They're gonna get here soon. Then I'll call a Lyft, if you want to share.'

'Did they say anything about depression?'

Michelle rubbed her eyes, now clear of makeup. 'They said Rose went through a depressed *phase* in high school, but she wasn't medicated. She was never psychotic or dissociative, nothing like that. She was just *moody*.'

'So, normal then.' Emory picked at her nails, searching Rose's exposed skin for any sign of marks. But, of course, there was nothing. 'Would anyone have spiked her with something like ketamine? Is that even possible?'

'At the wedding?' Michelle made a dubious face. 'Really?'

'Maybe someone did it as a joke.'

'That's the kind of thing that would show up in a test, though, right?'

'And it doesn't really fit, does it.'

'People do act weird on that stuff.'

'But why would anyone do it? And why was it just her?'

A shrug. 'I don't think it's drugs, to be honest.'

Emory hesitated, glanced at Rose again and sighed. 'Me neither.'

A polite knock on the door, and the doctor returned with a reassuring – but not happy – smile. 'I wanted to let you know we got some blood results back, and we haven't found any traces of recreational or date-rape drugs in her system. So, we can rule those out. Sometimes people spike drinks with stronger types of alcohol, but there isn't a significant enough level of alcohol in her blood to be concerned about. Even if it was an allergic reaction to a common substance, we would expect to see other symptoms like a rash, nausea, swelling, that kind of thing.'

Emory would never have admitted it out loud, but she had almost hoped the test results would show something. Even the clarity of something like Rohypnol would have been a relief, given Rose had made it straight from the dance floor to the hospital without any predator intercepting her. Ruling things out was good, but nothing was ruled *in*.

'Thanks,' was what Emory said instead.

'So what now?' Michelle asked.

'We'd like to proceed with an MRI as soon as possible, to check if anything is affecting the soft tissue of the brain.'

'Do you think she had a stroke or a blood clot?' Michelle looked nauseated.

'After an MRI we'd be able to confirm that either way.'

The doctor left the room with an apologetic nod, and Emory stood up.

'I'm going to call Lara. If Rose's parents get here, could you explain the *pretended to be her sister* thing?'

Michelle grimaced but didn't argue. 'You know, the only thing this reminds me of is something this guy at work mentioned happening to his girlfriend once. He said she seemed fine, no depression, no signs of anxiety, nothing. But she had a nervous breakdown, completely out of the blue, apparently from stress. He said one day she literally sat on the floor and cowered against the cupboards with her fists up, and just wouldn't stop screaming.'

Emory shivered as Michelle acted out having her wrists up to her face. 'What happened?'

'He called an ambulance, and she screamed until they sedated her and took her away. She was sectioned for a while but she's fine now.'

'Maybe this is a nervous breakdown.'

'Yeah. Maybe she was really stressed out with work.' Michelle's voice became shrill with false optimism. 'Maybe it's burnout. People generally recover from nervous breakdowns, don't they?'

'I think so.' Emory could hear her voice rising to match Michelle's, and wasn't sure she totally believed it herself when she said, 'Yeah, she'll probably be fine.'

CNN Breaking News @cnnbrk
Eight people declared unresponsive in possible drug-related incident at Hunter Mountain, NY. Story developing.

3.

Emory called Rose's parents at the hospital every day for a week, but there was still no change. They ruled out a stroke or a brain tumour. Aside from an intermittent racing heart, Rose seemed physically well. The hospital decided to insert a feeding tube, which Rose's mother told Emory about on the phone with the stunned, thin tone of someone who had staggered away from the scene of a violent incident. After that, Emory agreed to stop calling unless someone contacted her with news.

A few days later, the site of a small music festival at the Hunter Mountain Resort was sealed off in Greene County, New York. Some reporters were camped out in their cars outside the resort waiting for news, so Emory messaged her father, a forensic drug analyst, to see if he was involved in investigating the scene. Worst-case scenario, he said, it was a reaction to some illegal substance in circulation, possibly even exposure to an unknown pathogen. Though that was more unlikely, as only a handful of people were affected so far. But it was still a story, which meant Emory could take some time off worrying about Rose to focus on work.

The first thing she did was check if anyone had posted any interesting images from the site to social media. A survey from a few years back claimed that Americans checked their phones on average every twelve minutes, but Emory suspected it was way more. She hated checking the news. It was a self-inflicted torture, but she did it upwards of two hundred times a day. She had to. She was a part of it, and her decision to cultivate a more investigative personal brand meant immersing herself even more in current affairs.

Sixty per cent of staff writers were laid off during the last recession, and writing think pieces was hardly the most stable niche. Her little sister had moved straight back in with their father after graduating from Columbia; not because she wanted to but because there were no jobs and rents were too high. Emory was hanging on by the skin of her teeth in New York and she knew it. But worse than failure was the idea of giving in. She still thought that – contrary to all evidence – if she worked hard, if she did nothing but work, she could make it.

If her father got back to her with any answers about the music festival, then the story coming out of Hunter Mountain could turn into something. She just had to know for sure before pitching it.

The caffeine crash and the news had made her morose, lethargic. She thought about messaging Lara to ask after updates from the hospital. But she was getting ready to leave for her honeymoon, and was low-key still irritated at Rose for causing a scene. Emory didn't want to bother her with more drama.

Emory's phone vibrated against the table with a message from an unknown number.

Hey it's Yun (from the wedding, Mike gave me your number). Wanna grab a drink later?

*

'I'm glad you got in touch.'

'Really?' His smile showed a lot of teeth, like a kid. He was wearing a white T-shirt and jeans that were ripped at the knees. He looked younger than Emory remembered. But then suits had that maturing effect on men, and his hair was no longer scraped back, but falling over his eyes in boyish curtains as he inclined his head. 'I have a pretty memorable name, I'm sure you could've tracked me down.'

She slowly mimicked the gesture. 'Okay, I guess I could have.'

They met at a bar in Greenpoint and wedged on to a table by the window. The window was open but it wasn't cold, with the weather starting to turn now they were approaching the middle of May.

'Mike said you're a journalist.' He compulsively turned his drink – bourbon – around on the spot while speaking. 'It's cool you can make money doing that.'

'Not *that* much money.'

'If it's enough to live on, it's cool.' She had to lean forward to hear him over the bar chatter when he added, 'Hey, what happened to that girl? We didn't really know anything when we left the ER. Maybe we should've stayed, but we didn't think we'd be much help.'

'It's okay, there was nothing you could've done. I actually went over the next day.'

'Wait, she was still there?'

Recounting it to somebody else made it feel more real. 'She's still there now. She didn't get better. It wasn't a spiked drink or anything like that. They don't know what's wrong with her.'

'Holy shit. I mean, I've seen people drunk before but I've

never seen anyone do that.' He turned his glass again. 'Maybe it's one of those new things everyone gets hysterical about. You know, like bath salts? Makes people act like zombies, start biting and stuff.'

His nervous, breathy laugh – like his smile – changed his whole demeanour. Unless lit up with a moment of animation, he came across as aloof, almost cold. It was partly why Emory had smiled at him at the wedding. Most people's aloofness was just a mask for shyness, but not Yun's. His was totally authentic, which made it an amusing challenge to poke holes in.

'They tested her and didn't find anything.' For the first time that day, Emory felt cold. 'She still won't eat or drink so she's on an IV and a feeding tube. The last I heard they said it looks more like depression or anorexia, or a major dissociative episode. But it's somehow like all of them and none of them at the same time.'

'So she had a nervous breakdown. Maybe she was going through some really bad shit no one knew about.'

'It's possible,' was what Emory said out loud.

Privately, she'd started to wonder whether there could be any connection between what had happened to Rose and what had happened at the festival upstate. She didn't say it out loud for fear of coming across as insensitive. There were more important things, after all, than turning everything into a potential story.

'I'm sorry you and your friend had to deal with it though,' she said. 'It must have been pretty intense. Were you both okay?'

'Oh, I barely did anything, Andrew did all the actual helping.'

It was like he was used to people turning conversations

back to his tall, handsome friend. He started chewing the skin around his thumbnail, became aware of it and stopped.

She pretended not to notice. But it was hard, because she rarely stopped watching his hands. He had the most beautiful hands. Long pianist's fingers that made very precise movements, strong knuckles and veins.

A couple of times he saw her looking. A couple of times she looked away and drank her wine, and he smiled.

'Are you hungry?' Emory asked after about an hour.

'Now you're speaking my language. I'm always hungry.'

Yun picked up his bike and they walked along the water for as long as they could before cutting in around Williamsburg, heading for an Italian place Yun said was great. She wasn't that hungry, but she didn't want to go home.

The sun went down.

'Do you make enough money to live off your music? That's rare for New York.'

He shrugged. They were sitting in a garden out back while a blues band played in the bar inside. Fairy lights were strewn over everything.

'My parents said if I did music I'd go broke.' His tone was impassive, as if talking about someone else's parents. 'It's hard, but between the producing, writing, DJ-ing, I get by. I'd like to work less on other people's stuff and more on my own. I might get to soon. But I think that's how these industries work, siphoning off talent and using it to boost people with less talent and more family money.'

'How can you be so cynical? What are you, twenty-five?'

He laughed, twisting a fork into his spaghetti for a long time. 'Twenty-nine, but thanks. How can you be a journalist and not be cynical? The world is . . .'

He made a vague gesture at *everything*; a gesture which had become universal in the last few years. *Everything*. The overwhelming feeling that everything was out of control and only moving further out of control.

'Okay, the world *is* . . .' She imitated the gesture and almost knocked over her wine, catching the glass with her other hand and trying to move past it. 'But there are so many people trying to do good things. I read a lot about that too.'

'Trying,' he said, taking a sip of beer. But that was all he said.

In the bathroom – while the bass and drumbeat from the band reverberated through the wall – Emory took a long, hard look at herself in the mirror, and decided she was definitely going to sleep with him. Maybe tonight. That, she hadn't decided yet.

She fluffed her hair, and when she returned to the table she saw him looking at his phone with a bewildered frown. Naturally, she thought it had something to do with her.

'Are you okay?'

She didn't know what she expected him to say, but it wasn't, 'Did you hear about that festival at Hunter Mountain?'

As Emory sat down, she noticed other people staring at their phones with similar expressions. It's possible the memory had become exaggerated. Obviously not everyone found out at the same time, or reacted like it was anything other than a curiosity. But that's what it seemed like. Emory saw her own gut reaction of dread reflected in everyone else's faces.

She hadn't checked her own phone for a few hours.

Public health crisis in Hunter Mountain, NY, as 22 people now declared 'unresponsive'.

She scrolled further down, forgetting where she was. Her first instinct was to call her father and demand to know why he hadn't told her anything.

Drugs incident at Hunter Mountain resort: What they don't want you to know!

That one was from Fox News.

'People are saying the reason they've cordoned it off is because they can't move anyone.' Yun sounded tense. 'If people got sick that fast, and they're unresponsive, what if what happened to your friend –'

'My dad might know something,' Emory said, because she desperately needed to cut in before he finished the thought. 'He's a forensic – you know, a scenes of crime person. He might be there, I don't know. He usually tells me anything interesting, but it takes him hours to reply to messages, it's so annoying.'

Yun took another drink, his eyes fixed on some distant horizon inside his head. When he put the beer down, he mustered a half-smile. 'Maybe it's another pandemic.'

She laughed. She had no idea why. 'That's *all* we need!'

He carried on eating, and put his phone away.

They went inside and leaned against the bar to watch the band for a few songs, not looking at each other and also painfully aware of not looking at each other. It was too hot to be inside. As one song ended, Emory raised her hands to clap and felt him brush her hair back from her shoulder, middle fingertip grazing her neck. But when she looked at him, he wasn't looking at her.

She kept watching him until he reddened and announced, 'Let's go. Do you wanna go?'

While he unlocked his bike, she sent another message to her father.

Can you look at your phone PLEASE? Xx

'I live off Metropolitan.' Yun turned away from his bike. It sounded as though he had rehearsed all of the words in his head, but not the order in which he said them. 'I have a room-mate but she's away all summer. If you wanna have a drink or watch a movie or something, it's near here. You don't have to, you can say no, it's not like I'm expecting anything just because you come back. *If* you come back, which you're free to . . . not. Either way, it's fine. I mean, you don't *have* to.'

'I *know!*' Before she could second-guess herself, she added, 'I'm going to head home, but maybe next time?'

'Sure.' He didn't seem fazed, which was part of the test. 'I'll walk you home.'

'It's not that far.'

'It's dark, I'll walk you home.' He leaned his bike against the wall again and smiled. 'But if I am gonna walk you home, can I kiss you now? I'm gonna think about it all the way back otherwise and then it becomes an awkward doorstep thing . . .'

Emory laughed so explosively that she forgot to make it sound attractive. 'You mean you want to get it out of the way?'

'Yeah.'

'Thanks!'

30

But she didn't find it hard to step forward, swaying a little, and wind her arms around his neck, and kiss him until they were both giggling and slightly off balance. He tasted of beer and whiskey and he was smiling brilliantly when she pulled away. And she thought, *Oh shit, I really like him.*

Oh shit, because it was never a good time to realize you really liked someone. Realizing you really liked someone meant knowing on some level it was going to hurt.

Jennie Barrett @jennieeee

sorry the video cuts out when people started freaking out and running but you can kinda see they're going down like dominos! like they were setting each other off

4.

When Emory got inside she noticed a missed call from her father, and a message telling her to call him. It was nearing midnight, so she shut herself in her room and turned on the rattling air-conditioning unit under the window. She sat cross-legged on her bed and opened her laptop to take notes, before calling back and putting him on speakerphone.

Jeremiah Thomas sounded tired and faraway. 'Hello, sweet pea, you're up late?'

'I always work late.' She scrolled social media. 'I haven't seen anything about Hunter Mountain that isn't a leak, that's pretty weird. Is no one making an official statement?'

'No, we were given a stern briefing and signed NDAs on the scene. But, uh . . .' He made a clicking noise with his tongue that he only made when he was perturbed by something.

'What happened? Was it a drug thing?'

'Honey, if it is drugs I've never seen anything like it. The line that got out is *unresponsive*, as you know. But that makes it sound like people were unconscious. And they weren't, that was the thing. They were awake, they weren't . . . right. When the paramedics tried to move them, tried to give them water or medication, they –'

'Lashed out?'

'How do you know?'

Emory felt like the bed had plummeted several floors. 'I

33

saw something similar, the same thing even, at a wedding a couple of weeks ago. You know, Lara's wedding? I didn't mention it because it just seemed like one of those weird things, someone gets sick . . . But this girl, Rose, at some point in the night she just sat down in the middle of the floor. We couldn't make her do anything. She was awake, but when we tried to get her to stand up or drink something, she went crazy.'

'Is she all right?'

'No. Some guys took her to the ER and she's still in the hospital now, they have no idea what's wrong with her.'

Her father went quiet for a time, and Emory hoped in those moments of dead air that he was about to say something contradictory, something about the Hunter Mountain incident rendering the two events completely unrelated. And she could file a story about twenty-two people drinking contaminated water, eating bad vendor food, contracting a flu virus; anything but something so hideously unexplainable.

'You know what it looked like?' he mused. 'It looked like everyone had some kind of collective nervous breakdown. We were asked to look for traces of ketamine or hallucinogens.'

'That's what the doctor said about Rose too. They tested for ketamine and other drugs but they didn't find anything. She hadn't even had that much to drink.'

'I wish I could say something different, but we didn't find anything either.'

'Someone from the resort is going to have to make a statement eventually, right?'

'You'd think so when it concerns this many people. We're up to forty-eight affected and they're having the food stalls investigated. Food stalls! As if everyone on-site will have eaten the same thing. But the liability, this many people getting poisoned, some of whom weren't even –'

'I thought it was twenty-two?'

'It was. But people kept dropping even in the medical tents, like this thing is infectious.' The silence was heavy with the weight of whatever he was choosing not to say. 'Honey, I know you're a professional. So, I'm telling you this off the record, as your father.'

'What?'

'There were a lot of people, it was crowded. So no one knows exactly when this happened. But a Hunter police officer who arrived on the scene also became unresponsive. Somehow, whatever this is, one of the first responders came down with it too.' He cleared his throat. 'Now, I don't want you to worry about me. It's different for us, we wear protective equipment for a reason.'

'But that doesn't make sense. If it was contagious then surely a doctor would find something? It would be an illness, right? A virus?'

'It could be a bad coincidence, Emmy. Like I said, it was a crowded site, and everyone else was fine.' But he didn't quite believe this. She could tell.

'You know, if this has happened in New York multiple times in the last couple of weeks, it's probably happened elsewhere.'

'I don't want to panic anybody.'

'Me neither, but if something bad is happening, don't you think people should be warned as early as possible?'

'If it was a contagion, then surely other people from your wedding would have come down with it.' That was the thing about her father, he could never be cajoled into anything reactive. 'Have you heard of it happening to anyone else? The people who took her to the ER, for example.'

'No,' Emory admitted. 'Everyone else who went to the ER is fine.'

'And you're fine? Did you touch her at any point, try to help her up?'

'Yes but . . .' She frowned. 'Okay so, say I *don't* quote you directly, can I run with this?'

'You can't mention the police officer.'

'But I can file a story? And also put out a social media request listing the symptoms? That way I can find more people.' She repressed a shudder, goosebumps flying up along the back of her neck. 'If there are more people.'

'I can't see how that would do any harm.' He hesitated. 'I just don't think . . .'

'You don't think I should do it?'

'No, it's not that.' Something about his tone reminded Emory of the night he told her and Esther that their mother had died. 'It's just that, this isn't anything I've seen before. It was such an odd experience, the atmosphere. I wouldn't be surprised if a few people need to talk to a shrink after.'

Her lips felt dry. 'Are you worried?'

'I'm not worried. I know you're careful. If you're going to research it, I know you'll be careful.' Her father detested things that didn't follow a logical progression. People, too. 'It's just unusual, to get to my age and see something in your job you've never seen before.'

In the days leading up to the press conference at Windham Medical Center, Emory put out requests on all of her socials for people to get in touch with similar stories of sudden catatonia, people becoming unresponsive and aggressive when subjected to forced interaction.

Within hours, the emails started coming. Some were scary, there were always scary ones. The standard death and rape threats that came with simply being a woman online. But then there were the emails Emory sifted through in the corner of the coffee shop she had taken to writing in, and put into a separate folder marked *Notable Incidents*. First, they were just from other Americans, but then she heard from people in Croatia, France, Australia, Taiwan.

Croatia: A young woman working in a call centre for a credit card company was called into her supervisor's office – one of those glass-walled eggshells they called 'pods', which didn't really belong to anybody – to talk about an incident of misconduct on a recent call with a customer. The supervisor wanted to talk to her about brand damage and she tried her hardest not to laugh in his face at the absurdity of it all. *What has happened to your life?* she thought. *What has happened to your life that you should care about such things? Brands aren't real.* She was planning on resigning soon anyway, so maybe she didn't hide her contempt that well. At one point, her supervisor reached for his coffee mug and stopped, as if he had thought better of it. He froze that way, only dimly focused on the mug, like he had forgotten where he was. She said his name, several times, then waved a hand in front of his face, saying 'Hello? Hello?' A stroke, she realized. He must be having a stroke. She stood up, knocking her chair to the floor behind her. No one on the office floor rose from their seats for several minutes, continuing to take calls even when she ran from the pod calling for help.

Leaving your desk while still logged in was a disciplinary offence.

France: A dishwasher hauled some trash into the alley behind a Turkish restaurant in Lille, and spotted a local homeless woman asleep among the dumpsters. 'Get out of here!' he yelled, chucking the bags down. They had caught her stealing food they had thrown out before. 'Hey! You can't sleep here!' When he noticed her eyes were open, he thought she was drunk, and aimed a kick at one of the bags near her head. When she still didn't move, didn't even acknowledge his presence, he leaned down and tried to pull her up. That was when she began screaming, and he jerked away with three deep scratches down the side of his face.

Australia: This one came with a video file attached. A celebrity personal trainer was in the ER with her girlfriend of three years. As the PT explained to the phone screen with bloodshot eyes, they were at brunch and *she just got like this*. 'Baby?' – shaking her by the arm, which did nothing – 'Baby, can you hear me?' But her girlfriend's gaze didn't focus on her, or the phone camera. 'Baby, can you wake up?' Finally, she burst into tears. 'I just don't know what's wrong with her! What's wrong with her?' The video went viral on YouTube before Emory even had time to write and file the first story.

Taiwan: Two construction workers were taking a break, sitting on the edge of the scaffolding encircling a new office block. They were unpacking their lunches and swapping food when one of them went strangely limp, eyes glazing over. He didn't seem to move himself, so much as let himself be moved, by the wind or by gravity. He slipped away from the grasping hands of his colleagues, fell seven floors and landed on a man walking to work below, killing him instantly. The man who had been sitting next to him on the scaffold – the one who emailed Emory – said that whatever happened to his friend and fellow worker, it had taken him over mid-sentence. He lost his words, and the smile fell from his face faster than his body had fallen to the street. Like he had suddenly been given some very bad news. Or remembered something horrible.

Emory cut and pasted the description into the first few lines of her pitch, and sent it to her editor.

She got up at four a.m. to call a car to Port Authority, then spent over three hours on a $36 bus to get to Windham Medical Center finally, by cab, at nine a.m.

So many reporters had turned up that the conference was moved to one of the lecture theatres, and Emory scored a seat near the back, on the aisle. She could just about make out the resort rep's facial expression, which was like that of a general facing his troops after a heavy loss on the battlefield.

Ninety-five people who had been on the scene at Hunter Mountain were now afflicted, though their names hadn't yet been released.

The room was buzzing but it felt aggressive, put her on edge. The consultant psychiatrist – the independent one the resort hired after a neurologist leaked details about the symptoms to the public – stood up like someone preparing to be shot by firing squad. At least three cameras were on him, one from CNN and two others she couldn't see properly. Most were recording on their phones.

Emory was light-headed, like the cameras were on her,

and she felt an urge to live up to this moment. She loved her job, but this was the first time she'd felt like she was present for *a moment*, maybe even one of historical significance. Was it sick to think like that? To make this about her career aspirations? Maybe. But then, humans instinctively look for meaning in everything that happens to them. At least her search for meaning had helped some people. At least her initial story detailing the cases she'd heard about had allowed others to believe in the comfort of a narrative.

'Upon further examination, and with the greatest respect to Dr Wade's work in this area, it is my conclusion that the symptoms being displayed cannot simply be explained away by catatonic depression. We have not ruled anything out. It is still possible this is a drug incident or a contagious disease.'

The simmering aggression in the air turned to open hostility. People started talking all at once, causing the psychiatrist to raise his voice and the resort rep to stand, as voices rose like a hornet swarm.

'We need to conduct further tests to ascertain the presence of any hazardous biological agents, either airborne or in the water supply.'

'What about the other symptoms?' someone asked, causing the rep to snap, 'There will be *time* for questions at the end.'

The voices fell to silence, but it was not a respectful one.

Emory saw her phone wasn't recording and hit the video button again, and when she looked from the screen to the rep's face she could see – even from where she was sitting – that he was sweating. It was hot outside, but not in here. The air con was turned up so high it was practically cold, the noise from the units adding to the whir of angry activity.

'What needs to be stressed here, is there is no scientific

evidence of a connection between this incident or any other cases.'

A man stood up and shouted, 'Can you substantiate the claim that you've offered the families of the victims compensation conditional upon their disqualification from any future class action lawsuit?'

The rep yelled, 'Questions at the end!'

Someone else: 'Are you aware of a similar case at a wedding in New York?'

Emory's heart was pounding.

'Similar cases make it more likely this phenomenon is being caused by an unknown biological agent. I want to reassure you we are taking this very seriously. We can confirm some symptoms that all of the affected share so far. They are in a state that resembles catatonic depression, but become violent when forced to move, or accept food or water. Unfortunately, a full report will *not* be made public at this time, in the interests of national security.'

'What about the compensation?'

'Have there been any recoveries?'

Emory's eyes left her phone for a second, to watch the rep make a *wind this up* gesture just before leaning into his mic. 'I think it's best we leave things there.'

Again, but louder: 'But have there been *any* recoveries?'

She didn't stay to watch the rest. Security was already trying to herd these clammy, shiny men from the room before they had to look someone in the eye or get caught sweating in close-up by any of the cameras. Emory left her seat and hurried up the stairs, making her way through one of the doors at the back.

She was a good ten yards ahead of anybody else who took

the same exit, and her phone was still recording as she jogged out of the lecture building and headed for the grass verge that looped down and around towards the main entrance.

Security was waiting on one side, forming a human wall beside the car parked on the street. But there was nobody on the other side; not on the side of the building from which Emory emerged pretty much alongside the officials, whose attention was drawn towards the reporters following them out.

As she stepped from the grass to solid concrete, Emory stumbled. The psychiatrist reflexively caught her under the arms before she fell, and up close she saw his face was totally white.

She was hoisted roughly to her feet. The man's expression was uncomprehending, and she blurted out, 'What about the officer?'

He started walking. She started walking. For those few seconds, everyone surrounding them was too afraid to react to her unexpected presence, probably because she was small and blonde and white and everyone was recording.

As they reached the car, she tried again. 'What about the police officer? The one who became afflicted at the scene? Have they recovered?'

'I . . . I can't . . .' The psychiatrist was shaking.

A man screamed 'Fuck off!' straight into her left ear, making her duck as if someone had thrown something. A pair of strong hands yanked her forward by the collar, then pushed her so hard into the road that she fell flat on her back.

'Fuck *off*!' she heard again, from the same man, but it happened so quickly that she was looking at the sky and not at the rep who'd shoved her, or the crowd forming around the car.

Her hands were grazed and bloody and she was no longer holding her phone. She scrambled to her feet, more humiliated than scared, in time to see the rep throw it to the ground and smash it under the heel of his shoe.

'You fucking people!' he spat at her, his eyes bulging. 'Fucking *vultures*!'

She realized it didn't matter that he'd destroyed her phone, because everyone had filmed it.

The rep's face was bright red and the psychiatrist's was corpse-white, the two of them creating a bizarre colour spectrum with fury at one end and terror on the other. She almost started laughing at the indignity of it, the two of them bundling over each other into the car like Labradors.

But as they were driven away, it occurred to Emory that if both men looked that scared then maybe everyone else should be too.

What We Actually Know About the Hunter Mountain Incident

The 95 people declared 'unresponsive' at Lowdown music festival last week are displaying similar symptoms to an earlier case in NYC and several confirmed cases internationally.

By Emory Schafer | @emoryschafer | emory.schafer@therelay.com

So far no evidence of contagious disease has been identified by medical personnel, and it was also confirmed that Rose Hailey was not under the influence of either drugs or alcohol. A Hunter first responder has described the symptoms as most closely resembling those of catatonic schizophrenia; a form of schizophrenia causing those affected to 'ricochet between hyperactivity and under-activity.' Corresponding symptoms include stupor, little or no response to verbal interaction or instruction, and extreme agitation when physically provoked.

Another source at the University Hospital of Brooklyn remarked that this new form of catatonia also bears a striking resemblance to the rare psychiatric disorder Pervasive Refusal Syndrome (PRS), which is thought to affect only children and young adults. PRS is characterized by the refusal to eat, drink, walk, talk, or undertake self-care, and outbursts of aggression towards acts of help. Stressors include trauma (sexual, physical, and/or emotional abuse), witnessing violence, bereavement, relocation, and difficult transitions . . .

5.

After Emory's story broke, everyone's initial theory was that it was some sort of contagious neurological sickness. The news that a police officer had been affected decimated the theory it was caused by a party drug.

The evening after it was published, when shares hit almost 50k and climbing, Emory sent it to Yun. When she mentioned Rose being taken to the ER, Yun was described by name as 'a 29-year-old musician from Brooklyn', Andrew as 'a 30-year-old professor at NYU', and both of them as 'heroic'.

Andrew's only comment had been to message, *I'm really just an associate but it's nice to be promoted.*

If he was being honest, Yun found the attention flattering. That's probably why he didn't mind, why the sheer speed at which the experience had been converted into media, into money, didn't bother him.

In the initial message, Emory said she was worried she'd embellished the account too much, for the sake of drama. But pieces get edited, and Yun put everything that jarred with his memory down to journalistic licence.

Yun biked to a studio in Bushwick the morning after the story dropped, to go over a track with Derrick, the other session musician, while they waited for the vocalist to arrive. This process mostly involved drinking iced coffee, eating bagels from the deli around the corner from his apartment, and chatting shit while looking at their phones.

'That *was* you in the Hunter Mountain story, right?'

Yun grimaced. 'That is my name.'

'That's some wild shit. Did it really go down like that, with that girl?'

'It really wasn't that wild. She says in the piece the two cases might not even be related. It just *sounds* similar.'

'When you think about it, even if it isn't a disease, it does make sense.' Derrick adjusted his hat over his short dreadlocks. 'Who doesn't wanna sit down and just fucking yell at people if they try to make you do anything?'

'Yeah, is it an illness or living the dream?'

They both laughed. It was easier that way.

Derrick played back a guitar part on his laptop. 'We should put some mirrored vocals over this solo, it would slap.'

'I know, I did suggest it to her.'

'She doesn't know shit. Wish my dad could pay for me to put out mediocre tunes without worrying if any of it's good.' Derrick shook his head. 'Honestly, man, I don't know what you're still doing here.'

Yun checked his phone. 'She's only half an hour late.'

'No, *America*.' He shook his coffee and the ice cubes made a pleasant, clunking sound. 'It's not like I can go to Cameroon and make it big. But you could go to South Korea, make a ton of money and build some serious clout.'

'I've only been to Korea, like, four times.' Yun swallowed down the rigid, furious feeling that invaded his stomach whenever someone questioned his life choices. 'Anyway, I'm way too old to be a performer out there, and my Korean isn't that great any more.'

'Your music *is* great, though. And you sing better than

this rich chick does. I'm just saying, there's a road out for you right there.'

'I don't want to get out, though, I wanna get *in*.' Yun laughed darkly. 'Everyone here is obsessed with buying Korean stuff but turns out they still don't wanna work with any actual Asians. I can't even cash in on being fashionable.'

'You know I get that.'

They looked at their laptops again. The coffee had hit him badly, going straight to Yun's chest along with everything else he'd swallowed down. He felt bloated and acidic, like he'd crammed fistfuls of dense, poisonous air down his throat.

Yun changed tabs and brought up Emory's piece again, scrolling to the comments. A frightening amount of people seemed to think the Hunter Mountain incident was biological warfare from China, which of course didn't explain how it ended up also affecting a random person at a wedding in New York, or in Croatia. Someone else was certain it was due to radio waves. A man from San Francisco said that humans had irreparably altered the chemical composition of the air through pollution and ingesting too much plastic, and the body was now rejecting its new inhospitable environment. Way too many people thought it was a divine punishment due to the legalization of gay marriage in several states.

Derrick shook his coffee cup again, rattling the ice cubes. 'We should sample this.'

'Iced coffee is a great sound.'

'Right, it's not just me! I don't know if I'm crazy, or we could create a vibe like Sóley's first album. Or "The Sign" by Nujabes?'

'She'll hate it,' Yun pointed out, referring to the singer yet to arrive.

'We just won't tell her what it is. She won't know.'

In the end the vocalist never showed up. The last Yun heard of her, she'd moved back to her family's second home in New Hampshire. It wasn't clear whether she was affected by this bizarre sickness or not. Before it became standard procedure to start checking on people, a sizeable percentage of the afflicted died in their homes before anyone noticed their absence, making the real death toll almost impossible to determine.

'The resort got in touch and offered to pay for a new phone,' Emory said when Yun brought it up later, sitting on one of the tacky floating bars on the water off Greenpoint in the dying sun. 'I think the optics of attacking a journalist weren't great for them. Even if I wasn't technically where I was supposed to be.'

'It looked intense,' he said, having watched some of the videos. 'What did your dad say about it? Isn't he a scientist, you said? Like CSI?'

'He's *not* that cool.' She gulped back the overpriced, overdiluted beer with the same exhilarated expression that hadn't left her face all evening. 'No surprise here, but he keeps leaning towards a medical explanation.'

Yun made a non-committal noise, and she added, 'I can see you're not convinced.'

'Since when was catatonic depression infectious? No one caught my depression off me at college.' He shrugged, trying not to come off too weird or defensive. 'At least, not that I know of.'

'It's not *just* catatonic depression.'

'And if it's infectious enough to infect a random cop, infect almost a hundred people in one go, then how come you and I don't have it? How come Andrew doesn't have it?'

'I don't know. My dad is pretty annoyed I put that in the story, it was *technically* confidential.'

'Is he in trouble?'

'No. I started using my mother's maiden name for work before I graduated, so there's no reason for anyone to make the connection. Anonymous sources are just how most investigative pieces work.' She spread her hands. 'He'll get over it, that's what I mean. I probably shouldn't have done it, I just felt like people deserved to know the whole story.'

The bar moved beneath them, which made Yun feel drunk even though he wasn't. In the centre of every wooden table was a huge rainbow umbrella, which hadn't yet been taken down after Pride. Emory went to buy another round. There was a chill in the air, and Yun gave her his hoodie when she returned from the bar with their drinks and slid back on to the high wooden stool.

He inclined his head at her smile. 'What?'

'The bartenders were talking about my story.' She paused, as if worried about saying something insensitive. 'You know, I've been getting so many messages saying this is happening in a bunch of other places.'

Yun felt cold suddenly. 'They're probably just looking for attention, right?'

'I don't know, maybe. I don't wanna freak you out.'

'I'm fine, really.' He smiled, like it was true. 'Don't worry, you can talk about it.'

For some reason, he felt like she was holding something

back; information or maybe a hypothesis. But it seemed like an irrational suspicion, so he dismissed it.

'It's been kind of amazing, hearing people talk about it. I mean, really talking about it.' She frowned, like she was trying to perform a certain level of guilt to dilute her obvious excitement. 'Of course it's horrific. But it feels good to be able to provide people with information about it. This is really the first time I've felt like I know what my job is for. You know what I mean?'

The floor moved. He didn't *know*.

He held up his plastic cup. 'Well, cheers to that.'

After taking a drink, he surveyed the people around them and said, 'I read the comments, by the way. Did you see them? People are coming up with some pretty out-there theories.'

'I never read the comments.' She watched him over the rim of her cup. 'What do you think?'

He hesitated. 'I don't know. Obviously I don't agree with the whack-jobs who think we're being punished for equal marriage or whatever. Because why would anyone punish us for one of the only things we've done right? But at the same time, it's not like we haven't done a ton of other shitty stuff, as a species I mean.'

'But who would be punishing us?' For some reason she gestured at the water, then at the Manhattan skyline, as if at an invisible entity. 'Do you really think all bad things happen for a reason? Because of some malicious *intent*?'

'I'm not saying that, I'm just saying – there have been a *lot* of bad things, right? Like, more bad than good. I don't think it's irrational to think that maybe, somehow, we've brought this on ourselves. Maybe this is one of those diseases locked in

Arctic ice since the dinosaurs were around and we've melted it out.' He took another drink, longer this time, thinking, *Cool down, you need to cool down.* 'I thought you believed in God?'

'Not *that* kind of god.' She playfully tipped his hat off his head. 'You're the most Catholic agnostic I've ever met!'

Yun caught his hat before the wind carried it away, made a big show of outrage. 'Wow, that's uncalled for.'

'You're so into guilt, don't lie. I bet you're big on vengeance too.'

'The guilt thing I got from my parents, and I'm only into revenge when people deserve it.'

'How very Old Testament of you.' She laughed. 'You know how the Catholic Church gets people?'

'The snacks and booze?' he said. *Does my voice sound weird?*

'Yeah, it's sensory. That's why they have such beautiful art and architecture. It's also why they burn incense, have all these rituals around food and wine, the most interesting music. When you think about it, it's another thing you have in common.' She put her sunglasses on as the low-moving sun hit her face, making her glow. 'I majored in art history, so I had to look at a *lot* of Catholic art.'

'Wait, so you're saying *I* lured you in with music and liquor? That's the analogy you're making?'

She spread her hands. 'And didn't it work like a charm.'

'Well, it's not every day I'm directly compared to God, so I guess I'll take it.'

He bought another round, which somehow came to over twenty dollars. The bartenders were still talking about Hunter Mountain.

Emory's phone vibrated against the table where it was lying face down, and she turned it over.

Yun noticed the whiplash change in her expression, felt the atmosphere roll off her like a mist as she typed out a response to whatever she had just read.

'Is everything okay?'

The phone vibrated a second time.

'Um, no.' When she looked at him again, Yun had averted his eyes to make a point of not prying at her screen. Her voice shook when she said, 'Rose's parents called Michelle. Rose died last night.'

6.

Emory read Michelle's messages a few times before it sunk in.

Heart failure apparently.

They think it was the prolonged stress from not eating or drinking anything.

Yun raised his hand as if to reach for hers, or for her knee or her shoulder, but he appeared to decide against it and fiddled around with his hat instead. 'Fuck . . . I'm really sorry. Can that happen even when they feed people with tubes and stuff?'

'It doesn't always make a difference. People die from anorexia all the time, the stress puts too much pressure on the heart and everything else.'

Emory tried to work out if she was going to cry. No, she deduced after a few steadying breaths. Her mouth was dry, she felt a little dizzy and her hands a little numb. But she wasn't going to cry. Instead, there were only questions.

She messaged Michelle: *Did they mention any other symptoms?* And it wasn't Yun she was asking when she murmured, 'What does this mean for the others?'

'What do you mean?'

'Well, like I said, I've heard a lot of stories. And all those people at Hunter Mountain.' The beer was sitting heavy in her stomach. 'I haven't heard anything about anyone actually recovering.'

A brief silence, where Yun disappeared into his own head.

Michelle messaged back.

Her heart rate was still really high.

They said it was like a two-week panic attack.

'There must be someone though.' Yun's voice was unsteady when he spoke again. 'Statistically there must be at least one recovery, you just haven't heard about them yet.'

'You'd think if there had been a recovery, we'd all be hearing about it.'

Emory saw him make the decision to reach out and put his hand on her back at least three seconds before he did it. 'Hey, are you okay? Do you want to go?'

She didn't realize what she wanted to do before she met his eyes. 'Can we go back to your place?'

'Um, sure.' He failed to hide his initial surprise. 'You want to pick up something stronger to drink on the way?'

'I don't really mind.' She pushed her cup away.

He blinked as he slid off his stool. 'Okay.'

She perched perilously on his bike on the way back, while he stood up on the pedals. She turned her head to watch the traffic and felt a rush of bizarre, disproportionate happiness. Like she was in a music video and this wasn't happening to her but to some shinier, better version of herself.

They stopped outside a two-storey building on a pleasant, quiet road. Yun took care to carry his bike up to the second floor without making any noise, then went back down to double-lock the entrance.

'There's this old Italian woman who lives downstairs, Bernadetta.' He talked extremely fast as he poured two measures of Fireball Cinnamon Whisky. 'She owns the building. She hated me when I first moved in. Now she claims she doesn't

54

go to sleep until she hears me get home safe. She says she doesn't like it when I stay out late.'

Emory accepted her drink but only took a sip, listening with a patient smile. He was getting more and more flustered, pushing his hair out of his eyes, looking down at his hands, and eventually she shifted over and stopped his rambling with a kiss. They were already sitting on his bed anyway.

His demeanour changed again, a shocking duality. When he was pinning her down, running his lips along her collarbone and down past her stomach, he seemed like another person. It was like he kept several different selves locked behind unmarked doors, all of which were opened by different keys. His eyes were wild and almost black as he looked up at her and said, so quietly she could have lost it to the sound of their breathing, 'Fuck, you're so beautiful.'

She hesitated, and he must have felt the flicker of tension where her skirt was hiked up and his hand was around her thigh. 'Are you really okay?'

'It's nothing.' The irritation she felt at his question was more with herself than with him. She wanted to be able to give in to it, just invite the feeling in and let it overwhelm her, let him overwhelm her.

But she saw him internalize her moment of indecision, and when she tried to pull him towards her again, he stopped.

'Really, it's nothing,' she insisted, sitting up.

'Are you sure?'

'Yes, I'm sure!' She hated the manic edge to her voice.

Still holding her hand, he sat back on his heels. 'Yeah, I'm not big on doubt.'

'Do you not want to?'

55

He laughed, and stopped quickly when he could see it was the wrong response. 'No, I *want* to! I don't wanna give you the impression I don't. But maybe not when you've just found out your friend died?'

'We weren't that close!' Before the words had even fully left her mouth she was grimacing. 'God, I'm sorry. That sounded so awful.'

'It's fine.'

Rolling her skirt back down, Emory scooted back to the edge of the bed and reached for the glass of whisky she'd left on the floor. She sighed as the warmth in her chest turned to embarrassment. 'I can go.'

'You don't have to.'

'I probably should.'

'You sure you don't wanna talk about it?'

She tried to gauge his sincerity and was surprised to find no trace of obligation, quiet resentment, sulking; the way even the nicest of men reacted to having the promise of sex withdrawn. Taking another sip of whisky, she asked, 'Has anyone close to you ever died before? Anyone you know?'

He sat next to her and topped up his glass. 'My dad's mom. I was pretty young, though. Not so young that I didn't know what death was, I just don't remember feeling much about it. There was also this girl who killed herself at my high school, just before the SAT. There were all these rumours about how she did it so I don't know exactly what happened, but school was weird for a while. Like, they were offering counselling and stuff but we all still had to take the SAT. Only now we were being told to *reach out* and shit like that. I didn't really know her that well but everyone was freaked out. A lot of us just kinda stopped studying. I was smoking a lot. It was like we thought the same thing would happen to us if we carried on, acting like everything was normal.'

He didn't see her watching his hands as he talked, because he was watching them himself, turning them over and over each other, like he wished he was smoking, or doing something functional with them. 'What about you? Anyone else you know die?'

'My mom.'

She was grateful when he didn't overreact.

'Huh,' he said, in much the same tone he said everything. 'Was it recent?'

'It was eight years ago. I'd just started this internship and my sister had started college. She had a pulmonary embolism, at home.' Emory had become very good at talking about it, dispassionately describing the event in the formulaic way journalism grads were taught to convey news about a sudden bout of bad weather.

'Is your family okay?' he asked, which wasn't a part of the usual script.

She smiled. 'Is anyone's family *okay*?'

'Probably not.'

They didn't talk about her staying over. They watched a disaster movie in bed, laughing at the inaccurate science, and at some point he gathered her into his arms and they both fell asleep, which is why she woke up when he did.

She opened her eyes and saw him sitting on the edge of the bed, facing away from her and illuminated by the orange street light outside, creeping in through the thin blinds.

'Yun?' She reached out and brushed her fingertips against the small of his back. 'Are you okay? What's wrong?'

57

He was shaking.

She sat up and kneeled next to him, and he hunched even further over, putting a hand over his eyes. His mouth was contorted, his teeth bared. It scared her a little, seeing him like that.

'It's okay,' she said, putting an arm around his trembling shoulders, not really knowing if anything was okay or not.

A two-week panic attack, she kept thinking. *Like a two-week panic attack.*

He whispered something but she didn't hear it over the air con and his frantic breathing, so she leaned in and he inhaled deeply and said, 'What the fuck is happening?'

'You're having a panic attack.' She tried to sound calm, though the words threatened to lodge in her throat. 'Just breathe.'

He sat up straighter but didn't take the hand away from his eyes. Emory could see tears running from beneath his fingers and it sent a shiver up her spine.

'What the fuck is happening?' he said again.

Waking up the second time, Emory almost couldn't remember if it had been a dream or not. It didn't feel important now, not with Yun's arm around her, his forehead resting against her hair.

She didn't sleep well with others. Someone else breathing in the dark dragged at her nerves. She couldn't keep still either, chasing a tolerable temperature around the bed. If someone was touching her, she would move as far away from them as possible. Every ex-boyfriend would tell her this made them feel bad, and then she would feel bad, and resent them for making her have to wear earplugs every night.

So she was surprised she managed to sleep at all that first night, that she slept *well*.

His hand rested lightly in the curve where her waist met her hip.

She wished she hadn't washed her makeup off the night before, but that was only an echo of worries from many other mornings. It was gone as soon as she turned over. She didn't realize he was awake until her face was inches from his and the two of them seemed to melt into each other with closed eyes and, this time, no hesitation.

He dragged his shirt over his head and threw it away. 'I can't feel my arm.'

'Sorry –'

'I'll get over it.'

He kissed her again, touching her chin then her waist and up under the T-shirt she'd worn to sleep. She expected his hands to be cold, like hers, but they were as hot as the rest of him.

'Is this okay?' he asked.

She nodded. Still in that liminal space between sleep and consciousness, no awareness of what existed in the world outside of this. He wound his fingers into her hair and tilted her head back so he could find more skin.

When he brought his other hand up to her hair and kissed her more deeply, there was a part of her that worried he would grow bored with taking things slow for her benefit. It had been a point of pride throughout her twenties for Emory to act like someone who didn't have time for fore-play, because being anything other than immediately down to fuck seemed to be off-putting.

He opened his eyes. 'You all right?'

'Mm-hm.'

'You're not a big talker during sex, are you?'

She was surprised that she managed to laugh. 'I like feeling like I can just shut up for once.' But she flinched away from what she liked, in case it was too assertive. 'Unless you want me to talk?'

'No, it's fine.'

He seemed to hold his breath as he brushed his thumb along her bottom lip, followed his thumb with two slightly calloused fingers, which he only let out when Emory took them in her mouth.

A shudder went through him and his eyes momentarily fluttered shut. She wrapped both legs around him, drawing them against each other, and she could feel how hard he was. It was perilous, exciting, and she sucked on his fingers harder.

'Turn around.'

She could feel his breath against the nape of her neck. A hand went beneath the covers and between her legs, a sharp exhale against the back of her ear, and somehow she could tell he was smiling. She covered his hand with hers, guiding his fingers.

'Can I?' His voice was faraway, stretched thin, almost broken.

'Yes.'

'Yeah?'

'Yeah . . .'

He gently bit down on her shoulder, cutting off a low, guttural moan that sounded as though it came from deep within his chest. It was so easy to believe they would never leave, when they sounded this powerless. Locked tight against his chest, she knew he was thinking of nothing but her, pulling him deeper, like she was in possession of a gravitational force, not a woman but a sun.

'You feel amazing,' he was saying.

'Keep doing that,' she said.

She didn't know how long they stayed like that, so close she wanted to drown. The way he moved inside her felt slow and fast at the same time. The hand that was holding her against his chest moved to grasp her throat.

'Tell me when you come.'

'Yes, just . . . faster –' She shut her eyes tight, rigid with focus, teetering on the edge of feeling she was about to pass out or die, before something inside her finally came apart. 'Now! Now . . .'

'*Fuck.*' That was all she heard him saying. 'Fuck. Fuck . . .'

When they were both breathing normally, he shifted to look at her and brushed her hair away from her forehead, unable to stop a self-satisfied smile sprawling across his face.

She laughed. 'You don't have to look so smug, you know.'

'Sure.' He averted his eyes, making a show of cracking his knuckles, then looked back at her with his brows raised. 'But that was good, right? I'm really sorry about last night, by the way.'

'Wait, you're apologizing to me? Now?'

'Yeah, maybe I felt like I had a bit of . . . masculinity to make up for.'

'You're being ridiculous.' She laughed again as he covered his eyes. 'But your timing is impeccable, I guess.'

'*I* thought so.'

'Any more straight male anxiety to get off your chest?'

'Oh, I'm not straight.' He shrugged. 'But anxiety I can apparently still do.'

'Huh.' She wondered whether this new information mattered, decided it didn't. 'Well, it would probably be weirder if you *didn't* have anxiety, considering everything.'

'Yeah, maybe.' He let out a long exhale, and let his head fall to the pillow. 'I could literally sleep for another hour.'

It was then Emory remembered that things were still happening outside of this room. She rolled over to check her phone and saw her inbox: 4,800.

4,806.

4,812.

4,814.

Andrea Kleiman @andrea_kleiman

Replying to @fitzpo1999 @emoryschafer @therelay

idc how you rationalize it, publishing a story that was pretty much nothing but speculation when there is ZERO evidence any of these "cases" were related

Andrea Kleiman @andrea_kleiman

Replying to @fitzpo1999 @emoryschafer @therelay

if it's suicide clusters she liekly made the situation a million times worse, we've gone from less than 100 to 8k in america alone in 2 weeks. for clicks. tell me that's not journalistic malpractice!

7.

Emory wasn't the only reporter at Rose Hailey's memorial service, though she was the only one allowed inside. Others paced the sidewalk in front of Lara and Mike's Upper West Side apartment building. She had read a few pieces where Rose had dramatically been referred to as 'Patient Zero', even though that was categorically untrue if you took into account anywhere outside the US.

When she arrived at Lara's with Yun and his friend Andrew, several reporters accosted Emory by name, which made her all too aware she was now part of the story, when maybe she shouldn't be. Her Instagram following had doubled and her Twitter following was spiralling into six figures.

Recognition for her work was all she had ever wanted. But she hadn't reckoned on this amount of guilt. *So are you happy now?* Emory kept asking herself. *Are you finally happy now you've mastered the art of profiting from all this misery?*

She noticed some reporters instinctively move towards Andrew, who – as Yun put it – just looked like somebody. But Andrew ignored them, and they didn't have enough existing information about who he was to engage. Rose's mother, Penelope, had insisted on inviting him, as she wanted to thank the person who got her daughter to the hospital.

'We really didn't do much good,' Andrew said in the Lyft.

'It's not like you could have done anything different,' Yun said, frowning.

They exchanged a look, and Andrew offered a tight smile.

His wife wasn't coming, Yun had informed Emory before the car arrived, like this was something important she needed to know.

It wasn't that Emory disliked Andrew – her first impression was that he seemed almost impossible to dislike, which would make her suspicious of anybody – but she viewed him with a distant, benign envy. It felt rational, when faced with anyone who was both attractive and shared a language with someone you cared about that seemed to go beyond speech.

She escaped into the kitchen with Lara at the first opportunity, while Andrew's hand was being held in the vice grip of Penelope Hailey. Yun remained standing by, holding his drink just as tight. It was interesting to observe Yun around his friends; the indifference he projected around strangers was replaced by the anxious and slightly possessive air of an agent or manager.

'How are you holding up?' Emory asked, pushing the kitchen door to with her heel.

No matter how many times she came here, she was always stunned by how affluent the place was compared to her own apartment. She had slept on the couch a few times, and it was more comfortable than her own bed. The fact that the kitchen and front room were even separated by a door seemed like a luxury, let alone the Chemex coffee maker or brass fixtures.

Tanned and broader from the weeks of swimming on her honeymoon, with her curly hair bunched on top of her head in one of those messy buns Emory had never been able to pull off, Lara rolled her eyes.

'Oh, I'm *fine*,' she said, in the tone of someone who decidedly wasn't. 'All I had to do was offer the venue and drinks and I'm off the hook for everything else. Of course, her mom can barely *contain* her theory I pretty much owed them, because *I'm* to blame for all this somehow. You know, out of politeness I was like, *It's the least I can do*, and that *bitch* –' she was careful to whisper – 'just said, *Yes*. With this *look* on her face. And she's also gone out of her way *multiple* times to remind me there's no pressure, because the *real* funeral is in Ohio. Like she has *any* idea how much Rose hated Ohio!'

'I'm sure she didn't mean it like that.' It felt like the kind of thing she should say, with the woman barely ten feet away in the front room with the mismatched assemblage of her dead daughter's friends and colleagues. 'She knows it's not anyone's fault, but she's not going to be acting logically right now.'

'You know what's in Ohio? Neither do I. Corn?' Lara poured a bumper bag of chips into a glass bowl and glared at them. 'It's not just that it happened at my wedding, it's that we worked together. Like I should've seen it coming. Like there were warning signs.'

'I must have read thousands of emails about this thing and I haven't been able to make out any warning signs.'

'Try telling *her* that.' Lara opened another bottle of Pinotage to refill their glasses. 'Maybe the warning sign is there aren't any. It's like with mass murderers. Their families are never like, *Yeah we all saw it coming, they were a ticking time bomb*. It's always, *They were the life and soul of the party,*

66

the happiest person on God's fucking earth. Bullshit. Maybe the more well adjusted you seem, the more likely you are to just snap. The last thing Rose ever said to me was, "Mike's friend is hot." What kind of symptom is that?'

Emory drank most of her glass and held it out again. 'Yun?'

'Andrew. Though I see and appreciate your one-track mind and you'll have to tell me about him sometime when I don't feel like screaming into a pillow in my own home.' Lara had always been better at doing anger than sadness. She took a gulp of wine straight from the bottle and hid it behind a row of condiments. 'This one can be just ours.'

There was something different about Lara, now she was married. Maybe because marriage was one of those checkbox tasks people were meant to complete on their way to a meaningful, society-approved version of adulthood. The main difference Emory could observe would have been imperceptible to anyone who didn't know her well. But Lara was moving with more gravity, like her edges now reached the high ceilings and filled the impressive square footage of this apartment she and Mike owned, because the combined incomes of two accountants – and those of their respective parents – were enough to pay for a home rather than a temporary respite.

Emory couldn't imagine what it felt like to inhabit space you truly owned. Cities were hostile to anyone who couldn't count on the split rent and utilities of partnership. Being *one* person was more expensive than she had been taught to anticipate. She knew that Lara hadn't taken Mike's last name, but they did share a bank account.

She put her glass down on the granite countertop,

figuring it was better to stop drinking early. 'The last thing Rose ever said to me was, "This DJ is ass." Sorry.'

'No, she was right. He *was* ass.' Lara picked up a chip, then put it back in the bowl as if it disappointed her. 'I'm still really angry with her. Rose. I know you probably think I'm a massive bitch for saying this, but every time I think about it I . . . You know, the last time someone on our floor killed themselves he just threw himself in front of the L train. Why couldn't she do something like that? Like everyone else? She couldn't *just* die, she had to cause *this* much drama. You must have to really hate everyone, to decide you're going to die like that.'

A knot of panic was forming in Emory's throat. 'You really think they decide?'

Lara threw her a look that implied she was being pathetic. 'What else would you call it?'

During a slightly insincere monologue from Rose's line manager, Susanne, about the first time she and Rose had met, Emory scanned the front room and realized Yun wasn't there. He had designated himself the keeper of vices for the day, which meant those in the know kept pulling him aside to ask for an edible or cigarette. He had thoughtfully put the edibles in a container, so he wasn't flashing a label saying *Cannabis Cookies* in front of Rose's parents.

'I need some fresh air,' Emory murmured in Lara's direction before going to the master bedroom, where the window was wide open and voices were coming from the fire escape.

Yun was saying, 'Yeah but was it nominated for an award, though, musically *and* lyrically?'

68

Andrew: 'That's not the only metric by which things can be measured as good.'

'Grow up.'

Emory leaned out in time to see Michelle laughing. As they spotted her one by one, she was struck by the sudden conviction she was unwanted, an outsider to the trio who had been in the car with Rose.

'Em can settle it.' Yun gestured for her to come out before she had time to retreat.

It was the first time he had called her Em. She wasn't sure she liked it.

'Settle what?' She climbed out with some difficulty, given her bodycon skirt.

'The best song about the apocalypse,' Michelle clarified, passing a joint to Andrew and waving her hand to disperse the smoke.

'It's "My Kz, Ur Bf" by Everything Everything.' Yun put his arm around Emory's shoulders with a just-come-up smile on his face. 'He thinks it's "Nothing But Flowers" by Talking Heads. What do you think?'

'Well, I can't remember either of those so I'll have to say . . .' Emory glanced at Michelle, who looked ten pounds lighter; thinner and harder and wearing sneakers with her dress like she hadn't given a fuck about anything but comfortable shoes since being caught out in a hospital waiting room. 'I don't know. REM, "It's the End of the World As We Know It"?'

'No!' Yun collapsed against the railing. ' "My Kz, Ur Bf" not only tells a story, but it also has the line, "But now I can't find his torso, I guess you're separated". You know how much money I'd pay to write a line that funny?'

' "Nothing But Flowers" has the line, "If this is paradise, I wish I had a lawnmower".' Andrew stubbed out the last of the joint on the railing but didn't throw it, instead carefully balancing it upon the edge like he was going to take it with him later.

'That's not funny, that's sad.'

'They're both funny *and* sad.'

'*You're* both funny and sad,' Michelle interjected, making Yun laugh and Andrew smile.

It felt too late to ask for a cigarette, which would have established her place among the group.

'I like REM,' Andrew said.

Don't help me, Emory thought.

'I still think being nominated for an Ivor Novello has to be the decider, like objectively.' Yun released her shoulder in order to make his point more emphatically, and Emory realized with another irrational prickle of jealousy that she wasn't the only person he was like this in front of.

'So only the best songs get nominated for awards?' Andrew raised one eyebrow, the closest he could get to a combative expression. 'That's what you're saying?'

'That's not what I said.'

'You have to consider the wider implications, if you're going to make that argument.'

Michelle shook her head. 'That's why you don't argue with a professor.'

'I'm going to go back inside,' Emory announced to no one in particular, uncomfortable with the levity or maybe with not being a part of it.

' "It's like I'm watching the A4 paper taking over the guillotine",' Yun said as she ducked back through the window.

'The genius of those lyrics! *It's like I'm watching the A4 paper taking over the guillotine!*'

Emory entered the front room just in time to see Penelope Hailey slap Susanne across the face. The sound sliced through the air like a gunshot, followed by Susanne's shrill cry and a dramatic crescent of red wine falling in dreamlike slow motion across the cream carpets and down the back of one of the purple couches.

Mike, who had been so stationary the last few hours that Emory wondered if he'd gotten preemptively high before everyone arrived, snapped into action and ran to the kitchen.

Emory searched the cluster of people until she found Lara, who hadn't even risen from the couch. As her husband rushed back in with spray and a wet dishcloth, a muscle tensed in Lara's jaw. She rested her head on her hand and closed her eyes, as if sunning herself somewhere far away. Emory's stomach clenched and for a moment she wondered whether this is how it happened, with a look of peace.

Then Lara opened her eyes again, and rolled them in Emory's direction.

'She didn't kill herself.' Penelope Hailey was shaking, the raw heat of her rage almost shimmering in the air. 'How dare you!'

Susanne, her glass now empty, held her face and shielded her eyes, as if she too could see it, as if it burned.

Penelope Hailey adjusted the collar of her burgundy blouse, retied the little bow at the top. 'She *didn't* kill herself,' she said again, slower and louder, making sure the whole room heard it.

*

71

In the car on the way back to Yun's, Emory checked her phone and saw that over twenty people in Avilés, Spain, had been declared unresponsive at a concert venue. There were no photos, yet. She tried refreshing the page a few times, then looked across the car at Yun.

He was leaning his head against the window.

'Don't you think it was inappropriate to be laughing like that?'

'What?' He opened his eyes.

'When you were outside getting high, what if her parents had heard you?'

'They didn't.' He seemed confused by the accusation. 'You know what Michelle told me when they were making all those speeches about how they knew her? She said they met at the team-building night for new graduates at . . . wherever they work. The first time she met Rose she was snorting coke off her keys outside a bar. Michelle held her jacket up to hide her from the bouncer. Not exactly a story she could've told in front of her parents. Still a part of who she was though.'

The beginning of a headache was pushing against the front of her skull. Emory tried to cool it with her freezing knuckles. She refreshed the page but there were no further updates.

Yun followed her gaze to the screen, and leaned his head against the window again. He linked his fingers through hers and shook his head in anticipation of her saying something. 'I don't wanna know. Don't tell me, I don't wanna know.'

CNN Breaking News @cnnbrk
Last of the 95 catatonic patients from Hunter Mountain
confirmed dead this morning. 27-year-old Kasun Mayuran
died from heart failure after two and a half weeks in
hospital.

8.

If the news started murmuring about the markets being spooked, Yun had learned it was always preceded by the steady cancellation of all of his and Derrick's upcoming jobs. Any job in the arts was the canary in the coal mine when it came to the economy. He would be living in his overdraft for weeks before anyone even whispered the word 'recession'.

This isn't what he told Emory, who was the first to notice when he started making excuses to stop going out. According to her messages she was 'super busy', so he told her he was also super busy, and tried to block out the mounting anxiety when June rolled around, cases were spiralling into the tens of thousands, everyone declared unresponsive at Hunter Mountain was dead, and he hadn't seen much of anybody since Rose's funeral.

Bernadetta Bianchi, Yun's landlady, lived alone in the apartment below his. The second-floor apartment was bigger, but she suffered from arthritic hips and didn't like stairs. She didn't seem particularly worried about the escalating crisis, refusing to see it as any kind of crisis at all. Then again, she was in her seventies, and very few people over fifty had been affected. Yun wondered whether it was because old people were less likely to die in a way that could be mistaken for voluntary. Everyone his age joked about wanting to die, using it in the careless way other generations said 'Fine'.

In the absence of much else to do – and admittedly hoping the more he ingratiated himself, the more likely she would be to show leniency when his rent started being late – Yun found himself offering to do Bernadetta's shopping several times a week. After a few weeks of running errands he offered to cook, because by that point he needed the company, and he thought she did too.

'How is Jessica?' Bernadetta was rocking back and forth in a chair by the AC unit and the open window, in a diminishing patch of sunlight. She had only ever referred to Jarah – his most recent ex-girlfriend, or 'room-mate' as he had put it to Emory – as Jessica, because apparently her real name was too complicated. She looked older in the sun, as it reflected off the grey streaks in her hair, making them appear almost white, and more numerous in number. 'Why do I never see her any more? Did you two have an argument? Did she move out? What did you do?'

Yun stopped chopping carrots and looked over his shoulder. 'Which question do you want me to answer first?'

After they officially broke up – her breaking up with him, if he was forced to be technical about it – Jarah moved out of their shared bedroom and into Yun's music room next door. She had since decided to leave the apartment and the country entirely, staying with her parents until fall. Missing her became an irritant, like something was permanently lodged in his chest.

Bernadetta threw back her head and laughed. She didn't have a quiet laugh. 'You *did* do something! I know men.'

'Maybe go easy on the insults when this man is cooking you dinner.'

'I saw you come back with a blonde girl three weeks ago.'

'You're too nosy for your own good, you know that?'

A darker laugh. 'I know men.'

He put the carrots to one side, checked the oil was hot enough and started cubing the pork. 'We actually broke up a few months ago. She's been looking for a new place but obviously it's hard.' He gestured at the street with the knife, at the offending unattainable housing. 'Our schedules were too different.'

'That's sad, dear.' She pondered. 'You do stay out very late. Waking up after she was gone. That's no way for two people to live.'

'I had the same schedule when we met, it's not like she didn't know.' The apartment heated up intolerably quickly. He was sweating, but didn't want to look away from the stove. 'She knew I wasn't going to get a nine-to-five office job but after two years it suddenly became an issue.'

'You kids these days. *Happy*.'

She didn't elaborate. The word hung in the air with the steam. Yun wiped his forehead on his forearm. 'Have you got anything to drink? Something with ice?'

'Dan, I thought you'd never ask.' She heaved herself out of the chair and walked, groaning and fussing, over to the darkwood cabinet on the other side of the apartment, by her dining table. Bending down, cursing her lower back, she straightened up holding a bottle of Campari. 'There's lemonade in the fridge.'

He smiled, grabbing two glasses from the cabinet. 'Are you trying to get me drunk, Ms BB?'

'Don't be vulgar.' As she poured out some pretty generous measures over ice, she added, 'I'll have you know that if I were fifty years younger, I'd be out of *your* league!'

He laughed and held the cold glass against his face, before downing half of it. The ice fell against the side of the glass with a *clink*, and Yun wondered how Derrick was coping now he was out of work and cooped up with his four-year-old son. Mike and Lara had returned from their honeymoon in Mexico and discovered their firm was laying departments off. He wondered how his parents were doing, and whether his little brother was going to move out of their house or not.

That was what these twice-a-decade economic crises did to people: confronted them with the unbearable truth of their own choices. Caring for the children you didn't want, trapped with the partner you were bored of, stuck with the room-mates you hated, chained to the lease of a one-room apartment that had made you feel so free the first time you walked in the door.

'People deserve to be happy, don't they?' he said.

Bernadetta sat in her chair by the window with her drink in hand, but the sun had moved on. 'We never used to think like that, like we *deserved* anything. And looking at the way things are now, I'd say we were happier for it.'

'Oh, so in your day people were miserable and just accepted it? Sounds healthy.'

'Why wouldn't a nice girl who thought the world of you make you want to get a normal job to make her happy?'

'Because that's not me.'

'Jobs don't care about who you *are*. Are those clubs you go to at all hours of the night *you*?'

'What is it you think I do again?' He poured stock into the pan and put the lid on.

'Ah, I don't know about your *music*. I know I wouldn't like

77

it. But that's not the point. If she didn't make you want to change, it wasn't love. So that nice girl is better off.'

'By that logic, she didn't change for me either.'

'Women change for everyone. Men just don't notice.'

He felt guilty all of a sudden, but didn't know why. The emotion was there, but the theory she had posed was impenetrable to him. He checked the pan was simmering, pulled a chair out from the dining table and sat for a moment.

It was still light out. A gentle evening light that made this part of Brooklyn resemble a movie set.

'Didn't you get divorced?' he asked.

The speed at which she turned in her chair made him smile. 'What kind of question is that?'

'You mentioned it a couple of times. You had two husbands, right? Luke was the second one.' He pointed to one of the photos atop the cabinet. 'So you must have thought you deserved better at some point. Isn't that what divorce is for?'

'You think you're so smart!' Her sardonic expression made her look very young. 'Fill up my glass and I'll tell you.'

She tutted at him the whole time, and then refused to tell him until dinner was ready, because serious conversations were for the table.

'Could you *be* any more Italian?' Yun remarked.

'Don't be racist!' she snapped, making them both laugh.

The stew turned out pretty good, he thought. She said she didn't want him to *mess around with it* or *use any of those spices that give me a bad stomach*. But when she announced it was delicious and he told her it was a gochujang-based stock, she approved.

It grew dark outside as they ate. She put some Paul

Mauriat on the record player. 'Love is Blue'. He pushed his bowl away as she poured two shots of limoncello. He had never had a high tolerance for alcohol. It turned him red and confrontational, then tired, eventually sad. Bernadetta could undoubtably drink him under the table.

'I play a great piano cover of this. I'll record it for you if you want.'

'It's been a long time since a young man played me a song. What a treat!' She tapped a thick, sturdy finger against the tabletop along with the strings. 'You want to know about my first marriage, fine. My parents arranged it when I was seventeen. I was still living in Naples. My first husband was a *short* man I didn't even like. A friend of my father.' An evaluative look at Yun, then, 'He was shorter than you. Though that was far from the worst thing about him.'

'Did your parents not care what you wanted?'

'It wasn't done. You couldn't say no when your parents had worked so hard to secure your future. He had money. Who was I to complain? It was either that or run away, and I was never the running type.' She frowned. 'He was a careless man, with his money. With everything. I can't abide carelessness. Nothing to respect about it.'

'When did you move to New York?'

'I don't remember. Sixty-something. I didn't speak a word of American, and he set me up in a house. It was in Manhattan, but it was a *dump*, and he was away so much I barely even saw him. I was in this city that I didn't know, and I couldn't speak to anybody. So I begged him, I said, "Frank!" – that was his name – "I want to take night classes!" And he said, "What do you want to do night classes for?" And I said, "I want to learn to cut hair."'

She owned a small chain of salons in Brooklyn, two, maybe three. Yun knew that was how she had made her money.

'No way, is that how you ended up with the salons? You took night classes?'

'Well, you've cut ten years off my story.' She bristled, then appeared pleased with herself. 'But yes. That's where I first learned, and it's where I learned to speak the language too. The ladies there taught me. I used to walk from the Upper West Side all the way through Harlem, and I used to walk back at three, four in the morning. Men used to yell at me. I was terrified, but no one could've stopped me from going. I got so good that the woman who ran the class – she was *African American* – hired me at her salon sweeping the floor, and I had my first part-time job.'

'So what happened? Did you save up enough money and then divorce him?'

'No. I did save up some money, in secret, because he was a gambler. But I only divorced him when my father called me and told me I was going to.'

'What changed their mind?'

'He was back home visiting family and I wasn't there. They caught him messing around with one of my cousins. She was only thirteen. They had to pick which family disgrace to live with, and I was already in New York, so it was easier to keep me out of mind.'

'Wow.' The record player had stopped, and he got up to flip it. 'Did you ever see him again?'

'He showed up and threw a brick through the window of my first salon, here in Brooklyn, and I had the bastard arrested!'

Yun wasn't sure whether to laugh, but then she did.

'Luke was much nicer.' She looked at the photo on the cabinet, the one from her second wedding. Yun estimated that she looked about twenty-five, definitely younger than he was now. 'I was glad my father got to meet him before he died. I never appreciated how much he used to worry about me. I never realized it was worry, I always thought he was telling me I wasn't doing well enough for myself. I was so defensive. Like you.'

'I'm not defensive!'

As he took another sip of limoncello, he thought about his parents meeting Emory. They would politely dislike her, of course, but there wasn't much about his life they didn't politely dislike.

Bernadetta turned away from the photo. 'Kids don't think like this, but the best-case scenario is always that one of you dies.'

He wasn't able to hold her gaze. 'I'm not sure I agree death is the best-case scenario for anything.'

'It's the most important part of the vows. Till death us do part. Of course it's the best-case scenario! One of you dies, and you're together for long enough that you care about which one of you dies first. That's the best anyone can hope for.' She shrugged. 'Of course, the men usually die first. They're not built to deal with the other way around.'

A siren passed the window, and faded.

He felt choked up and couldn't drink any more. The room spun a little. 'I'll wash up.'

'Don't worry about the rent, dear. I know it's due tomorrow, but I haven't heard you going to work in a while, and I'm not going to act like some slumlord while the world is busy deciding whether to keep us or not.'

He would never have mustered the courage to ask. He leaned against the sink with an exhale which took three inches off his shoulders. 'Thank God.'

'Don't thank God, thank *me*!'

'I can't even file for unemployment. Everyone thinks being a musician is pretty much choosing to be unemployed.'

'I know you're a good boy, Dan.' Maybe he imagined the pity in her tone. 'What's your blonde lady's name?'

'Emory.'

'Isn't that a boy's name?' she asked accusingly.

He pulled on some washing-up gloves and spread his hands. '*I* didn't name her!'

She snorted. 'I'll call her Emily.'

What We Actually Know About the Catatonic Crisis

ERs report 'unprecedented surge' in mental health emergencies alongside record referrals. But medical experts are calling for calm, reiterating the symptoms of concern.

By Emory Schafer | @emoryschafer | emory.schafer@therelay.com

As of Thursday, cases resembling the catatonia were estimated to be at 25,103, with a further 4,775 deaths last week. The vast majority of these cases are confined to the US, with a reported fatality rate of 100%.

Doctors have blamed rampant disinformation for driving the recent spike in mental health emergencies, with patients reporting panic attacks and cardiac concerns. Dr Robin Hefner at St Luke's University Hospital, PA, has called the situation 'completely absurd' and claimed, 'most of these people are literally making themselves sick with anxiety'. Medical experts have reiterated that the main symptoms of concern are the combination of catatonic social withdrawal, extreme agitation and violence. Death eventually occurs within one to two weeks, due to an unnaturally elevated heart rate. But in order to be considered a legitimate case, it must have been preceded by both aforementioned symptoms.

'It is not one without the other,' says Lucia Fabrizio at the CDC. 'It is not any standard depressive episode, chronic anxiety, or even a panic attack. Though of course we understand that people are frightened and want to take measures to protect themselves. The best advice we can offer to those who are struggling is to reach out and talk to someone.

9.

Yun had to down one beer and half of a second before setting up his laptop in Jarah's partially vacated room to call Kevin. He would never have chosen to video-call with his brother, and Kevin would never have chosen a painful face-to-face inter-action with him unless guilt-tripped into it by their mother.

'Can you hear me?' Yun asked, resisting the urge to imme-diately reach for the rest of his beer.

'Yeah.' Kevin yawned, as if Yun had woken him up at seven in the evening. Kevin was a little taller than him, and lankier. The top of his head and eyebrows were out of frame and not being able to see his whole face made Yun uncom-fortable. 'What's up?'

'Mom said I should give you a call.'

A nod. 'Same.'

'Are they doing okay?'

'Yeah, they're downstairs,' Kevin replied, like that answered Yun's question.

Yun had a vague memory of the two of them being close when they were younger, when he still lived in San Diego. But he couldn't pinpoint the exact time they lost their grip on each other's personalities, when Kevin started having more in-jokes with their parents than with him.

'Did you have any luck looking for a place?'

'Nah.'

'Don't you have, like, friends?'

'Yeah but they don't have, like, rooms.'

'No one's had a free room in a year and a half?' Yun didn't bother to hide his disbelief. 'Right.'

'Well, yeah, but they're expensive.'

Yun sighed. 'Is Dad okay? Is his job solid?'

'They were talking about lay-offs, but it didn't come to anything. They're both pretty freaked out by the news though.' Kevin emitted a sputtering laugh from behind his hand, which reminded Yun that no one in their family had a normal laugh. 'Dad got this idea in his head that he was gonna build a pizza oven in the yard. I think it's how he's dealing with the stress. He was watching tutorials and talking a lot about bricks.'

'We don't eat that much pizza. Mom doesn't even *like* pizza.'

'I did tell him this. There was a whole debate about it and then he seemed to get quiet about the idea.' He pulled a dubious face. 'I'm not convinced he still isn't gonna do it. You can feel it. He just *needs* to go stand in a Home Depot.'

'It's like his version of a nail salon. He just needs someone in retail to observe him buying another saw.'

'It's weird how neither of us got into DIY.' Kevin reached off to the side and his hand returned holding a can. 'He's so disappointed I don't wanna become an engineer or something.'

'What do you actually wanna do, though?'

Kevin paused, and the silence was sharp. Behind him, his room looked the same as Yun remembered it. He thought back to the last time they'd spoken, which must have been Christmas. Had either of them progressed since then? Yun's room was the same. The room he was calling from was emptier.

Another shrug. 'I'm twenty-seven, it's not like I've got to decide now.'

'It's probably best you kinda decide.' Yun's fingers twitched towards the beer bottle, and he rubbed his forehead instead. 'You can't live there forever.'

Kevin rolled his eyes. 'Come on, man.'

'I'm just saying, some of us never had the option to live at home.'

'*You* moved to New York, no one forced you to do anything.'

'Okay, it was my choice to move to New York. But you have to admit I didn't get any help.'

'Dude, they didn't ban you.' He leaned forward so Yun could see his raised eyebrows. 'That shit ever get heavy? Carrying around that massive fucking chip on your shoulder?'

Yun drank some more beer to dilute the abject scorn in his tone. 'Okay, whatever. Sure. But come on, you were doing pre-law and now what?'

'Law sucks *balls*, that's what. Less than *half* end up passing the bar and I didn't even like it.'

'No one likes it.'

'Oh, so because you're miserable I have to be miserable too? Thanks.'

'What?'

Kevin leaned forward again. 'You heard me. You go on and on about how Mom and Dad judge you and *all* you do is project that shit on to me. Just because you're, like, thirty now and, you know what, you didn't make it. Tough shit! Most people don't end up living the dream or whatever, you're not special.'

Yun would have hung up if they were talking on the

phone, but it was awkward to end a video-call. The silence drifted on for long enough that Kevin filled it.

'And what's the point in talking about what I'm gonna do when we're literally in the middle of my third recession? I'm twenty-seven and it's my *third* recession! Maybe that's why Mom and Dad are okay with me staying here, because they know we're all fucked. Who gives a shit if I'm not doing pre-law? By the time you get to Number One on iTunes or whatever, we're gonna have a fucking billion climate refugees. So who gives a shit? No wonder people are sitting down and giving the fuck up.'

He looked behind him at the door, as if to check no one else in the house had heard him. In that moment, Yun let out the breath he was holding.

'Wow,' Yun said. 'Sounds like you've been wanting to say that for a while.'

'Yeah, maybe. Yeah.'

Yun took a gulp of beer and noticed his hand was shaking. 'I didn't realize you thought I was such a loser, good to know.'

'Well, to be fair, I always knew you thought *I* was a loser. You weren't subtle about it.'

Yun's voice was strained, pulled so thin you could poke a hole in it. 'You know music's not even like that. You don't just *make it*, like in a movie.'

'Yeah, all right.' Kevin rolled up the sleeves of his T-shirt. 'I'm gonna go. I hope you don't die and everything.'

'Yeah, you too.'

Kevin frowned. 'Didn't you see someone go crazy at a wedding? I've seen it online, but is it really like that?'

Yun wasn't sure what to say. 'It wasn't exactly like that. It's not violent, it's more . . . desperate.'

'Jesus. Do you think it's even a disease?'

'As opposed to?'

'Well, do you think it just comes over you? Or do you think they just choose to check out?'

'What, choose to die?' It was hideous to hear out loud. Of course, Yun had thought about it. He thought about it every day. But it seemed cruel to imagine people were choosing this fate for themselves. 'It seems like a lot of effort. If they wanted to kill themselves they could jump off a building or OD.'

'Jumping off a building doesn't work that well. It has to be over a certain height or you'll just paralyse yourself, or die later real slowly. It's inefficient. There aren't that many guaranteed ways to die, to be honest. People choose inefficient ways all the time.'

'Why do you know that?'

'Read it somewhere. It's why you don't take paracetamol either. Messes you up, really slow way to go. I read that some people wake up, get all relieved because they realized they didn't wanna die. But their kidneys are already fucked and they die, like, weeks later.'

'Shooting yourself has to be pretty efficient.'

'Surprisingly not.' It was the most Kevin had sounded like an aspiring lawyer in a while. 'Putting a gun in your mouth, a lot of people miss the brain and blow their jaw off. But the side of the head isn't a sure thing either. The bullet can get lodged in your skull.'

'So what *is* a good way?'

'Heroin.' Kevin failed to elaborate in a way that made Yun feel uneasy. 'Maybe this whole thing was started by a cult.'

'How would that even work?'

'I don't know, a newsletter?'

Yun laughed. 'Yeah, right.'

'It's not impossible. It's mostly affecting young people, right? Average age is, like, fifteen to forty. So if they are choosing to do this, maybe it's about making a statement. They're not just choosing to die, they're choosing to do it like this for a *reason*.'

'So like a protest? What would they even be protesting?'

'Dude, everything?' Kevin spread his hands.

They both drank, then exchanged goodbyes. Yun shut his laptop. He pushed the wheelie chair away from the desk and let it turn him around, staring blankly at what remained of Jarah's possessions. He was struck by the familiar feeling that someone else out there, or maybe several other people, were already living the life he was supposed to be living, because maybe he had been too slow or too unfocused, or just not good enough to attain it.

Maybe Kevin was right. That was a thought Yun had never had about his brother before. But what if he *was* right? Not just about Yun, but about everything?

Yun kicked his feet up to rest on the windowsill, watched the guy doing yoga on one of the low roofs across the street. He went to message Emory but decided against it, sending it to Jarah instead.

Can I call?

Her reply was fast: *What is it?*

He called her straight away, and it rang twice before she picked up. 'I hate it when you do that.'

'Aren't you bored living with your parents?'

'That doesn't mean I want to talk to *you*. What is it?'

'Can't I just call and check how you are?'

Yun turned on the camera, and after a few seconds of

irritable silence, she did the same. Her expression was one of resigned endurance.

'I don't know why you're calling me if you're bored,' she said, zipping her grey hoodie right up to the top. 'I know you're seeing someone.'

'How do you know?'

'I have this thing called *friends*, some of whom are also yours.' She shrugged. 'For the record, I don't mind. Is this about rent?'

'No, it's fine. BB actually gave us a waiver.'

She waited for him to say something else. She looked lovely, he thought, in that way women do when they're out of your life forever. Or maybe *because* they are.

'When we lived together,' Yun said slowly. 'I mean, when we were *together* together. Did you ever feel like I made you change things about yourself?'

Someone off-camera said something, and Jarah replied, 'Yeah, it's just Yun.' She turned back to him. 'Mom says hi.' She gave the question some thought, and walked to another room, giving him a skewed view of her sharp jawline. All the angles he used to press his lips against. But it felt wrong to think about her like that now. 'I don't know. Everyone changes.'

'Did I?'

'Um . . . No.' A trace of disappointment.

'When we broke up, you never really said why. You said things weren't working any more, which is fine, I'm not disputing that. But why? Was it because I never got a real job or made enough money?'

'No, it wasn't that!' She laughed, which shocked him. 'Oh my God, it wasn't *money*.'

'What was it?' He could tell that she knew what she wanted to say. 'Don't worry, I can take it.'

'Why do you want to have this conversation now? Are you dying or something? Have you joined AA and you're calling everyone you've ever wronged?'

'Ah, so you think I wronged you?'

'No! Not really. It just felt . . . too depressing.'

His beer was warm. 'I made you depressed?'

'No.' She grimaced, as she always did when he failed to be as precise with his communication as she was. 'It *felt* depressing. You know when you're depressed and you just do the same thing every day? The repetitiveness, the boredom, with yourself, with everything you used to like. It felt like that with you.'

'Wow.' Yun looked at his own face in the corner of the screen. 'I always thought you just wanted me to do better.'

'I wanted you to be happy, I didn't care what you were doing. It just got too much, watching you do the same thing over and over, and I realized you were never going to stop trying to become this imaginary version of yourself where you're happy *because* you're rich or signed to a big label or something huge like that. Even when things did go well, you were never happy because it wasn't like this ultimate fantasy you already made up in your head.' She took a breath. 'It was really hard to be around, to be with someone who was just never happy.'

She was right, he thought. So was Kevin.

'So I'm never gonna be happy. Is that what you're saying?'

'Well, if you're asking yourself these questions, you must really like this girl at least. Because I never felt like you asked yourself any of this with me.' She dodged the question, then snorted. 'Or you really are dying.'

10.

Emory took the subway into Manhattan, then three different buses up into the Bronx, finally making her way to City Island. Almost a three-hour journey because the buses were running a reduced service due to a staff shortage.

She was aware of City Island as a kind of novelty holiday resort tagged on to the Bronx, which on a map looked like a miniature Florida. Lara had talked about going there a few times, but – being from New York – neither of them ever managed to organize anything.

It was so hot Emory had to stop and reapply sunscreen in front of a moderately busy Crab Shanty, before turning down a narrow street off City Island Ave lined with small homes. She kept walking until she was almost at the water, checked the address in her phone, and approached a tiny white bungalow. A dark-blue Mercedes was parked in the one-car driveway, which looked out of place. It was almost the same height as the house.

A woman of about forty, with hair a similar shade to Emory's but for the inch of grey-streaked roots, opened the door. Shelley Walsh also had a black eye and a cut above her eyebrow. Stress had prematurely aged her.

'You have to walk around the back,' she said, indicating the side gate. She had one of those fancy accents that people on the Upper East Side sometimes put on. 'I can't let you in the house, no one else is allowed in until they test every-thing for *contamination*.'

She put the word in air quotes.

Emory walked around the bungalow and found herself in a grassy yard with a yellow-painted shed and a swing-seat. Shelley was already opening another gate, leading to a thin dirt track running behind the houses. It was lined with trash cans, discarded garden toys and people's bikes.

'I have to keep coming to the beach or I'd lose my mind inside that house.' Shelley lit a cigarette as her flip-flops made a dry smacking sound against the parched ground. 'I'm not even allowed to visit him. What was it you said your name was – Emily?'

'Emory.' She took her phone out. 'Let me know when it's okay to start recording. Of course, I'll only print what you're comfortable with.'

'Fine, fine.' Shelley waved a hand without turning around.

'How long has it been since it happened?'

'Five days.' It sounded like the act of smoking was regulat-ing her breathing. 'It's only been two days since they left me on my own, they kept coming back to take things. They took his shaving kit, can you believe it? And the remote controls. Not the TV, just the remote controls. So now I have to get up. I have to physically *get up* to change the channels. It's bizarre.'

Shelley was referring to the specialists from the Depart-ment of Health and CDC, who hadn't corresponded with Shelley since, or returned any of her belongings.

She and Emory emerged from the path on to a stony beach with an empty concrete walkway where two white weather-beaten chairs stood alone facing the water. Shelley took one, and Emory the other.

'This is usually full of sailboats and yachts.' Shelley gestured towards the unseasonably quiet Eastchester Bay. 'You can see Manhattan. It's the second horizon.'

The sky was larger than everything. It was overwhelming to look at even through sunglasses. It made Emory feel sick, like she was out on the water.

'Can you describe what happened? If you're comfortable with that.'

Shelley took a long drag, inhaling until the cigarette burned right down to the butt, then flicked it away and took out another. 'You could technically say it happened in his sleep. But the weird thing was, he seemed awake. So whatever happened to him, it must have woken him up at some point. Or maybe he was lying awake all that time after we said goodnight, and I fell asleep without even noticing the change.'

As Shelley lit her second cigarette, she stuck her little finger out and said, 'Swans.'

Emory looked back to the water, where two swans and four cygnets were passing by.

'I see more of them now fewer people are out on their boats. At least the panic has cut down on day trippers.' Shelley spoke around her cigarette while she retied the ribbon on the front of her pink summer blouse. 'I knew it had happened as soon as I woke up. He gets up earlier than me. *Got* up earlier. Got up at four a.m. because he liked to work out. I told him I couldn't see the point in that. Anyway, it doesn't matter now. Maybe he was thankful for those extra hours.'

Emory's mouth was uncomfortably dry and she desperately wanted to drink some water or apply some lip balm. But she didn't want to do anything that might stop Shelley from talking, so she continued to hold her phone on the arm of the chair while she chewed her lips. Shelley's account interested her because Shelley and Kian, being in their mid-forties, were a little older than the average case, and she noticed the general public seemed more sympathetic towards accounts of afflicted people who weren't in their twenties or thirties.

'I know this sounds terrible but I hoped he was dead. I hoped it was something quick that had taken him in the night. It would have been better.' Shelley tapped at her chest with her free hand, like she was trying to dislodge something internal. 'I called an ambulance, but at first I just shouted at him. I could see he was awake and, even though I'd heard the stories, I guess I just didn't understand why he wouldn't *get up*. I thought it had to be a joke. I didn't even think this thing was real!'

'It's an understandable reaction,' Emory said, seizing the opportunity to take out a bottle of water.

'My sister told me she had depression a few years ago.' Shelley said the word 'depression' like a slur. 'But it never made sense to me. What did she have to be depressed about? She described it as somehow not being able to get up or do anything.'

'It does seem similar.'

Shelley shook her head a little too aggressively, fiddling with her wedding ring. 'Trust me, whatever it is, it's *not* depression. No one dies from depression.'

For the sake of the interview, which she was planning to post on her personal website due to the increased traffic she was getting, Emory didn't contradict her.

'I tried to do CPR while waiting for the ambulance. I

know it doesn't make sense, it wasn't like he'd stopped breathing, but I didn't know what else to do. I slapped him a couple of times and that did nothing.'

'Is that how you got . . . ?' Emory indicated the bruising, the cut above her eyebrow.

'I know everyone says you shouldn't do that, you shouldn't move them or try to make them do anything. But he didn't do anything when I slapped him. I even threw some water on him. I was so angry –' Shelley's voice thickened and she paused. 'After CPR I tried to just pull him up. I was saying, "Kian, that's enough! You get up right now! Right now! Don't you dare do this, don't you dare!" And he hit me like he didn't even know who I was.'

A moment of silence, where Shelley seemed to drag her rage back from the water's edge and shove it back down. 'He didn't even look sad about it.'

'I don't think they're consciously doing that,' Emory said, in case it helped.

'Of course I know *that*. I saw it myself! You saw one, didn't you?' Shelley looked at her with an inscrutable expression. Disdain maybe, but not necessarily towards her. Towards everything. 'That's the only reason I agreed to talk to you. I think everyone else still thinks we're crazy. Or making it up. They sound like that when they call me, other journalists, I mean. I don't even know how they got my number here. We don't live here usually.'

She switched her cigarette to her other hand and took Emory's arm suddenly. 'Do you think that's why this happened to us? Be honest. Me and Kian only came here because it was going to be empty for the summer when our rentals cancelled. But we thought we'd be safer here. In hindsight, maybe we caught it on the way here somehow. Even though we took the car . . .'

'For what it's worth, I don't think that's how it happens.' Emory thought about taking her hand but decided against it. 'I don't think you can catch it, like a virus.'

Emory had noticed more people wearing face masks. Though whatever the catatonia was, it almost certainly wasn't a typical contagious disease. If it was, then Yun would already have it. So would Emory. So would Michelle, Andrew, and pretty much everyone else who had been at the wedding. These kinds of precautions might offer some illusion of control, but ultimately made no difference.

'That's something.' Shelley nodded and let go of her arm. Emory worried that Shelley was about to cry, but she didn't. Her composure was visibly shaky but firm. It reminded Emory of the skyscrapers designed to sway during earth-quakes. 'That's something.'

'If you don't mind me asking, if you wouldn't describe it as depression, what do you think it is?'

'They're already dead,' Shelley replied, faster than Emory was expecting. 'He did die in his sleep, in a way. Because whatever that was they took to the hospital, it wasn't my husband. He might have been able to breathe and fling his arms around, but plenty of dead things look like they're alive.'

A handful of dates into a potential relationship was a bad time for life to rudely cut in line and demand full attention. It had happened to Emory a few times. They were offered a new job and moved, or she was offered a new job and simply became more absent for longer periods of time, until one or both of them lost interest. He became busy. She became busy. And suddenly she and Yun hadn't seen each other for over a month. She wondered whether it would be too forward to ask where they stood. But they were hardly exclusive, and that might seem embarrassingly like caring. Maybe it was better to let it fizzle out, like these things usually did.

Emory sat at her kitchen table and went over the extra questions she had asked Shelley for texture: what kind of person Kian Walsh had been, his lifestyle, where he grew up, his relationship with their adult children. She also asked about his medical history. She wasn't under any illusions she was going to crack the case – the CDC still hadn't, and neither had the WHO – but at the very least she wanted to exercise some basic pattern recognition.

The violent act of giving up had happened to smokers and non-smokers, the fit and unfit. She had put a world map up on her bedroom wall, like a crazy person, using pins to indicate every reported case and cluster, but they didn't create a compelling visual. There were more cases in urban areas than rural, more cases in Western nations than in the Global South or underdeveloped countries. It skewed more young than old, more poor than rich, more towards people of colour than white. But then, didn't most things?

All these people had in common was the fact they sat down and fought to stay that way until they died from a heart attack, heart failure or sudden cardiac arrest brought on by the prolonged release of stress hormones, elevated blood pressure and heart rate. Sometimes all of this was preceded by palpitations, spasms or arrhythmias. Some patients had a history of heart disease in their family. Some didn't. But all died eventually, mostly within one to two weeks.

Emory had even tried to look up criminal records, but it all came to nothing. There was no indication the afflicted had done anything wrong, and no indication of what anyone else was doing right. No neat line between deserving and undeserving, which was what everyone wanted.

At lunch with her father after the Hunter Mountain presser, he had kept putting his fork down and saying, 'I just can't explain it.'

Every first responder and analyst who had been on the scene of the incident at Hunter Mountain was assigned mandatory therapy sessions. All of the people they had tried to help that day were now dead.

Dead things. Since talking to Shelley, the words were never far from Emory's mind.

'I can't explain it,' her father had said over and over, looking down at his salad with pure devastation. 'It almost makes you think . . .'

But he had never elaborated on exactly what it almost made him think.

When Emory called Shelley Walsh to follow up on the interview, she was informed that Kian had died of a heart attack in hospital the day after they had seen each other. She put her phone down and paced the apartment until she was exhausted.

Fuck this, she thought, before calling a car and going straight to Yun's apartment.

II.

It was almost impossible to find a place to buy ice cream without a line stretching around the corner.

Emory felt like they had been walking around Williamsburg for hours, and her shoes were starting to rub a blister on to the outside of her big toe.

'The reason kids can't get it is because they have no idea what's going on.' Yun indicated Derrick's son, Lewis, who was walking a little in front of them with his perpetually anxious father in tow.

Derrick smiled like someone who hadn't had much practice in it growing up. Even his most sincere smiles started on one side of his face, and if the other side managed to catch up his overall expression was one of surprise, as if positive emotions only ever crept up on him. She liked Derrick. She preferred him to Andrew, though couldn't work out exactly why.

'Kids like to be selective idiots.' Derrick stooped to keep a hand on the back of his son's collar. 'This guy knows exactly where his food is coming from but pretends he doesn't know the difference between a road and the sidewalk, or asleep and awake.'

'I'd love to have no idea what's going on.' Yun tickled Lewis on the back of the neck and put on a sing-song voice. 'You must be so happy!'

'Some kids have had it,' Emory pointed out, tying her

redundant jacket around her waist. 'Pervasive Refusal Syndrome is pretty much the closest working diagnosis anyone has, and that was around way before this.'

'Wasn't that mostly refugee kids, though?' Yun raised his eyebrows. 'That proves my point, right? They definitely know what's going on. If most adults over here experienced the level of fucking *knowing* your average refugee kid has, they'd throw themselves in front of the nearest train.'

'So you think self-awareness is the problem?'

Derrick laughed. 'Self-awareness is a massive problem, to be fair. Though I kinda get what you're saying. It can't just be that because, contrary to appearances, kids aren't totally stupid. They pick up on vibes. If something feels off, if me and his mom are arguing and we're all quiet and tense, Lew starts acting out. He doesn't know *why* he's acting out, but he picks up on the feeling.'

Like he had suddenly been given some very bad news. Or remembered something horrible.

Emory recalled a study from the UK that found around ten per cent of people who tried meditation or other 'mindfulness' practices experienced an increase in anxiety, depression, panic attacks, or sometimes full-on nervous breakdowns. No one was sure why a small minority suffered these adverse side-effects, but Emory suspected it was because a lot of people cultivated a lack of awareness for their own sanity. If you were suddenly to become *aware* – like the woman Michelle had told her about, who one day sank to the floor screaming against her kitchen cupboards – and were filled with nothing but horror and regret, what then?

Lewis ended up steering them into the most expensive ice-cream place any of them had seen so far, the kind of place where you could top a cone with edible petals. Emory somehow ended up spending almost twenty dollars on two cones, and by the time they left the shop – shutting her eyes to enjoy the final blast of the air con inside the doorway – Yun had liquid mint chocolate chip melting all over his fingers.

'I really admire people who go for mint chocolate chip,' Derrick said, taking liberal spoonfuls from Lewis's tub of mango. 'You've got real self-care going, brushing your teeth twice.'

'I admire how many times you've made that joke.' Yun went to put his arm around Emory's waist and had to rethink it due to the state of his hands. 'You're really comfortable with your old material, huh.'

Usually the heat made people lazy, but everyone's eyes seemed wide and trained on the ground, as if watching for black ice. If someone so much as crouched to tie their laces, a collective intake of breath rippled up and down the block. Emory had started avoiding sleep, sitting down, any form of rest. If she was always standing, always awake, she felt safe. Any hint of fatigue made her own body seem malignant, waiting to drag her down at any moment.

As they headed for Prospect Park, Emory's second scoop of pistachio neatly rolled off her cone and hit the sidewalk. 'Oh shoot.'

Yun fell to his knees without hesitation, attempting to use what remained of his cone to salvage the majority of the scoop without touching the ground.

'I'm not eating that off the sidewalk!' Emory shrieked.

'For nine dollars, *I'll* eat it off the sidewalk!' Yun snapped, licking the excess from the bottom of his cone with laser focus.

Lewis burst into tears, but Yun's sudden drop had already caused people to start looking.

Derrick muttered, 'Damn it . . .' before thrusting the tub of mango at Emory and throwing himself animatedly to the ground beside Yun. 'Hey, Lew! Hey, it's fine, look what Daddy's doing!'

'What *are* you doing?' Yun asked, getting to his feet and eating Emory's rescued ice cream.

Derrick rolled on to his back and kept waving both arms and legs at his son, like he was floating atop a dinghy and trying to attract a lifeboat. It didn't take long for Lewis to stop crying and start laughing instead. He sprang forward to grab his father around the waist, trying to drag him upright, and only at that point did Derrick get up off the ground.

Trying to quell Lewis's overexcited squealing, Derrick dusted himself off and gestured for his ice cream back. 'It's a positive reinforcement thing,' he said, as if that explained everything.

'So, like *Clockwork Orange*,' Yun said, making Emory wonder if he had actually seen the movie, or if she had misunderstood the phrase 'positive reinforcement'.

'Well, kinda like what we were talking about, Lew has started freaking out every time anyone sits down. It's unavoidable, it's all people talk about any more. He hears it on the TV, the radio, preschool. Sit down, and he's learned that people start screaming and crying. It's scary. So I figured the more I can make being on the ground something funny, the easier it'll be on him.'

Emory looked at Lewis, who seemed to have forgotten his own moment of hysteria and was far more concerned with getting his ice cream back. 'And it works?'

'Yeah, it works.' Derrick gave Lewis back his tub. 'Only problem is, I can't do it for too long in public. Had to practise loads at home to have it work that quick.'

'Why?'

'*Cops,*' Derrick and Yun said in unison.

'They see a Black man rolling around on the ground causing a scene, they're liable to think I'm having a *mental health incident.*' Derrick lowered his voice for his son's benefit. 'And they don't always go so well.'

They started walking again.

Derrick chuckled to himself. 'One time, a guy I worked with in the hardware store got fired and he sat down in the aisle until they carried him out. I couldn't get away with that, but respect to him. It's always bothered some people, randomly sitting down.'

'Maybe that's why they banned shop workers from doing it.' Yun shook his head. 'I never understood why retail managers get so pressed over whether the kids at checkout are sitting down or not. Like, customers don't care if they rest their legs on an eight-hour shift.'

'It's not for the customers, though, it's for the managers. It says, we own your body so you'll stand up if we tell you to stand up. Sit down and you're not playing along, you're not all submissive and jumping to attention.'

Hanging half a step back from their conversation, Emory opened her notes app and wrote, *Rest as a radical act.* Her fingers were sticky but the cone was gone and she vowed, not for the first time, not to spend such a ridiculous amount on tourist food ever again.

Yun was less bothered, but then he regularly ate things he dropped on the floor. The five-second rule meant nothing to him. As long as it wasn't visibly soiled, it was fair game. 'If I die, I die,' was how he put it.

Someone had sent her an email, marked urgent, about the Hunter Mountain 95, but she didn't have the stomach to read it outside in the sun. Putting the phone away, she caught up with the others, who were still talking about the petty indignities of minimum wage jobs, and hadn't noticed they'd walked on ahead.

Yun complained of stomach cramps all the way back.

'Why don't you just stop eating dairy?' Emory said, trying not to laugh as they turned the corner on to Skillman Ave.

'Because I'd rather die,' Yun retorted. 'Let me complain, it's part of the process.'

'It's a medical symptom.'

'It's a *process*.' Yun veered off the sidewalk and into the middle of the empty road.

Emory thought he was simply being dramatic. But instead he stopped walking, and looked up at the early-evening light making the low buildings seem golden against the sickly blue sky. There was an inhale – Emory's stomach clenching with fear, because she wasn't sure what was going to happen – and Yun suddenly lay down in the road. He rested both hands on his diaphragm, as if to feel the long sigh of relief.

'Are you drunk?' Emory tried to remember if she'd seen a hip flask. 'Get out of the road!'

'I just wanted to try it.' Yun gestured for her to join him. 'There are no cars.'

Emory's instinctive response was to tell him to stop being stupid, because there was *no* way she was going to lie down in the middle of a road in Brooklyn, just like there was no way she was going to eat a scoop of pistachio ice cream off the sidewalk. But refusal didn't come easily to her. Refuse one too many things and at some point she stopped being fun, even if the things she was being asked to do didn't strike her as fun in the first place. She hadn't spent a night at her own apartment for over two weeks and was amazed Yun didn't mind, every bit as much as she was plagued by the anxiety that, at some point, he would start minding. Especially if Emory stopped being fun.

Emory looked up and down the street to confirm there were no cars or, more importantly, witnesses, then went to stand over him. She hovered for a moment, worrying about her sundress, while he shielded his eyes and smiled up at her.

It was the most beautiful he had ever looked.

She dropped her shoulder bag and lay down next to him. 'It's hot!'

'But not fry-an-egg hot.' Yun took her hand, interlinked their fingers. 'It's nice.'

Emory craned her neck to check for cars. She was pretty sure one of the middle-aged men who lived opposite was sitting on his stoop a few buildings down, staring at them. She tried to tell herself that everyone in New York had seen weirder things.

The tarmac was abrasive against her skull. She couldn't remember the last time she had lain down on anything that wasn't a bed or a couch. Maybe she never had. She hadn't been one of those children who was partial to forts, caves, hiding places, or even throwing herself to the floor while having a tantrum. Unlike Yun, who still enjoyed flinging himself flat to the nearest surface to make a point.

'It's almost like you're not in the city, from this angle,' Yun said, his stomach cramps forgotten.

'We should move soon though,' Emory said. What Derrick said about cops had made her paranoid, and she thought the road seemed more hostile with your body flattened against it. The sky looked poised to fall.

'In a second.' Yun took out his phone and flipped the camera.

He took one shot of himself, then pulled Emory in. She was startled by the sight of her own face, as she always was when she looked into a phone camera. *Do I really look like that? That can't be what I actually look like, can it?* But then she remembered to smile and not search for a car, and instead lean the side of her head against Yun's, like she was the sort of person who could live in the moment.

'In a just world, they'd have to give us a reason to get up.' Yun raised himself on his elbows, gathered some momentum by rolling on the small of his back and kicked up.

He helped Emory to her feet, then went quiet while he posted the photos to Instagram.

There were tiny bits of gravel stuck to her calves. She brushed them off as she climbed the steps and opened the email about the Hunter Mountain 95.

The sister of a twenty-nine-year-old man named Calvin Huntsberger wanted to tell Emory that Calvin had attended the wedding of Michael Ellison and Lara Rodell the week before; the wedding where Rose Hailey had first been taken ill. She thought Emory might like to know, in case the information was relevant.

Suicide clusters, Emory remembered reading somewhere. Or something else contagious.

But it wasn't a virus, was it. It wasn't a virus.

On some level, Emory had known a connection like this was out there. It had occurred to her some time ago to cross-reference the list of wedding guests with the ninety-five afflicted at Hunter Mountain. But she hadn't. She was too busy. She forgot. It didn't seem relevant. Whatever excuses she went with, she knew it was because doing so could expose a link she didn't want to know about, a link that didn't fit with the narrative she had already created.

Emory didn't realize she had stopped in the doorway until Yun said, 'Em, are you coming in?'

He disappeared into his bedroom, and she heard him flop on to the bed, groaning. 'My stomach hates me and wants me to die.'

She wondered whether Calvin Huntsberger was the first to go down. With mass events, she was most fascinated by the ones who sat down first; the ones whose bodies were more sensitive to that unseen trigger. It was relatively easy to see what it was that triggered the others; witnessing those who were sitting down before them. But the first was beholden to a completely independent call to action. Or, at least, she had thought so. Now it was obvious that Calvin Huntsberger's call had been heard the week before, and he had taken the echo with him upstate.

Somewhere between Rose sitting down on the dance floor and Emory's story about her, what might have been nothing more than an isolated incident of mass hysteria caused by one freaked-out young man became a non-isolated incident of something else entirely.

Emory read about one case where dozens of children at a school were convinced they were sick, after one classmate fell ill and another claimed the smell of fresh paint in the cafeteria was a gas leak. In that case, a doctor who was called to the scene came to the logical conclusion, and used his authority to tell all of the kids and teachers that they were fine, there was no gas leak, nothing categorically wrong with them, and they should all go back to work.

But in this case, no medical professional was able to reach the scene first, tell everyone to calm down, and enable everyone to return to their day as normal. Because in this case, Emory had created the narrative first.

She had formed the connections, called it 'the catatonic crisis', called it 'the catatonia', and turned the isolated incident into a non-isolated incident. It wasn't a virus. It was no longer a simple case of mass hysteria. What if it was now just a narrative that too many people had accepted?

Emory came inside and shut the door.

She was about to tell Yun. She could feel the words forming on her tongue. But instead she ran herself a glass of water, deleted the email and never told anyone about it.

Sumi @Lucky13930

i hate this week i hate working from 9 until i sleep, makes me want to d word

12.

Some of Jarah's friends turned up to pack the rest of her stuff into a moving van, leaving only the furniture the two-bed apartment had come furnished with. They told Yun she was staying in Hawaii with her parents indefinitely, so he moved his instruments back into the spare room. Life seemed to lose any trace of intent, and he felt increasingly like he was watching things happening to him.

He didn't mind that Emory hadn't gone home for the last three weeks, because she gave him something to focus on. The summer warmth was only just starting to eke out of the air but he held himself like it was colder, shoulders hunched and braced for some sort of impact because at any moment it felt like death was going to burst into the room.

Yun collected his fried chicken burger from the Jamaican place five blocks down, and hung the bag over his handlebars, alongside the bag of cleaning products he'd picked up from the bodega for Ms BB.

As he cycled home, he noted the pop-up bars which had folded almost immediately after opening. One of his favourite sandwich places was boarded up but he'd been holding out hope that it might reopen. Everyone seemed to be advertising for new hires. No one wanted to work, apparently. No shit.

He turned off Metropolitan then on to Skillman, and came to a halt as someone's cat darted in front of the wheel.

The bags unbalanced him and he threw his foot out, catching the kerb as he stumbled and landed on one knee, taking the bike down with him.

'Shit . . .'

The cat didn't stick around. It was already gone, as if he'd imagined it. He straightened up and couldn't catch his breath. The jolt had shaken him, and his legs and shoulders hurt. He got off his bike and pushed it the rest of the way.

As he passed Ms BB's front door, he remembered he still had to carry his electric piano back upstairs. She refused to listen to a recording unless it was on vinyl, so in the end he'd played her his cover of 'Love is Blue' in person the other night, when he'd dropped off some shopping and stayed for a drink.

She didn't like Emory. When he asked her why, she said, 'She's someone who's learned how to act nice. I don't trust it.'

He pointed out that she'd liked Jarah specifically because she *was* nice.

'I didn't say she was nice, I said she's learned how to *act* nice. That's completely different!' Then she added that it shouldn't matter to Yun what she thought anyway. 'Men will do whatever they want until they can't stand it any more,' she said.

He couldn't work out what she had meant by that.

Emory was out, so he headed back downstairs after putting his burger in the oven to reheat.

He knocked on the door. 'Hey, it's me.'

No answer.

His first assumption was that Ms BB was out as well, but she kept her shoe rack outside the door. Like Yun, she thought wearing shoes indoors was unsanitary. All of her shoes were still there.

Knocking again, he put his ear against the door but couldn't hear anything. He went outside and crouched on the steps, trying to peer through the window, which was partially open.

Come to think of it, she didn't really go out that much, because of her hips.

'Ms BB?' He tried to get lower, see better.

The sun was too low in the sky to reach the street.

He kept telling himself it was too dim to see anything inside, but he knew he could see something. Something was wrong, because his body became cold and light, like he was floating outside of his own skin. He was shivering when he let himself back into the building. He tried to open her front door but it was locked.

Without hesitation, he started trying to kick it down. It didn't even occur to him what it might look like; that some-one might think he was trying to rob the place and call the police. That's how he knew – later when he really thought about it – that he had seen something, that he knew some-thing was wrong.

When kicking the door didn't work, he went back out to the steps and dropped into a crouch again. He took his phone out, called 911 and said, 'I live on Skillman Ave, I think my landlady needs help.' And when she asked him the build-ing's number, he snapped, 'Can you hurry! I don't think she's moving!'

He tried to kick the door in again but it wouldn't budge so he went back out and climbed over the railings, which dropped into the narrow, dank space between the street and the basement level. He didn't notice how badly he'd bruised his legs until after.

He climbed on to the trash cans, braced himself on the sill and somehow wormed his way through the half-open window, landing hands-and-face-first on the floor, and almost forward-rolling into her empty chair.

Shivering, though numb to any physical pain, he lay for a moment on the floor, aware that she was also lying on the floor. He kept telling himself that it was dark in here, that he hadn't really seen anything. But here they both were, lying on the floor.

He used the chair to support himself as he got to his feet. His phone had fallen out of his pocket so he picked it up. It was so quiet. He unlocked the front door, opened it and left it slightly ajar. It drifted open a couple more inches of its own accord, creaking towards him then coming to a slow halt.

He didn't know why his first instinct wasn't to rush towards her, to check if she was still breathing or if there was anything he could do. It's what he imagined a normal person would have done, a better person. But a large part of him knew there was no point. A larger part of him knew that he wasn't the type to run instinctively towards someone who needed help, let alone run instinctively towards the dead.

Crossing the room, he checked the stove was off. For some reason, he was worried about the gas.

She was by the dining table and had fallen on to her front. Maybe she had tried to support herself on it, when she first realized something was wrong. But he didn't want to turn her over or see her face. He didn't want to touch her at all.

He shouldn't even be in the apartment, not without being invited in.

He thought, *Jesus Christ, am I going to lose the apartment?* and the cold transformed into a rising panic in his chest. He knew he wasn't a good person, for having that thought. But he couldn't stop it.

Crouching down, he forced himself to reach out and adjust her grey cardigan, pulling it a little tighter around her shoulders. He clenched his teeth and averted his eyes when he took ahold of her wrist to feel for a pulse. She wasn't cold, but she wasn't warm either. The skin was alien and rubbery, like when you lie on your own arm in the night and the numb, heavy limb feels repulsive and fake to touch.

Yun stood and ran to throw up in the sink.

After rinsing out his mouth, dashing some cold water on his face, he approached her again. Just to make sure. But there wasn't any breathing, no blank and staring eyes. She hadn't given up. This wasn't catatonia. Ms BB had died the old-fashioned way.

His electric piano was wedged up against the bureau where the record player was, and he sat on the stool to wait for the ambulance.

When the medics arrived, they tried insisting Yun travel to the hospital with them for tests, but he refused. For one, he was uninsured and had no idea how much they'd bill him for it. And he didn't want to travel in the ambulance, with Ms BB in the bag. It wasn't a case of catatonia and, as far as anyone knew, death itself wasn't inherently catching.

They asked him if he had touched anything in the room. They told him not to touch anything else.

He paced around his front room – taking his charred

burger out of the oven and dropping it directly into the trash – until he heard the people from the Department of Health and CDC arrive. Then he watched from the stairs while they covered Ms BB's apartment in plastic, and started taking her things outside in bags.

They took the record player, took samples from a bottle of Campari, took things from the fridge.

'That's my piano!' Yun exclaimed, following them outside. 'She didn't even touch it!'

'You can have it back once we've run some tests. This is standard procedure now, when there's no definitive cause of death.'

'You think I haven't heard of asset forfeiture, you assholes!'

One of them turned to him and sneered from behind a black visor, 'We're not the police.'

When Emory got back, she found him lying on the floor in Jarah's old room on the phone to the letting agency. Someone told him that the place was co-owned by Bernadetta's younger brother, who lived in Milan, but he had little interest in doing anything with the building and would likely just let the agency move another tenant on to the first floor.

The relief would've knocked him down, had he been standing. He got up off the floor and let Emory make him some food. He couldn't even let her hug him for long. It was the first time in weeks that he didn't want to be touched. He felt like something was following him around and leaning on him; a black spectre with feathery, delicate hands that lifted all the hairs on his arms and made his skin feel infested.

'At least you don't have to worry about the apartment,' Emory said.

He knew that she meant to sound reassuring, but he was already thinking about the rent payments he would no longer be able to avoid.

Good people don't worry about these things when someone has just died. The guilt lodged in his throat. Would a good person look at the body of someone they knew and liked, their friend, and think, *Jesus Christ, am I going to lose the apartment?*

Am I going to get my piano back?

How can I cover both mine and Jarah's rent now?

These worries barged in front of anything that might resemble grief and jostled for place.

He should've been thinking about playing 'Love is Blue', or how she had told him, 'It's disrespectful to sit at a piano wearing a cap, take that ridiculous thing off!' But when he had finished playing, she stood up and clapped like she was at the theatre and announced, 'What a treat! What a treat that was!'

Yun should've been thinking about when Ms BB had said, 'You laugh like Luke, he could never laugh properly either. He laughed like a budgerigar and so do you!' And Yun had replied, 'Well, you laugh like a pack of geese, you hear me complaining about it?'

The bag of cleaning products from the bodega was still sitting on the floor inside the front door, where he'd dropped it.

He was thinking, *How am I going to pay the rent when there's no Ms BB and no waivers and no decent-paying jobs?*

When he went to get a beer, he froze in front of the open fridge. The sudden change in temperature made him feel close to tears. It spewed freezing air towards him and Yun wanted to collapse under the weight, the unbearable weight of knowing he had to carry on moving, continue to *try*, to wake up day after day and do this, do everything. He didn't want to die, he just wanted to stop, to cease, sit down. Maybe just sleep, for a year or maybe forever.

'Yun?' Emory touched his arm and she sounded concerned. 'Do you need anything?'

He wondered if she had somehow felt it, felt him slipping away. But it wasn't likely. She was just standing by him and searching for a way to help, like any normal person would. Like any good person.

He took out a bottle of Asahi and rifled in the drawer for a bottle opener. Then he turned to Emory and said, 'This might sound insane, but would you wanna move in?'

'It's strange,' Andrew said softly. 'I don't think I've seen anyone that out of it before.'

'Maybe it was that stupid drinking game.'

'Maybe someone put something in her drink. Nicola said she had her drink spiked once and it just wipes you out. One minute you're fine and the next you don't even know where you are. Total blackout.'

Yun shrugged. He was getting a headache and didn't want to go home. He had looked at the girl in the back of the car and wished he could feel genuine concern, but all he felt was dehydrated. Being driven through New York at night always made him melancholy.

Andrew kept staring unseeingly at the entrance to the ER like someone else trapped by their own relentless trajectory, like he wasn't driving his own car, and Yun realized they were still sitting there because he didn't want to go home either.

'Ah!' Yun remembered the joint in his pocket and produced it with a triumphant flourish.

'We can't smoke in a hospital parking lot.' Andrew paused. 'Actually, I can't. You can.'

'You can have one drag,' Yun said, holding it between his lips to light it.

'What if I have to brake suddenly?'

'Then we'll die, obviously.' Yun took a drag and offered him the joint.

Andrew looked at it for a couple of seconds before shaking his head. 'It'd be irresponsible.'

'Fine.' Yun exhaled and coughed. 'I'll smoke it, you can breathe near me.'

He started lowering the window and Andrew spread his hands in mild exasperation. 'I can't breathe it in if you blow it out of the car.'

'Won't Nicola mind the smell?'

'She doesn't care about that kind of thing.' He considered this for a while, as if there was an underlying importance to the statement Yun had failed to pick up on. 'I would describe her general mood as resigned, these days. If we start to bicker, she just walks out.'

'That's good, right?' Yun coughed again.

'It's because we both know, I think, we're not going to stay together. So why disagree about things any more? There's no point.'

'Fuck, man, I'm sorry.' It wasn't surprising to hear, though it wasn't a relief either. It was hard to watch someone like Andrew be unhappy.

'It's probably for the best.'

Another ambulance pulled up. They watched as someone was lifted out and rolled inside in a wheelchair.

'I'm sorry about you and Jarah,' Andrew said, swinging the spotlight back around. 'I feel bad that I haven't seen you since you guys broke up.'

'Everyone's busy, it's fine.' It wasn't fine. Hearing her name made his chest tight and his hands hot. 'It's weird her still living there, like nothing's changed but the sleeping arrangements. And it's so fucking *formal*. Like, she'll talk to me about dishwasher tablets and then nothing else.'

Andrew nodded. 'We'll have to move soon.'

It took Yun a moment to realize he meant from the parking lot. He closed his eyes and took a few deep breaths, then reached out to pat Andrew's shoulder. 'Come on, lean in.'

They shifted in their seats to lean across the divide until they were inches apart. Yun kept his hand on Andrew's shoulder as he took a long drag, holding the smoke in his mouth before exhaling into the heavy, heated air between them. He kept his eyes open, watching as Andrew closed his and parted his lips to draw Yun's breath into his lungs.

The anxiety that had been sitting in Yun's chest now felt like a pleasant buzz, a flutter, as Andrew leaned away to exhale.

'Thanks.' Andrew smiled, a little flushed, and touched his hand.

'No problem.' Yun squeezed his shoulder, then opened the window to throw the stub out. He settled back in his seat and slid down a little, feeling stupid suddenly. 'Look, man, even if you do – get divorced, I mean. You'll be fine.'

Andrew was playing with his hair. He seemed unsure. 'I

saw you disappear from the wedding with that bridesmaid. Maybe you just need to meet the right person?'

Yun laughed, but it felt more like uncontrollable sadness. 'That's my problem. *Everyone* feels like the right person, I can't even tell the difference any more. I ride the subway and see someone reading a book I was just reading and think, *Wow, maybe it's you*. It happens all the time. Someone looks at me and it's just *them*. You know what I mean?'

'You read?'

This laugh felt real. 'Fuck *off*.'

'Yeah, but no.' When Andrew turned to him he seemed bemused, and wasn't laughing any more. 'I've never felt that.'

Andrew and Fin

'I won't live in your world. I will live as if your world has ended, as indeed it deserves to end. I will live as if my gesture of refusing your world has destroyed it.'

– Curtis White, *The Spirit of Disobedience*

13.

'You're not here,' Nicola said when they'd both agreed – at least they agreed on this – that separation wasn't working, therapy wasn't working. Their problem was the state of being married in general. 'I don't know how else to explain it, you're just not here.'

'Did you use to be present, Andrew?' the therapist asked him during a session in late October, approximately six months after Mike and Lara's wedding. Incidentally, on the exact day US case numbers were reported to have surpassed six figures, with deaths lagging slightly behind.

Andrew wanted to explain that he always felt engaged with every event in his life, at first. But the grounding was never permanent. Enthusiasm turned into something bland and lumpy in his mouth, something he could no longer swallow while pretending to enjoy it. All he had learned about love by the age of thirty-one, after two long-term relationships and one marriage, was that it seemed like nothing more than the recurring, soul-eroding process of finding out he didn't feel for someone quite as much as he'd *hoped* he would. That all of his relationships felt like a pale, diluted imitation of something, but he didn't know what. Something he'd seen on TV maybe. Definitely not what he'd seen in his parents.

Of course, he could just be depressed.

'I'm not depressed,' he had told the therapist his parents

made him see in his teens, after his mother first got sick. 'I'm not sad, I just don't *feel* much any more.'

But that was apparently a symptom. So he took citalopram, switched to fluoxetine just before graduating high school, then to sertraline after his father died, when fluoxetine made him want to sleep twenty hours a day.

Sertraline was fine, even if sometimes it was hard to sleep. It was fine, but then he never thought the problem was with his own brain. The problem was everything else. There was an absence in the world. An absence he sometimes thought a partner could fill. But they only made him feel the absence more keenly, until it became hard to even look at them.

Andrew didn't have the heart to tell Nicola that, to put it so plainly. *I never loved you anywhere near as much as I'd hoped I would.* So, he agreed with his wife's assessment. He agreed to the end of his marriage.

On that day, instead of attending the conference taking place at Columbia, Andrew went to the Met. He always went to the Met when he felt on edge, when avoiding other people and too much time alone with his thoughts.

It was a routine. Wherever he travelled, wherever he lived, he cultivated routines. The same coffee shops, restaurants, parks. He found these places quickly and settled in, and that way he never had to think too hard about what he was doing. There was no dead time. He could focus on another article or syllabus. His work stopped him from thinking. That was the good and bad thing about academia. He was overworked and underpaid, but it left no room to contemplate what was absent.

Another routine: he headed to the Mark Rothkos first. It wasn't quiet, but it wasn't as busy as usual, after lunch but before the close of the workday. Andrew tried not to notice how public spaces seemed less busy now, as if people were trying not to catch sight of each other. Both the afflicted and unafflicted were shrinking back into themselves.

Someone was standing in front of *Untitled (Blue Divided by Blue)* but that was to be expected. He stopped and hovered off to the side, looking at the painting from a slant.

A minute passed before Andrew looked at the other person, and the act of looking seemed to affect them both like a physical touch, causing them to turn and face each other. The directness caught Andrew off guard, as did the fact the boy's cheeks were streaked with tears. He realized he wasn't a boy, but a young man. A young, strikingly beautiful man.

Strikingly beautiful wasn't an assessment he usually made about someone. But it wasn't a value judgement, just an observation. Though he felt this observation in his gut, and his chest.

In the time it took for him to react and dismiss his own reactions, the young man smiled at him, wiped his eyes and said, 'Sorry, you're probably waiting to look at this.'

'It's fine. I don't want to rush you.'

'I've been here long enough.' The young man bowed his head, a slightly nervous mannerism, and backed off to sit on one of the benches in the centre of the room.

Andrew stepped in front of the painting, but looked over his shoulder.

The young man sat cross-legged, staring at his phone. He was wearing a black beret and a brown leather bag across a khaki parka. He could be a student, but he wasn't one of Andrew's. He would remember if he was. Yet the tingle of familiarity was there. Maybe he was an actor.

Andrew turned back to the painting, mystified as to why he was dwelling on this momentary interaction. It wasn't in his nature to dwell on anything. His mind simply refused. Everything but work skimmed off the surface.

He had never cried in front of *Untitled (Blue Divided by Blue)* before, or any painting. He didn't really cry per se. Only at certain songs, which he stopped listening to in college because the sensation scared him, left him feeling hollow and disturbed, like everything in the world had rotated imperceptibly sideways and thrown him physically and mentally off-balance. Exactly like he was feeling now.

The slight tip of the world seemed to nudge him to turn around, allow him to break from routine before he could overthink it. He went to the bench and sat beside the young man wearing the beret.

'There was a study,' he said, as if this was a normal way to open a conversation with a stranger, 'of which paintings people cried in front of. And the paintings most people cried in front of were Rothko's.'

A beat passed. The young man looked up from his phone, but didn't seem startled. Then a smile, which emphasized two sharp dimples in the hollows of his cheeks. His eyes – his huge eyes – were glassy, but he was no longer weeping. He said, 'At least you don't think it's embarrassing.'

His accent was unusual, but England came through strongest.

'Why this one?' Andrew indicated his head towards the painting, now framed between two more people several feet away.

'I don't know. If so many other people cry, there's probably nothing special about my reaction.'

Andrew wanted to contradict him, but he didn't know why, or with what.

The young man continued, still looking distantly at the painting. His side profile was full of straight lines. 'It's something about the colour, I think, those particular shades of blue. It should be optimistic. But then he painted it four years before he killed himself, so maybe not. It doesn't make me feel sad, it makes me feel more . . . homesick.'

'Where are you from?'

'Not for my actual home.' The young man smiled more widely, revealing small and endearingly uneven teeth. 'Sorry, I'm not explaining this very well.'

'There is a word for that. A student of mine told me about a word in Welsh, *hiraeth*.' Andrew wondered for a second whether he was being boring, but those eyes were on him, and he felt unable to stop. 'It's also difficult to explain, but it conveys an emotion which is something like homesickness, nostalgia and regret all rolled into one. It's a longing for home, but it's a home that's not specified or definite. It's not a physical place, not a home you can really return to.'

For some reason, the words curled themselves around his gut.

The young man nodded with increasing bemusement. 'Are you a teacher?'

Oh, you are *being boring.*

'Lecturer in Philosophy, so I apologize if I am lecturing. It's not like you asked for an audio tour.'

'No, it makes sense. *Hiraeth*. It's scary to consider we're at the mercy of so much we don't even have names for.' This smile was a little different.

129

Andrew realized he was staring, and quickly averted his eyes, looking towards *Untitled (Blue Divided by Blue)* again.

'That was a segue into asking you *your* name,' the young man said. 'I'm Fin.'

'Andrew.'

It was wordplay, Andrew knew that. This young man being at his mercy was not the implication. That was not a *rational* thing to infer here.

'Sorry but I have to ask, do I know you from somewhere?'

And it was the incline of his head that made Andrew remember, these same features with a black eye just beginning to swell, a hand covering half his face, the other waving him away as he asked if he was all right . . .

Fin put it all together before Andrew said anything. 'Were you at a wedding a few months ago?'

Andrew had never liked the cafe, too white and shiny and full of mismatching sculptures. He didn't mind it today, though. They found a table and sat opposite each other, Andrew with his usual almond milk flat white and Fin with an oat milk latte.

Neither of them was from New York, or even the USA, originally. Andrew was born in Vancouver, and Fin – the son of an Irish mother and Irish-American father – had grown up in London and moved here three years ago.

Fin took off his coat and let it hang over the back of his chair. He was wearing a white turtleneck that dwarfed his tiny frame.

Andrew put his phone on silent.

'Sculpture leaves me cold, I think.' Fin cast his eyes about. 'Maybe I'm uncultured. But I feel like we're losing out on some essential experience if we're not allowed to touch them.'

'So you're the sort of person who likes touching exhibits in museums.'

'It adds an element of danger.' Fin's eyes crinkled over the rim of his cup.

'Maybe it's not sculpture that you don't like, it's the environment. Maybe we're not meant to experience them when they're artificially separated from us.'

'I like that thought.' His dimples became even more pronounced. 'I bet you've never touched anything you're not meant to in your life.'

He means the exhibits.

Andrew looked at his hands, unsure whether it was appropriate to smile. 'Have you ever seen Bernini's thigh?'

'Have I seen *what*?' Fin choked on his coffee, and laughed in a way that made Andrew want to make him laugh again.

Andrew scrolled through images and handed his phone across the table. 'He was an Italian sculptor, there's a thigh he's famous for. It looks so real, the texture.'

'Oh, I *have* seen this.' Andrew's eyes dropped to the way Fin unconsciously flexed his hand against the white tabletop. 'We looked at this sculpture for some choreography once, because of the way she's being held in the air. It would actually be disappointing to touch it and find out it's cold.'

'You're a dancer?' Andrew found the word strangely hard to say. Its implications were more sensual than the word 'thigh'. One was made of stone. One wasn't.

'Yeah, my scholarship was to a dance academy downtown. Ballet.'

'Wow.' He wished he could say something more interesting

but the air in the cafe suddenly felt far too close for such high ceilings. 'I don't think I've met anybody who does that for a living.'

'Not for a living *yet*. And the merit scholarship was fortunate because of how much it cost just to move here. It's why I live so far away since moving out of dorms – international students don't get financial aid.' He looked off to the side with an anxious clench of his fist, like the statement picked at a newly healed scab. 'But I graduate in a year, so I've hung in there.'

The youngest he could be was twenty. Andrew felt uneasy doing the mental calculations. He wasn't sure when dance students graduated, whether it was earlier or later than typical students.

Fin remembered he was still holding Andrew's phone. When he offered it back, their fingertips touched briefly, and Andrew tried not to meet his eyes. As he returned it to his pocket, regret weighed heavily in his hands. He felt strongly like he was remembering something, but also that he was remembering it wrong.

It's projection, Andrew told himself. *You are on the brink of divorce. Of course you associate touch with regret.*

'It's ironic,' he said, because he wanted to pass something back to Fin, but couldn't use his hands. 'What you said.'

'What did I say?' Fin cradled his cup in both hands but didn't drink.

'That Bernini sculpture depicts the Rape of Proserpina. It's ironic that the form would punish someone who gave in to the urge to touch it, given you said it would be less gratifying to touch than observe. So sometimes things you find beautiful are only meant to be appreciated from a distance.'

God, shut up, he thought. *He's too young to find you interesting.*

Fin inclined his head. 'You're right. Maybe the urge to touch everything is something well-adjusted people grow out of. And if you don't grow out of it, you're basically still a toddler running around trying to put everything in your mouth, always prone to shoplifting by accident, that kinda thing.'

'Have you ever touched the Rothko?'

'No!'

'That's surprising.'

Fin turned in his chair to take a sip of his latte. He seemed as though he was trying not to laugh, but it pulled at some desperate, unknown part of Andrew's gut, watching him look away.

Eventually, Fin turned back. 'They literally seem to move the longer you look at them. With Rothko it's more like they're trying to touch you.'

'That's interesting when you consider the one we were looking at.'

'Why?'

'Blue is the colour that light casts when it doesn't quite reach us.'

'So you're saying, blue is the colour of light that tries to touch us but can't. That's . . .' Fin pulled his lip between his teeth, then smiled. 'That's hot.'

You don't have to go to this panel, Andrew thought. It didn't matter if he missed one.

Fin looked directly at him in that way only the very young are able to look at other people. 'I don't have to be anywhere for a few hours. Do you want to go somewhere else?'

14.

As they were heading to a bar, Andrew reasoned Fin had to be at least twenty-one.

They took the 6 train towards Midtown and talked about their families. It was the longest conversation Andrew had had in months where nobody said the phrases 'psychogenic catatonia' or 'psychogenic death'. 'Psychogenic' was the new buzzword in the media, and had become the eternal subject of discussion in Philosophy departments all over the country since some psychologist with a huge social media following first used it in a televised interview.

Psychogenic death was the phenomenon of sudden death as brought about by giving up on life, most often triggered by trauma, or severe emotional responses such as shock or fear. Psychogenic catatonia referred to the condition preceding it. Though they were often used interchangeably.

'Psychosomatic' was sometimes used but it wasn't as fashionable, due to the prejudice carried by many that psychosomatic was simply a word doctors used to mean *not real*. The original phrase was coined by a professor in 1942: 'voodoo' death. But obviously no one was using that in any official capacity. A flashier term was coined by medical officers during the Korean War, 'give-up-itis', or GUI, to describe the process by which prisoners of war gave up all hope, stopped eating and speaking, and quickly died. As with voodoo death, people only tended to use that one online, or on the right-wing news channels.

'It's a strange situation.' Fin looked down at his drink. He had ordered a mojito, and Andrew a daiquiri. 'My ma worked so many jobs so we could get by. But my father is, like, Forbes rich. He's actually married and has his own family. My mother signed what amounted to an NDA and he put some money in a trust so I could just about afford to go to university, if I wanted. And that was it.'

He didn't know Fin's father, but Andrew conjured an image in his mind and was repelled by it. 'He's never tried to get in contact with you?'

'No. I have a feeling I might not be his only illegitimate child.' Fin didn't offer a smile so much as a thinning of the lips. 'Do you want to hear something funny?'

Andrew felt duty-bound to his smile somehow, his laugh. 'Okay.'

'He's based in New York. I only applied to academies here to . . . I don't know.' There were so many emotions in his face that Andrew couldn't identify. 'Every so often, even today, I get off the subway at Rockefeller and go to his office building. I've rehearsed what I'm going to say.'

Andrew's heart lurched when he thought of him standing in front of the painting. It was the strongest physical reaction to an emotion he'd experienced in months. 'What happened?'

'Nothing.' Fin drank some of his mojito through a straw. 'At the last moment I just leave, usually walk to the Met instead. Or somewhere else. Sometimes I go sit in Bryant Park.'

The bar was starting to fill up. A gentle hum of activity

that barely registered with Andrew, who knew nothing but Fin's careful, softly spoken voice. 'Are you planning to go back again?'

'I never plan to go back. It's not like I want his money. And my ma is already proud of me enough, I know that. She's amazing. I shouldn't need any more.'

'It's not always rational, what we want from people.'

Fin leaned his elbow on the bar with a dark laugh. 'Well, I've known plenty of people who would rather have had the money than the father. So maybe I'm better off.'

There was no explanation for why Andrew felt an urge to hug him then. He didn't like hugging people, Yun aside, and at times Nicola. It would be inappropriate to hug someone he didn't know. He noticed his leg bouncing on the bar stool, an anxiety symptom that hadn't manifested in years.

'Do you think that sounds heartless?' Fin asked, almost as if he was expecting Andrew to leave.

'No, what you did was brave,' he said. The urge to hug him had arrived alongside a visceral idea of what Fin would feel like in his arms, and Andrew didn't go through life wondering what other people would feel like. 'Walking away, at least you exercised control over your choices.'

'Don't get ahead of yourself. I still have time to cancel out all my good choices with bad ones.'

'Some people never learn how to make good choices. What are you, twenty-one?'

For a beat, Fin's expression said, *I see you*. 'I'm twenty.'

'But how . . . ?' Andrew gestured around the bar vaguely.

'It's a fake ID, like pretty much everyone uses.' Fin's smirk became more pronounced. 'Though I can't imagine you ever using one. How old are you?'

Andrew ignored the question and ordered another round from the bartender. Technically illegal, but he realized he didn't care. A glance at his phone told him that several colleagues were trying to get ahold of him. But Andrew put it back in his pocket and decided he didn't care about that either.

Fin finished his drink and accepted another. 'What do your parents do?'

Andrew had hoped not to get into this. He was having a nice time. But it felt rude to evade two questions in a row. 'They're dead.'

Fin's face fell. Both of Andrew's hands were in a defensive position around his drink, so when Fin reached for him, it was his knee he squeezed. 'I didn't mean to make you talk about it.'

'It was a while ago.'

The words came out coherently. But it was dangerous, the jolt of heat which accompanied that touch. Like someone had struck a match along the inside of his thigh.

Andrew exhaled as Fin withdrew his hand and hid his face. 'Jesus, and me saying all that about rather having money than a father. Tell me to shut it, please, I talk some shite.'

'It really is fine. And you were probably right.'

Fin eyed him for just long enough to make Andrew uncomfortable.

'Are you hungry?' he asked.

'We could . . .' Andrew thought about the conference, the final panel, the unanswered messages. 'Did you not have somewhere you needed to be? I don't want to keep you.'

'I don't actually have any plans, I only said that to seem

enigmatic.' Fin blushed a little. 'Or to give myself an out if you started to seem like a potential murderer. You can keep me if you want.'

It was a joke. Andrew knew that. But he felt the weight of regret in his hands, in his chest, and didn't know what kept putting it there.

They took the subway to Washington Square – so far from the Upper West Side that Andrew could no longer kid himself he was going to see any of his colleagues tonight – and found a place in Greenwich Village where they could eat outside on the small terrace. It wasn't warm. The shadows lengthened, and the heaters cast Fin in reddish light. He said his school was near here. He talked about how ballet was about moving in perfect lines. You had to be fluid, but every action also had to be precise enough, at every stage, to create a still flawless enough to be considered art.

It was exactly how Andrew would have described the way Fin moved, but of course he didn't say that.

When the evening turned crisp, Fin suggested they move inside. They sat on one of the couches running along the back wall, Fin beside him, squeezed up against his hip. Looking down from this angle, Andrew noticed a tiny mole on his left ear.

Fin swirled his Amaretto Sour around his glass. As if he felt Andrew's gaze, he tipped his head back on the couch, looking up through heavily lidded eyes. Andrew could feel the pulse of the just-too-loud music through the seat.

Turning his head a little, Fin said, 'Isn't it great, when you end up on one of these accidental dates that somehow takes over the whole day?'

It would be absurd to pretend he hadn't heard him. 'Is that what this is?'

The angle of his head was an invitation, Andrew realized.

He had never kissed a man, told himself he had never even thought about it.

Haven't you? That's not true, is it?

Tension crept into Fin's smile. 'Isn't it?'

Andrew wasn't sure what to say. 'I'm older than you.'

'I really don't care. Kiss me.'

Andrew's body started to react to the order before his mind registered it. His eyes dropped to Fin's lips and he tried and failed to haul them back up.

'I can't.'

A flicker of hurt crossed Fin's face. 'Are you embarrassed?'

'No!'

What Andrew couldn't find the words to say, was that he couldn't kiss him here. If he did, he wouldn't be able to stop. If he kissed Fin here then he would have to touch him. That, he was certain he had never felt before.

'I live near here,' Andrew said, suddenly seized by a powerful fear that Fin would leave.

Fin looked away, but only to gulp down the last of his drink. He stood up and there was a split second where Andrew felt the absence of his body, before he turned and offered his hand. 'Well, you'd better take me home.'

'Where was the last place you felt truly at home?' the therapist had asked him four weeks ago.

'Nowhere,' Andrew replied, truthfully. 'I think home is in the routines we make for ourselves, the familiarity we build. But I don't think I've ever felt *at* home. Like I belong to a place.'

'Why do you think that is?'

'I think we all have to live somewhere, but I don't think homes exist, in the romantic sense of the word.' Andrew thought about his parents' separate bedrooms. The bedroom his mother left less and less, then remained confined to towards the end. The bedroom he never set foot in again, after it ceased to be her room. '*Home* is just a lie our brains tell us about permanence.'

When he and Nicola separated, not long after the wedding, he left their place in Carroll Gardens and moved into an apartment building several blocks down from the Elmer Holmes Bobst Library. When Yun asked him why he was leaving when it was technically his house too, he pointed out that it was easier for him to move out than her, and it honestly hadn't occurred to him to make her leave while they tried to sell the place. Nicola was from a good family – just good enough to appease his – but Andrew had inherited enough money from his parents to last two lifetimes.

The interim apartment was perfectly fine, but he became self-conscious when Fin walked in, looking around with sharp eyes. Andrew took off his jacket and paused in the doorway, watching this mysterious, elegant creature suddenly roaming about his home.

'Can I get you a drink?' He gestured towards the kitchen and thought, *What are you doing?*

Stalling, he realized once he was on the other side of the kitchen island. He was stalling.

'I'm fine, thank you.'

Fin began to slide the pins out of his hair that had been

holding the beret in place. With precision, he placed them one by one on the granite countertop.

'Let me take that,' Andrew said as Fin put down his bag and began to take off his coat.

It wasn't even off his shoulders by the time Andrew got to him, and in reaching for it he had inadvertently encircled Fin in his arms. He smelled of some bitter fragrance that had faded during the day and become sweet. Fin looked up unwaveringly – almost a head shorter than him, Andrew noticed, now they were standing this close – and let his coat drop to the floor.

'You don't do this very much, do you?' Fin said, still holding the trace of a smile.

Andrew inhaled sharply as Fin took one of his hands and walked him back half a step, until he was leaning against the kitchen island. They were barely touching and already Andrew felt wrecked, all self-control wrenched out of his hands. Had it been a mistake, to follow this feeling? Feeling nothing was never this terrifying.

As if he sensed the thought, Fin pressed the underside of Andrew's wrist to his lips. A shockwave spread through his veins, but it somehow steadied him.

Andrew's fingertips brushed against Fin's cheek, and came to rest on his neck as he dipped his head to kiss him. The world became small, narrowed down to just the two of them. His lips were full, soft and slightly chapped. Fin leaned into him and suddenly no amount of close was close enough. He opened his mouth to Fin's tongue and tried to search out parts of him to hold; his waist, his face, the smooth skin of his back underneath his sweater.

With a hungry expression, Fin pulled away for a second.

He brought his thigh between Andrew's legs, drawing attention to how hard he was. Andrew flinched but dared not move in case he did something wrong, something to make Fin pull away and leave.

Fin sank to his knees with such grace it punched the breath out of him, and Andrew blurted out, 'Wait.'

Fin's hands were on his belt but he stopped. 'Do you not want me to?'

Andrew's first instinct was to say he didn't like that, because that's what he always said. Now, though, he had to rethink it, maybe rethink everything. It seemed many things were no longer true.

A disgrace. The thought came to him in his father's voice, about a boy he had known at school called Eric Hahn, who was transferred after something happened with another boy. Or was it a teacher, like him? The boy everyone talked around, but never seemed able to talk about. *A disgrace to his family.*

Andrew said, 'You don't have to, if you don't want to.'

'I want to.'

Andrew reached down to cup his cheek, and because he didn't know what to say or how to come to terms with what was in his hands, he just nodded.

As Fin tugged at the elastic of his briefs Andrew felt a dangerous squeeze in his abdomen and it occurred to him, as Fin touched him, that if he watched he would come immediately. He wrenched his gaze towards the ceiling just as Fin ran his tongue up his entire length, and something in him seemed to capsize, caught by the fall of a wave.

'Is this all right?'

'Yes . . .' Andrew put a hand over his eyes.

'Do you want me to continue?'

142

'*Yes!*' His forehead was clammy. 'Please . . .'

When Fin took him fully in his mouth, Andrew held both hands over his eyes and trembled.

He thought of all the times he had pulled away, looked away. How many times he had lied to himself and others, so accustomed to being numb, sleepwalking through his own life, never letting himself think about what could be, if he let himself want.

This wasn't a new discovery, not really. It wasn't as if he and Yun hadn't lived together during sophomore and junior year. It wasn't as if he hadn't seen it or heard when Yun had brought someone back. The guy from the football team who Andrew didn't like, or the other guy from the coffee shop he also didn't like.

Why are you thinking about him now?

Lying to himself then, too. Headphones on for the evening after listening a little too long. Late morning, coming into the kitchen to see Yun with a towel around his waist, cracking eggs into a measuring jug, hair wet from the shower, and Andrew lying, lying, lying to himself.

Tears sprang to his eyes.

Andrew reached down again, this time to touch Fin's hair.

Fin's grip tightened on his hips and he let out a moan, a moan Andrew felt vibrate through the deft pressure of his tongue.

Trying to stop himself proved futile. He was coming, hard. He screwed his eyes shut for what felt like minutes on end. His knees were weak and he felt unstable. A final drag of pleasure, then the sudden coolness of empty space. Sound returned, and Fin sat on his heels with the back of his hand over his mouth.

'I'm sorry!' Andrew exclaimed, the heat of gratification turning seamlessly into shame.

'What?' Fin looked up at him, blinking tears out of his eyes.

'I haven't . . .' The confession would make it worse. Andrew couldn't tell him he hadn't done anything like this in years, that he couldn't remember the last time with Nicola and even if he could he wouldn't want to. He stumbled over his words, unable to believe he had managed to cut short something that felt so life-altering. 'I'm so sorry.'

'Why are you apologizing?' Getting to his feet, Fin adjusted his briefs and smiled with no trace of self-consciousness. 'That was good, right?'

'I didn't realize it would be over so quickly.' He forced himself to say it. 'I've never slept with a man before.'

'I know.' Fin took his hands, unfazed. 'And the night's not over, don't worry. Not unless you want it to be?'

'No.' Andrew let himself be led, only vaguely steering the way to his own bedroom. 'No, I don't want it to be.'

'I believe that no man ever threw away life, while it was worth keeping': Can Hume's 'Of Suicide' Provide a Modern Moral Framework for Analysing the Causes of Mass Psychogenic Death?

Jeremy N. Bogan

The British Journal of Philosophy and the History of Ideas

Vol. 96, No. 1 (Oct. 2021), pp. 63–85

15.

Fin Keohane woke up in a bed that, it took him a few seconds to remember, wasn't his own. For one, he couldn't hear his room-mates making an unreasonable amount of noise. Secondly, he was warm.

A prickle of irritation with himself, for not going home. Then he turned over and found himself facing Andrew, who was not only awake but fully dressed and typing on his laptop as though he had been awake for hours.

It was not Fin's first time hooking up with someone he had met the same day. It wasn't even his first time being someone else's first time. It was, however, the first time he had stayed the night in a long while. He was far more at ease with catching the last train, a late-night bus, or calling a car as a last resort. So he wasn't sure why he had accepted Andrew's offer of a shower, taken one of his shirts to sleep in, why he had downed a medicinal glass of water before falling asleep laughing about . . . He couldn't even remember what they had been laughing about.

Having not shared a morning after with anyone since Emilio, he felt unpractised.

Andrew didn't seem to notice. He glanced down and curled his hand around Fin's head to scratch the nape of his neck. 'Morning.'

Well, this is nice, Fin thought, feeling himself becoming drowsy with warmth before reminding himself he shouldn't have stayed over, and now things were going to get awkward.

'How long have you been awake?' Fin asked, sitting up and rubbing his eyes.

'I wake up at five no matter what, so I went to the gym and thought I'd reply to some emails.'

'Oh, you're one of *those*.' Fin leaned against the head-board. 'I'm usually the same. Sorry, I don't know why I slept so long.'

'It's only nine. I didn't want to wake you on a Saturday.'

Fin regarded him, trying to come to terms with perhaps the most handsome man he had ever seen in real life. The strong jawline, defined cheekbones, the full lower lip; everything that had made it so easy to ghost his date and pursue this instead. Ah yes, this was why he had stayed over.

'Do you want some coffee?' Andrew asked. 'What are you doing today?'

Fin didn't have much resolve in the first place, and while he couldn't quite believe Andrew was as earnest as he appeared, the excuses Fin would have reached for seemed flimsy. The commute back to Flushing on the 7 was going to be miserable whatever time he did it.

He shook his head. 'Nothing that important.'

Andrew smiled. 'Are you hungry?'

What are you doing? 'If you're offering me breakfast, I won't say no.'

'Okay.' Andrew shut his laptop and swung his legs off the bed, only to pause, and turn around like he had forgotten something.

Fin's breath caught in the back of his throat as Andrew leaned in, very slowly, as if with every centimetre he was

147

giving him the chance to refuse. Fin closed his eyes, let Andrew kiss him, and thought, *Oh no.*

'You can stay here,' Andrew said as he got up. 'Sleep more if you want.'

That would've been one step too far. He could come around to the idea of having this man make him breakfast, but he was not going to lounge around in bed. He followed Andrew to the kitchen and sat at the counter reading the news on his phone while Andrew made exceptional coffee in his stove-top coffee pot. Ground the beans himself, because of course he did.

'Do you like eggs?'

Fin looked up from his phone. 'Yes.'

'Do you like salmon?'

An even wider smile. 'Yes.'

Andrew was out of good bread, so Fin offered to go to the deli around the corner. Still wearing Andrew's shirt under his coat, he took the elevator down and noticed again on his way out that the building was opulent enough to have a doorman.

It wasn't often he allowed himself caffeine. The weightless buzz made him feel he was walking several feet off the ground, and as he hit the fresh air he replayed a mental highlights reel from the day before. It shocked him to remember how much he'd talked about his father, having never broached the subject with Emilio. But Andrew felt safe to talk to. He also seemed interested in Fin as a person and not just a body, something he wanted to mould and take from. Not that it didn't give him a different type of buzz, recalling the expression of awe as he'd guided Andrew's hands, showed him how to touch him and where, how his eyes had been blown so wide.

Both shins connected with something on the sidewalk and Fin stumbled.

'The fuck?' he mumbled, before he knew what or who he had tripped over. Apologies didn't come naturally to him.

He looked down and his body went cold. An urge to recoil, keep walking and pretend he hadn't seen the man in the navy peacoat sitting in the middle of the sidewalk, shoulders slumped and staring, unseeing, straight ahead.

Fin cast his eyes about for assistance but everyone was carefully not looking at them. Edging back a step, not wanting to get too close, he waved a hand in front of the man's eyes. 'Hello?'

Nothing. It wasn't even ten a.m. on a Saturday. The high from the coffee became a rattling in his chest. There was something he was meant to do, but he wasn't prepared for this. Fin took out his phone and opened the app; the new one people could use to divert a driver already working for Uber or Lyft, and call on them to take an afflicted person to the nearest hospital. Payment for these rides was requested from emergency contacts after the fact. So it was rare, though not unheard of, for yellow cab drivers to accept them without payment up front.

Crouching down in front of the man, Fin searched his inside pockets for a phone or wallet, anything that contained emergency information. It was only when he tried to read the man's driving licence that Fin realized he was crying.

He wasn't sad, damn it. Or frightened. He was angry. He wasn't ready. Not today. He couldn't deal with this today. He wiped his eyes, read the name 'Marcus Damian Sheridan' and checked the phone, which was locked. People skirted around them, and Fin was bitter that he had been the one to stop. If he hadn't, someone else would have, and he would be on his way back to Andrew's with fresh bread by now.

Avoiding looking at Marcus Sheridan, Fin found a slip of paper in his wallet. *In case of emergency, Lex*, written in neat handwriting, followed by a phone number and insurance information, which had to be recorded in the app by the time the car arrived or they wouldn't take them.

A car was still seven minutes away. There weren't enough of them, people kept saying. Cases were rising too fast going into winter and there weren't enough excess drivers. Also not enough hospital space, even with the uninsured left to fend for themselves. Some had written wills stating their preference: in the event of catatonia, they would choose to stay at home with their families.

In case of emergency, Lex.

It occurred to him that he didn't have Andrew's number, so he couldn't tell him why he was delayed.

He didn't have the guts to call, so he sent a message to Lex with the tracking number for the car due to arrive in five minutes. Whoever Lex was, they would always remember this message, Fin thought, as he quickly deleted all trace of it from his phone. They might think about it later while Marcus Sheridan twisted and thrashed away from all attempts to give him water, hands crammed into protective mittens to spare the nursing staff the scratches. They might wonder why the fuck they had offered to be an emergency contact. Because you never offer to be an emergency contact thinking about the reality of receiving that message, or that call. It's a name on a form, until the deadweight of duty and obligation are dropped unceremoniously across your back.

Guidelines stipulated that if you came across an afflicted person in a public place, you should stay with them until help arrived. Fin didn't want to. No one wanted to. But if Fin left, someone might take the opportunity to rob him or worse, and Fin could do without that on his conscience.

Some of the afflicted had also been killed. That was the other thing people didn't want to talk about. Not just by family members in their homes, but by people who happened to be passing by, who felt something dark and bloody unfurl in the backs of their minds at the sight of them, who decided they would be better off, the world would be better off.

Fin couldn't remember exactly what those men had said in court. *They're dangerous! We don't know what they are! It's not like anyone ever comes back!* A crowdfund was set up for their bail and legal defence. No one was certain whether it was justified or not, though a lot of people acted like they were. True, no one had ever come back. But Fin thought the violence towards the afflicted found its origin in an insidious, familiar urge to punish. As if sitting down and refusing to go on represented an intolerable act of insubordination.

Sitting on the kerb with his feet in the road, Fin waited.

Like everyone else, he spent a lot of time wondering how it happened, and whether it would creep up on him one day, whether he would return home to find one of his housemates, or all of them, rendered intolerant to living. He watched the increasingly vague announcements and he read everything he could get his hands on: about dopamine and adrenaline and cortisol, about how stress can cause the body to flood itself with calcium, about MDD and schizophrenia, about disassociation and psychogenic death, about Resignation Syndrome and Pervasive Refusal. All the varied and useless hypotheses that averted neither catatonia nor vascular collapse.

Like everyone else, Fin told himself it couldn't happen to him, because he didn't *want* to die. And it was still hard to detach this phenomenon from the idea the afflicted chose it. It didn't help that there was still no medical evidence to the contrary, to appease the parents, wives, friends, who had lost their tempers and screamed, '*Just eat something! For God's sake, just eat something!*'

Fin didn't have a proper emergency contact. On his registration form he had put the name of an administrator at his dance academy. He couldn't think of a friend close enough for the role, and no living family were in a position to help. His mother couldn't afford an unexpected flight.

If it was ever him sitting in the middle of the street, someone would call his teachers. A couple of them might even lament what a talent he had been, but his place would be given to someone else. He couldn't imagine any of his fellow students would visit him, except maybe to tell others they had, to demonstrate they were a good person, while privately celebrating a little less competition when it came to post-Christmas performances and the graduates preparing for company auditions.

Fin pushed his cold hands into his sleeves. The car arrived, and the driver wordlessly put on a visor and protective gloves to help lift Marcus Sheridan into the vehicle. Then he was gone; the problem transferred into someone else's day.

Was that 100,000 in the US now? 100,001? Fin checked the figures several times a day. Whatever the exact number, he felt the additional one more keenly than the hundred thousand or so preceding it.

Fin walked the rest of the way to the deli and bought a warm loaf of sourdough. Andrew seemed like a sourdough kind of guy. He wasn't sure what made it healthier than normal bread. Better branding, he suspected. Most of the students at his academy didn't eat carbs at all, especially the women. Bread was bread was bread. Fin sometimes bought a sandwich at the weekend, ate it while walking in another part of town. He didn't tell anyone else about it but felt paranoid the others could somehow smell these moments of weakness on him, or worse, *see* it.

On his way back to the building he suddenly stopped. The weightlessness was now a feeling of being *too* light, like he might dissolve if someone knocked into him. It was as if he could no longer move his feet. He wanted to, but he couldn't.

If he carried on walking back to Andrew's apartment and had to face his smile, his soothing voice, a hand on his shoulder, he would start to cry again and he wasn't sure he'd be able to stop. He couldn't stand to be looked at like he mattered, when mattering to someone was this dangerous.

They didn't have each other's numbers. They didn't even know each other's full names. Right now, at least, Fin knew he wasn't anybody's problem. Andrew would get over the absence of bread.

He turned and walked towards the nearest subway.

A gust of air rushed to meet him as he jogged down the steps at the subway entrance, hitting his still-wet cheeks. He was cold, he realized, because he was wearing only Andrew's shirt under his coat, and had left both his jumper and beret in the apartment.

16.

He and Nicola had agreed to spend a few hours every Sunday afternoon sorting through their possessions at the house. So far these visits were only mildly unpleasant. Both were bored of not getting along, and found there was nothing left to argue about.

The day after Fin had left to buy bread and never returned, they started dividing up the plants. By four p.m. they were halfway through their second bottle of Sauvignon. Nicola was in the recliner with bare feet pulled up underneath her, and wearing a sweater that reminded him of Fin. Andrew was sitting on the floor beside the couch, pushing pots back and forth across the coffee table.

'You should take the aquatic terrarium,' Nicola indicated with her head, topping up her glass.

'I bought that for you.'

'You bought most of them for me but realistically I can't take everything. You've been on more of an emotional journey with it than me. I could never really get excited about algae.'

'I don't think that was me getting excited, I think that was having an anxiety attack.'

She nodded sagely. 'Yes, I could recognize the transference.'

'Okay, I'll take the swamp. You should take the begonias.'

A roll of the eyes. 'You work from home more and they're so high maintenance.'

'They're so temperamental I don't think they'd even survive a journey back with me today.'

'They're going to have to move eventually.'

'Well, let's give them longer to live then.' He sighed. 'I'd
find it too depressing if I took them back tonight and they
had a meltdown. Think about what we just said – when the
plants have a meltdown, I have a meltdown.'

'Okay, I'll keep them.' Nicola waved the bottle, and they
both stretched so she could pass it to him. 'Actually, the cool
thing about begonias is that name-dropping them in front of
plant people comes across as a real power move. That being
said, I'm keeping the Chinese Evergreen and Devil's Ivy.'

'I want to keep the Devil's Ivy.' As if to emphasize the
point, Andrew slid the pot to his side of the coffee table.
'You can't keep all the low-maintenance plants, my apartment doesn't get direct sun.'

'You're not going to stay there forever.'

'I don't know that.' He folded his arms. 'I've repotted it
three times.'

'Is that like the plant equivalent of changing a diaper? Do
you think it's imprinted on you?'

'Yes!'

She laughed, and waved the plant away. 'Okay, okay.'

Andrew could hold his wine even less than he could hold
his spirits, but he had got into the habit because Nicola liked
it, and it made them laugh more easily. He had worked late
the night before and risen at five this morning. Back to his
habits, making sure he didn't have too much time to
himself.

It was what he should have expected. That was how
young people dated these days, wasn't it. Casual, with little

formality. Andrew was convinced he had probably scared Fin away by suggesting he stay over, and then suggesting he stay for coffee, and breakfast. Absurd to think that was the way to do things with a twenty-year-old whose last name he didn't even know.

'Are you feeling okay?' Nicola asked, and he realized he had zoned out.

'Yes, sorry. I was miles away.'

'You seem sad. Not about this, I mean you've looked sad all day.'

It was so easy for her to make these frank emotional assessments now they were no longer beholden to each other. Honestly, he preferred it, and he thought she did too. He didn't like to dwell on regrets, but he and Nicola had always made much better friends than romantic or sexual partners.

'I've just been preoccupied.' He sipped his wine, thinking of the white jumper and black beret folded neatly in the second drawer of his dresser.

Ironically, the only person he would have felt comfortable talking to about this kind of thing was Nicola. She was smart in a logical, methodical way. She looked at problems from all angles and approached them headfirst. In direct contrast to him, who didn't so much feel his way through life as approach all uncomfortable situations with eyes stubbornly closed.

'Aren't we all. You can't even read the news any more. Every time someone calls me I think someone I know has come down with it.'

'Do you still think you'll move in with your parents?'

Nicola tipped sideways in the chair until her legs were

hanging over the side. 'Dad needs more care anyway, and it seems like a good time to keep everyone close. Do you think you'll stay in New York? You were always floating the idea of leaving. I thought I was the one keeping you here.'

Andrew had to admit, all his previous ideas about what he might do with his life seemed insignificant. Thinking about New York now, Andrew thought about Fin. Or maybe it was the idea of Fin. New York had the potential to be a completely different city, one that had become visible only with a slight altering of his perception. Maybe that's why people stared at paintings for so long. Long enough, and they really do see something else.

'Andy.'

'Hm?'

'Is something going on with you?' Despite everything, it was shocking how well she knew him. There was a lot to be said for the pattern recognition that came from the sort of daily familiarity he and Nicola had shared. 'I know we're not in therapy any more but there's no reason you can't talk to me about things. Compared to anyone else, I think we're doing pretty well at getting divorced.'

'We are, aren't we?'

'This is how compulsive straight-A high achievers divorce.'

'Well, you know in my family, A stood for Average.' He smiled. 'I don't want to ruin this.'

'I don't either. But I hope we'll still be able to talk to each other. It would be a shame not to.'

It had always been easier to remain silent. But not with this. Every time he tried to force it down where it belonged it would lash out, howling and twisting away from him like the afflicted.

'There is something,' he said, unsure how to proceed.

His expression must have been foreboding, because she leaned forward. 'Does someone you know have it?'

'What? No, it's nothing like that.' Andrew shivered. The day before, he had walked to and from the deli, terrified he would find Fin sitting on the ground. It had been both a relief and a desperate sadness not to find him. 'Look, I would like to talk to you about it. But I'd really appreciate if you didn't talk about it with anyone else. Apart from your therapist, if you want. Obviously I wouldn't stop you from doing that.'

Nicola exhaled slowly. 'You didn't cheat on me, did you?'

'God, no!'

'Can you just *say* it?' She gestured for the bottle. 'You're scaring me!'

'Just give me a minute.'

'Well, how bad is it?'

'It's not bad, it's . . .' He covered his eyes with the palms of his hands, and the gesture took him back to Friday night so vividly that he snatched them away. 'I think I might be . . . No, I don't *think*, I know. I like men.'

He took a large gulp of wine, fists clenching and unclenching where they rested on his knees. It took him a while to remember Nicola had wanted the wine bottle, and he picked it up and found her staring at him with such open-mouthed disbelief it would have been funny, if she hadn't at that exact moment started to laugh.

'I'm sorry!' Spluttering and hiding her face. 'Oh my God, I'm sorry! I don't mean to laugh, I'm just . . . I wasn't expecting that. I don't know what I thought.' She laughed harder and tried to stop herself, cheeks furiously red. 'I'm *so* sorry, I think I'm hysterical. I'm not laughing at you, I promise, I just wasn't expecting that. Right, okay. I'm okay. Sorry.'

All of Andrew's worst-case scenarios seemed to already be off the table. She hadn't stormed out. She hadn't started crying or throwing things, and she hadn't spat in his face. It had never been Nicola's style, but those reactions hadn't felt out of the question.

'Okay.' She swiped the bottle and drank some more wine, placing both feet on the floor. 'Okay,' she said again, as if talking herself through it. 'Okay! So you like men. You like men, that's fine. Okay. How long have you known?'

'I've been asking myself the same thing. I didn't know for sure until, well, Friday, to be honest.' He registered the exaggerated raise of her eyebrows, and added, 'All right, maybe I did know. Or suspected. But not explicitly. It's hard to explain. It was more like I knew something was wrong, but I thought I was just depressed. Or maybe I was depressed *because* I knew something was wrong.'

'Well, it's not . . . wrong,' she said in such a careful tone it made him want to hug her.

'No, I know. I know *it's* not wrong. I mean I knew something was wrong, with my life.' He glanced at her again and she was looking off to the side. The silence worried him more than her laughter had. 'I'm sorry. Are you okay? I didn't mean to spring this on you.'

'I'm not sure.' She gave the question some consideration, retying her hair in its ponytail. 'I am glad you told me, I think. No, I *am* glad you told me.'

'You are?'

'Yes! What a huge thing to not even know about my own

159

husband. I always thought *I* was the problem. Not that you were . . . Not that *this* is a problem, I don't mean that. Even though clearly it was a *big* problem. I just mean . . .'

'I know what you mean.' He grimaced. 'I am sorry. I'd understand if you hated me.'

'I don't *hate* you, Andy.' She sat back in the recliner with a sigh. 'The only thing that's changed is now I actually know what's going on inside your head for once. It's a relief, to be honest. You probably don't want to hear this but it does explain a *lot*. God, I always thought you just didn't like sex. How did I not notice?'

He felt overcome suddenly, his throat tight. He reached out and found her hand and she squeezed. Neither of them said anything.

For some reason Andrew was thinking about one night in college when he and Yun had stayed up playing Bowie's 'Ashes to Ashes' over and over because Yun couldn't describe the specific emotion it made him feel. Andrew was sitting on the floor and Yun was crouched on his bed, high on Adderall, deep frown-line between his brows and stock-still with focus, muttering, 'Euphoric . . . regret? Euphoric regret? Euphoric regret?'

He played every cover he could find, for *research*, stopping again to fixate on A Perfect Circle's live cover, jumping down to lie flat on the floor, which was where – Andrew had learned – Yun preferred to dwell when dealing with strong feelings. 'The guitar gives it so much more space to expand into,' Yun smiled, eyes closed and fingertips fixed to the floor, as if soaking up the bass. 'Can you feel it?' And Andrew had looked down at him and replied, 'Yeah.'

Nicola hadn't noticed because Andrew had perfected the

art of making sure Yun didn't notice first, so he could stand in front of him in that kitchen. Yun cracking eggs with a towel around his waist and lowering his voice to say, 'I can't believe I fucked a guy who actually listens to the Dave Matthews Band,' while Andrew laughed. Drops of water fell from Yun's hair and he flicked it out of his eyes as he started to whisk the eggs with chopsticks. 'The Dave Matthews Band, can you believe it? How embarrassing.'

Andrew got out of the car with two tote bags full of house-plants, put one on each shoulder and tried to walk as evenly across the lobby as he could. It was too late to cook. He would have to get takeout from the Thai place around the corner.

He was trying to reach for his phone in his inside pocket without dislodging either of the bags. For this reason, he didn't look at the hallway until he was almost at his door.

When he did, he stopped several feet short.

Fin was getting up off the floor, where he had been sitting against the wall. He was also carrying a tote and shoulder bag, and started talking very fast before Andrew could say anything.

'I think your doorman assumed I had a key. If he thought I was going to wait in the hallway he probably wouldn't have let me up.'

Remembering his keys, Andrew went to unlock the door. Fin took a respectful step back. He had no idea what to say so he settled for logistics. 'How long have you been here?'

'Oh, only a few – hours.'

Andrew flipped on the light and put the bags of plants on the kitchen counter. It was obvious why Fin was here.

Andrew had no use for acknowledging that the sight of his face made his chest hurt, like the thing which was now alive inside him was clawing to get out.

'It's okay, I've still got your things.' Andrew tried not to look directly at him. 'I'll get them.'

'Wait!' Andrew turned, and was shocked to see that Fin seemed to be on the verge of tears. 'It's not about the stuff, it's . . . I wanted to say I'm sorry.'

'You don't have to apologize. I don't know how to do these things, I probably made you uncomfortable.'

'No!' Fin took a second to compose himself, after the exclamation came out strangled. 'It wasn't you, you were . . . I was walking to the deli and there was a man, and I had to use the app, for a car, I mean, and then I don't know what came over me, I just left, I just had to go home.'

'Are you all right?'

Fin looked at him like no one had ever asked him that question in his life, then seemed to catch himself, and put his own tote bag on the counter.

'I brought your shirt back,' he said, as if that answered Andrew's question. 'There's bread in there, by the way. I did actually get some.'

It must have taken a lot of courage for him to come back. Andrew had walked away from enough in his life. He knew how hard it was to retrace your steps, especially if you had gone to great lengths to forget how you got there in the first place. Kicked dirt over the footprints, erased all evidence that might provide another person with a reliable map of how to love you.

'I've had a long day,' he said, fatigue seeping into his voice.

He noticed something in Fin's face flicker and fall. 'I was about to order some food.'

'I'll leave.' Fin stared at him, stricken. 'I really am sorry.'

'It's fine.' He meant it. 'You're more than welcome to stay for some tea, or anything. I won't be drinking, but you can have anything you want.'

'Really? I'd like that.'

'Tea?'

'Sure.'

Andrew crossed the room again, and as he approached the kitchen island Fin took a step to block his path. He wasn't looking up at him, but his expression was determined. As Andrew stood holding his breath, Fin raised both hands and gripped the lapels of his coat.

'You can kick me out if you want, I wouldn't blame you. You probably want nothing to do with me after all this. But I'd really like it if we could just start over as if I never left.' He still wouldn't meet Andrew's eyes, looking at his own white knuckles. 'Could we . . . ? As if I never left?'

It was no longer a question of whether it was a good idea or not. It was only a question of what made him happy and what didn't. Fin's face was so easy to touch, to tilt towards his own. It was easier than anything he had done in his life, easier even than lying.

'I feel like I'm going crazy,' he said to Nicola at some point, when they were sitting side by side on the floor in front of the couch and he had unexpectedly burst into tears. 'Is this a nervous breakdown and I'm too afraid to see it?'

'I don't think you're having a nervous breakdown.' She

patted his knee. 'I think you're experiencing some normal human emotions for the first time.'

'It's horrible.' He couldn't catch his breath. 'It's unbearable, how do people do this?'

'Oh, I know!' She laughed, agitating the finger where her wedding ring used to sit. 'It is unbearable, I know.'

17.

Everything that came next felt easy. Almost too easy for Fin to tolerate. They were both such pedantic and orderly people – his own messy hiccup notwithstanding – falling into a new routine to accommodate each other felt like the most natural thing in the world.

Admittedly, Andrew was doing most of the physical accommodating. He lived so close to the academy that he wouldn't hear of Fin hauling himself to and from Queens every day, even though he'd been doing it for months.

'Why deal with the journey when you can sleep here?' Andrew remarked, after Fin asked one evening – as he did every few days – whether he should go home. 'The 7 is hell.'

'I've *always* said that! Like it was designed by a mole rat.'

'Do you want to go home?'

Fin hesitated. 'No. But this is your place.'

'It's not really my place, it's temporary.'

'Well, it's more your place than my place.'

'You can think of it as your place too, I don't mind.'

Fin did mind. He felt an urge to push back against Andrew's perfect edges, against the edges of this place, which was far nicer than what he was paying rent for. He ran his fingernail in and out of a nick in the kitchen island while Andrew marked some essays. 'But do *you* want me to go home?'

Andrew looked up from his laptop like he was being silly. 'No, of course not.'

'It's okay if you want some space, I wouldn't be offended.'

'I know.' And he would smile as if to say, *I am not getting tired of you*, and Fin would almost – not quite, but *almost* – believe it.

Between twelve and twelve thirty, when their lunches most often synced up, Fin would walk to Andrew's office with a falafel wrap from the place on MacDougal they both loved, which was a block away from the Thai place they also both loved. Andrew would make him mint tea because Fin didn't drink coffee on weekdays unless it was decaf, due to the way caffeine and sugar affected his breathing and coordination.

They were late workers, early risers, and obsessively health conscious. Andrew was already in the gym by the time Fin woke up at six, and Fin would stay late, using the studios for hours after classes ended, only stopping when Andrew messaged to ask if he'd eaten.

Seven weeks passed and Fin would have said it went quickly if he hadn't been analysing every moment to death, waiting for the hammer to fall, the disaster, or just a hint of irritation to creep into Andrew's eyes, warning Fin that his presence had inevitably become caustic.

Andrew would leave eventually, but he might stay interested a little longer due to novelty. That's why it was better when Fin chanced upon someone who had never acted upon who they really were before. They didn't know when they were supposed to leave.

It was almost seven on a Friday evening when he received a message at the studio. He knew that always staying late, even with no rehearsals scheduled, didn't single him out as uniquely dedicated, but identified him as someone a little older than the rest, with something to prove.

But he was a little older than the others, and he did have something to prove.

He flopped, sweating, to the floor where his phone was plugged into the wall.

A friend invited me to his DJ thing in Bushwick tonight
Short notice but do you want to come?

Would he mind?

I think he'd prefer lots of people there :)

Ok what time?

It starts at 11 so no need to rush home
We can grab some food before we go

。(*^▽^*)ゝ

Fin wondered whether Andrew had meant to say 'home', and why it made him want to cry. He picked himself up, gathered his things and rushed home earlier than he had done in years, kissed Andrew harder than he had the day before.

This is not your home. He is not your home, Fin kept reminding himself. *No matter how much he feels like he is.*

For all the hours he spent making sure his hair was perfect, that he was flawless, irreproachable to behold, Fin didn't muster the courage to ask the obvious question until they were in the back of a car crossing the Williamsburg Bridge.

'How are you going to introduce me?'

Fin had insisted on making frozen margaritas before they left the house, so Andrew was already flushed and affectionate, hand on his knee. 'I was planning on saying, this is Fin.'

'You know what I mean.'

'How would you like to be introduced?'

It was automatic for him, to make it about what Fin wanted, which would be fine if Fin could handle the pressure, if he didn't always think he was about to make the wrong move. 'Do your friends even know?'

'About you?'

'Do they know you're gay?'

Andrew had little problem walking the walk, but still couldn't quite talk the talk. Even now the word gave him pause as he tried to wrangle his way around unfamiliar terminology. 'No, they don't know that. But it's not the kind of thing I'd send an email about. I'd only mention it if we were seeing each other in person.'

'Like tonight?' A little push.

'If you want.' A little push back.

He would announce it tonight if Fin wanted him to. Maybe that was what being in your thirties was like. You really did stop giving a fuck about other people's opinions.

Andrew searched his face for the right way to de-escalate, like he was talking Fin back from the edge of a tall building. 'I thought it'd be presumptuous to introduce you using specific labels when we haven't talked about it yet.'

Fin glanced at the driver, who was wearing earphones, or politely pretending not to listen. 'I guess two months isn't that long to have been seeing each other.'

'But it's not insignificant, the way we have been seeing each other.'

Oh for fuck's sake, Fin thought, wishing that just for once Andrew could be anything less than perfectly good. He had to turn away and lean against the window.

'I'm sorry if I offended you,' Andrew said, as if he had

ever been offensive for a moment in his life. 'I just didn't want to presume.'

Because you left. That's what Fin heard.

But I also came back! he wanted to protest. *I came back and waited for you.*

He had never done that before, not for anyone.

He sighed. 'You haven't offended me, I just wondered.'

Throughout the exchange, Andrew hadn't taken his hand off his knee. That was a good sign. Fin tried to relax. It probably wasn't that deep. He was afraid Andrew's friends wouldn't like him. A lot of people didn't. It was a sixth sense cultivated at school, singling out someone who desperately wanted to be liked. Sure, they wanted to touch him. Wanted to fuck him, sure. But all that want coursing through his veins repelled them, like an underlying smell of rot. Fin *wanted* with all the wide-eyed grasping of someone who'd never *had*, and no matter how viciously he polished the surface everyone could see it.

Ballet was a process whereby the dancer honed the body, conditioning it to be able to move gracefully beyond the point of pain. But Fin had never managed to achieve that same perfection in his face. He observed himself in the mirrored studio walls, up close in the bathrooms, and he figured that no matter how much he trained, some things were innate. He held all of that ruthless, consuming *want* in the tension in his jaw, in the guarded, metallic sheen to his eyes.

He watched Brooklyn pass by and felt sick.

'Well, they're my friends,' Andrew said after a few minutes had passed. 'But it should be up to you whether you want to ah, deal with them in that way tonight. They're

169

good people, but they'd be curious and want to ask you a lot of questions. They'd be well meaning but intense, that's all.'

In a game of relationship chicken, Fin would back down every time. His general inexperience trumped Andrew's specific one.

'Maybe not tonight then,' he said, still looking out of the window.

Even though he'd been the one to bring it up, he felt like this had been a test, and he had failed.

One of the best and worst things about Andrew Zhou was how often he could look at Fin and know exactly what he was thinking.

'There will be other times.' Andrew brushed his fingers against the back of his ear, so Fin shivered and turned to smile at him. 'I would actually like you to meet them more than once.'

Wards for the 'long-term catatonic,' patients remaining in a catatonic state for three weeks or longer, have been shut after a New York Times investigation into 'truly inhumane' conditions - article

nytimes.com/2023/12 . . . ⬏

18.

Yun started having a nightmare and then it came true. There was a metaphor in that series of events somewhere, for why he no longer felt able to think about the future.

Derrick got in touch in mid December to let him know that a friend of his, who managed a club in Bushwick, was looking for a DJ to take over a four-hour hip-hop set after a cancellation. Yun made him up the rate for the short notice, and used the difference to pay Derrick to drive his stuff over in his van.

He sent an invite to everyone in his contacts, though the only person he really needed there was Emory. She had seen him play guitar and piano in the apartment before but never doing this. The stakes felt high; his first real opportunity to pull his best self out of the closet. Whenever he'd dated before, there was a period of almost total performance lasting about six months. During that time they would see only the best version of Yun, the one with potential, a relentless upwards trajectory, no baggage or problems to drag into their life. But he'd never had that time with Emory, and it was starting to scare him. If he could show her *this*, he told himself, then she could tolerate everything else. To tolerate the real him, the everyday him, she just had to know this other, better Yun existed. That would be enough.

The club was in a converted theatre. Derrick gestured with his drink during the guitar band who were on before him, saying, 'You can still see those old-timey columns and balconies. Looks like the place where Lincoln got shot.'

It probably wasn't that old-timey, Yun thought. Most buildings more than a few decades old were empty blocks of luxury apartments or rubble by now. There was a church by the river in Manhattan that wasn't even a hundred years old, but had been designed to imitate a thirteenth-century French cathedral. He only retained this information because Andrew insisted on walking him and Jarah up there one summer years ago, and talked for a long time about the construction and elevator technology.

Derrick hadn't been out in a while on account of his family. Yun hadn't been out on account of being broke. As far as he could tell, they were the two main reasons people stopped doing things. Not because of age. Being in your thirties meant nothing. But by then, people tended to have acquired things that gradually cut them off from all the places – bars, basement venues, galleries, converted theatres, anyplace after midnight – they imagined more exciting lives were taking place. Long-term partners, multiple jobs, more demanding jobs, babies, mortgages, debt, traumas, physical injuries or sometimes just too many failures.

As the band finished, people filed out and even more filed in. Nerves crept in around the edges of the one drink Yun had allowed himself. Suddenly he didn't want Emory to come.

'You ready to do the thing?' Derrick yelled over the music.

Yun checked his phone. Emory was already on her way with Lara and Mike. Andrew was on his way with a friend; he assumed someone from work. 'Yeah, sure, let's do the thing.'

For the first hour he didn't overexert himself, sticking mostly to newer music. It was the ideal crowd. Young, but not so young as to be self-conscious and ironic. Late twenties to early thirties, with a smattering of the Brooklyn media crowd, but not too many white people.

Emory, Lara and Mike arrived just before midnight. Emory waved at him, wearing a tiny black dress over cycle shorts and one of his plaid shirts tied around her waist.

He got out his phone and held it by his waist out of sight.

Can you not look so hot please I'm trying to work

Yun felt sixteen years old again as he searched the crowd and found her, laughing at her phone.

Derrick brought him a second drink and he took a sip of what tasted like cheap Scotch. He put it down out of easy reach, because he liked to observe the social dynamics of clubs as one of the only sober people in the room. Young women and girls – some of whom looked alarmingly young – gravitated to the front and centre, and the men – some of whom looked alarmingly old – watched them from the edges. It only worked because everyone was too drunk and too immersed to see how creepy the bigger picture was.

Every so often a woman would climb on to the stage to scream requests in his ear. Sometimes they stayed too long. A few years ago, every slightly swaying and flushed woman who climbed up to yell in his ear and brush her fingertips along his forearm felt like a possibility. He used to measure the success of the night in how many numbers he collected. It was how he met Jarah, though she hadn't given him her number right away. She brought him a bottle of beer and a bourbon chaser, smiled and climbed back down, forcing him to look for her afterwards. Now these women made him anxious, unable to multi-task, always leaning away towards the monitors. He never used to worry this much during sets when he was young. He never used to be so preoccupied with the worst possible outcomes, so scared of everything. Now he needed the second drink.

The floor got busier. Sweat dripped from the ceiling and the air was dense. Derrick hollered into his ear at one a.m. to tell him there was a queue out front. Yun played a few classics, his remix of 'Kinda I Want To' by NIN, slipped in some Korean hip-hop, and whatever he did everyone loved it. He wondered if he could get away with some Pet Shop Boys, because he knew it would make Andrew smile. He had time to read the room, further assess. He began to drag out a few transitions. Derrick plugged in his guitar and played over a track they had created together, which Yun said he'd only play if the place was on fire. He knocked back half a pint of water, picked up the mic and started to rap. They hadn't rehearsed together in weeks. It could have been a disaster but, somehow, it wasn't.

He felt lifted up by some terrifying energy as the shifting, almost fluid floor of people directed their attention from each other, towards the stage. He couldn't see Emory, because he found it easier to blur his vision and stare over the top of the crowd rather than into it.

Derrick was the opposite. He got off on seeing the whites of people's eyes, whooping and dancing and creating in-jokes with everyone down the front.

Yun felt strong in a way he hadn't in years. For the rest of that set he could've punched both fists straight through a brick wall. He spotted Andrew in the crowd. It was easy because he was tall and women stared at him. He looked happy, uncharacteristically relaxed. Yun didn't recognize whoever he was with, maybe one of his students.

For the last half-hour, Yun threw out the heaviest rap tracks, the classics that made people scream and grab their friends. Emory brought him a glass of water just for an excuse to kiss him, and he couldn't hear what she said but she was smiling more widely than he'd ever seen. She gestured down at Lara and Mike, who were dancing together like a couple of college kids. Yun was looking for Andrew again, lost in euphoria, when Emory gripped his arm too tight.

Following her eyeline to the second-floor balcony, he became aware of people streaming down the stairs.

With an abrupt zooming sensation, the room dragging itself away from him, the sound changed. Yun realized it was because Derrick had stopped playing. Across the stage, he saw his mouth form the exclamation, '*Shit . . .*' Eyes to the club, and the people below them pulled away from each other in white-faced panic, revealing the bare floor covered in crushed plastic cups and splashes of spilled drinks. And the ones left behind, sitting amongst the debris.

A crowd flowed across the room from the stairwell, dodging and skirting around the vacant islands. One person falling and righting themselves, another sitting down, then another, then another, dropping as if something unheard was passing between them.

Yun stepped back and almost tripped over his own cables, dragging Emory with him as he stumbled. He didn't notice how tightly Emory was holding his arm until he saw the bruises left by her fingers later. He wasn't even aware of what song was playing while the venue emptied out in what felt like seconds. He only felt the beat pulsing through his soles.

Derrick was in his face suddenly. 'Move! Let's move!'

They moved. Yun helped Emory down from the stage, and she pressed against his hip to avoid touching the sitters, as if one of them might grab her. Some were bleeding. They must have been stamped on, but the pain hadn't moved them either.

Yun stopped by the cloakrooms, turned back and noticed they were all still facing the stage.

'Come on!' Derrick gave him a shove before darting out of the exit.

Emory tugged on his hand, her expression pleading.

Yun pulled out of her grasp and walked to the stairs, watching his step.

'Yun!'

He ignored her. The overriding emotion propelling him wasn't fear, but anger. He wasn't scared of them, not like everyone else. It sounded insane – he hadn't said it out loud to anybody, not even to Emory – but as the numbers climbed higher, as it became more and more common to see them in the street, to see bars and restaurants evacuated, hundreds of people standing shivering on sidewalks while the cars and ambulances arrived, Yun started to feel like a predator had its eyes fixed on the back of his neck. That whatever this thing was, it was following him.

There were more on the second floor. They seemed grouped towards the centre, with fewer of them scattered around the edges. One of the guys closest to the balcony was still holding his phone. He and another girl were facing each other, as if they were talking when it happened, or had discussed it beforehand.

Yun leaned over the railing, and when he turned back he repressed a shudder at the sight of them all looking at him, looking straight through him. He crouched down, tried to meet the eyes of the guy wearing the Nike hoodie and expensive-looking watch, tried to work out if he had left the house wanting to die tonight, whether wanting to die had been a passive or active force in the man's life. He felt the common urge to grab the front of the hoodie and shake him. Something about them almost made an outburst of violence feel preferable to whatever this was.

The lack of focus in their eyes reminded Yun of the look on Jarah's face as she'd moved her stuff from one room to another, while he had stood in the doorway and cried, forcing her to knock into his shoulder every time she had to pass. 'Why don't you just go out?' she kept saying, skirting around him and refusing to let her eyes land. 'Why do you always have to make things so hard?'

A third floor functioned as a VIP room. Yun got to his feet and found another half-dozen up there. They almost lined up with one another, he observed, craning his neck over the balcony again, like something descended upon them from above.

Going back downstairs, he saw Andrew waiting for him by the exit. 'Fuck Your Ethnicity', Kendrick Lamar, was pounding from the speakers and everything was very still. Yun remembered how he thought it funny at the wedding, when no one thought to turn the music down.

'Yun?'

Andrew had come closer, and Yun was startled to realize

he was standing next to him, hand hovering above his arm, like he thought touching him might cause something bad to happen.

He had started having a nightmare. Sometimes he was home in San Diego, or his old school, sometimes on Skillman. Once, he was in a supermarket he hadn't set foot in since he was a kid. But he was always running, and there was nowhere to go. He never caught sight of what was pursuing him and his feet worked fine. He would run until he woke up and Emory would hold him, sometimes for hours, until he fell back to sleep. He hadn't only asked her to move in because of the rent; he had never been good at sleeping alone.

It wasn't that he couldn't run, it was that there was nowhere to go.

'Do you think the music makes it worse?' He didn't raise his voice, so he couldn't be sure Andrew heard him. 'Is it something about music? Do you think it makes them feel everything too much?'

'Let's go outside.'

Yun looked down as he felt Andrew take his arm, fingers curling around the underside of his bicep, as if anticipating the need to grip tighter and hold him upright.

Reynard @thankfulforass

little known fact about ww1 is the astronomical fatality rates weren't unplanned or even unfortunate, they were actually factored into the battle plans /thread

Reynard @thankfulforass

Replying to @thankfulforass

commanders calculated how many to die per week so they had reinforcements to immediately replace them without any delay to the war machine, this was called 'normal wastage'

Reynard @thankfulforass

Replying to @thankfulforass

late stage capitalism does the same, that's literally what these deaths are. it's also why no one cares. not enough have died to impact capital or the rich, they're just normal wastage

19.

Emory spent two hours on the train from Penn Station and her father met her at Hudson in a new yellow truck. Jeremiah Thomas was a nerd who had always looked like a nerd, with the perpetually hunched shoulders of someone who spent most of his time sitting in a chair looking down. He looked different now. He looked like someone who had been standing upright and carrying things for days. Farmstrong, Emory supposed you would call it.

'What the hell is that?' She gestured at the truck as they hugged.

'Oh, that? Isn't it a beauty! I wanted to name it, but your sister wouldn't let me.'

'You wanted to name your *yellow* truck. What?'

'Helios.'

She laughed as he lifted her case into the back. 'That is actually a good name.'

'Making sure the sun rises every day. What's not to like?'

'Aside from the fact it's a truck so probably not great for the whole global warming thing.'

'I guess that doesn't matter so much now.' Then he hugged her again, for a long time. 'I'm so happy you made it. I can't wait for you to see the new place!'

It wasn't a long drive, most of it through fields. She didn't ask again, why he'd sold the house upstate they all loved. He seemed happier, which was the only thing that mattered.

She didn't have the emotional bandwidth to cram any extra worry into her head, was happy to listen as he told her about the emptying towns, the locals moving away since the resort incident, about how the land was 'a hell of a deal, a once in a lifetime deal', how there was a river branching off Schoharie Creek they could swim in during the summer.

She hadn't found out about the move from him, but from Esther. Her sister's only comment on moving further into the country and the sudden quitting of his job had been a text.

Think Dad's having a nervous breakdown lol.

Yun had flown back to San Diego the week before. Before he left he made her a Christmas-themed playlist for the two-hour journey. One of the tracks was a cover of Kate Bush's 'December Will Be Magic Again' by a guy called Wojtek Godzisz, because Yun loved to introduce her to things she had never heard of.

'Is that it?' Emory exclaimed when the house came into sight at the end of a narrow road lined with an archway of brown trees.

She exclaimed with genuine excitement, like a quarter of a million weren't projected dead by Christmas.

During the hour they waited outside the club for the sitters to be removed, Emory thought it was going to snow. The air filled with floating particles of ice, but they landed like rain. Derrick broke protocol and started loading equipment into the van before anyone arrived, to make sure it wasn't requisitioned.

In all that time, Yun didn't move from the edge of the sidewalk out front, chewing at the thumbnail of the hand that wasn't ice-cold and clutched between Emory's. Since he finally joined them outside he had gone quiet, his gaze directed at something she couldn't see. At one point he looked at Andrew and his friend, eyes narrowed, then back down at the road.

For the whole week after the incident, Yun's brow stayed lowered, always staring at something she couldn't see. In every spare moment he compiled theories, scrolling through forums and socials looking for the most obscure and outlandish speculations he could find, a carousel of conspiracies she could practically see spinning behind his eyes. He didn't sleep so much as drift away and hover just under an unsettled surface, sometimes for a few hours but sometimes for only minutes. If they fucked he would pass out for longer, though the intensity that used to turn her on had shifted a gear in the wrong direction and was now disconcerting. His eyes were red and his hands were always moving, the inside corner of a nail always bleeding.

The night before he flew to San Diego she had pushed him off her and snapped, 'I feel like pain medication! If you can't sleep then for God's sake talk to somebody. I'll pay, I don't care, just *talk* to someone!'

He spread his hands. 'I talk to you.'

'I'm not a therapist!'

'You're my girlfriend?'

'Exactly!' She was trying to sound angry and hated herself for sounding more like she was pleading. 'I'm not a therapist, I don't know how to help you!'

She didn't have the guts to say what she was actually feeling, which was that she couldn't stand the way he looked at her any more. The longer he went without touching his

183

keyboard – unplayed since his landlady had the stroke – the more he touched her like he was searching for something. His eyes would flutter shut, and she could kid herself for a moment that whatever he was looking for he could find, right there, with her. But afterwards something seemed to descend upon him, softening his expression into one of disappointment, like he had become newly aware of something he hadn't – until now – fully realized he'd lost.

The only time Yun showed an interest in anything unrelated to the catatonic crisis was when Emory tried to distract him by bringing up Andrew.

'Andrew's straight, right?' she checked while working in bed one evening, delicately casual.

Yun had a bottle of beer halfway to his lips, eyes on his own laptop screen, but he put it down. 'Yeah?' A trace of concern, like there always was when she asked any direct question about Andrew. 'Why?'

She didn't like his expression, so notched her tone over to playful. 'Did you not see that guy he brought with him the other night?'

'I wasn't really paying attention,' he said, and she wondered why he was lying. 'One of his students, right? I told him to invite anyone.'

'He's not one of his students, he's a *dance* student, at a ballet academy. He was at the wedding, remember?'

She pretended to still be typing, finishing another piece about another family. When Emory had interviewed the parents of a catatonic seven-year-old, they said she had been taken to a better place. She was too good for this world. It was the best of them who were leaving. Emory thought about that sentiment all the time, but couldn't believe it. She had to believe the best of them were still here, or at the very least, that the catatonia had no target. That, at worst, it struck with the painful, arbitrary randomness of a disinterested god, or disinterested universe. Everyone had to die eventually, so this couldn't be about who was good and who was bad. It couldn't be. It was about who was gone, and who was still here trying to carry on. That was all they had.

'Huh.' Yun frowned, and she saw something register in his face that he quickly dismissed, or chose not to share with her. 'Well, we lived together for two years so trust me, if he wasn't straight I would know.'

She glanced over, trying to gauge if he was going to say anything else. But he remained silent, scrolling through the CNN updates for what might have been the fifteenth time in the last hour, picking at the raw skin of his bottom lip.

Not for the first time, it occurred to her that she was never the one allowed to fall apart.

'That's it! Outside of town, close enough for convenience. Best place to be.'

She hadn't realized how big the house was. He must have used his savings to afford it, or the money her mother left behind. It wasn't one house so much as three or four separate buildings linked by walkways or conservatories. One was made of exposed brick, another painted white. Plus what looked like a gigantic red barn, with a smaller barn next to it.

'Dad, this is insane.' She got out of the truck, pulling her coat tighter as her breath became mist. 'There's a barn! Why do *you* need a barn?'

'We keep the trucks in there,' he replied, hands on his hips and beaming. 'Also some supplies. Good to have some canned food on hand, for emergencies.'

'Trucks *plural*?'

'Your sister needed one too. And she suggested we get a couple of dirt bikes, for traversing the land. Or just for fun.' He pushed his glasses up his nose. 'Come on, I'll show you around out here before we go in.'

'Where's Esther?'

'At a meeting with a realtor. There's a couple of empty houses nearby we think we can buy and rent out.'

Maybe he is having a nervous breakdown, she thought. Or maybe he was a genius. Either way, over thirty years into Emory's life her father had become unrecognizable. He went through something of a manic phase after his wife died, which manifested as spending hundreds of dollars on a collection of vintage maps, and hundreds more on obscure art prints. Esther confiscated his credit card, and after those few weeks had passed she said she heard him crying every night for a few days. He signed off work for a month with stress and then, one day, he was back to normal. He sold the maps, and most of the art, and nothing more was said about it.

'We own all the land up to that row of trees,' he said, indicating a place in the far distance. 'There used to be a horse pen in this field but me and your sister took the fences down on account of not having any horses. And we own all the land that way, right down to the river. It's only about fifty acres but we're looking to get bigger.'

'Why?'

He looked at her like he hadn't anticipated the question, a

186

little dazed. 'It seems safer, a lot of wide open space,' he said eventually. 'Follow me!'

They walked together around the main house. Emory typed out a quick message to Yun, to let him know she had arrived. She saw an enclosed yard, and some sheltered chairs next to a heater. They took a path down towards the nearest copse of trees, which became a dirt track, then hard, frozen ground. She was wearing her city trainers and kept glancing down, paranoid about the mud.

Her father glanced at the phone. 'It's a shame your fella couldn't make it up here.'

She smirked. 'My *fella*?'

'Well, whatever you call him.'

'Boyfriend. Boyfriend is still the term we use. His family live in San Diego so he's staying there for a few weeks.'

'I'd sure like to meet him.'

'You'll meet him at some point.'

'And living together, that's still going good?' He was nodding to himself repeatedly, looking at her in the carefully non-judgemental way he adopted when wanting to feel out a sensitive subject. 'You've never gone and moved in with anyone before. I've gotta say, honey, I was surprised. We both were.'

'Well, I'm glad I can still be surprising. But yeah, it's good.'

'He does his fair share of the work?'

'His mom raised him right, you'll be pleased to know.'

'Okay then, if you're sure. I just never imagined it, you know.' When she waited for him to elaborate on exactly what he meant, he added, 'You, with a musician.'

'*You* were a musician in college.'

'Yeah, but I was no good. And your mother set me straight.' He hugged her with one arm and laughed. 'We were thinking of cutting some of these trees back. Looks like it's turning into a forest over here.'

She nodded, like that was something she would have an opinion about. 'Yun is sweet, Dad. Don't worry about it.'

He rubbed his hands together and blew hot air into them, frowning. 'I am sorry you had to see another one of those incidents. I would always rather you tell me, but I do worry. I worry about both of you. At least your sister is here, not caught up in it in the city.'

'Honestly, with all the work I've done on it, it doesn't shock me any more. Yun takes it harder than me. *Way* harder. I worry about him.' The truth of the feeling couldn't be contained in such a banal statement. She worried about him so much she felt feverish, like the emotion itself was a virus. 'I don't think it's any safer here than in New York. New York is just denser. We see it more because the odds are higher.'

'You might be right. But I have a theory that, whatever it is, whatever happens, lightning doesn't tend to strike twice.'

She hadn't wanted to bring it up. It seemed safest to never look a crazy person in the face and tell them they were being crazy. But she endured enough conspiracies from Yun and her father was a scientist; he was supposed to be immune to this kind of thing.

'Are you serious? You bought this place because you think it can't happen here?'

'It's why the land was so cheap,' he explained, as if he was answering another question. 'Though I don't understand. I would've expected prices to go up, given it's statistically unlikely to happen on the same scale in the same area.'

Emory pinched the bridge of her nose. 'There's no evidence it can't hit the same place twice.'

'But striking in the same place as the first mass event? Less likely.'

'This isn't even the resort, it's not the *same* place.' When his smile didn't fully hold, she felt bad. But not bad enough to backtrack. 'Did Esther know why you were buying this place? Didn't she try to talk you out of it? This is insane, think about it. Why would you even *want* to live here? Aren't you going to go back to work again? Do you really want to commute that far?'

'Of course your sister knew. I thought you worked it out for yourself long before we got here.' His expression was slightly pitying, like he hadn't expected this uneducated reaction. 'But it's exactly like I said. Call it what you like, I personally think it's logic. It happened here, on Hunter Mountain. The chances of it happening again, at random, on the same scale, I'd say they must be close to zero. Of course the risk is still there, but it's smaller. Isn't that something?'

Emory wondered how she was going to explain this to Yun, then realized she wasn't sure who he would side with.

'This is *insane*,' she said again, hands in her pockets and shaking her head at the yellowed grass.

'You'll get used to it, Emmy, I promise.' Her father smiled, and put an arm around her shoulder. 'After a day or so, especially when you realize you're totally safe, you'll feel much better.'

She had never seen her father speak with such conviction about anything. It hit her suddenly, that he had no intention of going back to work.

'And, honey, it's such a relief. When we're back at the house and it's warm and we're all together, you'll realize we're away from it now. I promise, it's such a great feeling! For the first time since this whole thing started, I've been able to stop thinking about it. You'll be amazed by how easy it is to not think about it.'

20.

Like for so many thousands of other families, it was a tradition – as far back as Yun could remember – for their parents to drive them all down to Chula Vista's Christmas Circle.

They crawled along in a line of cars, Kevin and Yun relegated to the back seats once again, their parents up front. Everyone's windows were down and there was an endless rotation of Christmas songs on the radio. They could have walked, probably would have been less hassle, but they never had so they never would.

'It's so nice they still did it this year,' his mother remarked in Korean as Kevin and Yun started jostling each other, craning to catch sight of the sign first.

CHRISTMAS CIRCLE: NEXT RIGHT.

'Sign!' Kevin yelled in English, making everyone in the car flinch. 'Sign!'

When they were kids, Christmas Circle had turned into a game of family bingo, based on who could loudly announce the sighting of certain landmarks first. There were no prizes save for bragging rights, and the landmarks were the arbitrary choices of the kids they used to be.

'You're lying!' Yun snapped, unclipping his seat belt to hang out of the window. It was balmy outside, and flying in from New York during the holidays always left him with a kind of temperate whiplash. 'I can't even see it from *here*.'

'It's right there.'

'Well it's there *now*.'

Their father grimaced. 'Dan, get back in and put your seat belt on, do you want to lose your head?'

'At three miles an hour?' Yun slid back into the car and levered himself roughly into the middle seat alongside Kevin. 'There's no way you saw that, you get worse every year. And you *know* sitting on the right is an advantage so why would you lie?'

'I'm not even lying, get back in your own seat.' Kevin shoved him. 'This is why we can't play family games any more, you're such a fascist.'

'Can I swap places with Mom then? For fairness.' Yun raised his eyebrows at his father in the overhead mirror, who adjudicated on such matters.

Yun Ji-hoon shook his head wearily. 'You lost scissors rock paper, it was fair. Everyone stays in their seats.'

'Why *wouldn't* they do it this year?' Kevin shrugged, returning to their mother's original statement. 'It's not like everyone can just cancel Christmas.'

'Maybe out of respect?' Jeong Hui-sun reapplied her lipstick in the mirror as they came to a halt just before the turn-off to Whitney. 'These are military families, they might have thought it was inappropriate.'

'Are they still military around here? I thought that was just the people who started it.'

'Most of them are still going to be military, aren't they?'

'People move.'

'Dads are dads, whoever moves in they'll do the light show no matter what.' Kevin hung his hand out of the window, like he wished he was holding a cigarette between his fingers. 'This whole thing is like a monument to the focused competitive energy of dads.'

Hui-sun frowned. 'I could do better. The dinosaur house is lazy.'

'You mean the Jurassic Park house?' Yun gestured at the glowing sign.

'The T-Rex lived during the late Cretaceous period,' she replied. 'Everyone knows that.'

'Can we turn the radio off if we're gonna talk?' Yun implored, still hot-eyed and tired from staying up drinking grape soju and watching *Die Hard* with Kevin the night before. 'It's really throwing me off.'

One of the houses on the corner featured a neon crucifix with the garish caption HE IS RISEN.

'That's not right,' Ji-hoon commented as he turned the radio down, judging the misguided Easter sentiment.

'Does that not count as a misspelling?' Yun asked.

'*No!*' Kevin spluttered, appalled. 'No, it does not!'

'Well, it's technically a misspelling if it's supposed to say Merry Christmas and they've gone with Happy *Easter*.'

'No, no points,' their father confirmed. 'It's not a misspelling.'

'Ha!' Kevin shook his head at Yun. 'You're being really ugly right now.'

Yun mouthed, *Fuck you*, while Kevin made the jerk-off gesture.

'Are Emory's family Christian?' Hui-sun asked.

'I think her dad is a scientist. Like, a crime-scene scientist.'

Yun checked his phone out of habit. Emory had sent a message earlier when she arrived, but had been silent ever since. Now he no longer had to divide the holidays with Nicola's parents, Andrew was with his aunt and uncle in Vancouver. Mike and Lara were apparently in Aspen, like every year.

'She's just kinda generically Christian,' he said, flipping his phone case shut. 'She doesn't go to church or anything.'

Hui-sun's eyes narrowed. 'That doesn't sound very Christian.'

'I think she's Christian in a *census* way.'

'Will she be visiting? I'd like to meet her.'

The succession of questions made him feel cornered. Since Ms BB vocalized her dislike of Emory, Yun had become convinced his mother would dislike her too. Or, even worse, draw attention to the fact that Emory was making more money than him. 'I don't know, I'd have to ask. Of course she'd like to meet you guys, because she's nice. But we haven't talked about it yet.'

'*Creepy Santa!*' Kevin banged his fist against the door. '*Fuck!*'

'Dan!' Ji-hoon coughed, as if covering a laugh.

'Can you both calm down?' Hui-sun pulled her handbag on to her lap and twisted around to hand Yun a banana, before handing another to his brother.

Yun rested it on his knees, wary of being distracted.

Kevin started eating.

They all silently observed a *Nightmare Before Christmas* scene on the left as the car rolled to a stop again. On the right was a flashing American flag. A church-style luminous noticeboard beneath it read IN HONOR OF THE 229,992.

'He must have had to buy a ton of number sets to write that,' Kevin said.

'How morbid,' Hui-sun replied.

'I'm just saying, who has *three* nines ready to go?'

'Distasteful,' Ji-hoon muttered.

'He must have to update it all the time.' Yun turned the banana over in his hands.

'Other people exist,' their father elaborated as they moved on. 'Not just Americans.'

'It is mostly Americans now, though.'

Kevin shrugged. 'There are still a few in Europe.'

'Baseball house.' Hui-sun pointed through the wind-screen at the Tony Gwynn display.

Yun and Kevin hadn't known the story behind it when they were young, so they always called it the baseball house. A glowing number 19 and a life-sized cut-out of Mr Padre, a Black right fielder for the San Diego Padres.

'It's not really fair when you're in the front,' Kevin said.

'Yeah, that's just a lost point now.' Yun unzipped his jacket. 'Can I have some water?'

Hui-sun passed a bottle from her bag. 'Did you say Emory was spending the holidays on a farm?'

'It's not a farm, it's land with some houses on it. That was how she described it.'

'She's *gentry*.' Kevin exchanged an *ooh* expression with their father, adopting a ridiculous British accent. 'Does she have *peasants*, my lord?'

Ji-hoon chuckled and contributed, 'Feudalism.'

Hui-sun turned in her seat. 'Do you have photos?'

'Yes, but if you're all gonna be like this then you're not seeing any.' Yun punched Kevin on the shoulder and shouted *Palm trees!* as they passed the house, which this year also sported a family of snowmen wearing sunglasses, and glowing neon palms on their lawn. Their 'Merry Christmas' sign was spelled with a double 's': MERRY CHRISTMASS!

Yun punched him again. '*And* a misspelling! Yes!'

'Err, violence?' Kevin appealed in the overhead mirror but Ji-hoon waved the complaint away.

Hui-sun checked her hair in the sun visor. 'Does she have brothers and sisters?'

'She has a younger sister, who's a lot younger. That's it.'

'Have you thought about marriage?' His mother stopped pretending to be concerned with her makeup, meeting Yun's eyes in the overhead mirror pointedly. 'Does she want children?'

'Jesus, no!' It was like a question from another universe, as bizarre as asking if either of them had considered space travel, and it made Yun feel just as nauseated. 'No! I mean, I don't know if she wants kids. But no. *No.*'

'Yeah, after four nos we get it.' Kevin smirked. 'Can't think of a worse time to have kids, to be fair. You'd have to be certified insane.'

'Okay, enough questions now. *Thanks.*' Yun folded his arms and tried to sink down in his seat, only reconsidering when he realized he couldn't see out of the windows from that position. 'And yeah, wouldn't having kids now basically be, like, pre-emptive child abuse?'

They passed a gold-and-green archway, and Hui-sun leaned her elbow on the car window ledge, looking sad.

'I guess it could be,' she said. 'But some of us were born during wars. Do you think it would be better for them to have never been born? Things are always bad, somewhere.'

Everyone stopped talking, watching the houses and light displays. Yun saw Kevin brace as they approached the final corner. The queue of cars ground to a halt, and the two of them peered over the heads of people walking outside, trying to catch a glimpse of the final house, just out of sight.

'Are we tied for points or what?' Yun checked.

Ji-hoon checked his phone, but didn't say anything.

Yun put the banana in the back of his father's seat, and looked at Kevin.

His brother had raised the visor of his cap so he could see better, sitting the hat right back on his ears. As he went for his seat belt Yun opened his door, leapt into the packed road and sprinted for the sidewalk.

He heard their mother calling them as Kevin also scrambled out of the car.

Yun had weaved around a few families before Kevin caught up and grabbed him round the waist. They wrestled with each other and Kevin kicked him in the shin as he tried to trip him. Kevin was slightly taller, so by the time they came upon the last house on the block, Yun was dragging him back by his shoulder while Kevin had him in a loose headlock.

There were some bemused and worried looks as they stumbled, and both started yelling, 'Same door! Same door!' at the sight of the house, which still had an identical front door to their old house.

'You're such an *asshole*,' Kevin hissed, elbowing Yun in the ribs.

Yun snatched the cap off his head and threw it into the street in retaliation.

After Kevin retrieved it, they stood by the last house waiting for their parents to crawl the last twenty yards in the car.

A curtain of blue fairy lights hung across each window, and one of them held a glowing white dove. Yun was struck by a sudden, ice-cold fear that this trip would be the last time they ever saw each other. His mother's questions, his father's deadpan expression and strange mechanical-sounding chuckle, it could all be gone. It *would* all be gone eventually, but he didn't know what would happen if it was sooner than he was ready for.

Yun thought about the bag of cleaning products he had brought for Ms BB, which had stayed on the floor by the front door for days.

'When did you get strong?' Kevin asked, nudging him.

'Ah, it's embarrassing, I got another job so I'm cycling a lot for deliveries.'

'It's money, right.' Kevin shrugged, then chuckled. 'It's funny how it's still here.'

'What, the door?'

'Yeah, like . . .' His shoulders started shaking as he laughed harder. 'Like, in twenty years why would you never change your door?'

'Are you high?' Yun started laughing too, not because Kevin was funny but because his laugh was. 'People don't change their doors.'

'It's just funny. It's just funny that it's still here and it's still the same door.' Kevin rubbed his eyes, and the laughter died off. 'I wonder if it really is the same up close, or if it's just the same colour. I kinda don't wanna go look, just in case. I don't wanna ruin it.'

A father tailing his excited five-year-old caught up and tucked the label back into the neck of his T-shirt. Yun remembered seeing Andrew do that a week ago, with the guy who wasn't his student. It was nearing four a.m. and they were still standing in an awkward, shivering circle on the sidewalk outside the club; Mike and Lara having long departed in a Lyft and Andrew and the not-student loitering in muted solidarity as the paramedics took the last of the sitters away.

Yun had glanced over at Andrew, feeling a sickly mixture of embarrassment and guilt, and said, 'You can go, you really don't have to wait here.'

Andrew shook his head and said, 'We don't mind.' And the guy – *Fin*, the guy he now remembered seeing in the corridor where he first kissed Emory, he was called *Fin* – gave him a small smile, as if in agreement. Watching another ambulance depart, Andrew tucked in the hood of Fin's coat so it was no longer inside out, but it looked for a moment like he had moved to put his arm around his shoulders, and stopped.

We don't mind. Not I. We.

'Dude, you all right?'

Yun remembered Kevin, and turned away from the father and son. It was really none of his business if Andrew had made a new friend. He was getting divorced. He probably would go through a phase of wanting to hang out with weirdly younger people.

The line of cars was still unmoving.

'You know all that stuff you told me about, like, killing yourself and stuff?' Yun took a long inhale through his nose. 'I found all that info on, like, one website.'

'Yeah, I read it all on this blog. I can't remember.' Kevin put his hands in his pockets and started walking, slowly.

Yun walked alongside him, taking them a little further

away from the car. 'Were you searching for it? It kind of only comes up if you search for it.'

Kevin sniffed, rubbing his red nose. 'Yeah.'

He didn't say anything else.

Yun spread his hands. 'Are you, like, all right?'

Kevin smiled. 'Relax, it's cool. I looked it up once, just to . . . I don't know, see? It didn't sound great. Even opioids, like the heroin option or Oxy. It works, it's a great way to go. But getting resuscitated, apparently it's the *worst*. You'd have to be a hundred per cent sure someone wasn't gonna walk in.'

Yun felt a sensation like an abrupt drop, in his hands and his chest, parts of him that were suddenly weak. 'But you're okay now, right? You're not actually *going* to.'

'Nah, man, nah, I'm not big on the risk of pain.' He shrugged, like his reasoning was obvious. 'And I couldn't do that to Mom. She'd never get over it, so it's just not a realistic option right now.'

Yun wished he had imagined the disappointment in his little brother's tone, the slight abrasion of resentment.

He sighed. 'I get what you mean.'

They stopped walking and waited for their parents to reach them. Yun's jaw ached, which reminded him he should probably talk to someone about getting a mouth guard like Emory kept telling him to, like that kind of thing was free. But it seemed so inconsequential, the knowledge that he was clenching his teeth in his sleep. If he sold a few good songs, then he could afford all the dentistry he would need in his thirties to fix all the problems caused by the stress of his twenties. And hopefully some other apocalyptic event – climate change maybe – would spare him having to grapple with the fact that retirement as a prospect no longer existed for most people his age. That seemed like a better plan, in the long run. Kick the can down the road for long enough and there might not even be a can or a road any more.

He looked at Kevin. 'Have you thought about trying yoga?'

Kevin started laughing so hard that by the time the car reached them they were both crying.

不想跪着，又站不起来，只好躺平，"躺平的韭菜不好割。"

21.

Two days after Christmas, Andrew flew back to New York to surprise Fin for the New Year, via San Diego to surprise Yun. He rented a car, booked into the Hilton in Del Mar for two nights, and in a fit of worry told Yun he was also catching up with some friends who taught at UCSD, which was a lie.

Only you could think San Diego is a logical stopover, Yun messaged when Andrew alerted him to the visit. *But it'll be good to see you obvs.*

Fin didn't even know he had left Vancouver. It was easier, if neither of them knew his reasons for being here. Less worry that way. Less pressure. But he barely slept the first night, and spent most of it sitting on the balcony, trying to read and listening to the freeway in the bizarre warmth.

He was going to tell Yun, he decided. The right words wouldn't come every time he tried to write a message, and he couldn't think of anything more mortifying than a phone call. The only way the conversation could happen was in person, especially as he and Yun hadn't seen much of each other since the summer. Or at least, it felt that way.

In the morning – one p.m., which was the earliest Yun could be convinced to do anything – he picked Yun up from Kearny Mesa and they walked the Razor Point Trail towards the coastline in the Torrey Pines Reserve. They had been here before, though Yun complained a lot less this time around.

Yun had become broader at the shoulders, harder but

thinner. Due to the hours spent cycling, he had abs for only the third time in his life, he proudly announced. As he talked, Andrew felt more aware of the underlying construction of his face than usual, the sharp, angry edges of his cheekbones and V-shaped jaw.

'I'd be such a liability in an actual apocalypse,' Yun said, leaning on the wooden fence a few feet back from the cliff edge and pulling at the neck of his black shirt. 'I'm really fit but I need to eat every two hours.'

There was something surreal about seeing Yun out of what Andrew considered his natural habitat. No dim light, the grey-black-beige-grey of New York backdrops. Just Yun turning to face him, back to the sea and sky. He looked too real for this kind of landscape, a human person trapped in a crude painting.

'What do you mean, an *actual* apocalypse?'

'I mean compared to the shitty fake one we're in right now, where the world is ending but we all still have to work.'

A little way along from the outpost, part of the cliff had recently plummeted, and the austere greenery flourishing among the rocks and sand seemed to be crawling its way over the edge in its effort to spread. 'Do you wish it was worse then?'

'They're predicting half a million by the end of January and then it'll drop like cases dropped almost everywhere else. The only reason anyone still cares is because it's weird. If it was a bad flu season hospitals wouldn't even bother keeping a tally. It's such a poor fucking effort.' Yun shrugged, moving a hand as if it was itching to hold a cigarette. 'I'd rather everyone sits down, fucking *everyone*, and I get to stop paying rent.'

Andrew watched the ocean for a moment, and when he looked at Yun again he realized something had shifted. Until he met Fin, he had never before met anybody with a more direct gaze or louder thoughts than Yun.

'What made you visit?' Yun regarded Andrew, brow lowered. 'I don't mean to sound suspicious, but you're not the most spontaneous person. Makes me think you have big news or something.'

'We didn't get to talk a lot that night at the club. I just wanted to know you were doing all right.'

Yun's expression softened, and Andrew relaxed, feeling he had gotten away with it for now, could lie for a while longer. Though he had little idea why the prospect of telling Yun was triggering such anxiety. Yun should be the easiest person to tell, especially compared to Nicola. Maybe it was the abrupt change of weather. The warmth of the breeze on the coastline, knowing it was December, made him feel wrong-footed.

'You know, I haven't even told Em this,' Yun said, hands in pockets, hands out of pockets. 'Sometimes I think it's following me.'

'It? You mean, the catatonia?'

'I know it's crazy.' Yun grimaced, tried to cover it with a smile. 'It's not a *thing*. It's not a villain who hates me personally. But sometimes it does feel personal somehow, the way nothing ever gets better. Like I wonder, am I here to just watch everything get stranger and worse? And it makes me so fucking angry.' He swallowed, turning again to rest his forearms on the fence, eyes on the backs of his hands, flexing and unflexing. 'But I'm not angry about the right things, I don't give a shit about any of those people. I know it sounds bad but I really don't. I'm angry that I was doing kinda okay for myself, I felt like things were coming together with my music and everything, and then the world fucks it up for me again. It's like my brother said . . .'

His voice trailed off into the white noise of the sea.

It had occurred to Andrew more than once that the way Yun faced off against life with both hands balled into fists seemed at once brave and also incredibly lonely. He carried himself with a frustrated grandeur so palpable it made most people nervous; like the bastard son of royalty who would never inherit.

Main character syndrome, a girl at college called it. Though Andrew would describe him like that unironically.

Yun's face was blank for a second, as if he had forgotten what he was going to say, or knew what he wanted to say but couldn't bear to repeat it out loud.

I'm going to tell him, Andrew resolved, his mouth going dry. He couldn't let Yun leave today without telling him.

'Well, if it's following you, it's following me too,' he said, thinking that this should be easy, it should be easy . . .

The smile Yun turned upon him was so serene Andrew didn't need to hear the words out loud. It said *Thank God you're here*, and anything else Andrew might have said at that moment stopped in his throat.

'Do you want tacos?' Yun said, taking his arms off the fence and walking back towards the car. 'I'm *so* hungry.'

'How's work been?' Yun asked, sprawled at the foot of Andrew's bed at eleven p.m., balancing a whiskey-Coke on his chest. He had been saying he was going to call a car for the last two hours, but every time he got up to reach for his phone he ended up smoking weed on the balcony instead.

He couldn't let Yun leave without telling him. He couldn't.

Andrew sipped his minibar gin and tonic and put it on the bedside table. 'Oh, fine.'

'Are your students okay?'

'Not really. But okay, considering.'

'I've been thinking about it and maybe things aren't even that different now. People have been killing themselves by the tens of thousands for years and no one really cared until they aligned on method.' Yun sat up and shifted alongside Andrew, leaning against the headboard while he topped off his drink. 'A more public-facing method. Do you remember when the suicide veil went up?'

When Andrew was a sophomore, two students had thrown themselves from the upper floors of the Bobst Library. A strange rumour went around that they became hypnotized by the black-and-white optical illusion of the floor in the lobby below, and the university put up Plexiglas barriers to stop any more incidents. Several years later another student made it over the Plexiglas, and an architect was hired to design an aluminium enclosure, turning the atrium into a golden-patterned waterfall. Andrew thought it was beautiful when he returned after completing his PhD and saw it for the first time, before he learned why it was there. Some people called it a suicide veil, which made sense to Andrew because it didn't deal with the problem of students wanting to die; it just made sure the university didn't have to clean them up.

He contemplated exactly how much of a fit his department head would pitch if he brought up the suicide veil as a case study in his Ethics class.

'I should call a car,' Yun said, but didn't reach for his phone.

'You can finish your drink.' Andrew indicated his drink. 'Or you can sleep here, I don't mind.'

With a comic lack of hesitation, Yun slid down the headboard and made himself comfortable. He rested his drink on his chest again and looked up with a self-satisfied smile, like he had been waiting for Andrew to suggest it. 'Not gonna lie, I am literally dying to spend a night away. My parents are still getting up at six for some reason and I never get back to sleep.'

'I have to get up at eight, latest.'

'Still an improvement.' Yun sat up to take off his shirt and throw it across the room, where it landed on the back of the grey chair pulled into the desk. 'Visiting family is funny, you can eat all the food you want but can't get a moment of peace.'

'I know what you mean.'

Andrew's aunt believed the psychogenic death epidemic was a distinctly *American* disease, due to the highest numbers of afflicted and dying being from the United States, Britain and Western Europe. 'Americans are so lazy,' she said to Andrew as soon as her grandkids were safely in bed, and he suspected the sentiment had been pacing back and forth under the surface all day. 'They don't know how to work. They have nothing to be sad about, nothing to be tired about. Their government lets them do whatever they want and here they are, ungrateful. Undisciplined. *Lazy*. I would say they are like children, but as children we were more disciplined.'

Andrew had glanced at the kitchen door, wondering whether he could sneak any leftovers upstairs and also why, at the age of thirty, he still felt guilty drinking alcohol in front of his family.

'*You* were always so disciplined,' she said, taking his silence as tacit agreement.

Andrew found it excruciating to be complimented. Even more so, to be complimented for the things he had done to survive.

Has she considered the UK and US are just exceptionally bad vibes? Fin messaged, when Andrew shared her theories with him.

His stomach clenched as Fin crossed his mind again, and Yun shuffled out of his sweatpants and hurled them on to the chair along with his shirt. Without spilling a drop of his drink, he levered himself under the covers, put his hand behind his head and exhaled for such a long time it made Andrew laugh.

'Make yourself comfortable.'

'Thanks, I will.'

Yun smiled more widely, and Andrew felt jolted into the past, six or seven or maybe eight years ago, to whenever they had last done this, when their friendship had felt more important than anything else, certainly more important than any other kind of love.

'I miss living together sometimes,' Yun said, like he could read Andrew's mind.

'How's living with Emory?'

'She's cool.' Yun shrugged, vague and non-committal.

'Do you love her?'

Yun laughed, like the question or maybe the whole idea was absurd. 'I don't know, what the fuck is love anyway?'

A beat, where Yun looked up at him with an eyebrow slightly raised, and the expression reminded him so much of Fin that Andrew picked up his drink, gripped it tightly in both hands and said, 'I'm actually seeing somebody.'

'Wow.' Yun sat up on his elbows and put his drink down. 'Is this like a divorce rebound thing? Or a *thing* thing?'

'I have asked myself that and I think it's the latter.' He pretended not to notice the way he was still skirting around pronouns. 'We're living together.'

'That's fast, don't you think?' A hesitation. 'But then I probably can't talk . . . So, what's she like? You should have invited her to the club and introduced us.' In the split second Andrew didn't reply, the corner of Yun's mouth twitched, and he looked away and muttered, 'Ah, fuck.'

The ensuing silence was suffocating.

'Em was right, wasn't she? You did bring them to the club. Right?'

Regret left a bad taste in his mouth, regret at his own cowardice. By letting Yun talk, he had managed to avoid saying the words out loud, but now felt as though he couldn't own the confession. For some reason, he was sure Fin would be disappointed in him, for not summoning the courage to say what he really meant.

'Fin didn't want to make an event of it that night and I couldn't find the right time to tell you,' he said, attempting to regain some control. 'I wanted to tell you in person.'

'Ah, so that is his name.'

'Yeah.' Andrew began to smile involuntarily and stopped himself, because Yun wasn't smiling.

'And he's a dance student? So, pretty young then.'

'Younger than I would have expected, I suppose.'

'I wouldn't say that's the unexpected part.' Yun took a long drink, didn't look at him, instead leaned forward on his knees and looked straight ahead. 'Did you always know? Like, this can't be the first time you realized . . . ? Was it?'

'I don't know.'

'You don't *know* if you knew you were gay or not?' Yun frowned, and it felt like an accusation. 'Or what? You go both ways?'

'No.' He was gripping his drink too tight, flustered. 'I don't think I've ever gone both ways. I know that, at least.' The laugh that came out was shaky, and it didn't make a dent in the way Yun was looking at him.

'So this guy, this is the first time anything has happened?' His tone was as disbelieving as it was offended, and even though logically Andrew would have considered Yun the easiest person to tell, he realized he had known on some level it was going to be this hard. 'Did it start at the wedding? I don't know why you wouldn't have mentioned it to me then.'

'It was after the wedding. I ran into him at a gallery.'

'And?'

'And, what?'

A chill invaded the air. Yun's expression freezing over. Then he released Andrew from the intensity of his gaze, picked up his drink and shrugged. The expression was gone, but the chill remained. 'Okay,' he said.

'Okay?' Andrew was a little out of breath, like they had argued. But this wasn't an argument, was it? It wasn't an argument. They wouldn't have argued. Not about this. 'Are we okay?'

Yun shrugged again. 'Sure. I'm happy for you. We'll all have to go out when we're back.'

The words were staccato, no weight to them.

Andrew wanted to ask what was wrong, but didn't want to draw attention to the fact something *was* wrong. He wanted to explain, but didn't know what else needed to be

211

explained. He wanted to go back and tell some other version of Yun, the one in the kitchen with the towel around his waist, hair wet from the shower and smiling. He wanted.

Yun announced he was going to sleep, and went to the bathroom to use Andrew's array of skincare products. When he returned, the harsh outline of his body, the set of his shoulders turned away from him, seemed unfamiliar. Andrew switched off the bedside light and listened to his breathing, waiting for him to say something that never came.

He woke up once, needing the bathroom, and found Yun was asleep on his left arm. Andrew considered moving, but couldn't bear to wake him. When he tried to flex his fingers, he couldn't feel them. The weight of Yun's head was heavy but his expression was at peace.

Yun would never describe himself as a morning person, but the version of Yun that Andrew missed most was Yun in the morning, when he was younger and his fists were momentarily lowered and he laughed more easily, and whatever furious electricity propelled him now hadn't caught up with him. He missed Yun so much, yet he was right here, asleep on his arm. He missed his best friend. But they still were best friends, weren't they?

Waking up a second time, Andrew flexed his fingers and Yun was gone.

22.

'And Sophie Martin, she's pregnant.'

'How do you know? I thought her account was private?'

'I saw her yesterday, she works at the Lancôme counter in Selfridges.'

'No way!' Fin poured himself some Shiraz and carried his eight-year-old MacBook Pro – the most expensive thing he owned – back to the sofa, where he set the glass on the coffee table and flopped on to his stomach in front of the screen. 'I never graduated from online stalking people from school into *actual* stalking, you're way ahead of me.'

His mother set the phone on the counter, giving him a view of the ceiling as she took something out of the microwave. She had just finished a double-pay shift at the credit card company she had worked at for the last six years. She had worked every Christmas and New Year Fin could remember, and never understood why everyone didn't jump at the chance for double pay when, 'You don't need a whole day to eat a bird and play some George Michael.'

'Ah well,' she said as Fin heard the sound of peeling plastic film. 'I have more experience. I looked up Wish, she's still alive!'

'I do check on her sometimes. She'll probably outlive us all. She must have been *seventy* when she first let me start practising at the studio. It was only my third lesson when she tripped over these ladders a construction crew left lying around. She went flying, smacked her head, everyone was saying to call 999. And she just got up and told the girls to stop fussing. Carried on like nothing happened. Fall like that would've done Nana in! Still the best advert for carrying on with ballet I've ever seen. She just wasn't *old* like other old people are.'

'Are you looking after your back?'

'I didn't have a spare pillow for a while but I've been sleeping with one under my back and one under my knees. I always thought the knees thing was weird but I totally get it now. Andrew finds it funny.'

'But school is okay?'

Fin thought about his last evaluation, the teacher with the shitty 'stache who invited him out for a drink twice, then offered him nothing but scorn dressed up as some tough-teaching-radical-honesty bullshit. *You're just not a leading man.*

Fin thought about that for days, but didn't tell anyone. *Not a leading man.* Five syllables, five beats. He could take it to class, grit his teeth and count along to it like a waltz. *Too short to go pro.* Another five syllables. That one he had at least heard before.

'Finlay? They treating you well?'

'It's fine, I guess.'

'You sound so American now.'

She said it every time, but so far no one in New York had mistaken him for one of their own. Fin hadn't lived in Dublin since he was four, but after twenty minutes speaking to his mother, he could hear her accent creeping back into his inflections.

'You should write to Wish.' Ma took the phone through to the front room and propped it against something. In the background, Fin could hear the Christmas Special of some quiz show. 'She always saw something special in you, she'd love to know how you're doing.'

'Yeah . . .' Fin swallowed down the guilt with a mouthful of wine, put the glass on the floor so it was easier to reach. He was good at falling out of touch with people; she knew that about him. 'I'll write to her before graduation.'

'Best not put it off.' She frowned. 'I wish you weren't spending the holidays on your own.'

Two of Fin's former classmates were in the hospital, slowly wasting away in one of the few London wards still given over to the catatonic. They had started dating in Year 11 and stayed together the last four years. Fin wondered how that worked on multiple levels. Childhood sweethearts, as a concept, had never made sense to him. How did two people stay together during years where surely they should have changed, shed their childish former selves? He found it hard to believe it was possible without both parties deluding themselves, or deluding the other. Either way, someone pretending to be something they weren't.

How they became afflicted together was a whole other question, which Fin didn't want to think too much about. There was still no evidence of viral or bacterial cause, so the scientific consensus was now that people were – whether consciously or subconsciously – bringing it upon themselves. Maybe one or both of them had always been unhappy. It was only now they were offered a language with which to adequately express it.

As soon as Fin realized choice-theory was taking hold, he knew insurance companies here would abruptly stop covering treatment, and employers would stop handing out sick pay. And he was right. Many companies, including Andrew's university and Fin's academy, announced their new policies just before Christmas. It was now considered the individual's choice to stop working, to use up resources, to die. No one else was at fault, and there was no external cause for them to assume liability for. Friends and family alone were now responsible for overseeing their quiet, slow and selfish deaths.

And the deaths were coming quicker now, usually within a week. Everyone suspected it was because families were euthanizing them. No one knew if it was kinder, but it was undoubtably easier than dealing with the grappling and scratching, the snarling and spitting, the silence, the limited visitation to the long-term catatonic wards, which most medical staff were refusing to work on, for fear the malaise, the unhappiness, was infectious in a way they didn't yet understand.

So far only two Black women had been prosecuted for hurrying the wretched process along. One down in Texas, and another in Alabama. Because the crisis that everyone thought would change everything hadn't actually changed anything, just dug deeper into the existing cracks. Like the last one, and the one before that.

At the club, Fin first noticed something was wrong when a man knocked into him, bolting for the exit. He thought a fight had broken out. Then a landslide of bodies crashed into him, slamming him against another wall of bodies surging from behind him. All he could think was, *Don't go down, don't go down*, because if he lost his footing he knew he would die. He had visions of fingers breaking, a foot crushing the back of his neck. The floor vanished from under his feet, and it wasn't until he was moving with the crowd that he realized a pair of strong arms was tight around his chest. He was hit with a blast of cold air, and suddenly he was outside.

In the seconds it took for everyone else to stream out, Andrew took his face in his hands and asked, 'Are you all right? Are you all right?' while Fin gulped for air, shaking before he even noticed the cold.

Andrew had held his freezing hand tight, and didn't speak for a long time in the car on their way back from the club. Though when he eventually spoke, Fin knew what he was going to say.

'Who's your emergency contact?'

He feigned thinking about it for a beat. 'My academy.'

Andrew turned, and Fin squirmed under his obvious shock.

'Don't look at me like that, it's only been two months! I think changing my emergency contact would've been *more* presumptuous than you calling me your boyfriend, don't you think?'

'But not even your mother?'

'What could she do in an emergency, jump on a plane? Quickly fly over to lift a car off me?' Fin grimaced, and wished he was able to reach for a more mature shield than sarcasm.

'You think I wouldn't want to be the first to know if something happened?'

He was completely sincere. Fin didn't doubt that any more.

'Honestly, I haven't even thought about it.' He pretended to look out of the window. 'It's not going to happen to me anyway. So it doesn't matter.'

'If it doesn't matter, then why not put me?'

'You know what, fine.' With as much passive-aggression as he could muster, Fin took his informational card out of his wallet, crossed out the number of his academy administration office, and wrote down Andrew's name and number. 'You know what this means. You'll get a call now, if something happens.'

'That is the idea.'

'I don't want you to feel obligated. If something happens you can call my ma. This isn't *Marguerite and Armand*, you don't have to watch me die as a final romantic gesture.'

'Fin.' Andrew looked at him as if he was insane. 'How could I *not* be obligated?'

He couldn't think of anything to say to that, so he glanced at the driver and said, 'Can we please not do this now?'

When Andrew fell silent, Fin swore he could hear what was coming next. Some variation of *I can't do this any more*, or maybe *This isn't working out*. Andrew was too thoughtful to say that kind of thing in the car, so he bit back tears and squeezed his hand a little tighter.

Well, Fin thought, they'd had a good run. Better than he could have hoped for and arguably more than he deserved, because God knows Andrew was more patient than most. But there was a limit. It was fine. Expected, even. Fin had got through break-ups before and he would get through it again. Living in a shittier apartment made him stay longer at school, so in a way it was beneficial, not to get complacent. It had only been a matter of time before the initial novelty wore off and Andrew realized he could do better, that he could date someone with a cool job, a job at *all*, someone smarter, older, someone who knew how to do this, someone whose father never left, who didn't need so fucking much.

They were about two blocks from the apartment when he said it. Fin was so far down his well of self-pity he almost missed it, and he turned from the window. 'What?'

Andrew hesitated, like he hadn't anticipated needing the courage to say it twice. '. . . I'm sorry.'

'You're sorry?'

'I know it's early, I just had to say it. I've been thinking about it for a while. You don't have to say anything.' He rubbed the tiredness out of his eyes, but didn't let go of Fin's hand. Only then did he say it again. 'I love you.'

It was like he didn't understand that relationships were all about power. They were about control, about who could endure the longest without visibly caring. Andrew was always giving his power away without a thought, like he wasn't ceding anything.

But maybe he wasn't. Because even while in that moment Fin was aware he could have said anything – used this leverage to steer them both in any direction he wanted – what he actually did was break down and ugly-cry at four thirty in the morning in the back of a Lyft car.

So much for power.

Fin knew he didn't have to spend the holidays alone. When he told Andrew he wanted to save the money so Ma could come over for graduation, Andrew offered to pay for the plane tickets. When Fin turned him down, Andrew then asked if Fin wanted to come to Canada to stay with his aunt and uncle. When Fin turned him down again – pointing out that his family didn't even know Andrew was gay, and he had no desire to star in a Hallmark movie pretending to be a stray orphan for two weeks – Andrew insisted Fin at least stay in the apartment to look after the plants, and check in every day.

That, Fin could manage.

After calling Ma, he rolled on to his back and checked his messages. Andrew hadn't sent anything since yesterday, and they hadn't spoken over FaceTime for three days. He tried not to read too much into the drop-off in communication, considering how family tended to monopolize time.

The last time they spoke, Andrew had escaped to his room and called him for twenty minutes at the end of the day, propped up against his headboard with a glass of brandy. He looked drained, as he always did after teaching, or any situation where he was forced to be social for a prolonged period of time. Though in lieu of seeking real-life acceptance from his remaining family, Andrew was reading a book on a history of homosexuality in China, and delighted in sharing this education with Fin.

He told him of a story from the Song Dynasty, in which a student of writing called Wang Zhongxian sought out a famously beautiful writer and teacher by the name of Pan Zhang. The two fell in love at first sight, and lived together for the rest of their lives.

Woozy after his fourth glass of wine and a few scoops of sorbet, Fin tried not to drop his phone on his face as *Home Alone* played in the background. 'Let me guess, they both died.'

'Well, yes, though they died at the same time. Apparently a tree grew over their grave, and its branches grew to embrace each other.'

'That doesn't sound real. I know this can't be as whole-some as you're making it sound.'

'It was wholesome *until* they died. No love stories would be wholesome if you include dying.'

'I agree. No love stories *are* wholesome, unless you lie, or lie by omission.'

Fin reached for his glass again but the wine was gone. As was the case in so many great ballets, he had always believed – if you stripped away the illusion of easy-flowing beauty, the insidious narcotic-thick bliss designed to cloud your better judgement – love was about blood and gore, and what you were willing to rip out or cut off. And what you had to be willing to cut off usually amounted to a lot more than clothing. It was surprising Andrew wasn't more overtly morbid in his outlook. But then there was no way of pre-dicting the fallout from watching your parents separate and then slowly, stubbornly die of different cancers within four years of each other.

'What would be the point if stories were only limited to truth?' Andrew said, sounding amused. 'There would be no art.'

'Fewer kids would be fucked up by fairy tales. You know what really happened at the end of *Snow White*? At the wed-ding they made the step-mother dance in hot iron shoes until she died. *Little Mermaid*? After she gave up her voice, the prince lost interest and she killed herself.'

'They're different versions of the same story, they just fin-ish earlier. What if both are true? Both *are* true. People live happily ever after *and* they die. Maybe that's the point.'

'I know I've said this before.' Fin looked at him and smiled. 'But you'd get on really well with my ma.'

Andrew took the comment as it was intended. Basically as good as an *I love you*.

'Maybe there is something to be said for the fantasy,' Andrew said, after a sip of brandy. 'Deep down, people know just how unlikely their happiness is. The only thing we can at least be honest about is we want things to work out, and that's what these stories are really about. It's not about the lie, it's about the fact there is value in *wanting* to be happy.'

The sound of a key in the lock brought Fin back to the present, still staring at his phone, wondering what to write, and procrastinating on the task of getting up and drinking more wine. He sat up, listened to the front door open, and wondered for a moment if he had fallen asleep on the sofa and was dreaming.

'I just don't think anyone can spend their whole lives together without lying to each other,' Fin had said, pushing back, as he always felt the need to push back.

And Andrew had smiled at him – just as he was smiling at Fin now, walking into the kitchen, dragging his suitcase – and said, 'Back then, a whole life wasn't so long.'

23.

'Your dad could be on to something, asking you to move upstate. It might actually do the two of you good, getting out of the city.' Lara stood on her toes and tapped her card on the bar top to see if she could get any attention. But the bartender started serving someone else, and Lara turned back to Emory. 'Even if your dad is having a weird episode, you could still make a couples break of it. Better than doing something *really* insane to fix your problems, like hiking together. Or camping.'

'When have you ever gone camping?'

'Not recently, thank God. It was one of the first dates Mike took me on. A hike and *then* camping. I compare all subsequent events to how bad that night was.'

'It can't have been that bad if you married him.'

'I remember it vividly. I reached over, I held his hand – *very* chaste! – and said, "Mike, I hate this. Never make me do anything like this again." Maybe that's when I realized if we could get through that, we could probably get through anything.'

Lara wedged her elbow further on to the bar to order a lime and soda, which caused Emory to raise her eyebrows.

'What, are you pregnant or something?'

'Don't be ridiculous.' Lara seemed to swallow her own laugh. 'I just had a heavy one last night.'

Emory felt her smile flicker. 'No, you didn't.'

'Yes, I did. Why are you being weird?' Lara busied herself with checking her bangs in the mirror behind the bar as she paid. Emory hadn't seen her since before Christmas. Her hair was much longer and her face had filled out in a way that made her look healthier, younger. 'You can drink on your own for once, can't you?'

'Oh my God . . .'

'What?'

'You *are*!'

'Can you *shut up*?' Her tone was a little wild.

'Lara!' Emory put her hand on her arm. 'This is good news. You can tell me.'

'I didn't want to tell anybody.'

'Well, you can tell *me*, silly.' Emory shook her gently. 'It *is* good news, isn't it?'

Lara rubbed the bridge of her nose and didn't answer.

She didn't say anything else until they found two free chairs and sat at the edge of someone else's table, bags on their laps. Lara watched Emory take a sip of wine and sighed. 'For what it's worth, I hate not drinking. As if things aren't stressful enough. This!' She raised her lime and soda with disgust. 'This is no life.'

'Mike does know, doesn't he?'

'Of course he does. He would *also* notice if I stopped drinking.'

'How long?'

'Nine weeks.' She grimaced. 'Urgh, listen to me, I'm measuring things in weeks like one of *those* people. Just over two months.'

'Are you going to stay in New York?'

'I don't know.' She covered her lips with her fingers, like

what she wanted to say was too horrible to utter aloud. 'What I'm actually thinking is, should I be having a baby at all?'

'You think it's too soon?'

'No, I mean *ever*. It just seems selfish. What life is a baby going to have now? I mean, people are giving up, just sitting down in the street and giving up.' She spread her hands. 'A baby is a *person*. I have to think about what their life is going to be like, and I can't see any way it's going to be good.'

'If anyone can give a child a good life, it's you and Mike. You're doing so well, you've both got good jobs, you've got the money.'

'Rose *died* at my wedding!' Lara averted her eyes, took a breath. 'I know technically it happened a few weeks later but that's not how everyone remembers it. I've been talking to my therapist about it, about my *own* wedding. I can't put someone else through all *this* just because I want them, just because I want to meet them. That's not a good enough reason. Is it?'

Emory drank some more wine. Lara drank her lime and soda and looked even more dejected.

'What does your therapist have to say about everything?' Emory asked, changing the subject. 'My dad was seeing a therapist and all it did was make him quit his job.'

'Mine says my problem is with "life's inherent uncertainty".' Lara pulled a face. 'I feel like my problem is actually with all the certainties. Like, how the world is going to turn into a cremator in thirty years and, you know what, we definitely won't stay in New York because the city is going to end up in the Hudson. That's why it feels *insane* to have a baby right now.'

Emory's wine was almost gone but she didn't want to get in line at the bar again.

'So, you think everyone should stop having children? What if it gets better? It could.'

'Yeah, right.' Lara's eyes filled with tears and she rifled through her bag for tissues. 'More likely, it ends up hating me. Because I thought I should just carry on as normal and do something as stupid as *have a baby* after thousands of people decided killing themselves was better than trying to live through this shit-show.'

'Have you talked to Mike about any of this?'

'He basically said he'll go along with whatever I decide.' Lara rolled her eyes. 'It's nice that he's supportive but it's also fucking frustrating. Going along with whatever I decide is awesome when we can't decide where to eat, but not so great when it's about something important like whether we should have children together.'

'So what are you leaning towards deciding?'

'I'm leaning towards having it.' Her tone was apologetic, as if continuing to pursue any form of happiness was such an ostentatious luxury it should make her worthy of scorn.

On some level, Emory thought she might feel that way too, and had felt that way for a long time.

At the end of January – when it was still freezing but everyone was resisting the oppressive urge to stay inside sitting in front of the space heater – they went down to Red Hook on one of Yun's rare days off, with the intention of meeting up with Andrew and Derrick.

They stepped off the subway carriage on to the platform,

and into an unexpected crowd of people heading outside in a slow, shuffling mass.

Commuting hours were long over, and Yun glanced at his phone, which had no signal. 'Was there anything on today?'

'It could be a pop-up thing.'

'Oh God.' He fell dramatically against the handrail. 'It's too cold for a pop-up.'

'We'll find you a drink and a patch of sun to bask in like a lizard.'

'That's all I want.' He shifted to lean against her instead. 'If there's a flash mob, I'm leaving.'

As they reached the top of the steps and began to file out of Carroll Street and on to Eileen C Dugan, she noticed a lot of people were wearing white. Yun had also noticed, and they both tensed.

'Is it a protest?' Emory reached for her phone.

Keeping ahold of her hand, Yun stepped a little ahead and raised up on his toes to peer over the crowd, which filled the road as far as they could see. Cars were at a standstill all the way down 3rd, unable to turn around or move forward due to the mass of people. A man had gotten out and was hanging over his car door yelling, 'Get out of the street!' at no one and everyone.

'Hey,' Emory turned to a young woman next to her, wearing a white puffy coat, 'do you know what this is?'

'It's a vigil!' The girl smiled. 'They're happening all over. There's, like, three in Brooklyn today, and Manhattan. Do you want a flyer?'

Emory glanced at it. Whatever this was had been organized by what she assumed was a religious group. Someone she had never heard of. *#wearwhite*. 'Who are The Genesis Org?'

'I don't know,' the girl replied airily. 'I figured they were some progressive thing from Greenwich Village. That's where their address is. They could be students at NYU?'

Yun looked uneasily at the crowd as Emory let go of his hand to read the flyer. He scrolled through his phone as they drifted towards the sidewalk, where it was easier to move. Crowds made him nervous, he said. When Emory pointed out how ironic that was coming from someone who wanted to be a famous musician, he said he didn't mind being above them; separated from them, on stage. He just couldn't stand being in them. Too many people in one place and they felt threatening, hostile and erratic. Like something that wanted to kill you. Like the ocean.

There weren't any destinations specified on the flyers. Only places to gather.

'Where are we going?' She turned to the girl again, but she had vanished into the hum of bodies and misted breaths.

Emory raised her phone to snap a few shots of the street ahead. Looking at them, she estimated there must be at least a hundred people. She vaguely recognized the hashtag from social media, but hadn't paid much attention to it. Police officers were flanking the road and directing traffic, so it must have been authorized. But she was unfamiliar with the concept of a gathering or protest with no purpose, no leaders and no speakers.

Yun was typing. 'I'll tell Andrew and Derrick to stay where they are. There's no point trying to get a drink around here.'

'Should we go back? We can go if you want.'

To her surprise, he shrugged. 'I don't know, we're here now. Let's see what it is. At least it's not a flash mob.' He smiled, and she relaxed a little. Looking over the flyer, he raised his eyebrows. 'All the places on here are really nice neighbourhoods. Must be why the cops are so chill.'

She knew this was code for *white*, but he had chosen to say *nice* instead on account of being surrounded by so many white people.

They ducked off the main road to grab some takeout coffees, then joined the slow walkers on Court Street. She would have preferred a protest. This felt too much like a funeral, which she had always found to be pointless. And she hated anything involving a colour scheme. There was something repulsive and unnerving about uniform accessories and clothes. Everyone acting like they were united by anything. She was wearing a white trench and it made her want to take it off.

Suddenly feeling sick, she dropped the rest of her coffee in a trash can and caught up with Yun as everybody came to a halt at an intersection. Everyone looked so young; teens and twenties, early thirties at most.

'They don't have a website.' Yun gestured with his phone. 'The Genesis Org. I thought I'd check.' He frowned and touched her cheek. The tips of his fingers had softened since he'd stopped playing guitar. 'Are you okay?'

'Just light-headed.' She rubbed her eyes.

As she said it, the ground seemed to move away from them. It took her a few seconds to realize it wasn't them who were moving, but the rest of the crowd, kneeling in unison right there in the street. No noise, no chatter, no signal she could discern. Everyone moved as one, until she and Yun were the last two left standing.

Mass events were rarer now, almost unheard of outside

the US. But she still heard about them occasionally. She searched everyone's eyes, heart thumping and her hands going cold. Then she saw people glancing at each other, lips moving, and realized this wasn't another mass event, but something staged.

Yun's hand moved to her shoulder and he pulled them both to the road.

She crouched, not wanting to touch her knees to the cold tarmac.

Most of the people around them had their eyes closed. A couple next to Emory had their heads bowed. Their lips were moving, but silently. Praying, it hit her with a wave of nausea. This small crowd of people were kneeling and praying in the street, acting catatonic. It couldn't have filled her with more terror if they had started throwing petrol bombs. At least then, people would have had the good sense to run.

'We should go,' she said.

He wasn't listening. He was typing something into his phone without looking at the screen.

'*Please* can we go?' Emory hissed again, making Yun put his phone away. 'I don't like it!'

'It'll be pretty noticeable if we get up now.' But he still wasn't looking at her, and his voice was barely above a whisper. But for the sound of the overhead expressway, the white noise of cars, Emory had never heard a New York street so silent. 'Let's just see what happens.'

She refused to let herself sit or kneel, so she crouched until the balls of her feet burned and her ankles started to ache. She couldn't catch her breath. Someone was taking photos from the edges, and she turned her face away. She looked instead at Yun, who was sitting cross-legged, watching the mass prayer impassively. It was the most comfortable she'd seen him look in a long time.

'You've gotta admit,' he murmured, 'this shit's pretty powerful.'

Since returning from San Diego, Yun had been dragging a palpable cloud of anger around in his wake. It followed him from room to room. But whenever she asked about it, he said he was fine. She hated the word 'fine', the more she and Yun leaned upon it. *I'm fine. It's fine.* The skin around Yun's thumbnails getting redder, more swollen. *Fine.* All the while, that skin around his thumbnails getting rawer and rougher. He was good at hiding his feelings, but his fingers told the real story.

She thought getting his keyboard back would make him happier. He would sit in front of it, circle around it, but wouldn't play a note. He frowned at the keys like they were a book written in another language. Occasionally, he sat with his arm slung around his bass guitar, but it seemed more about the comfort of the stance than anything else.

Of course, she knew what it was about. It was about Andrew, or about his parents. But she couldn't ask him about either of those things, and it was like constantly having to walk past a locked room in her own house. All she really knew about his parents was that his mother was a teacher and his father worked in insurance. Also, that they were uniquely terrible; somehow both smothering and neglectful in a way only Yun was allowed to criticize. As far as she could tell, what Yun wanted from his parents was impossible. He wanted them to have made him happy.

His feelings towards Andrew were more opaque, more closely guarded than she was comfortable with. Initially, she had diagnosed the issue as anxiety; maybe Yun was a little jealous of his wealthy, popular friend, in the same way Emory was jealous of Lara and everything she had, everything she seemed oblivious to. But it wasn't that. If she mentioned Andrew, Yun had a way of looking at her with a kind of muted outrage, as if he couldn't believe she would dare utter his name.

'We're going,' she said at a normal volume, standing up.

As she rose above them, she thought the crowd were going to turn their faces towards her. But they didn't. To her relief, it was as if she hadn't spoken or moved at all. So she walked away, weaving around and stepping over people in her hurry to get back to the subway, and she heard Yun get up to follow her.

'Em, wait, I'm coming!' Walking down Huntington Street, past some uninterested police officers and a serene row of redbrick houses, he caught up and took her arm. 'Hey, are you okay?'

'I hated it. I'm sorry, I just hated it.' She gestured back towards the road. 'What do they think they're doing? Who are they helping by doing that?'

'I didn't think it was that weird.'

'You don't think it was kind of gross?'

'I thought it was, I don't know . . . nice?'

They carried on walking.

Yun took the lid off his coffee and gulped down the dregs. After disposing of the empty cup, he put his arm around her. 'Come on, we've been to some pretty intense marches and you usually just go all Louis Theroux. Why don't you write a piece about it?'

'I don't want to write another *piece*.' The word came out with more venom than she anticipated.

'Fair enough.'

A flash of disappointment that he hadn't understood something she couldn't fully explain, but felt deeply. It crept around the edges of her deep-seated fear that Yun didn't really know her, could never know her, or didn't want to.

'Derrick says they can meet us up at Bergen, if we hang around here.' Yun was looking at his phone again, and she saw him pocket the flyer.

Emory's therapist – a calming, Yale-educated former professor she had been seeing for the last two weeks – claimed she was trying to travel in the opposite direction to grief. Away from personal grief, but also the collective grief of the moment. She said it wasn't an uncommon reaction, but it wasn't sustainable either. Time will give you the illusion that you've put some distance between you and trauma, that you can stand up and walk away. But that time is elastic. The further you try to pull away, the harder it will snap you back.

Emory Schafer @emory_schafer

Tone notwithstanding bc some of my dms are legitimately terrifying, but I think it's fair for people in general to be questioning the utility of journalism right now. I know I am. I hear you, I promise.

Emory Schafer @emory_schafer

Replying to @emory_schafer

400k Americans dead and I can't say what I've actually done while they were dying. A folder of articles feels pathetic tbh. I feel like one of those people who stand on the beach waiting to film the tsunami.

24.

They met up with Derrick, then Yun and Emory, outside a bar on Bergen styled like an English pub. There was nowhere to sit so they walked to a place nearby that had long banquet-style tables and exposed pipes snaking across the ceiling. Something about the harsh lighting made Andrew anxious. Or maybe it wasn't the lighting.

'It is weird how we have more cases than other countries.' Emory gestured with her wine glass, referencing a recent story about an isolated mass event at a hotel in Milan. Eight people had drowned themselves in the pool while twenty-two watched, unmoving. 'The US and Western Europe make up almost the entire global death toll. But Finland only had five, plus one of the alleged recoveries.'

Andrew appreciated that Emory was fine and conspicuously making up for the fact Yun clearly wasn't. He sounded okay when they spoke on the phone to arrange this, if maybe a little short. Now the air around him looked corrosive. Even Derrick seemed on edge, sitting next to him.

'Doesn't Finland have, like, fifteen minutes of sun all winter?' Fin nudged Andrew with his knee under the table, which made him remember to lower his shoulders. 'Maybe their bodies are hardwired to wake up after going into hibernation. Like muscle memory.'

'Wouldn't *living* count as muscle memory for most people?'

Yun's eyes were fixed on his fingers as he scraped the label off his beer.

Fin shrugged. 'Not for everyone.'

'What about that guy going around who thinks he's Jesus?' Derrick wondered aloud, and everyone immediately knew who he was talking about. 'Most people who claim to have recovered just wanna start their own cult, right? No real doctors have confirmed anyone actually recovering.'

Eddie E. Cooper was a forty-nine-year-old actor based in LA who had been in one semi-famous so-bad-it's-good horror movie back in 1990, then a shitty sitcom cancelled during its third season. He famously auditioned for the part of Ross in *Friends* and didn't get it. He'd spent years doing shows in small late-night comedy clubs, and almost thirty years later had finally returned to the spotlight.

'From *obscurity* to *scurity*!' Fin had laughed when he read the story.

A couple of weeks ago, Eddie E. Cooper had apparently been catatonic for twenty-eight and a half hours before waking up, shortly after he was found by his housekeeper and a car had taken him to the hospital. Before he miraculously recovered, he had punched the woman in the throat and beaten her so viciously she almost lost an eye. While afflicted, of course. His housekeeper wasn't working for him any more, but she wasn't contradicting his story either. He was now going on a national speaking tour.

'He said it felt like falling into a pitch-black hole, and you just keep falling.' Emory recited the words like someone who had heard them far too many times. 'Scammers have really latched on to the *falling into a black hole* soundbite, because it sounds scary enough to get clicks but plausible enough for anyone to believe it.'

Yun shook his head, as if disagreeing with someone who wasn't present. 'I don't think it feels like falling.'

'Do you have a theory?' Andrew ventured the question, because Yun hadn't said anything directly to him yet.

He noticed Emory take a larger gulp of wine, as if anticipating that Yun's answer was also going to be something she had heard far too many times.

Yun met Andrew's eyes across the table and blinked like he hadn't expected to see him there. 'Well, they all sit down, don't they? They sit down and can't get up. Whatever this thing is, it weighs something. It's *heavy*. It must feel more like being crushed.'

The first week back after the holidays, a student from Andrew's Phenomenology and Existentialism course arrived during office hours to tell him about a poem by César Vallejo called 'Stumble Between Two Stars'. He wanted to talk about the line 'Beloved be the ones who sit down', which was quoted a few times in a movie about the end of the world made by the Swedish director Roy Andersson.

'Do you think it means anything?' he asked, wide-eyed, making Andrew feel like he always felt when confronted with eager students. That he didn't belong here, on this side of the desk, with them looking at him like he had any answers.

It made him feel even more like a fraud every time the predatory urgency of academia coerced him into immediate responses, so he asked Ahmad to come back in a couple of days and they could talk more fully about it then.

Beloved be the ones who sit down.

He read the poem several times, then watched the movie with Fin.

> *Beloved be the child who falls and still cries*
> *And the man who has fallen and no longer cries!*
> *Pity for so much! Pity for so little! Pity for them!*

'Do you think he might have known something like this was going to happen?' Ahmad asked when they talked again. 'Do you think that's why Vallejo wrote it? Maybe that's why Andersson made a movie like that?'

Andrew thought about the blindfolded child being led towards the cliff edge by society's elders, pushed over the edge on the off-chance it would give the old another few good years, bankers flogging themselves in the streets, endless traffic jams, people trying to escape entropy and finding nowhere to escape to, and said, 'I think the point is, Vallejo realized something was already happening.'

While at the bar waiting for their drinks, Fin remarked that Emory was extremely pretty in the way blonde women in seventies cults were pretty. Wholesome, but could and would absolutely kill someone if necessary. He also insisted this was in fact a huge compliment.

'He hates me, by the way,' Fin added as he took his mojito back to the table, not giving Andrew time to either contradict or reassure him.

Emory joined Andrew at the bar with some bills between

her fingers, and let out a long breath like she had been holding it for a while.

'It's not you,' she said, like everyone had made a prior agreement to only talk about Yun. 'He hasn't been sleeping well.'

'Can we add another Sauvignon?' Andrew asked the bartender, waving away Emory's money.

'He's never slept that well.' He intended it to sound supportive but realized it may not have been taken that way, when Emory stiffened a little and turned away towards the bar. 'I mean, when we lived together he would go to sleep around the time I was getting up, so I suppose he's improved since then.'

Emory managed a smile. 'I don't know when he found the time to actually study.'

'Well, he didn't have to.' Andrew was signing for the drinks and assumed he heard her wrong.

A small laugh as Emory took her wine, like she thought he was joking. 'Well, he must have done at some point, right?'

'No, I mean . . .' Somehow, the whole premise of the interaction had shifted. 'He didn't.'

She looked similarly wrong-footed, and hesitated with one hand still on the bar top. 'Wait, what do you mean?'

'Yun didn't go to college. I knew him at college, obviously, but we didn't meet there.' It was horrendously clear, from the look on her face, that Emory had no idea Yun never went to college. His lungs felt saturated, tight.

'But you lived together.' Something wasn't clicking. He could see the panicked recalibration going on behind her

239

eyes. 'He's never mentioned what he studied but you guys always talk about . . . *at college*.'

'Well, *I* was at college. Yun knew loads of people at NYU because he was a DJ, and he played in a load of different bands.' There was no way he could make this better. Andrew knew this even as he searched for any words which might make it better, cast light on the situation without making it more humiliating for either of them. In the end, he settled on, 'We met at a party.'

'You met at a *party*, of course . . .' She said it almost as if it was something she was remembering. 'Sorry, I just assumed. I mean, I forgot.'

His cheeks were hot, and he felt strangely like he had transgressed, inadvertently become a wedge and inserted himself somewhere he hadn't been invited in the first place.

Emory recovered herself before going back to the table. He took his and Fin's drinks over, motioned that he was stepping out for a moment, and thought he could feel both Fin and Emory watching him out of the corners of their eyes as he walked away.

Outside the bar the light was fading. Yun was smoking a regular cigarette, which should have served as another sign something was wrong. He rarely smoked anything but weed.

Andrew opened the door but didn't step out, and Yun didn't turn. Somehow, Andrew felt that he already knew whatever they said to each other here – and the way it was said – would come to define them in a way that haunted him.

'Are you all right?' Andrew asked.

'Yeah.'

'Is there something you want to say?'

'No.'

Andrew turned to head back in, but heard Yun inhale as if to say something.

'You know the reason he got punched in the face at the wedding is because he fucked around on his boyfriend with one of the waiters.' Yun spread his hands but couldn't keep the vitriol out of his tone. 'Maybe you don't remember. But me and Em saw it happen, so maybe you should think about whether he's the sort of guy you wanna hang out with.'

Someone across the street laughed a little too loud and Yun flinched.

'We're not *hanging out*,' Andrew said slowly.

'I just thought you should know.'

'I did know.' Andrew was forced to move closer to Yun when a group of people tried to leave the bar by squeezing past him. 'I'm not saying I knew the specifics. But either way, it's no excuse to assault someone.'

'I'm not saying it was justified,' Yun said, though his face said the opposite. 'I'm saying there's precedent. He's not someone you should trust, that's all.'

'Is there something wrong here?'

Yun laughed horribly, in a way he had never laughed at Andrew before, and flicked the cigarette away. 'This *really* isn't about me.'

'It doesn't seem like that. It seems like you're angry.'

'Why would I be angry?'

'You tell me.' Andrew tried to find a way to elicit something constructive. 'Are you angry I didn't tell you sooner?'

Yun snorted. 'You know what, I'm sorry I said anything. Honestly, do whatever you want.'

'So that's it?'

'Yeah.'

They had never had a proper fight; not that Andrew could remember. He had never found him intimidating the way other people did; snobbish occasionally, spiky, and often impossible to read. But none of that provided any context for this. All Andrew had to grapple with now was the wall of painful moving parts, the one he came up against every time he tried to think back.

Yun bringing him coffee in the morning, even though he didn't like mornings. A dull ache. Playing their guitars on the floor or the couch while high, when Andrew still had the time to play the bass he ended up giving to Yun. A sharper ache. Yun coming home drunk and passing out on the couch. Yun coming in sober and talking until he fell asleep at the foot of his bed, or right alongside him, left arm numb.

'If that's how you feel,' Andrew said, feeling that something buried deep in his muscles was being wrenched clean out of him, 'maybe we shouldn't talk for a while.'

'Fine.' Yun offered nothing but another shrug.

So Andrew went back inside the bar and sat down next to Fin, who did not ask him about it.

25.

'I don't think you can technically be late to a protest.' Fin raised his eyes from the cupboard under the sink, saw Andrew moving closer to the front door. 'Relax, I'll be five minutes.'

'You did say fifteen.'

Fin emptied the cupboard of bottles of bleach and kitchen cleaner, pulling out a tub full of rubber gloves and fossilized sponges, a spray can of furniture refresher they never used. 'It'll take longer the more you distract me.'

'Are you sure it wasn't just a spider?'

'I know what a spider looks like.'

'It was probably just an ant.'

'You live on the tenth floor, if there's a bug up here it's not *just* anything.' Fin reached for the flashlight on the counter and shone it into the vacated space, surrounded by a small fortress of cleaning products. 'Is anything actually happening?'

'It sounds like the police don't know where to start, there's so many people.'

'If the crowd's that big, they can't arrest everyone.' Fin shone the light from corner to corner and found nothing. 'God knows this country has tried.'

Andrew was scrolling through his phone, other hand in his pocket and trying his best to look casual. Like many people from church-going Christian families, Andrew lived like he was perpetually accountable to someone unseen who was keeping score, building up to one final perform- ance review at the end of his life.

'Why don't you go on ahead and I'll find you?' Fin pulled on the rubber gloves. 'I'm just going to give this a once-over.'

'Can't we do this when we get back?'

'The protest is still going to be there in fifteen minutes.' He stood up to run the tap, filling the tub with an inch or so of warm water and adding a dash of bleach. 'It'll last all afternoon and probably tomorrow, and the next day –'

'But do you *need* to do this now?'

The question was gentle. Fin still tensed, sat back on the floor and said nothing. He soaked a scouring sponge and began to scrub at the base of the empty cupboard.

'They're estimating there are more than ten thousand people.' Andrew put his phone away. 'I don't want us to get separated.'

'Are you taking the subway?'

'There's no point, it's growing so fast downtown we could get there in ten minutes if we walk.'

'Then I'll be literally five minutes behind you.'

'Okay, I'll message you in five minutes to check where you are.'

Andrew patted his pockets to make sure he had his keys, wallet and phone, and Fin let out the breath he had been holding as he left.

The acrid chill on the rim of his nostrils was reassuring; nothing could escape bleach. He ran the solution up the sides and top of the cupboard, then went over it again with warm water. He couldn't see any trace of where the insect had been, so before he put everything back inside, he ran bleach over the spray bottles and cleaning products until he was satisfied everything was disinfected, and nothing was where it wasn't supposed to be.

He stood up to tip the water and bleach solution into the sink, took off the rubber gloves and checked his phone.

Cleaning the cupboard had taken nine minutes, but what surprised him was that Andrew hadn't messaged yet. When Andrew said he would message in five minutes, he meant five minutes. He didn't do approximations.

Fin supposed the now five-minute vacuum was evidence of Andrew's irritation, and tried not to think more about it as he put on his coat, shoes and a scarf. But before he reached the front door, he felt a phantom itch on the back of his neck and along his right shoulder blade. He checked his phone – Andrew still hadn't messaged – and took off his shoes again. In the bathroom he took off his scarf, coat, jumper and shirt in front of the mirror, scratched the back of his neck and scalp, then got dressed again.

By the time he went to leave the apartment, the five-minute punishment was up to eleven minutes, and his wrist and the inside of his right thigh itched. It was possible, he thought, that whatever bug he'd seen on the floor could have ended up on his person while he was cleaning.

Diverting himself away from that mental image, he messaged Andrew, *Where are you?*, and started walking fast uptown.

When he looked at his phone again, it hadn't been read.

Fin scratched the back of his head, surreptitiously scratched his stomach under his shirt. Even as far down as Greenwich Village the streets were packed, and he knocked shoulders with someone he didn't acknowledge.

'Watch it!' a man snapped.

'Blow me!'

Another message: *Hey I'm cutting through the park, where are you?*

Looking up, Fin realized with a lurch of anxiety that getting on to Fifth Avenue was going to be a nightmare. So he took a left with the intention of looping back around. Scrolling through social media updates, he saw police had started blocking people from joining the sit-down on West 18th and West 39th.

Andrew still hadn't read his messages when Fin turned right on West 11th, and joined a fast-moving snake of people towards Fifth.

Fin sent another: *Basically on 5th.*

Sent another: *On 5th.*

Wrote another: *Can you look at your fucking phone?*

Deleted it.

It had occurred to him that Andrew was agitated about the protest because he knew some of his friends were going, including Yun. Yun, who Andrew insisted had no problem with Fin, but who wasn't speaking to him right now for reasons unexplained, and supposedly unrelated to the way Andrew had asked, 'We never really talked about the wedding, what happened there?' in bed a few days after they all went for drinks.

'It was basically over with Emilio but I knew he was never going to break up with me, so I helped things along.' It was a rehearsed line. Fin had envisioned having to explain himself at some point, so he allowed himself to concede, 'It wasn't a great idea, but we'd been in a bad place for a while. I just wanted it to be over.'

246

Andrew considered this, turning back to whatever he was reading on his iPad. 'Why did you think he wouldn't break up with you?'

Because he felt sorry for me.

But Fin couldn't say that. He would not draw attention to his own weakness, lower his own value. 'He wasn't that kind of guy, he didn't do conflict very well.'

Andrew didn't ask the next question, despite it seeming so obvious: *Is that the way you'd break up with me?* He didn't ask, so Fin didn't answer, even though he wanted to. He wanted to say, of course not. He would never choose to do things like that again, given the choice. He would never choose to do things like that with Andrew.

But Andrew didn't ask.

It was becoming impossible to navigate the throng of people and keep checking his phone, so Fin made his way along the outskirts. Even the sidewalks were packed, people taking photos and watching those at shin level, sitting in the street.

His breath caught and Fin stopped, trying to comprehend the scale of what must have been over a thousand people within his sight, sitting down. Some were wearing white and some weren't, in keeping with some hashtag or another. An indistinct roar filled the air, from chatter and the overhead news choppers, and the few motorists still complaining. But the sitters themselves appeared still, most of them silent and artfully staring. Marcus Sheridan sitting on the sidewalk near the deli, multiplied infinitely.

Everyone looked very young.

Fin reached out to hold on to someone but remembered Andrew wasn't next to him. He realized he was subconsciously rubbing the back of his neck, where Andrew sometimes liked to rest his hand when they were in public.

The messages were still unread.

Fin had never seriously considered losing Andrew, especially not to this. He seemed too overwhelmingly adult for that kind of thing. But unless he was teaching, Andrew never left his messages unread.

He wrote: *If this is about staying behind to clean the cupboard then it's a bit of an overreaction, don't you think?*

Deleted it.

His coat was zipped up too tight, his chest and head and hands tingling, pins and needles all over his body. He needed space. Wavering on his feet, Fin waded into the crowd, stepping around people who didn't look up at him. It was like walking into a river, and as soon as he saw a space on the ground both large and small enough to accommodate him, he sank to the road cross-legged, eyes fixed on his phone.

Read. They had been read. He waited for the ellipsis to appear, shoulders up, hands beginning to shake, but it never came. The messages had been read. Andrew wasn't afflicted, wasn't lost. He just wasn't replying.

How long had it been since he stayed at his own place in Flushing? Four months? More like five. He thought of Cassius hoarding dirty plates in his room and insisting he wasn't, until Fin had let himself in while he was at work and found them piled in his closet, a veritable tower of mould. When Fin first moved in they had a room-mate from LA who used to insist that eating a spoonful of Vaseline a day was good for the skin. Another room-mate brought a stray dog home that she'd found outside the subway, which infested the whole place with fleas. Fin was already well acquainted with how to kill unkillable things. So for a while, he had grown his nails a few millimetres so he could pluck the fleas from where he would look down and see them leaping up the side of the bed to his mattress. Sometimes they made it as far as his laptop, chasing after the light. It wasn't enough to squash them – fleas were immune to blunt force – you had to get them between two nails and decapitate them, guillotine-style. But Fin's lone defence didn't make a dent in their numbers, and they hadn't kicked the infestation until everyone agreed to douse the dog in solution and let off flea bombs while they sat in a bar around the corner waiting for the toxic smoke to clear.

He didn't want to go home. The prospect made his skin crawl, made him itch on the inside. *But this isn't your home*, he thought. The mantra he had forgotten. *Andrew isn't your home but he feels like he is. God, he feels like he is . . .*

I'm not going to move, Fin decided, scratching behind one of his ears. He wasn't going to get up. He was going to sit here until the cops dragged him up, spitting and kicking. Of course, he couldn't do it forever, couldn't quite bring himself to refuse life, if only on account of his ma. But the thought was comforting. It was decisive, almost safe. It made him feel held firmly by the back of the neck.

His phone vibrated and he looked down to see Andrew calling. He wished for a second – wished with all the bitterness he could taste on his tongue – that he was the type of person who could ignore a call from someone he loved.

He answered, 'Where are you?'

'I'm so sorry.' Something about Andrew's voice was blurred. 'I'm on 6th. Can you come and meet me on the corner of 28th and 6th? We need to take the subway uptown.'

'What do you mean? I told you where I am.' Fin turned his head, trying to find a landmark.

'No, it's not that. I got a call.' And for once it seemed as though the words weren't there waiting for him. 'I got a call,' Andrew said again. 'I got a call from Emory.'

Yun and Andrew

You simply go out and shut the door
without thinking. And when you look back
at what you've done
it's too late. If this sounds
like the story of a life, okay.

— Raymond Carver, 'Locking Yourself Out,
Then Trying to Get Back In'

26.

Boy meets girl at a wedding and the groom sits down in the street to die.

Yun shut his eyes. No grainy speakers, just road noise and Lara screaming. The harsh light of day on Riverside Drive. When he opened them again, reality remained in a kind of slow motion, then the street came back into sharp focus as Lara shouted at Emory, 'Get *off* me!' and proceeded to try to drag Mike up by the front of the grey hoodie he had worn running. Andrew and some blond guy – one of their neighbours – darted forward in unison to grab Mike's arms, which jerked upwards as if on strings and started swiping with rigid, clawed hands.

Emory tried to pull Lara away and the four of them lurched sideways like a rat king, while Yun stood rooted to the spot feeling like he was about to vomit, eyes fixed on Mike's snapping, contorted face, the sudden excess of teeth. A gargled snarling sound came from Mike's throat, not quite drowned out by Lara's screaming or the neighbour yelling, 'Woah woah woah!'

Lara clutched her cheek where Mike had caught her with one of his flailing arms, and aggressively shrugged Emory off, elbow snapping back into her nose.

Yun took an automatic step forward but Emory waved him away with bloody fingers. 'I'm okay! I'm fine!'

Andrew and the neighbour managed to pull Mike

away – simultaneously acting as dead weight and thrashing like an animal, all fists and nails – and let him drop the short way back to the ground.

'We should call an ambulance,' the neighbour suggested for the twelfth or the twentieth or maybe even the thirtieth time. Because they had been doing this disturbing dance for twenty minutes and the only visible changes were more cuts and bruises.

Someone ushering their gawping kids past, giving them a wide berth. Another woman pretended to be absorbed in her phone. Yun took a shaky step backwards and stumbled over the bag of groceries from Whole Foods that Mike had dropped.

'Are they still taking them at the ER by Columbia?' This came from Andrew.

The neighbour dialled 911, apparently having lost his patience. 'If we call an ambulance, they'll take him wherever there's a bed.'

'Are ambulances still taking them?' Andrew sounded quietly devastated by his lack of knowledge. 'I haven't had to call one for a while, I don't remember.'

Oblivious to the discussion, Lara sank to her knees and burst into tears, crawling a few feet to touch Mike's face, keep shaking him.

'We can get a cab if the wait is too long.' Emory fell into a crouch, her hand on Lara's arm and speaking slowly for her benefit. 'We'll all get a cab, okay?'

'Hey, do you want a Xanax?'

And Yun remembered Fin was also there, standing to his left. He was about to reply with something scathing but realized yeah, actually, he did want a Xanax.

'Do you need to sit down? You kinda look like you need to sit down.'

'No.' Yun took the pill and shoved both hands in his pockets, then turned and went to sit on the steps outside Riverside Church.

To his annoyance, Fin followed.

Emory looked over with alarm but Yun raised his hand weakly. 'It's okay,' he called, his voice thin. 'It's just normal sitting down.'

While the others kept trying – snapping their fingers, gently shaking him and slapping him and saying *Mike Mike Mike* like he was still in there – Yun shut his eyes again and took several deep breaths.

'Were you close?' Fin asked, already using past tense. 'Did you know him that well?'

'Not really.' Yun wished he could stop himself from blurting it out so fast. 'I knew him at college but Mike's one of those guys who was everywhere, friends with everyone.'

Yun wondered how many people would visit Mike in the hospital or at home. They would get their visits in early before he began to waste away, before his skin appeared stretched too tight over his skull and turned grey, fists clenched so hard his hands would bleed, before all the blood vessels around his eyes burst from trying to throw up the feeding tube.

'I only met him a couple of times, and not since the wedding.' Fin adopted what sounded like a well-practised tone of neutrality. 'I remember seeing you there.'

Yun didn't say anything, because it felt like a trap. He watched the neighbour jog to the roadside, either searching for the ambulance or about to flag down a cab. Emory's nose was still bleeding, and she wiped it on her white coat, leaving a smear of red across the right sleeve.

'What do you think got him?' Fin wondered out loud.

'Sometimes Whole Foods makes me want to kill myself.'

Fin nodded in a way that reminded Yun a little of his brother. 'I get it. Sometimes I watch people walking around in grocery stores with their families and kids they obviously hate and they just look dead inside. There's nothing more depressing than listening to other people talk about what they're gonna buy.'

Yun wanted to find a way to disagree on principle, but had to begrudgingly respect Andrew for hooking up with a twenty-year-old who was smart enough to sound this jaded.

He stared at the discarded Whole Foods bag, thought about Ms BB for the first time in a long while and sighed. 'I think it's because when you're at a grocery store, you're always thinking about having to feed yourself for another week. It's so fucking *boring* feeding yourself all the time.'

'It's boring doing most things you have to do every day.'

The neighbour managed to hail a cab. He and Andrew tried to find a way to lift Mike without provoking any violence. They had to carry him smoothly, like he was a tray of water glasses, or royalty. Mike's feet, his Adidas sneakers, dangled serenely in mid-air.

Yun stood up, feeling like he should offer to do something. The cab could only fit four so the neighbour offered to stay behind. Emory and Lara sat either side of Mike in the back. When Andrew went to sit up front he turned and seemed surprised to see Yun and his boyfriend outside the church.

He faltered, like the sight of them together was jarring.

Fin raised his hand to wave. 'We'll follow you.'

'We're going to Mount Sinai but if they don't have room we'll try Harlem,' Andrew was saying, to Fin. 'I'll message you, I promise. I'll let you know where we end up.'

Yun didn't say anything, because he didn't know what to say, because he and Andrew still hadn't uttered a single word to each other. He looked past Andrew for Emory, but she was turned towards Mike and Lara, and wasn't looking at him. He was vaguely aware of Lara crying; a grating, monotone sound like a power drill.

All the doors to the cab slammed shut and Yun wished he felt an urgent need to follow. Maybe it was the Xanax kicking in. Everything had become quieter and slower, and his limbs felt heavy.

'I'm gonna pick up some things from their apartment, bring them to the hospital.' The neighbour had a bruise coming up on his cheek, and gave them an awkward smile before walking away.

The sun was sharp. Even going into spring, the sun retained the bitterness of warehouse lighting.

'Do you want to get a cab?' Fin asked.

'Not really.'

It was probably the right thing to do. But Yun knew how it was going to play out. They would sit there, and sit there, and sit there by Mike's bedside, until the hospital decided whether they could spare the room or to send him home. And no good would come of it either way. But if Emory noticed his absence, he wasn't sure she would forgive him.

A nauseating, viscous contempt sat in the pit of his stomach, and Yun realized he hated Mike for doing this, for putting him in this position, for doing this *to* him.

'Yeah, I guess we should get a cab,' Yun said.

But despite his announcement, he didn't move. So Fin took that as his cue to walk to the kerb and look for a car. He glanced back a couple of times, as if to check that Yun was still there, and Yun took the opportunity to really look at him. The skinny yet muscular legs and his soft, effeminate side profile. Long lashes. So unlike anyone Yun had ever been interested in.

Fin seemed to sense the observation, and turned to look at Yun with a similarly evaluative expression. His hand was in the air as his eyes travelled from Yun down to his phone, and he made the stance look graceful.

For a visceral moment Yun wondered how he and Andrew fucked, but to think about it felt like a capitulation, like it was what Fin wanted him to think about. So he cut the image off before it could progress or disrupt anything, and went to join him by the side of the road.

After another cab ignored them, Fin lowered his arm. 'I don't really do hospitals, to be honest. Do you want to go get fucked up instead?'

Yun tried to recall if Mike had ever seemed unhappy, and came to the quick and deflating conclusion that, out of the three of them, Mike actually seemed like the happiest. He was happy in a laid-back, apolitical way Yun disdained. So why would Mike, of all people, go out for a run, pick up some groceries from Whole Foods and a shake from Shake Shack, and only make it halfway home?

'I got the impression he was one of those guys who knew a lot of people, but would probably lend his car to help anyone move house.' Fin was drinking a vodka-soda and had offered to buy the first round.

They were sat at the window table in a sports bar eight blocks down, and Yun was drinking a Campari and lemonade, which had turned into one of his regular orders since Ms BB introduced him to it. The alcohol mixed well with Xanax, in that after one drink he already felt pretty out of it.

'Mike was kinda like that,' he said, glad they were sitting next to each other facing out towards the street and not opposite each other. That way, he could stop talking at any time and people would think them strangers who had arrived separately. 'Andrew helped me move house.'

Fin took the statement as it was intended and nodded, accepting the assertion that Yun had known Andrew for longer. 'So why aren't you guys talking?'

Fair play. Yun would have taken the shot too, and even he had been surprised by the way Andrew managed to blank him today. Yun knew Andrew had a gift for shutting things out; his brain functioned like emergency doors designed to block a fire or flood. But he had never envisioned that talent being directed towards him.

He knew he should apologize, but didn't feel he should have to apologize first. And he sure as hell wasn't going to apologize through Fin.

'It's no big deal,' he said, and Fin gave this some thought.

If Fin contradicted him, it meant acknowledging Yun held some special status in Andrew's life, and he wasn't going to admit that. Yun watched him out of the corner of his eye, thinking *Yeah, fuck you*, and waiting for the inevitable agreement and change of subject.

'He really cares about you,' Fin said, inclining his head.

Yun swallowed. 'What?'

'Did you guys use to have a thing?' Fin sipped his vodka-soda, unblinking.

Yun wished more than anything that his first reaction hadn't been to laugh. It wasn't a proper laugh. Not provoked by this being in any way *funny*. It was nothing more than a tell, a moment of panic; the verbal expression of fight or flight.

'What makes you think that?' Yun exhaled, feeling hot, and checked his phone.

Emory hadn't messaged asking where he was, which felt pointedly worse than if she had.

'I reckon your type back then was probably guys who didn't realize they were gay, am I right?' A smirk. 'I only hazard a guess, because that's my type too. It's not generally linear, the sexuality thing. Not unless you're lucky, or *really* straight. And I guess what I mean is . . . Andrew's not exactly a linear person, is he?'

Yun didn't know what that was meant to fucking mean. 'If you mean I didn't expect him to fuck someone ten years younger than him with obvious daddy issues, I guess you're right.'

It was a shot in the dark, but Yun could tell that barb landed.

'He's just not as good at acting fine as he thinks he is.' Fin seemed used to bringing up certain subjects with the aim of making others uncomfortable. 'I find it hard to believe nothing happened.'

'You ever heard of *friends* as a concept?' Yun sneered. 'Friends fall out, they get over it, it's not that deep.'

'Sure, I understand if you don't want to talk about it,' Fin said with infuriating certainty.

He sat back in his seat to drink the rest of his vodka-soda, and Yun found himself stricken with a vicious, stinging envy, that his hair wasn't as thick and he had never been this self-assured, even at the same age. He wondered whether it was a generational difference, or being an athlete, which gave you a fundamental comfort in your own body civilians could never attain. Of course, Fin was the kind of person who could look at anything they wanted, *anyone*, and pursue it with everything he had. All at once Yun could see it, how he and Andrew had happened. It probably felt so effortless. All someone like Fin would have had to do was ask.

Fin pushed his empty glass away, raising one eyebrow. 'Your round.'

'So he hasn't messaged asking where you are?'

'They're in Harlem, Mount Sinai turned them away. I said we'd be along soon.'

Accepting defeat, Yun went to the bar and shouldered his way between some students to order.

Many ERs no longer accepted the catatonic because in theory hospitals existed for treatment, not for the dying or already dead. A drain on resources; that's what people were saying more openly now. They were a wilful, selfish drain on resources. They were calling the new cases 'copycats', as cases started to drop towards the end of February. Numbers no longer threatening to soar much higher than half a million, and even if they did end up hitting three-quarters of a million by this summer, it would be easy to round down. Not infectious, like a real disease, just childish imitation.

Nothing inside the human brain or the human body could be pinpointed as the cause. Nothing small enough to be seen under a microscope or opaque enough to be observed on a scan. It seemed more likely to Yun that the catatonia was something so vast it couldn't be perceived with the eyes. It could only be felt, like an ache soul-deep.

According to the socials, the crowd downtown weren't budging. For all the people dragged away by police, dozens more were arriving and sitting down in their place. Fox newscasters were calling for the National Guard to be brought in, and Yun tried to remember if he had asked Derrick about extra gas masks.

He opened a message to Emory, and closed it.

He opened a message to Andrew, and closed it.

Opened it again, closed it again.

He opened a message to Jarah. *Saw you're back in NY, let's catch up?*

When he returned to his seat, Fin was on his phone. 'No change,' he said. 'Mike, I mean.'

'Of course there fucking isn't.'

Yun was the only one who – upon seeing Mike sitting on the sidewalk – hadn't tried speaking to him, hadn't gone through the motions of trying to get him to focus, react, snap out of it. Any tests the doctors still ran were for data collection and nothing else.

Fin put his phone away. 'I'll get us some shots after this one, then we should go.'

'I never even liked Mike that much.' Yun might have said it in part to shock him, but it was also the truth. 'Honestly, this is the most interesting thing he's ever done. I'm amazed he had it in him.'

'Well, I won't tell anyone.' To his surprise, Fin smiled in a way that made Yun think for a second he might even be flirting. But then, it was possible Fin might flirt with everybody. Rather than a calculated decision, it was simply how he interacted with the world. 'Why didn't you like him? If nothing else, he seemed . . . likeable.'

'He was always so fucking cheerful.' Yun could no longer work out if he was having a good time or not, but it was refreshing to speak freely. 'Scratch the surface and there was just more surface. The thing about trying to be friends with everybody is it doesn't fucking mean anything.'

'At least people can surprise you, eh. There was a moment at his wedding where I thought . . .' Fin shrugged, something in his eyes went cold. 'I don't know what I thought. Anyway, he clearly wasn't all that cheerful.'

Fin was going to go home later, and Andrew would be there.

The thought reminded Yun to hate him.

But Fin's assessment of Mike made some sense. Everyone Yun knew who was deeply, terminally unhappy at least tended to be unhappy in understandable ways; overburdened by their own resilience, or beaten down by any glimpse of the future. Happiness was so grievously boring to witness, it almost defied aspiration. The only way it manifested now was in filtered, Instagram-friendly snapshots, with neat borders and carefully defined limits. Four a.m. alarms and green juices, meditation, jogging, yoga, gratitude lists and whatever soundtrack happened to be trending. All any musician had to do to make it big was soundtrack fifteen seconds of someone else's perfect life.

Is that it? Yun would think, scrolling through image after image of what everyone was meant to want. He wasn't grateful. He refused to be grateful, for any of this. *This can't be it. This can't be fucking it.*

27

Emory made another round of coffee in the Chemex for her, Lara and Mike's parents, while listening to a news podcast. The host, Jamie Clarke – a journalist who became famous for an investigative piece about men who had been caught assaulting catatonic women in hospitals and prisons – was talking about how one of the unexpected side-effects of the psychogenic death epidemic was the unemployment rate hitting its lowest point in decades.

The scent of strong coffee filled the kitchen and Emory found the frother in the sink, unwashed since the last time she'd used it. Already she felt more awake. The smell alone sent a message to her brain. It didn't matter that she hadn't slept more than three consecutive hours in a week. In a few precious minutes, it would feel as though she had.

She would never admit it, but she found it harder to be around Lara than it was to be around Mike, who she considered gone the moment she saw him sitting down. Even though Lara had long stopped crying, there was an electric, violent miasma following her from room to room that only Emory seemed able to withstand. Lara's grief was possessive, magnetic. It demanded she and Emory moved in tandem, offering her hand for Lara to dig her nails into, Emory acting as the other side of her brain, reminding her to eat and drink.

Jamie Clarke was saying, 'Assuming it burns itself out by the summer, following the pattern of other pandemics, we

could actually be looking at a situation where it has bene-
fited the economy.'

'Well, Jamie, if you look at the demographics most
affected,' the guest replied, some House representative whose
name Emory kept forgetting, 'we're looking at entry-level
jobs, the service industries and various young professionals in
their thirties and forties. These were the jobs decimated during the last recession, the most competitive openings. But of
course this is still an extremely precarious situation. We're
probably facing a short period of social unrest, as is usually
the case during these crises. But previous models point to that
levelling out within a few months.'

Emory put one more sugar in her mug than usual, and
made a mental note to go to the bodega and get more bread,
eggs, ramen . . .

Jamie Clarke said, 'So if cases stop escalating when they're
expected to – and we are already seeing a significant slow-
down in some regions – you're saying we could actually be
looking at an overall improvement to the deficit, in the
long term?'

'There are of course other factors at play. The money
saved in social security could be outweighed by the increased
cost to social care, kids left without parents, the elderly left
without family carers. But don't forget, we're also talking
about a generation of people who were already significantly
delaying having children, which has at least relieved the state
in that capacity.' The guest made a noise that sounded a little
like laughter. 'All things considered, if whatever this outbreak turns out to be follows previous patterns, we hope to
see minimal disruption to the economy, and maybe even a
slight improvement.'

A waitress in LA told Emory during a phone interview that you couldn't go anywhere in the city without smelling smoke from the overloaded crematoriums, though Emory also wasn't surprised there had been a lot of cases in LA.

'That really is quite incredible, Mark,' Jamie said breathlessly.

'Well, it *is* an incredible situation, Jamie. It is exceptionally rare to see a situation where an economic surplus decides to just remove itself.'

'I think I always knew on some level he was going to let me down like this.'

It was the first thing Lara had said in half an hour, having been silent on the walk from her apartment to the coffee shop, then all the way through Central Park to Bethesda Terrace, where they were sitting opposite the fountain. Occasionally Emory had stolen a glance at her and found Lara with her eyes closed, taking deep, measured breaths. Her therapist had been talking with her about ways to stay grounded.

'You know statistically,' Lara went on, taking a sip of cold coffee, 'women stand by their husbands when they get sick. If the woman gets sick, it's more likely their husbands will abandon them. I read somewhere that nurses treating women during a cancer diagnosis often have to prepare them for divorce too.'

Emory didn't say anything.

Lara made a noise of disgust. 'There's something so weak about men. If it was me instead, do you think Mike would've cut and run? Maybe all this *is* just another way to cut and run.'

'I'm not sure that's how it works.' Emory tried to remember if she had read any corresponding data about spousal abandonment during psychogenic death, but nothing sprang to mind. It was possible no one had studied it yet; the process often happened too fast.

'Didn't you say more men had been affected than women?'

'I think estimates are at like . . . sixty-eight per cent?'

'So seventy–thirty. It makes sense.' Her gaze followed the people walking past them, alighted on some joggers standing by the fountain, as if one of them were to blame. 'I gave Mike the talk about how we were going to co-parent, how it was *actually* going to be fifty–fifty. We were going to hire a nanny, and I wasn't going to run around after work looking after our kid while he chilled out and played video games. And after all that, he literally decides to die instead. I'm surprised he was able to arrange anything without me scheduling it for him. You know I used to make all his doctor appointments? I know his great-aunt's birthday because I reminded him to call her every year. He couldn't even remember the code to get in and out of the basement. He used to ask me every time he took the trash out, like, once a week.'

Lara put her coffee down to rest her head in her hands, massaging her forehead. She was shaking, as if letting the anger out only created space to fill with more.

'At least I know I can raise a kid alone,' she said, letting out a long sigh. 'I was pretty much already looking after one.'

Emory watched a woman with a dyed purple underlayer and wearing a huge peacoat, walking to the fountain holding a large piece of folded cardboard. Another preacher, she suspected. They were popping up everywhere these days, though they couldn't seem to agree on what stance to take regarding psychogenic death. Emory heard as many New Age types – usually environmentalists – proselytizing in favour of it as she heard evangelicals raging against.

'Don't you ever get tired of doing everything for him?'

It took a second for Emory to realize this wasn't a rhetorical question.

'I don't do everything for Yun,' she said, starting to chew her lips. She sipped her coffee again to distract herself from the nervous habit.

'Bull*shit*. When was the last time Dan Yun pulled his weight in your relationship? Where *is* he?'

'He works longer hours than I do, it's a harder job.'

'He doesn't have a harder job.'

'It is *objectively* a harder job.' Emory tried not to look at the woman's cardboard sign, because she knew reading it would only annoy her. 'It's easier for me to clean up after myself, I'm at home all the time.'

'No, I mean where is he *now*? Right now. Where has he been since this happened? He didn't even bother to turn up at the hospital and you haven't seen him since. *God*, I wish I had a cigarette.' Lara picked up her coffee again. 'Do you ever check his phone?'

'Of course I don't. Did you check Mike's?'

'I checked his phone and email at least once a week, I'm not stupid.'

'Did it help?' Emory snapped.

'What?'

'Well, it must have given you some *great* insight. Did he schedule this in his iCalendar?'

Lara looked away and Emory felt shitty for the outburst.

It would be a lie to say she hadn't contemplated, once or twice, how much easier it would be to live with her father and sister. But she told herself that life was hard for everyone right now, and she shouldn't give up on what little she had just because everything was hard. And it wouldn't always be this hard. It couldn't be.

'Sorry.' Emory grimaced. 'You're right. It's not like Yun is perfect.'

'No, I'm sorry. I just worry about you. You know the only one of Mike's guy friends who visits is Andrew? I've seen more of that fetus he's dating than I've seen of Dan Yun or the rest of them. My mom doesn't even sleep any more, she tracks down, like, eight home remedies a day. Mike's dad is useless, my dad is useless . . .'

'They just don't know what to do.'

'And *we* do? Or do we just get on with it? And they let us?' Lara noticed the woman with the cardboard sign and purple hair and sat forward. 'Great, who's this *bitch*?'

The words scrawled across the cardboard in red paint said THEY ARE THE LUCKY ONES.

The woman yelled, 'We shouldn't be afraid of them, we should celebrate them!'

'Here we go.' Lara rolled her eyes.

'These people aren't diseased or sick. They're more attuned! They know humans have long outstayed our welcome and have committed to doing what needs to be done to rebalance the planet!'

Barely anybody sitting around the edges of Bethesda Terrace reacted, though one group sitting on the fountain picked up their drinks and moved. Someone near Emory muttered, 'Why don't you join them, then?'

'Humans aren't becoming diseased! Humans are the disease! If so many are finally hearing the message from Mother Nature to move on, shouldn't we take notice of them?'

The coffee wasn't helping with the exhaustion any more. Emory suspected it was making things worse, writing a cheque in the mornings that her body had to cash every afternoon. After three p.m. she could barely think, barely walk, barely keep her eyes open. This went on until midnight, when she felt too awake again.

'It's time to face the truth, less people is what the planet needs!'

'Fewer,' Emory hissed under her breath. '*Fewer* people.'

'This isn't an illness, it's a calling!'

At first she thought Lara was crying. But when Emory looked at her properly she realized Lara was laughing, leaning against the wall with her hand over her face.

'Jesus Christ, these nutjobs . . .' Lara wiped her eyes, and the levity dropped from her face with shocking swiftness. 'You know, Mike's parents keep talking about taking him back to their place on Long Island. I might just let them. What do you think?'

Emory didn't realize she had stood up until she was already walking. She heard her coffee cup drop, was aware of Lara saying, 'Babe, where are you going?' But her decisions weren't conscious as she approached the woman chanting, 'This isn't an illness, it's a calling!'

The only coherent thought Emory remembered later was *Shut up! Shut up! Shut up!*

She grabbed the cardboard sign and wrenched it out of the woman's hands with such force that she stumbled and almost fell, bending it over her knee before throwing it away.

The woman gaped and exclaimed, 'You!', which only made her angrier. Emory didn't remember slapping her until Lara recounted the story. The next thing she was really aware of was being knee-deep in freezing water, the woman screaming and clawing at her like a cat as Emory dragged her over the stone edge and into the fountain.

'What the *fuck* are you doing? Are you *crazy*!'

Emory looked at the woman coolly before pushing her hard in the chest, sending her falling backwards into the water, wailing and thrashing. Then Emory turned and clambered out, shivering. The water climbed up her jeans, her trainers squeaking against the ground as she walked away. She noticed a couple of people were filming on their phones, could hear the woman screaming, 'What the fuck! You bitch!'

Lara grabbed her by the arm and dragged her away, saying, 'Oh my God, that's the best thing you've ever done! I swear, the *best* thing you've *ever* done!'

Her feet were numb, patches of wet hair clinging to the side of her face. Emory let herself be hurried away, fists clenched, the inside of her head ringing with the urge to go back and hold the object of her rage underwater until she drowned.

Nadia Keller @nadia_keller
Are we journalists really not going to talk about how Calvin Huntsberger's sister revealed the link between the first two incidents reported and Emory Schafer's irresponsibility and negligence in creating this story?

28.

'So, how many have you had so far?' Warren Calder returned from the counter with a flat white and black Americano to accompany their sandwiches.

'None,' Andrew replied, moving the plate to line up with the edge of the table.

Fin was running an errand over lunch, so Andrew accepted the Philosophy Department Head's invitation to lunch in a coffee shop around the corner from the Bobst Library. He suspected Warren liked him because Andrew's presence made the department feel diverse and progressive when, in reality, it was neither. In fact, the main reason Andrew hadn't mentioned he was gay to any of his colleagues was because he was certain that if it got back to Warren he would try even more aggressively to be his friend, considering it a form of activism.

The two most common types of question Warren asked were about the political situation in mainland China and Confucianism, neither of which Andrew had any great insight into but hadn't told Warren because he wouldn't know any better. In recent months he had mostly wanted to talk about psychogenic death and department policy, which at least made for a change.

'I've had three already this semester.' Warren shook his head. 'Not three all at once, but in total. I'm looking forward to Spring Break. All I do is write emails but it's getting to the point where, what do you say? There are only so many times you can say condolences before it starts to feel like you're at fault. Though maybe I am, maybe I've had three because my seminars aren't as interesting as yours!' He laughed.

'Do you just teach around them?' Andrew asked, trying not to sound judgemental.

'I know the policy is harsh but we can't keep wasting teaching hours every time this happens. It's not fair on the other students.'

Andrew resented the fact that Warren showed up to work with his hair greasy and unbrushed, wearing his jeans a size too small and his jacket a size too big. The kind of professor who cultivated an air of scruffiness because he knew a certain type of student would mistake it for genius. The same sentiment would never be directed at Andrew, who went to great lengths to present himself immaculately and would never dream of wearing casual shoes to work.

'I'm not sure it's fair to expect them to keep learning in that situation either.' Andrew kept his tone neutral. 'Is that not equally disruptive?'

'It's usually not apparent until the end of class anyway. I've only had to take a hard line with it twice. I told everyone in the incoming class if they wanted to leave they could, and I wouldn't penalize anyone for non-attendance as long as they caught up using someone else's notes. Almost everyone stayed.' He spread his hands. 'I don't know what else we can do. This isn't like the Bobst, where they can put barriers up. It's really out of our hands.'

Andrew took a bite of his sandwich to avoid answering. He did not think it was out of their hands, really did believe part of their job as teachers was to make students' lives easier, not harder. But he couldn't say that.

His silence must have said something, though, because Warren looked at him over the rim of his coffee. 'Your grading has been high.'

'I don't see the point in harsh grading while everyone is going through something unprecedented.'

'I don't remember anyone giving me higher grades because I was having a hard time. At some point, you have to suck it up. That reminds me, I was going to ask if you could help out rewording the departmental policy on essay extensions and finals. Letting people know that if they need mental health support they should email the support team and not their individual professors. We're snowed under with emails right now.'

A bland, soupy feeling had settled in Andrew's chest, which he attempted to wash away with more coffee. 'Sure.'

'And regarding the phrasing in our student communications, we need to make sure we're expressing sympathy but not anything that can be construed as liability, what with parents threatening lawsuits. We absolutely can*not* say sorry. No apologizing.'

Andrew glanced at his phone and said he had to leave early to teach a class.

With five minutes left on the clock at the end of his lecture on Guy Debord and the Situationist International, Andrew turned off the projector and took questions.

'If he was so against the idea of film and TV, why did he make films?'

'It wasn't film or TV per se Debord had a problem with, it was with the concept of mediation, how direct communication has been replaced by communication only as presented by media. We speak how people in sitcoms speak and act out concepts like love according to how we see it presented, rather than organically. It's about *watching* replacing *living*, how we are encouraged to be passive spectators rather than participants. To Debord, our relationship to media makes our ability to intervene in our own lives harder. Maybe someone who theorized or believed in that tendency would think they were in a better position to be a film-maker, though of course you may disagree.'

A young woman down front raised her hand. 'You said Debord killed himself, right? So what's that, a direct intervention or more spectacle?'

Andrew gave it some thought.

'Could it not be both? I don't think it's coincidental that Debord killed himself when on the verge of becoming a celebrity. But he also wrote in an epithet a few years before that –' Andrew checked on his laptop – '"All my life I have seen only troubled times, extreme divisions in society, and immense destruction." I don't want to avoid this topic when it's relevant, so anyone who wants to leave and not hear any further discussion of current events is free to do so.' He paused, as class was technically over anyway, but no one left. 'So, if we apply this theory more broadly, would you not also say our current epidemic of mass psychogenic death could be read as both a direct intervention *and* a spectacle, in the most literal sense of the word?'

'Would it not be more spectacle than intervention? Because it's, like, the most extreme form of passivity?' The way the student raised his eyebrows made Andrew think of Yun. He smiled, then remembered not to.

'You could read it like that. But it's also important to keep in mind that refusal is historically one of humanity's most powerful forms of intervention to provoke change. Strike action, for example, or sit-ins, mass peaceful protesting. Whether you agree with these methods or not, they are referred to as direct *action* because that's what they are, regardless of the fact the action itself is *refusal*. One of the key symptoms of the catatonia – though the one that receives the least analysis – is that the afflicted will fight back to maintain that state. Ergo, it is not a passive state.' He felt a little short of breath. 'So, I seem to have argued myself into a position that this is more intervention than spectacle. You could also think the same of Debord's suicide, or suicide as a whole, but we can talk about this more thoroughly another time if you want to focus a seminar on the subject. If anyone wants to disagree with me about this specifically or discuss it further, you can send me an email or drop by during office hours.'

Andrew packed away his laptop and reference books, slung his bag over his shoulder and waited until everyone had vacated their seats before leaving. He checked his phone during the short walk between lecture halls. Fin hadn't checked in, which was unusual but not unheard of.

A few students were loitering outside the lecture hall chatting. When he preceded them inside, Andrew noticed two students sitting near the back, and stopped.

His footsteps suddenly seemed loud on the hard, cheap carpet.

'Are you here for Ethics?' He raised his voice but knew there would be no answer.

They must have been here for a few hours.

Andrew searched inside his head for where he had filed away the rehearsal of how he would act in this situation. But then the door to his left opened and students began to file in, only to falter around the bottom of the stairs when they spotted the ones already there, eyes front and unmoving, like the lecture had already started.

He was supposed to be the adult here. Whether he felt able to or not, he had to take control of the situation.

'Wait outside, please, don't let anyone else in.'

One of the girls hesitated. 'Do you need help?'

'No thank you, Shauna. I'd rather none of you have to deal with this, so I'll come and get you when I've sorted something out for them.' He dropped his bag and went to make sure the door was closed behind them.

The students were both young men, both white, sitting in the same row with one empty seat separating them. Their notepads and books were still on their desks. One of them still had his bag between his feet, and the other had his backpack on the seat to his left.

Andrew sat in the row in front, so he could search their pockets and bags for student IDs, insurance information and emergency contacts.

Reese Earl Wylan and James West McKinney. Andrew sent messages to the numbers on their cards, adding that he was happy to wait with them until someone arrived. Then he called student support to add their names to the list of afflicted, before going online and adding their insurance status to a pick-up request.

A vehicle wouldn't be available for two and a half hours.

There were fewer of them now only one car company was providing the service.

Andrew went to the door and stepped out. 'There will be no class today,' he announced to the students gathered in the hall. 'I'll email everyone my slides and notes, and answer any questions next lecture or during my office hours.'

One of the boys rolled his eyes. 'Isn't it university policy to just teach around them? I don't mind, I'm paying for this class.'

'I don't care what the policy is. I'm going to wait with these students until someone arrives who can take care of them. That is my lecture in Ethics for the day.'

Andrew surveyed the rest of the students. No one else looked like they wanted to argue, but he suspected a few would send emails to Warren.

He returned to the lecture theatre and squeezed past a pair of knees to take a seat between the two boys, all three of them facing the lectern. He thought about Warren's obsession with liability. No one was allowed to say sorry, yet the only thing Andrew felt the urge to do was apologize, and keep apologizing. Not just to the students on either side of him, but to all of them.

Using 'sorry' as a form of condolence wasn't really a concept in Mandarin. 'Duì bùqǐ' was only applicable in situations where your actions had wronged someone else, so saying it in the face of death wouldn't make sense unless you had killed them yourself. What his family said was 'Jié'āi shùnbiàn', which loosely translated to 'Restrain your grief and accept the inevitability of change'. Sometimes it was just 'Jié'āi', and the rest was implied. Any literal translation into

English came across as too severe for Andrew to feel it comparable to the flippancy of 'sorry'.

Maybe 'duì bùqǐ' would be more appropriate. Maybe Andrew had wronged them, maybe the university had. Maybe everybody partaking in this spectacle was in the wrong?

A handful of first years came in, and Shauna said, 'We'll wait with you, if you want. We don't really mind about the class.'

They sat in the rows immediately in front and behind them, and Andrew knew from emails and office hours that at least four of them had lost a friend or a family member in the last six months. Everyone was tired, running grey in the cheeks. The young had lost some essential colour. He made a mental note to extend his office hours from five onwards, so anyone affected by what had happened could come and talk to him. He wished more tenured staff were making extra accommodations, but it seemed to be falling mostly to the contractors and adjuncts.

'I know we don't get much opportunity to talk to you directly about it,' Andrew said, trying to walk the difficult line between formal and approachable. He had never cared if his students found him cool, but he did care that they felt able to talk to him about difficult subjects. 'But how are you all doing? Are you okay?'

For a few seconds, no one said anything, not wanting to be the first to speak. Then one of the girls in front said, 'Oh, we're fine,' in a deceptively even tone, before she put her face in her hands and burst into tears.

29.

When he was fourteen, Fin spent a lot of time in the school library using the computers to search for information about his father; articles, gossip columns and Wikipedia entries about him, about the oil company, about his father's other family. He didn't want to do it at home in front of his mother, which would feel like betrayal.

But one evening over dinner, he had looked his ma in the eye and asked, 'Is he really my father?'

'Why would I lie to you about something like that?'

'Like Father Christmas,' he said, confident in his logic. 'Was it just easier to say he was some famous businessman and then it stuck?'

She appraised him for a while with admiration, as if she was glad he was smart enough to ask, to not take anything at face value, even from her. 'Well, you look like him, don't you?'

She waited, nudging him towards his own conclusions.

Fin knew he looked like him. His ma was fair, blue-eyed and petite. But while most of his features were cut-pasted from her – shapely lips, small teeth, thin nose – Fin's heavy brows, long lashes and dark eyes belonged to a different kind of face.

Eyes like pools of oil, his ma said more than once.

'Yeah, we do look alike,' he conceded.

She gave him a wry smile. 'If I was going to make

something up, don't you think I'd have picked someone like Enrique lglesias?'

No sitters on the subway today. Fin hadn't seen any for a while. Following the public service announcements, and the slight drop-off in numbers, etiquette dictated that no one reported them on trains any more. It was too disruptive to keep stopping the service, so people were advised to move them only if they were blocking a doorway, and the driver on the final service of the night would do a walk-through and report them all in one go. Fin suspected homeless people had been taking advantage of this policy to sit and sleep on the subway without being harassed, if they managed to keep very still. Good for them.

He forced himself to reread the email informing him he wouldn't be receiving a callback for the Boston Ballet. He moved it from his inbox and into the separate folder of rejections, from Cleveland, Austin and the Joffrey in Chicago.

The rejections didn't surprise Fin; very few of his fellow graduates would make it the first time around, or second, or ever. What surprised him was how little he cared. He used to identify so strongly with Apollo, the great coming-of-age role, constantly striving and evolving towards an inevitable destiny. Now it was within his grasp, only for Fin to realize he didn't give a shit about ascension when faced with yet another mountain.

Another email, from yesterday, from a choreographer he'd met through a dating app the year before. They hadn't hooked up, just exchanged messages and hung out a few times when Fin was in the early stages of seeing Emilio. He had moved back to LA and was now saying that a friend – the stage manager on the most recent run of *Chicago* – was looking for a new assistant.

He asked for the fussiest, meanest gay I knew. If you'd ever consider moving out here, I think you'd be perfect.

Fin was immune to flattery but easily succumbed to accurate descriptions of himself.

He put his phone away and resolved not to think any more about the emails or rejections. Not today anyway. He was coming up to Rockefeller Center, and he got up and walked down the carriage. He took his earbuds out and put them away as he exited the station. He thought, *This is the last time I'm going to do this*. But he thought that every time he walked up to this huge building, this gold entrance, hoping whoever was behind the front desk wouldn't remember him when he stood up as straight as he could, took a breath and said, 'I'm here to see Richard Sullivan. Eighteenth floor.'

The man – the same man as last time, though he didn't appear to recognize him – looked at Fin over his glasses, disinterest and suspicion jostling for place. 'Do you have an appointment?'

'My name's Fin Keohane, he'll know who I am.' He was breathing, but it felt like the oxygen wasn't reaching his lungs.

'Can I see some ID?'

Starting to sweat, Fin took his passport out of his pocket and handed it over.

The man behind the desk looked at it for what seemed like a needlessly long time, muttering Fin's name under his breath, before giving it back and pressing a button on his phone. In all the times he had been here, Fin had never made it as far as calling up.

'Finlay Keohane,' the man said into the phone, not looking at Fin. His suit was immaculate behind the bulletproof screen. 'For Richard Sullivan. No appointment.'

He hadn't told Andrew where he was, never wanted anyone to know his whereabouts during these visits.

The man's eyes flicked to him once, twice, as he put the phone down. He folded his hands in front of him, not unkindly, but with finality. 'You'll need to come back with an appointment.'

Fin was prepared for that at least. 'Could you please call again,' he asked in a tone honed from working weekends in retail when he was fourteen and fifteen. 'I'm his son.'

The man looked at him for a beat, decided he wasn't a threat, and picked up the phone. 'Finlay Keohane for Richard Sullivan. His son.'

This time, the man didn't look at him while he listened to whatever was said on the other end of the line. He put the phone down, folded his hands again and said, 'Richard Sullivan isn't available. You'll need to come back with an appointment.'

'He isn't here?'

'He isn't available.'

'Can I make an appointment here?'

'You'll need to contact Mr Sullivan's assistant to do that.'

'But you said, I'm his son?'

'I did say that, yes.'

'What did he say?'

'I didn't speak with Mr Sullivan. Can I help you with anything else?'

Without meaning to, Fin glanced over the man's head, his eyes landing on the nearest camera on the wall. The man followed the glance and lowered both hands to his lap, out of sight.

It would be easy to leave. There was no one standing behind him, no added humiliation. None of the people walking past his right shoulder towards the elevators looked his way. It was only him and the man behind the screen.

Another look around the foyer. 'I'll wait.'

'Sir.' It wasn't a term of respect, it was a warning. 'You can't wait here. This isn't a waiting area.'

'I can stand.' Fin crossed his arms. 'I don't mind.'

'You need to come back when you have an appointment.'

'I need to see him today, so I'm happy to wait.'

'Sir, if you do not work here and you do not have an appointment with anyone in the building, I'm going to have to ask you to leave.'

Fin could see two security guards approaching out of the corner of his eye. Both were white, carrying guns. Either they had been observing him already, or the man behind the screen had a way of calling them over, some button concealed under the desk.

The shorter of the two said, 'Time to go, buddy,' and attempted to take Fin by the arm.

When Fin shrugged him off and stepped away, they seemed surprised. Everyone misjudged how strong he was at first, due to his size and stature. He was small, but had enough strength hidden in his legs to kick clean through a human spine.

'Come on, no need to make this harder than it needs to be.'

The two of them adopted wide stances, blocking his path to the elevators.

'I agree.' Fin sprang back another step as the shorter one

moved to grab his arm again, evading his grasp with ease. He already knew things had escalated to the point where he would never be allowed back inside the building, and he looked the guards up and down with unrestrained scorn. 'Harassing me won't make you taller.'

It was by far the stupidest thing he had ever said to someone with a gun.

He ran, three pairs of feet pounding towards the entrance. Fin hit the doors, burst on to the street and took off south.

In the choreographed version of life in his mind, Fin sometimes entertained a fantasy of taking the elevator up to the roof of his father's building and throwing himself off it. He had always preferred Giselle's original death – stabbing herself with Albrecht's own sword – and not the later iterations, in which her death was reduced to a weak heart. One instance of uncharacteristic Russian squeamishness around death – suicide, and their refusal to portray it onstage – resulted in a moment of violent agency and defiance transformed into her body's surrender to feminine frailty.

But Fin never thought seriously about killing himself, only a stage death.

He arrived ten minutes late for his third class of the day, and wouldn't be hearing about his audition for the *Giselle* showcase for at least another hour. The outside of his right foot smarted, Fin noticed during a break two hours in, as he sat towards the back of the studio and listened to the familiar *thwack*, *thwack*, *thwack* of ballerinas beating pointe shoes against the floor.

One of the senior teachers stepped in, glancing at him once before casting her eyes over the iPad in her hands. 'Finlay Keohane.'

Emotionally he felt nothing, but he became aware of the sweat turning cold between his shoulder blades, a juddering sensation in his stomach as he scrambled up to catch the door before it swung fully shut.

He found himself walking down a corridor ten minutes later, holding a printout and wondering whether any of this mattered, knowing he should feel happy and aggravated that he didn't. Eric Whelan caught his shoulder on his way out and said, 'Hey, I really like your Albrecht,' which must have been hard for him. If it weren't for the recently broken toe, both of them knew the role would have likely gone to him and not to Fin, who had been told he was 'not a leading man', but it seemed the Director – for inexplicable reasons – disagreed.

Fin remembered too late he may have owed Eric a smile of gratitude or acknowledgement, but when he looked up from the printout he was gone. The outside of his right foot hurt and it must have been from the abrupt turn he took outside the building on Rockefeller, skidding and twisting, his bridge absorbing too much impact. It needed ice.

He messaged his ma, because her happiness was easier to relate to than his own. Then he messaged Andrew and headed home. And Fin *was* home, he kept remembering with breathless relief. He had finally, after weeks of negotiation, stopped paying rent for the room he hadn't seen since last year, and Andrew seemed more relaxed now he no longer had what must have looked like one foot jammed in the door.

'And this was the role you wanted?' Andrew checked, chopping Japanese aubergines and justifiably confused by the lack of presence behind Fin's eyes.

'Yes. I mean . . . yeah, it is!' Fin forced himself back into the room, leaning on the kitchen island and looking up from his right foot, which he was rolling against the floor with a satisfying ache. 'I am happy about it. I'm just shocked, I guess.'

'I know you've explained the plot before –' a smile, because classical ballet was outside his field of expertise, and he enjoyed reverting to the role of student – 'I might have forgotten some of it . . . But why did you want this one? Why Albrecht?'

It was so rare that Fin got to talk about ballet with someone he wasn't directly or indirectly in competition with. No effort, just letting his words go into free fall. Again, he told Andrew about Albrecht, the lord disguised as a peasant who catches Giselle's eye and allows her to dance. Her devastation upon discovering his true identity, the existence of a whole other family, his engagement to another. How she dances and dances until she dies, only to be embraced by the Wilis, the enduring souls of other women destroyed by betrayal, neglect and heartbreak. He describes how Albrecht weeps over Giselle's grave, and she is offered the chance to kill him the way he killed her. How, for whatever reason – whether viewed as weakness or stupidity or maybe a relentless strength – Giselle refuses, choosing instead to fight the puppeteering steps of the Wilis, dancing one last time with Albrecht and shielding him from the ghost women until sunrise, when she finally leaves him, broken and exhausted but alive, by her grave, now adorned with a red flower. 'Did Albrecht deserve mercy? Maybe not. You can definitely argue that no, he didn't. But I think that makes her benevolence even more powerful.'

Andrew dropped the aubergines into the steamer, and said, 'You don't think he's evil.'

It was neither a statement nor a question. Fin blinked and noticed his eyes were watering. 'No, I don't think so. Plenty of dancers interpret him like that, ham up the rich guy routine, play him as a villain with no humanity or remorse. But that seems too easy. Calling him evil lets everyone off the hook somehow, turns the whole story into nothing more than a cautionary tale. I've never thought of Albrecht like that.'

Something expanded in his chest, and he tried to breathe around it as Andrew asked, 'So why do you think he let her fall in love with him? Was he not leading her on?'

'He was just a kid.' Fin looked at the floor again, leaning on his instep until the pain reverberated up his ankle. 'So many people forget how young Albrecht is, characterize him as an adult. But when you're young and naive, and love feels so new, you don't think about consequences, can't fathom that people die, or that some things you do can't be undone, or that one day everyone you love won't be there any more. He doesn't disguise himself to seduce anyone, he hides his identity to enjoy a moment of freedom. And he's terrified when Giselle dies because of him, for the sake of a romantic daydream he had about being someone else. Because he did love her, and if he didn't he wouldn't have gone to her grave. Why would he have gone back if he didn't really love her? He goes back because he can't live with himself. They're both just kids, who end up dealing with these huge, permanent issues of life and death too young, and neither of them is ready for it or equipped to deal with it. Maybe when Giselle chooses to let him live, he wishes she *had* killed him instead. That he has to carry on isn't a reward, having to live *isn't* mercy . . .'

Fin tried to catch his breath, realized he was crying, and quickly bowed his head and covered his eyes, because very few people were attractive criers and he didn't think he was one of them. Letting all these words spill out had tipped him forward and now he was sobbing with such intensity it felt like he was about to retch something up.

And Andrew put his arms around him and leaned Fin's forehead upon his shoulder, and Fin tried to apologize but couldn't. But it didn't matter, he realized. It didn't matter, because Andrew just held him and let him cry, and didn't ask him to explain anything.

You've seemed really depressed recently ♥ Do you think
seeing a therapist would help?

Anonymous

Phrygia1188

3 days ago

My parents suggested it but tbh I don't think these
problems are things I can CBT my way out of. They're not
irrational, they're actually happening. What could a
therapist say about any of it when they're just another
person?

 0

30.

Cycling was unbearable in warmer weather. Yun resented how the monotony and physical burden of his temp job – now his sole job for almost a year – made him dread the onset of April. His muscles ached so frequently the pain faded to background. The dehydration headaches were more intense, grating at the front of his skull, but he took painkillers for those.

Cases had dramatically tailed off around the three-quarters of a million mark, as most world leaders, political commentators and scientists had predicted. Not a bang, but a slump, and Yun couldn't work out why he felt no relief. As he remarked to Emory, people had even given up on giving up. There was something almost sad about it.

Just under a year since Hunter Mountain, mass catatonic events were almost unheard of now, and it was rare to see more than one or two sitters at a time. The last incident Yun had seen was two weeks ago, when the cops blocked off the street to unceremoniously drag them out of the road. He was redirected along with the rest of the traffic, making him fifteen minutes late on his delivery and the assholes didn't tip.

The headache crept back to the fore as he let himself into the building carrying his bike at around midnight. He stopped for a few minutes at the foot of the stairs, bike leaning on his hip outside Ms BB's front door, listening to the young couple who had lived there the last six months watching TV.

His bones felt heavy yet his skin stretched so thin. A strong gust of wind and he felt like he could be lifted clean off the ground and flown through the air, were it not for the shapeless mass of emotions weighing him down.

'Why the fuck does everything feel so heavy?' he complained to Emory, months ago.

'Everything *is* heavy,' she replied.

He had no energy to climb the stairs, but he had been standing in the hallway for so long that he began to wonder what he was doing there. That was all he asked himself now. Every minute of the day he would catch sight of himself, as if through the eyes of someone else, and ask himself how he was always somewhere other than where he felt he was meant to be.

Getting out his phone, he checked Jarah's Instagram, LinkedIn and work Twitter where he didn't have to be careful about hiding his screen. Nothing new. The most recent photo was three days old; an ironic reposting of a black-and-white vintage billboard depicting a pudgy white family packed into a car, caption declaring WORLD'S HIGHEST STANDARD OF LIVING: THERE'S NO WAY LIKE THE AMERICAN WAY! Followed by another photo of the NYPD ramming protesters in Manhattan four blocks up from where he and Emory had been in February, right before she received the call about Mike.

The last photo of Jarah's face was posted shortly before he messaged her that day and received no reply. A selfie in the elevator at her new workplace. The mild thrill of checking her social media was starting to wear off in the absence of interaction. He had stopped looking for her in the streets, stopped taking routes past the bars they used to drink at and places where she liked to eat. It was almost impossible to run by chance into someone you knew in New York, and if you did it was always someone you disliked.

Eight days ago was the post about her brother, Leo, who had died back in Hawaii. When Yun saw it he almost called her, but he didn't in the end, because it wouldn't really be about Leo.

What am I doing?

Picking up his bike, he went upstairs.

The bedroom light was out and Emory probably asleep, so he went straight to the bathroom and showered sitting in the tub with the shower head in his hand. He hesitated before joining her, but only because he knew he should spend a few hours at the piano before going to sleep. He had started a song two weeks ago, but could only summon the strength to work in short bursts. One frantic day and night of songwriting followed by weeks of fatigue, unable to even open the studio door. He couldn't face it tonight. Like every other night, he was too tired, too guilty for the hours spent doing so much else, but not the right things.

No matter what time it was, he should spend some hours at the piano. He could hear what he should be playing, but it felt so much better to be asleep. Sleep was the only time he was able to put anything down, drop the weight he was carrying. He was living for being unconscious in a way he never had before.

'Are you sure you're not depressed?' Emory used to ask a lot.

He said no every time, and part of him really believed it too. 'I'm just tired,' he said.

All the time.

Yun rolled a cigarette and went back downstairs to sit on the stoop. His lighter was almost out of fluid, and the skin on his thumb was inflamed by the time he got it lit. He thought about calling Andrew out of habit, and also because it would annoy Fin to see a call coming in this late.

He video-called Jarah instead, on the off-chance she was still up.

She didn't pick up, but a few minutes later a message came in: *I hate it when you do that, stop it!*

Yun called again, and this time she answered, camera turned to the ceiling. 'What do you want?'

'I just wanted to see how you are, is that a crime? I'm really fucking sorry about Leo.'

'You don't seem to be getting the message but I *don't* want to talk to you!'

'What happened? It wasn't a sit-down, was it?'

'He was *canoeing*! Now what else do you need to talk about?'

This part, Yun hadn't given much actual thought. All he knew was that over the last few months, he had been willing something in his life to have taken a different turn, been different in some fundamental way. And it could be different, he was sure of it. He just needed to work out where he made the wrong turn.

'It isn't about one specific thing,' he said, stubbing the cigarette out only part smoked. He didn't like smoking, but he couldn't afford weed right now and needed something to do with his hands.

'Are you kidding me?'

She never took kindly to people who talked in generalities and he should have remembered that.

The screen lurched as she picked the phone up to take it somewhere else, but he was pleased to note that when she sat down again he could see her face. Her hair was shorter now and it suited her. Suddenly he didn't need the cigarette any more. He had read somewhere that, after a break-up, seeing an ex's face again, even in a photograph, induced the same chemical reaction in the brain as cocaine. More than once he considered walking into Jarah's new firm and falling to his knees, but so many people sank to the floor nowadays he suspected the gesture had lost its impact.

'I like your hair like that,' he said.

'I *don't* care.' She looked at her nails. 'Thanks. Now tell me why you're calling in one sentence max, or I'm hanging up.'

'*Fuck*, I don't know, okay! But I'm really starting to feel like we made some kinda mistake –'

'Unbelievable.' She shook her head. 'I knew it. I knew you weren't calling to ask about Leo. You're so manipulative!'

'Come on, that's harsh. Is it so insane that I just wanna talk through the idea?'

'Yes! It's been a year! We talked about it at the time!'

'Are you seeing someone else now or something?'

'Aren't *you*?' Her expression was dangerously close to pity. 'Because last I heard you were living with someone. You know what, I feel really bad for her because I don't even have to imagine how she's feeling. And I bet she doesn't know you're calling right now.'

'Oh, so I'm a piece of shit for just wondering? Like no one ever wonders how things could've turned out different?'

'You haven't learned anything! First of all, you're not *just* wondering, you're calling me looking for something. Second of all, it's *always* someone else's fault. It's always someone else's job to make you happy. You blame your parents, who are some of the nicest people I've ever met! Or you blame *this* exec or *that* producer, or me, or your *current* girlfriend! You think other people are just staff, don't you? And you're always *so* unhappy because *someone* isn't doing their job. But it's never you. *This* is why we can't be friends, Yun. Because if we were, then sooner or later I'd just get a shitty performance review for that too!'

'Wow.' Yun screwed his eyes shut for a moment. 'Well, you know what, I don't remember anything ever being your fault either.'

'Is that a joke?' She leaned closer to the phone. 'The only reason I picked up when you called is because I feel like if I don't, you'll end up sitting in some hospital starving yourself to death and it'll be on me. Do you think I don't already feel like that about Leo? Like I didn't do something right, like I could have done something different that day?'

The call had gotten away from him somehow. She sounded like she was about to cry and he felt like he was about to cry. He had cried in front of her enough.

'It's not your fault,' he managed to say. 'It's no one's fault.'

'Honestly, I have no idea how you, of all people, have made it this far. You make everyone around you feel like they aren't good enough and you don't enjoy anything, I thought you'd be one of the first to sit down.' She stood up, and the camera swung away from her face towards the dark ceiling. 'Don't call me again.'

He panicked, knowing they were never going to speak again. 'Okay, fine, I love you then.'

'Fine, I love you too. Please don't call me again.'

'I'm sorry, all right?'

'*Please* don't call me again.'

Yun went inside and got into bed next to Emory. She kissed him as he was falling to sleep, and he barely felt it.

Emory was writing at the kitchen table with her glasses and headphones on, when Yun got up in the early afternoon. He carried his bike downstairs, clipped on his helmet and put on 'Feather' by Nujabes. It was cool when he set off, cycling to piano and low-fi hip-hop. Maybe his favourite musical combination; something he could feel above his head and below his feet, as if he was expanding into a space outside of his body.

Traffic was a little backed up on Metropolitan but clearer towards the intersection.

Someone was running up the sidewalk and he turned to watch them go, before remembering to keep his eyes on the road.

A crowd was forming near Lorimer Street subway. He didn't want to pull one of his earbuds out, so he fixated on the cops trying to disperse them as he approached. Everyone was gathered around the subway entrance looking at something on the ground, the cops gesticulating over their heads.

Yun didn't want to look too hard, but he did look, unlike the guy running up the sidewalk with arms flailing. He craned his neck, because he had to see, had to see what was on the ground. Then the people were all gone. Suddenly, he lost them.

Everything went quiet but for a rushing in his ears, and he had no understanding of what had happened, or where he was, until his stomach dropped and he realized he was suspended in the air, the sky and cars and the avenue blurring as he plummeted to the street, his vision bleeding white.

He didn't lose consciousness but the impact – as the road rose to meet him – knocked him out of himself. All he could see was sky and he couldn't move. He thought he must have broken every bone in his body, but couldn't feel a thing.

How long had it been since he called his parents? Or Kevin? He didn't call Andrew. He should have called Andrew. Did he tell Emory he loved her before leaving? Of course he hadn't . . .

People above him threw their hands around, faces wide. He tasted blood but still couldn't feel any pain. He couldn't feel anything. He thought about Kevin and how he should not tell him about this, about how dying really did feel like nothing.

Then he was gone.

31.

They didn't talk much in the car on the way back from the hospital, both looking at their respective phones and Yun on the verge of falling asleep after his second dose of prescription painkillers. His right arm was going to be in a cast for three months, and he made a big show of saying he could ride a bike one-handed, if it came to that. But he didn't have a bike any more and now couldn't afford another.

At one point, Yun turned to Emory in the car and announced, 'It wasn't even a sitter, what happened by Lorimer. It was just someone having a heart attack, but everyone panicked.'

She wasn't sure what to make of this information, and nodded.

When they got home, Yun disappeared into the bedroom to call his mother, while Emory went and sobbed silently in the bathroom for five minutes, before coming out and calling the hospital's billing department to see what they could get written off. But it turned out Yun had to make the call himself, so she sat at the kitchen table waiting for him to get off the phone.

The second doctor she spoke to at the hospital had said, 'By the looks of it, he landed like a martial artist, just slapped the road with his whole arm,' and when he left the room Yun drank some orange juice through a straw and snorted from where he was propped up in bed, 'Do you think he only said that because I'm Asian?'

Before that there had been the crying in the car, on the way to the hospital. The crying on the steps, waiting for it to arrive. Emory couldn't remember the last time she had cried like that, especially in public. She didn't cry at anything, really. Not any more. Yun was the crier in their relationship. But when Andrew called her she felt shaken, as if gripped by a huge, merciless hand and slammed to the ground. She cried so hard it physically hurt.

She was working when Andrew called, explaining in a distant and unfamiliar tone, 'Hi, Emory. I got a call from someone saying Yun has been in a road accident. He's alive, but they said he's in surgery. I just . . . I'm at work. I don't know why they called me.'

He sounded apologetic. Whenever Emory envisioned something going wrong in her head, she had never assumed Andrew would be the one calling her.

Without thinking, Emory had said, 'He's allergic to penicillin,' and Andrew replied, 'I know.'

- *Emergency Room Visit Fee: $1,500*
- *Surgeon Fee: $1,854.87*
- *Surgical Treatment of Humerus Fracture: $17,911.00*
- *Non-surgical Treatment of Wrist Fracture: $2,565.00*
- *Ambulance Fee: $1,222.79*
- *X-Rays: $428.99*
- *Application of Upper Arm Cast: $242.00*

That wasn't even all of it. But it was all Emory could stand before looking away. If Yun had been travelling half a second faster he would be dead, she reminded herself, as she read through the list of numbers Yun was still refusing to look at.

The arm was broken, and his collarbone. He had bitten

301

through his bottom lip and one of his ankles was swollen, though somehow not fractured. A thin bandage around his head held some gauze in place, but the head wound wasn't severe because his arm and shoulder had absorbed most of the impact.

'Fuck, my laptop . . .' Yun muttered under his breath as Emory sat in the chair next to his bed trying to add everything up.

If the car had hit him, rather than him hitting the car, he would be dead.

'It's just a laptop, we can get another one.' The words sounded like they were coming from someone else. She felt no connection to them. 'Don't worry, we'll get through it.'

' "We'll get through it" is what people say about cancer. I'm not totally uninsured, I think the company can cover stuff up to ten thousand. Is it more than that?'

'. . . Yeah.'

She didn't know how else to put it. She didn't know how to say that only having medical expenses covered up to ten thousand was pretty much the same as being uninsured. She wished she could force optimism into her tone, but she couldn't find any.

Yun had met her eyes and asked with a weak smile, 'Can I even afford the car home?'

It wasn't until he emerged from the bedroom that Emory really noticed the extent of the bruising. His right knee and thigh were almost black, mottled with an angry purple and burgundy, as was his left wrist. One of his knees was bloodied and raw while the other was covered with bandage and gauze, like his head. Dried blood in his hair, on his left cheekbone, smeared diagonally across his chin.

He smiled and she almost collapsed. A fist took ahold of her heart from the inside and tried to drag her to the floor. Love was so heavy. The weight of one human life was so heavy. And she was so angry with him she could barely breathe.

'This is wild,' Yun said, indicating his phone. 'Kevin said someone filmed it. They thought there was gonna be a mass event with everyone crowding around, so they caught it on their phone and it's literally on YouTube.'

He started laughing as she went to look at the screen, making it shake. A police officer was yelling into a small gathering of people, 'Move back! Ma'am, I am once again asking you to get back!' Into a radio: 'We need an ambulance to Metropolitan / Lorimer subway.' Someone screamed and everyone turned – including the phone – in time to see Yun smash into the side of a dark-blue car, fly over the handlebars and vanish, landing in the road as the officer shouted, *Jesus Christ!'*

Emory didn't say anything. She had to move away, in order to stay quiet.

He hadn't even been looking at the road. He hadn't been looking at the road and now they had this list of numbers to deal with. He hadn't even been looking at the road and now everything they had was going to be crushed and fed like minced meat through the accident-to-bankruptcy pipeline. He hadn't even been looking at the road.

And the hospital called Andrew first.

It didn't seem appropriate to think about that at the hospital, but now Emory allowed herself to question why exactly *the fuck* they had called Andrew first.

Yun was still looking at the video with this doped-out

smile on his face and she wanted to shake him, scream in his face.

She said, 'You have to call the billing department and say you can't pay. Just keep saying you can't pay and they'll reduce it. I don't know if it'll be by much but it sometimes works.' She ran herself a glass of water and swallowed the anger down, because even if she did say something now, he wouldn't hear it. 'But you *have* to call them, do you understand? Do you want to call them now?'

Yun was only half listening. Still looking at his phone, he said, 'You know, this is the most views I've ever had.'

When Emory woke up the morning before, she had thought it was later than it was. Almost every morning on Skillman, a portly middle-aged Italian man from down the street walked up to the building opposite theirs and conducted a yelled conversation with another portly middle-aged Italian man leaning out of his second-floor window. It would go on for about half an hour, both of them discussing articles in their respective newspapers, the man upstairs sometimes disappearing back into his apartment to grab fresh coffee. Their voices annoyed Emory for about a week, until she got used to it. She didn't know how she would live without it now.

But it wasn't them. She looked at her phone and saw it was only five a.m. Five a.m. and only then did she become aware of Yun's absence as she heard his voice creeping into her consciousness, singing quietly through the wall.

Trying to keep quiet, she got up and stepped out of the room, leaning against the door to Yun's studio with her robe wrapped tight and her feet cold against the floor. She would have been annoyed at him for waking her up, if she hadn't heard Yun singing for . . . long enough that she couldn't remember what it sounded like. He paused to adjust something at the piano, began again, and she realized she couldn't make out the words because he wasn't singing in English.

She knocked softly and let herself in.

Yun started, dragging his headphones to his shoulders. He was working by lamplight, squinting a little. 'Sorry, was I being loud?'

'No, I was just sleeping light.' She gestured at the piano. 'Are you writing something?'

'Nah, it's a cover.' He moved along, letting her sit beside him on the stool. It reminded her of the night they met and she was about to say so, but Yun was already pointing at his laptop screen. 'I felt rusty, so I thought I'd try out a song I've been meaning to do something with for a while. I don't think it needs any guitar. I might harmonize my own backing vocals but I'm not sure it needs that either.'

'What's the song?' she asked carefully, not wanting to make him self-conscious or embarrass him into silence. It felt fragile, this spark of the old Yun she could see in the air. If it wasn't cultivated, something as arbitrary as a stubbed toe could shut him down again for months.

'It's called "Diphylleia grayi". I guess it's a song about loss, but *Diphylleia grayi* is this little white flower whose petals become see-through when it rains. Another name for it is the Skeleton Flower.' He took his phone from the top of the piano and scrolled through some lyrics in Hangul, almost smiling. 'There's one part that really gets me. At the end there's this line, repeated over and over until it fades out. It translates to "Time passes", basically. You could hear the

305

song as being about a break-up, losing someone, whatever. But the sadness of the final line is about the generality of it all. *Time passes.* It's not about losing one person, it's about how eventually everyone loses everything. And when you listen to it, the repetition of that line fades out before the song ends. The song ends on its own time, but that final line disappears first. That's how life works. Time passes, everything fades out, the song carries on without you.'

He glanced up at her, to make sure she was following.

Emory smiled, trying not to cry.

There was a split second where his frustration clouded over, where he seemed almost disappointed by her presence despite his best efforts, as she had sensed so many times. Only this time she knew, she knew for sure. She felt it, in the way he looked at her. He would rather be explaining all of this to someone else.

'Anyway, this is the kind of vocal I'm trying for, this falsetto.' He brought a performance of the song up on his phone for her, eyes fixated on the screen while she watched him, thinking about things that became transparent when exposed to how harsh life could be, fading out under the pressure. 'I just think the song . . . the vocals, that line. It's one of the most beautiful things I've ever heard.'

32.

Almost a year to the day since Mike and Lara's wedding, and the global death toll limped over one million with no leading stories. The US was no longer expected to reach 800,000, Yun learned as he lay in bed scrolling through his phone. The hysteria was all but over; another blip to be analysed by sociologists and historians, turned into articles and essay questions further down the road.

At least he wasn't noticing the headaches any more. The rest of him hurt too much. He had gone from constant movement to inertia in the space of a day, and spent almost two weeks in bed, high on prescription painkillers and slamming through nine seasons of a sitcom. His parents mailed a box of snacks and sodas from San Diego. Kevin and Derrick sent him funny videos. Kevin remarked that he was lucky to score an Oxy prescription.

Emory wrote all day in the front room, brought him food and coffee, but she was quiet. Her brain got loud when she got quiet but he pretended not to notice, as his bruises faded from black to purple, green to yellow, the bandages came off, and his cuts began to scab over and itch.

The visible healing only reminded him he was on borrowed time and finite sympathy. The closer it got to rent day, the louder her silences became, and the more painkillers it took for Yun to sleep without thinking about the bills, tallying up exactly how much his life was worth. It may have been financially preferable for everyone if he had died.

He couldn't sleep on his side, couldn't sleep at all at night. During the day he didn't so much sleep as pass out, counting down the minutes until it was medically advisable to take another painkiller. Emory would curl up near him but she couldn't lean on him, or touch him. She would lie awake until he appeared to fall asleep – faking it for her benefit – then turn away.

He wondered if she was going to leave him, and whether he could blame her if she did. He was down to one functioning arm, and everything that gave him purpose and meaning and joy demanded two. Jarah had also acted like this, right before she ended things. Whirring mind, reproach in her eyes.

When Yun could finally walk again without limping, he got up to make himself a sandwich. Emory had her laptop open on the kitchen table, glasses on, looking at a spreadsheet. Paper covered the tabletop but he avoided looking at it. But doing everything one-handed made him awkward and loud, and as he tried to take out a chopping board, she turned in her chair.

'Can you come here and actually try to engage with this? Please?'

He was wrong-footed, rigid with shame. 'I don't see how a spreadsheet is going to help.'

'Well, can you help me *think*?' Her tone became shrill.

He shrugged. He really didn't know what else to offer. 'It is what it is.'

'Rent is due in *four* days and after this month I can't afford this place on my own!'

'This isn't my fault!'

'I didn't say it was! Can you just . . . ?' Taking off her glasses to pinch the bridge of her nose. 'Can you come over here, please?'

Replacing the chopping board with some commotion, he went to sit next to her. The sight of the paper up close made him nauseous and his leg started to bounce. He couldn't stand the way she was looking at him.

'It would help if we could even deduct the ambulance.'

'Sorry, I would've told them to put me in a cab but I was busy being unconscious.' He chewed the ragged skin around his thumbnail. 'Maybe you could've mentioned it when they called you?'

He jumped as she smacked her hand to the tabletop. 'They didn't call me, Andrew did!'

'What?'

'They called him first, because apparently he's your emergency contact and I'm not. *He* didn't mention it either, so if you're that pissed about the ambulance then take it up with him.'

Yun tried to remember if it had occurred to him to remove Andrew's name from his emergency contact information. But he had nothing, nothing but the hurt, to realize Andrew had called Emory, but hadn't come to the hospital to see him. The bitter taste in his mouth, resentment that he'd even *wanted* Andrew to come. And something even deeper, some ugly part of him that hoped Andrew would feel regret, guilty even . . .

'I didn't realize,' he said, cringing at how flimsy it sounded. 'He's good in a crisis, that's all, I never thought to change it.'

'I don't care.' She wasn't looking at him as she affirmed it to herself. 'I *don't* care.'

He tried to change the subject. 'I could sell my guitars.'

'You'll never get them back.'

'I need a new laptop more urgently, I can't work without one.'

'You can't *work* at all.' She took an audible breath. 'We need to give notice.'

'Why don't we clear the second room and rent it out?'

'They'll raise the rent.'

'We'll sublet.'

'Even if the agency didn't find out, this isn't big enough for three people.'

He sank lower in his seat, saying nothing. He had lived here for seven years. Three days after he first moved in, a man came over to fix a Wi-Fi box to the front of the building. Ms BB came out and screamed the street down until he came out and yelled from the steps that he had no idea they were gonna nail a new box to the wall but he needed the internet to work so could she stop being such an *ass* about it. And she laughed at that. He had Derrick and a few other people over a week later, and he didn't have furniture yet so they put beanbags on the floor, drinking beer and passing the laptop around to pick the next song for the playlist. Jarah came back here the first night they met and he was so in love he couldn't think straight. Emory set up an obscene indoor lights display for his thirtieth birthday. So many coloured fairy lights packed into the front room it was enough to give someone a seizure.

But it wasn't just all the living done here, it was the dying. Since Ms BB died, he had been looking out for the place on her behalf. If he left, someone else would move in who didn't remember this building was hers. If he left, and didn't come back, he felt like she would still be lying awake, waiting to hear him get home safe.

'I've talked to Dad about it,' Emory continued, sounding as if she was treading carefully. 'I think we should take him up on his offer –'

'No.'

The response was out before she even finished the sentence.

'There's no other option.'

'It's humiliating.'

'Why? Plenty of people live with their parents. My sister lives there and it's not like –'

'Look, my parents said if I worked in music I'd go broke, this is just –'

They talked over each other, getting louder and louder, angrier and angrier, as they rushed to the ends of their respective statements.

'This is absolutely ridiculous, I really can't with your –'

'– proof that of course I'll never be able to support anyone –'

'– insecure breadwinner bullshit right now!'

'– let alone a family if I can't even support myself!'

'Can you just *not*?'

She put both elbows on the table. He picked at his nails.

'It's the only way we can pay this off,' she said with finality.

'It's *my* debt and I don't wanna live in *Nowhere*, America, with your weird dad who hates me.'

'It's *upstate* and he doesn't hate you.'

'You said yourself you think he had some kind of nervous breakdown.'

'That was just when he quit his job and bought this new

place. He's been better. Being in the countryside could actually be nice, we'd have more space.' She spread her hands. 'It's not like we can move in with your parents.'

'Well, I'm sorry this hasn't been *Crazy Rich Asians* for you.'

He closed his eyes so he wouldn't have to deal with her expression. He might have coped better, if she had said she was leaving him. Realizing she was staying brought the full extent of his uselessness home. She was settling for this, for less than she deserved, and he was letting her.

When the silence went on for too long, he opened his eyes. 'Why don't I go back to San Diego and you stay here, get a room-mate?'

'So, break up?'

'No, Jesus . . . I didn't say that. I just mean that you don't have to leave.'

'But you would. So how does you living on the other side of the country, over the option of us living together, *not* equal breaking up? Do you want to break up?'

'No! It was just a thought. Forget it.'

Arms folded, mouth set in a grim, hurt line, she sat back and surveyed him. 'Okay. Do you have any other ideas?'

He didn't. She knew he didn't.

She shrugged in an uncanny imitation of him. 'Let's hear it then. What's your plan?'

He wanted a painkiller. His collarbone ached. 'What exactly did you say to your dad?'

'I said you were in a car accident and you're not insured, so we have to stay somewhere else for a while. That's literally the truth.'

'It's not *literally* the truth, I'm not uninsured, it just doesn't cover it. What did he say?'

'He said it was fine, they have loads of room and he'd love to have us.' All of this was said in a low monotone as she shut her laptop and gathered the papers into one pile. 'I know you don't want to, but I don't know what else to do. I don't want to move out either! Do you really think I want to leave New York?'

It was sweltering inside the cast. Even with the sling, it was hard to move around, hard to sit or stand upright. 'I don't,' he said quietly, tears of embarrassment springing to his eyes.

'You don't, what?'

Don't cry. The only thing that could make this worse is if you cry.

'I don't have a plan,' he said.

It was hard to comprehend the scale of his failure. One lapse in concentration and the small space in the world he had managed to carve out for himself was swept away. Fine, the building might not be his. But surviving for so long in this city – this neighbourhood, this street, the studio in the second bedroom – was more freedom than anyone ever believed he could attain.

Emory reached out to touch his good shoulder, and tried to sound convincing when she said, 'You know this isn't the end of the world, right?'

Hui-sun answered Yun's call with her camera switched off. 'What's wrong?' she asked in Korean.

It was a running joke in their family that no one called each other without warning unless someone had died.

'I'm fine, just checking in,' he replied in English. 'Can you turn your camera on?'

A pause, then her face appeared, pixelated and gaze slightly down, looking at him rather than at the camera. 'Are you sure everything is all right? How is your arm?'

Yun had to take a beat, let the dangerous urge to cry again wash over him and leave. 'I just thought I should let you know, I'm gonna go with Em and stay with her dad for a while. It's no big deal, it's still in New York, but I kinda can't work until my arm gets better so it makes sense.'

Hui-sun gave him a pointed look. She had never raised her voice at either him or Kevin growing up, and Yun often wondered how two such laid-back people managed to bring up two boys, never mind how she also managed to control whole classrooms. Whatever it was with his mother, her authority was something in the brows, which he had been lucky enough to inherit.

'You could come home,' she said.

That crumpled wanting-to-cry feeling came again, but not without anger. After the first few years in New York, his parents had stopped asking him about moving back in. On the one hand, he was relieved when the light nagging ceased. On the other, he had missed it, resented the apparent lack of concern. He would never have taken them up on the offer, but they didn't know that.

'It's really fine,' he said, struggling to meet her eyes. 'Em's dad has a big place. It's in the country, which could be nice, I guess. It's only temporary so we should stay near the city.'

She seemed hurt, but accepted it. 'Do you need money? Can you explain the bills? Your father was asking what you owe.'

'We don't need to go through all that right now.' He felt sick. 'Em got me on an interest-free payment plan and we got some stuff discounted when I called. Apparently I might get assistance if I send them tax returns and stuff. So as long as the company pays out, I probably won't end up owing that much. Ten thousand or something? Maybe less than that.'

'But can you pay? We can help. We're so worried about you, Dan.'

'You don't have to worry. Em is still working, she's doing really well actually. So she can help me out and, er, there's probably some work I can do.' He didn't know what. His skin was crawling with shame. 'But I can't ask you guys to pay my rent, and I just need to pay off something each month from the bills to show I'm paying *something*. I'll be fine.'

Something thwarted in her expression. 'You know you can always ask.'

'I know, I know.' He forced a smile.

'And your shoulder is okay? Are you in pain?'

'I mean, it hurts but I'm on great medication.'

She nodded, disappointment written in the set of her mouth, the softness of her gaze. Disappointment in him, herself, or maybe with the way all of their lives had turned out. Yun could read his mother's emotions in her face, but not his father's. In contrast, Ji-hoon was the kind of man who acted like his facial expressions were precious data to be stolen. He took pride in no one being able to guess his opinion on anything until he declared it.

Kevin and Yun had grown up so loud, so exuberant, in trying to elicit a smile from him, just one smile. Then Yun arrived in New York City and realized there was power in being unreadable, aloof. It made people either try harder, or

315

not try at all. It was why Emory had approached him in the first place. She had told him so.

It was only two years ago – when Yun had commented in front of Hui-sun over the holidays about their father's introverted nature – that she told him that wasn't the case before they moved to the US. Ji-hoon was quieter in English, she said. Even though they both studied abroad, Ji-hoon became frustrated with the extra effort needed to express himself exactly how he liked. So he chose to be enigmatic instead, preferring to be thought of as cold, rather than incompetent or imprecise.

Yun didn't know how he felt about that revelation, now it was too late to stop himself from forging his own personality around it. The more he found out about his parents, the more he wished he hadn't. He couldn't forgive them, for being human, for not getting parenthood right the first time, for not raising him better able to deal with *this*.

'I should go,' he said, as if there was anywhere he could possibly be going. 'But I'll let you know how it goes, the whole moving thing.'

Yun wished he could force himself to say something kind to Hui-sun, like he knew she had always done her best. But he didn't say anything.

What We Actually Know About the Psychogenic Death Epidemic (First Draft)

Just over a year after the first cases were reported, mass psychogenic death has receded in the US and Europe to only a few dozen isolated cases per week, with scientists now treating the outbreak as a particularly pervasive case of 'mass hysteria'. So, what really happened?

By Emory Schafer | @emoryschafer | emory.schafer@therelay.com

I don't know, I don't know anything I don't know fucking anything, I don't know what the point of any of this is, no one knows what the point of any of this is

33.

It was nearing seven thirty when they headed out to D&J. Yun didn't see the point in shopping for food if they were leaving in less than two weeks, but Emory needed to get out of the apartment more than she cared about a few days of food waste. She hadn't particularly wanted Yun to come, but he insisted.

Some emo pop from the early 2000s was playing faintly. Other than that, the store was quiet. Mostly single people coming by after work to pick up dinner. Emory leaned heavily on the cart, dropping in potato chips and hummus.

Yun walked half a step behind her and seemed preoccupied, staring at the shelves and displays of fresh produce like they had done something to offend him. She was too tired to ask him what was wrong. Something was always wrong – or maybe *she* was wrong – and she was so tired.

For most of the day she had been at Lara's, who went back to work for a month but was signed off for another two weeks' personal leave when it became apparent that throwing herself into work wasn't having the intended effect. Work reminded her of Mike. It was where they had met.

'They said I have to cite stress and take it as sick leave if I want more time off,' Lara explained while they watched season three of an old TV show. 'Because if I take too much sick leave they'll have grounds to try to fire me before I take any actual maternity leave. That's the cheapest scenario for them.'

Emory hadn't known what to say to any of this, exhausted by her terminal inability to help anybody. The week before, she had tried to call Michelle for the first time in a long while, and discovered her cell phone was disconnected. When she checked Michelle's socials, all the accounts were gone.

'Do you know if Michelle is okay?' she asked Lara, who seemed nonplussed by the subject.

'I don't know. The last time I saw her at work before she left, she'd cut her hair really short. And she lost so much weight, so lucky.' She shrugged. 'I think she has family in New Zealand or something.'

'Yeah, really lucky,' Emory had murmured, like background noise.

It was a second or two before she noticed Yun was no longer behind her. She turned and saw him standing in the middle of the aisle, staring at a wall of cookies. His cast was held across his chest, his frown deepened.

Emory checked her phone to keep an eye on the time. Sometimes the medication made Yun space out.

'Do you think we were ever right for each other?'

She looked up, but Yun's gaze was still on the cookies. 'Sorry, what?'

'Do you think we were ever right for each other?'

Her voice was quiet. 'What kind of question is that?'

'It was just a thought.' Infuriatingly, he looked at the floor.

Emory had dropped the subject before, but not now. 'That's not *just* a thought. What are you trying to say?'

'I don't know.' A shrug. 'Everything happened so fast this past year.'

'You asked *me* to move in.' Her voice rose and she tried to steady herself. They were still alone in the aisle, but people would hear them.

'Yeah,' he agreed, though he sounded dubious, like she was making things up.

'Are you kidding right now?' She couldn't believe he was doing this, while she was pushing a cart full of food under the too-bright lights. 'We've just given notice, we're about to leave and *now* you want to have a relationship discussion? Are you punishing me or something?'

'What?' He looked at her as if she had lost her mind. 'No.'

'Well, it feels like it. So far you've managed to make pretty much everything feel like my fault, so if you want to say something to me then just say it!' She threw up her hands, almost dropping her phone. 'Say *something*!'

He looked as though he was wishing he could fold his arms. 'Sometimes I feel like the only reason we ended up together is because we were both there . . . when everything started going to hell, when people started dying. Would we even still be together if it wasn't for all that?'

The anger left her in one punctured exhale, and she couldn't catch her breath again. 'Why are you saying this now?'

He met her eyes and she wished he hadn't. 'I don't know.'

Some tears had worked their way loose and ran down her cheeks. 'So you want to break up, that's what you're saying?'

'No! I mean, I don't know.' He grimaced, but his tone sounded like he was posing a dare. 'I don't think you're happy.'

'*Don't* put this on me, don't you dare! If you wanted out so bad then why didn't you just *go*? Why didn't you just break up with me so I could move on? So I didn't have to leave New York, so I didn't have to keep trying so hard like an *idiot* when you never even cared! All I've done is try to . . .'

She stopped, breathless, like she had been running and running and abruptly run out of track. 'No. No, I can't do this.'

'What do you mean?'

Emory wiped her eyes and rested her forehead against her phone, eyes closed. 'I'm not doing this with you. I don't care any more. Just do whatever you want. I'm going.'

'What, you're going *now*?'

'If you want to come too then come.' Her hands dropped to her sides. 'I won't hold it against you, if this is you just freaking out or whatever. But I can't do this passive-aggressive bullshit any more, I'm not going to wait here for you to *decide* if you want to carry on being with me.'

Then she turned away, leaving Yun and the cart in the aisle, and walked out of the store.

'How many people, do you think?' Yun had yelled above the sound of car horns, standing on his toes to watch the crowd crawling up a gridlocked Fifth Avenue. It was around this time that Mike must have been on his way home from Whole Foods uptown. 'Few thousand?'

'*Get out of the road and clear the area immediately!*' The voice over the megaphone rose above the horns. '*This is your last chance to clear the road or you will be detained!*'

Emory checked her phone. It was 11.59 and everyone had stopped. Even if they wanted to, it was almost impossible to get out of the road. Too many people, packed in too tight.

'*Clear the area or you will be detained and placed under arrest!*'

Yun turned to Emory, moved his black mask from where it had been sitting under his chin to cover his face. 'Cops aren't so friendly now, are they?'

There were more nerves in her smile than his. Yun was

looking for Derrick, couldn't see him anywhere in their vicinity, and typed something into his phone. Then he took Emory's hand and – along with the rest of the crowd, at exactly noon – they sat down.

It was the quietest Fifth Avenue had ever been. People took photos from branded doorways and a wall of riot police blocked the road about two hundred yards up from where they were, with more sitters beyond them. Yun was right. It definitely was thousands.

They had brought two backpacks, two cartons of milk in case of tear gas. Phone numbers written down their arms in Sharpie. They had shatter-resistant goggles, water, N95s, a first aid kit, and no demands. That was what the news anchors and the op-ed writers and the journalists and the senators had the biggest problem understanding. A protest with no public leaders and no demands. If she was being totally honest, Emory didn't understand it either, until she saw a post from an editor friend who ran an online outlet she had written for a couple of times.

All these old politicians and billionaires are pretending not to understand, because they're terrified of the level of change required to give people a reason to carry on living.

Ever since that post went viral, in a way one vague demand had formed. Emory saw it appear on signs and T-shirts. It trended online every day that week, before it tapered off and became uncool.

Give them a reason to live.

Give us a reason to live!

Give us a reason.

She sent a photo to her father, then became as still as the rest of them. She thought again of the woman Michelle had told her about in the hospital, on that first grim morning, talking across Rose's catatonic form. Emory couldn't imagine herself cowering in a corner, screaming until people came to take her away, ask what was wrong and give her drugs, give her whatever she needed. Not that she didn't want to. Surely everyone wanted to give up at some point in their lives, let someone else take over. But Emory couldn't imagine actually doing it. She couldn't imagine things being so bad that she would embarrass herself, inconvenience everyone around her, to that extent. She imagined she would simply carry on feeling the way she did now, like she was always on the verge of suffocation but never quite cut off from air.

Emory hated being this close to the ground, where it was colder, where her ankles burned and her knees hurt. Some people said it felt freeing to imitate the catatonic, let their eyes go blank and limbs go weak. Some today would never get back up. Some ended up in prisons or hospitals or were left in the street for friends to carry.

Her neck ached from craning towards the line of officers in the distance, so she let her eyes rest on Yun instead. He had withdrawn his hands into his sleeves, which warmed hers too. She could feel his pulse under her fingers, and swallowed back that terrifying need to somehow climb inside another person through their ribcage, disappear inside them.

There was no simple way to measure the meaning of being so present in someone else's life, but she still felt like something of an interloper in his. He was recklessly attractive and magnetic in a way that kept people trailing after him. He detested saying 'I love you' and claimed he didn't see the point in stating and restating the obvious, but Emory worried that – even though they lived together, talked about maybe getting a cat, spent every night together – Yun might still, secretly, not like her. Or at least, not like her as much as he had liked Jarah, or liked other things.

Emory often wondered whether he had felt the same way with Jarah. Jarah, who was two years older than Emory and looked younger. Jarah, with a naturally full upper lip. Jarah, with the younger brother who had died recently in an accident while canoeing. Jarah, who had moved back to New York and taken a job with a PR firm that couldn't be more than five blocks from where they were now. Jarah, whose Instagram and LinkedIn and work Twitter and locked Twitter Emory still checked four times a day, out of habit. She spent a weird amount of time wondering whether they would somehow be friends, if they had met under different circumstances. If they were friends, Emory thought she might be able to work out, through sustained observation, what magical formula might make Yun love somebody.

But any time she was close enough to feel his pulse, like this, smell the smoke on his clothes mixed with his deodorant that smelled faintly of bergamot, she wanted to push herself clean through him. He was here, right here, right in front of her, and she couldn't explain why she felt so heavy with *want* for someone she already had.

Emory watched the crowd again. 'No one has ever explained what exactly the white is supposed to symbolize. Is it some religious purity thing?'

'In some cultures it means death. It's more like what you'd wear at funerals.' For a moment Yun's thumbs rubbed apologetically across the backs of her hands, as if he was talking about something he shouldn't be talking about. 'Or when you're in mourning.'

Emory looked at him and felt like she was drowning suddenly, like she had to force the words out before water filled her mouth. 'You're such a terrible person to love, you know that? I hate it, sometimes I really hate it.'

Yun smiled, but there was nothing sardonic about it. In less than an hour, Lara would call her, and he would act as if he had all but forgotten the exchange.

'I know,' he said, squeezing her hands and laughing, as if he had come to the absurd realization that *yes*, she actually did love him. 'I fucking know.'

And he didn't sound sorry.

Emory went back to the apartment, packed her things and called a car to take her to Penn Station. By the time it arrived, Yun had made it back from D&J and was sitting on the steps outside. She didn't know how long he'd been there, and they didn't speak as she passed.

In the car, she let her father know she would be arriving late into Poughkeepsie. She decided to hold off on any crying until she got to Penn Station. It would be less embarrassing there. Penn Station was depressing enough; no one would even notice.

She bought a one-way ticket and dragged her case on to the concourse, pausing only to call Andrew. 'Sorry, I know it's late,' she said before he could speak.

'Is something wrong?'

She paused, assessed her reasons for calling. She no longer wanted to cry. Her voice was steady. 'I'm leaving the city earlier than planned. We weren't supposed to move until next weekend. I don't really know what Yun's doing. I don't even know if he knows what he's doing . . . But I think it might help if you talked to him.'

'Right.' There was no trace of judgement in his voice. He had always been so fucking *nice* to her.

Emory chuckled under her breath, knowing she sounded cruel. 'Look, you know he's never going to speak to you first or apologize for whatever happened between you two. So you might as well talk to him.' She took a breath, let the humiliation settle. 'To be honest, I think you're the only person he actually listens to.'

Before Andrew could say anything else, she ended the call.

She wished she had a cigarette, but she didn't have time to buy a pack and smoke one before her train. She had always felt kind of envious when Yun smoked, watching him surrender to whatever vice he felt like following in the moment.

Lara had asked her to move in, and she'd said no. She probably should have said yes. Maybe she still could, once Yun made a decision.

She also probably should have said goodbye, Emory thought, as she went to catch the 21.45 train. But she was too tired to feel any corresponding emotion. No guilt. Too many parts of her had been chipped away, left scattered around the city with other people. Maybe she should have spent more time and more care retrieving them, had the sense to not give so much away in the first place.

But leaving them behind instead, she felt lighter. Now there was less of her to go around, it felt like a relief.

34

'You're really going over there *now*?' Fin said, sitting at the kitchen island pretending to look at LA real estate after Andrew called a car.

Andrew returned from the bedroom with his jacket. 'It sounded like it could be an emergency.'

'Why don't you just call him?'

'Emory just left. She left the city, I should make sure he's okay.'

'So why don't you just call him?' Fin kept very still, and spoke slowly. 'It's late. And it's not like you've been talking, he might not want to see you.'

Andrew paused, like he was giving it some thought. But he had already decided he was going. It was only ten p.m. and he didn't fully understand Fin's reservations. The true origin of many of Fin's reactions was still a mystery to him, much like Yun's.

'I'll be back before midnight.' Andrew offered a smile of reassurance as he grabbed his keys and wallet from the counter.

Fin watched him go without returning the smile, eyes narrowed.

Andrew checked his phone repeatedly in the car, anticipating a follow-up message, but nothing came. Fin may have been right about calling first, but Yun needed to be surprised into any confrontation. If given a warning, or extra time to rehearse the situation, Yun would either shut down completely or become more snide. Andrew knew this from experience.

What Andrew didn't expect was to arrive on Skillman and find Yun sitting on the steps outside the building, finishing a cigarette. Somehow he was managing to roll them, even with his right arm in a sling and cast.

He watched Andrew get out of the car, laughed, and rolled his eyes so theatrically that his whole body slumped to the side. 'Huh. She called you, didn't she? Great.'

Andrew realized he was drunk as Yun righted himself with some difficulty and stubbed the cigarette out on the ground. Without looking at Andrew again, or saying anything else, he picked up the bottle sitting on the step beside him and went inside, not bothering to shut the main door.

It was the first time they had spoken in months and it already hurt. Andrew waited at the bottom of the steps, wondering whether friendships burned out in the same way epidemics, hysterias and protests do, then went up.

Yun was running a glass of water when Andrew shut the front door behind him.

'This is the secret,' he said, taking a sip of water before a larger gulp of cinnamon whisky. 'Drinking a glass of water between every drink.'

'What medication are you on?'

'Oxy. It's *so* great.' Yun dropped to the couch.

'Yeah, people tend to like it too much.' Andrew sat at the other end and searched the information on his phone. 'I don't think you should be drinking, it increases the risk of side-effects.'

'Oh, shut *up*.' Yun scowled. 'What are you doing here? I didn't *ask* for you.'

'Emory sounded worried.'

'So you're here to give me a pep talk for her? Since *you're* not worried.'

'Of course I've been worried.'

'You didn't even come to the hospital.'

'How was I supposed to know you wanted me there?'

'It was you who said we should stop talking.'

Andrew took a slow breath. 'Drinking always made you mean and angry.'

'Yeah?' Yun took another drink, eyes unfocused. 'Nothing makes you mean, does it? You're always so fucking perfect. You never say anything wrong, do you?'

'What's your problem?'

'Oh?' Yun smirked sideways at him. 'So, you can get angry?'

'I'm not angry, I'm . . .' Andrew was irritated that by pausing to choose the right words, he was proving Yun right. 'I'm confused, as to how something good happened in my life and it has somehow become all about you.'

Yun levered himself off the couch to go drink some more water at the sink. His cheeks had filled out and his hair was ̶onger again. Even held back with a sweatband it was hang-̶ around his chin. Instead of sitting on the couch, Yun ̶ed his bottle of whisky, leaned against the wall on the ̶de of the room and slid to the floor.

̶'t even know what you're talking about.'

̶ndrew said, and Yun pulled a derisive face. 'You ̶m with him, you made that pretty clear. And ̶ldn't mind if this was only about disliking ̶e has to like everyone else. But I don't ̶u're this angry with me. I thought that, ̶'d support me the most.'

'I don't have a *problem* with you suddenly realizing you're gay and wanting to fuck a twenty-year-old, okay.'

'But you're acting like I betrayed you.'

'Well, you fucking did!' Yun looked away and started fiddling with his hair.

Andrew had been relatively comfortable wading through the shallows of this inevitable conversation, but now felt he had walked into a steep drop. 'What do you mean?'

'Nothing.' He shrugged, as well as he could using only one shoulder.

'Why do you feel like I betrayed you?'

'I don't.'

'That's not what you just said.'

'I guess I'm just confused too!' Yun gesticulated with his good hand, and took another drink. 'I guess I'm just confused, why you never mentioned it. It's not like I wasn't open about it with you! But you never mentioned it, the whole time. And we were *living* together.'

'I didn't –'

'God, can you let me *finish*?' Yun raised the bottle to his lips, then stopped and put it down, looking like he was fight ing back a wave of nausea. 'Do you know how insulting that you never thought about me? I guess you didn me. Or maybe I just wasn't good enough for t Andrew Zhou. Everyone wanted to hang out with Zhou, everyone wanted to fuck Andrew Zho stopped fucking hearing about it! The coole me was that *you* were my best friend, and I d I didn't mind. Because I hated everyon fucking college, I couldn't stand *anyone* only fucking person I ever . . .'

He cut himself off with an almost panicked expression, then glared, as if Andrew had been the one goading him into saying something that even he considered a step too far.

This was their first real fight. What happened before could be considered an altercation or disagreement. But he hadn't expected an argument between them to feel this way. Even minor confrontations, the type he had at work, reminded him of displeasing his parents as a child, made him feel rigid and choked up. What he felt now was a rush of anguish and regret, and a love so powerful and so unlike what he felt for Fin that Andrew found it hard to speak.

'I didn't realize,' he said at last, not totally sure what he was referring to.

Andrew looked at his hands, and noticed the only light in the room was coming from the pallid glow above the stove. He resisted the urge to go and flip the main switch on the wall. Fin hated using the big light too. He wanted to ask what Yun had been going to say, before he stopped himself.

I'm the only person you ever – what?

'Fuck . . .' Yun mumbled, suddenly pale. 'Fuck, help me up!'

Yun reached out with urgency and Andrew scrambled off the couch. He swayed and stumbled towards the bathroom, catching the doorway with his good arm, falling back into Andrew, then lunging forward to throw up into the sink. Andrew held his waist as he leaned against the porcelain, keeping him on-balance.

'I'm fine!' Yun snapped, before vomiting again.

'Did you eat?' Andrew waited while Yun ran the faucet, swirled water around his mouth and spat it out. 'Do you have any food here?'

'No.' Yun shrugged him off as they left the bathroom, holding his forehead. 'I just need another painkiller.'

'You need to eat something.'

'I *need* another painkiller, my head fucking *hurts*.'

Andrew went to fill a glass with water and search the cabinets as Yun sat on the couch shivering. There was nothing in the fridge. He would have to order something.

'Drink this.' He took the water over to Yun and stopped. 'What are you doing?'

Yun looked up at him with bloodshot eyes, rolling the whiskey bottle back and forth over some pills on the coffee table. 'It makes them take effect faster. Otherwise it takes hours.'

'Stop doing that.'

'What?'

'That!' Andrew slammed the water down and snatched the bottle. 'It works on a time-release for a reason, it's not safe.'

'Give it back, I need it!'

'Can you think for a second?'

'I think I know how my own meds work.'

Andrew swept the crushed pills off the table.

Yun whirled around and Andrew caught his elbow.

'Can you calm down?'

'Do you know how much these cost?' Yun pushed him away. 'Why don't you just leave me alone? I didn't need you to come here!'

'Yun . . .' Andrew sat down and looked at the space between them, which felt years wide. 'I don't know what's going on here. What's going on with you?'

He laughed, and stopped abruptly. 'Nothing,' he said,

chewing his nail, then he laughed again. 'Nothing! Isn't that obvious? There's nothing going on with me. I have *nothing* going for me.'

'You're going through a tough time. It happens.'

'It's never not been a tough time.' The hostility melted out of his shoulders. 'I used to be okay hoping the next thing would work out. I'd at least . . . get stuff done, out of spite. I don't know what's wrong with me, but I can't do it any more. What's the point in trying all the time if everything just keeps getting harder?'

'I think everyone's felt like that this past year.'

'No, they haven't. Some people care and most don't.' Yun took a long drink of water, before holding his head again. 'People don't change. Everything gets harder and no one fucking changes. Apart from you, maybe.'

'I haven't changed.'

Yun didn't appear to have heard him. 'You know, I'm not surprised Em left. I kind of wanted her to. Not because I don't love her or anything, but I'm just holding her back. She's so good at doing things. I'm so sick of *doing* things.'

Andrew put a hand on the back of his neck, which felt easier to do than it ever had before. Yun flinched, but didn't move away. He shut his eyes, and a couple of tears ran from them.

'I'm going to order something, you should try to eat.' Andrew turned his attention to his phone and pretended not to notice.

Yun forced down some plain rice, vomited again, then had some soup and another painkiller. By the time he seemed too wiped out to continue the argument, it was ten to midnight. Andrew helped him to bed, placed another glass of water on the table and pulled the cover over him as best he could. He eased the sweatband off Yun's head and his forehead was clammy.

'Sleeping on my back sucks,' he muttered. 'I wake up and can't feel my toes.'

Yun's breaths seemed quick and shallow, and Andrew wasn't sure if he had swallowed or chewed the last pill. He sat on the other side of the bed, leaning against the headboard, and decided to wait a few more hours, to make sure Yun didn't stop breathing or vomit in his sleep.

'You don't have to stay.'

Andrew looked down to see that Yun had opened one eye, and laughed.

'So what is it about him?' he asked, rotating his good shoulder against the mattress. 'Except for the hot-and-twenty part.'

'Twenty-*one*, now. And you admit he's hot. Congratulations on an actual compliment.'

'Well, I guess, if you're into that kind of thing.'

'He actually reminds me of you a lot.'

'Yeah? I don't see it.'

'He's really quick and intelligent. He's funny, but he has a fatalistic streak, and he's stubborn. That's what reminds me of you the most, I think. You both act like you're here to fight the whole world.' He forced himself to stop talking, feeling like he had said too much, or too much of the wrong thing, because what he wanted to say was, *And I fell in love with him like I fell in love with you. I love him so much I feel weak with it, but I'm here because . . .*

'It sounds like . . .' A pause. 'He sounds all right.'

Something in his chest hurt. He was glad it was dark. This

was why it felt different than it felt with Fin, he realized. Whatever this was, this had never made it into daylight. He wondered if a love not properly expressed mutated into something jagged and unwieldy like metal, something that could kill you. He wondered whether that was why his parents had lived as if confined to different cages, and died in separate rooms.

When they were both in therapy, Nicola said that all the things you repress hide themselves deep within your muscles, finding the places where you're weakest, and only make themselves known when they're killing you later. He was the happiest he had ever been – deliriously, terrifyingly happy – and he woke up some mornings with his whole body sore, fighting for breath, like he had worked out too hard or been thrown down a mountainside. He half expected to find bruises on his skin but there weren't any. Whatever it was, the impact was internal. Sometimes a feeling of dread would wash over him when doing something totally innocuous. He would be marking essays, and a shame and selfishness hotter than fire would well up within him, and he would walk to another room and try not to hyperventilate. And he cried so easily now. He hadn't realized that all his repression was only accumulating a debt. That this was the trade-off. The price of happiness. In order to feel happy he had to feel everything.

'You know you could ask me to pay the bills off, if you wanted,' Andrew said, because he couldn't say anything he wanted to say out loud. 'The last few months, it really doesn't matter to me. I just . . . I need you to be okay.'

Enough time went by that Andrew thought Yun had fallen asleep.

'. . . Obviously I wouldn't ask.'

'You can, though. You can ask me for anything.'

He felt Yun nudge him with the backs of his fingers, and he took his hand and held it. His heart was loud and he felt unsteady, like he was trying to stand in strong wind at high altitude.

'I did think of you,' he said.

'Hm?'

'You said I never thought of you.' Andrew looked down. 'I thought of you.'

Yun didn't open his eyes.

35

Midnight came and went while Fin was doing stomach crunches in the living room with his phone on the floor next to him. He didn't check the clock again, instead doing twenty more burpees, twenty more jump-throughs, then twenty more push-ups. His whole routine took around thirty minutes each set; an hour and a half in total. When he checked his phone again, his shirt soaked and clinging to his shoulder blades, it was almost one a.m.

Andrew was an adult. Fin wasn't going to message and cajole him into coming home. These were the facts of the matter: Andrew's best friend stopped talking to him when Andrew started seeing Fin, his best friend's girlfriend had left him, Andrew had gone to his apartment in the middle of the night, and hadn't come back. If he walked in the door right now – Fin craned his head to check again – then it would be okay. It might be okay. But he didn't.

Fin knew Andrew wasn't the type to cheat. But he didn't have the self-awareness to see all of his actions coming, and there was often nothing more dangerous than a person fundamentally convinced of their own goodness.

Andrew loved him, Fin knew that too. He had asked several times if Andrew was sure about committing to the first guy he had ever slept with, if he was sure he didn't want to experiment, join the apps, try dating, see who and what else was out there. But Andrew always said no. He said he was happy, and Fin believed him.

But, all of these things taken into account, he still wasn't home. Another thing Fin had learned – filed away in case it ever became relevant – was that whenever Andrew said 'we' or 'our' when telling a story, he was always more likely to be referring to Yun than his ex-wife. The habit caused Fin to wonder if, by noticing this, he was once again aware of some fundamental, inevitable truth in Andrew's life before Andrew was.

Fin got off the floor and showered. When he checked his phone again it was 01.27. He made sure none of their plants needed watering, checked on the bonsai tree on the bedroom windowsill, tidied the front room, made a list of things they needed to pick up from the store over the weekend.

It took several more minutes to brew a valerian tea, and fifteen more minutes to drink it sitting in the kitchen, checking his phone the whole time. Approaching two a.m., he put the empty mug down, nudged it with his finger, nudged it again, and again, until it fell off the counter and broke.

At 02.03 he sat at the foot of the bed and waited.

Fin hadn't been that interested in attending a wedding with Emilio's accountant friends – especially with his interest in Emilio waning – but he also wasn't someone to turn down free food and drink. So he wore his tightest trousers and spent a lot of time at the bar, drinking along to the DJ's 'Roxanne' drinking game and looking for his way out.

He had already decided this night was going to be the end of something and the start of something else. He just didn't foresee the specifics.

338

The house lights were a little too bright; unflattering. He didn't like chocolate fountains or talking about Business majors. He didn't like himself, not any more, not the version of himself in this relationship. His mother had warned him about getting stuck, becoming so mired in sunk-cost fallacy that you stay longer than is good for you. He tried to tell himself that not wanting to do something any more *is* a good enough reason alone to stop doing it.

But he couldn't tell Emilio that. You couldn't actually tell people you just didn't want to be with them any more. There had to be a better, more socially acceptable reason.

He ordered another tequila, giddy on the free-bar high. A couple next to him were having quiet words because one of them wanted to leave early. Emilio danced to The Killers with the accountants while the bride danced with one of her bridesmaids, a rail-thin blonde woman who looked too happy to be an accountant.

Fin looked once or twice at a youngish waiter with slicked-back hair, tall and thin enough to make his waistcoat seem dandy rather than formal. He leaned one elbow on the bar and thought, *Turn around, turn around, turn around*.

When he did – because they always did – Fin smiled with only one side of his mouth. The waiter looked away to gather a couple more glasses. But Fin continued watching in a state of wolfish calm, as the waiter couldn't help but smirk to himself, then look back, at which point Fin allowed his smile to broaden to both sides of his face.

There it was, his trapdoor falling open with a *smack*.

He scanned the dance floor again, secure enough to let his concentration lapse, and noticed one of the bridesmaids leaning over the bar next to his shoulder to swipe a bottle of bourbon. Impressed, he watched her leave with an Asian guy Fin had scoped out earlier, but decided looked too much like hard work.

Emilio was calling him to the dance floor, and Fin figured that given what he was planning to do later, he could take one for the team and try to dance to Maroon 5.

It wasn't that he didn't like Emilio, he thought, as he let his hips and shoulders move to the beat. But Emilio had already created a vision for his future so detailed and ordered that Fin didn't see any room left for himself. Emilio knew what years he planned to be promoted at work, what kind of house he wanted to own, he knew he wanted kids and he knew he wanted two (adoption, not surrogacy, because it was apparently better for the environment), he knew he always wanted his parents and grandparents to live nearby, and that he wanted to live in New York or Philadelphia or Boston or – if he was being adventurous – Chicago.

And who was Fin to argue with any of it? Fin couldn't claim to know what he wanted out of life. But he began to have nightmare visions of waking up in his thirties – unthinkable in itself! – and trying to organize a dinner party for a group of suburban accountants after one of his adopted children had thrown up in the car.

God, no . . .

'Hey! Hey, Mike, this is Fin. You remember?'

Emilio was introducing him to the groom, and Fin allowed himself to dance slightly off-beat in a show of heterosexual camaraderie. Hard to do, as he actually liked Whitney Houston. 'Nice to meet you again. Cool wedding!'

'Ah, thanks. Must be your turn soon!' Mike clapped Emilio on the shoulder, flushed and stupid.

'Oh, I'm holding out until I can read more of the Yelp reviews on marriage,' Fin said, when Emilio smiled at him a little too widely. 'I guess you'll just have to let us know how great it is.'

'Yeah, yeah.' Mike nodded, and for a second it seemed as though he was talking only to himself. 'This is it!'

Fin felt cold suddenly, despite the tequila, and looked around for his waiter. When he saw him leaving the room with a trolley of empty glasses, he announced he was going to the restroom and followed.

They both walked in silence until they reached an elevator and went down a floor. He wished he had brought a drink, for the sake of having a prop. He looked the waiter up and down in the enclosed space, observed the long fingers and large knuckles, and the waiter let himself be looked at. Not quite as attractive as he'd hoped, viewed up-close under the elevator lights. Now Fin noticed the uneven shave, and evidence of a sad lack of skincare routine. But he had a gift for making the best out of almost any situation.

'That DJ is trying to kill us,' Fin remarked. 'Who makes Whitney Houston follow Maroon 5?'

'I know,' the waiter said, 'it's homophobic.'

'Do you often do this at weddings?' he asked, clocking the bridesmaid and her catch coming out of the ballroom to their right.

'More than you'd think.' The trolley rattled and clinked. 'Did you really come down here to talk to me about weddings?'

'I guess not.'

They found themselves in a back room full of shelving and wine bottles, tables upon tables of half-drunk drinks. A white bin and a black bin liner full of glass. No food waste at least, Fin noted as the waiter parked the trolley. He still had some class.

Fin allowed himself to be pushed back against the wall and the waiter kissed him sloppily, all tongue and teeth. This wasn't hot any more. The novelty had worn off. But he was here now. The least he could do was see his decisions through. Music thumped through the ceiling, faint whooping. The waiter ran his hands over his chest and around his waist and between his legs. Pressed against him, Fin could feel his sharp hip bones and dry, rough skin. Fin didn't particularly want the waiter touching his face so he pressed insistently on his shoulders to put some distance between them. It was difficult to stay aroused, even with the waiter on his knees. He screwed his eyes shut and tried to think of something nice, ended up thinking about Emilio. As the waiter moaned and deep-throated his cock, Fin felt like he wanted to cry but didn't. When it was over he did up his trousers and walked away before the waiter had even got to his feet.

He checked himself in the elevator mirror. No stains on his suit, cheeks flushed, hands clean. A small bite mark on his neck, but that could be anything.

None of it mattered in the end, because it was the look on his face that gave him away. Emilio watched him return as if he had been watching the door for a while, and when Fin smiled, Emilio didn't.

Maybe this wasn't a good enough reason to end something. Emilio wanted proper things, adult things. All Fin wanted was to not do this any more.

'You disappear for fifteen minutes and you seriously think I can't tell you've fucked somebody?'

It was hard to look at Emilio, so Fin blurred his gaze and directed it somewhere over his right shoulder. If he didn't look at Emilio, he wouldn't recall any of the reasons he had liked or maybe loved him.

He rubbed his eyes for effect, uninvested in his own performance. 'I'm drunk,' he mumbled. 'It just happened.'

Stevie Wonder was playing. 'I Believe'. Fin watched Mike slow-dancing with the woman he had just married, and thought his face seemed strangely blank. Then the light changed, and he was smiling again. Maybe he had been smiling the whole time.

'Everything I've done for you and you're gonna stand there and make excuses? You're messed up, you know that? You think just because you go around looking like that people will do whatever you want while you treat them like shit. Well, I've tried and tried with you, and I'm sick of it!'

A young woman wearing a teal dress got up from her table to head to the bar, cutting across the dance floor. Someone caught her arm and yelled at her to come dance with them, but she laughed and mimed getting a drink, only to take four more steps and stop.

'Have I wasted a year of my life? Please, explain! You owe me that much, don't you think?'

'It's been ten months, not a year.'

'*That's* all you have to say?'

Fin frowned, but not at Emilio. The girl was just standing there. People were dancing in her vicinity, moving around her, but she had stopped. An odd expression crossed her face, as if she'd remembered something which hadn't occurred to her in a while. She exhaled, and her shoulders dropped with relief, or surrender. Then she sat down in the middle of the floor.

He watched some drunk guy bend to pull her back up, clearly thinking it was some sort of joke.

He wondered how Mike had managed to make 'This is it!' sound so wretched.

Fin said, 'I think there's something wrong with that girl,' and snapped backwards with a flash of white as Emilio hit him. Trapdoor falling open with a *smack*.

As he regained his balance and tried in vain to open his left eye, he heard the men around him shouting; a woman let out a scream. He stepped backwards on to someone's foot and that someone caught him, asked, 'Are you all right?'

'Sorry, sorry . . .' Fin still couldn't see, holding his face.

The stranger gently eased his hand away. 'Maybe someone should take a look at it.'

'No, really, it's fine.' Fin's eyes watered as he tried to blink his vision clear.

'Are you sure?'

'Really, you don't have to do anything.' Hot with embarrassment and irritation, he flinched away from the stranger's concern, and Fin remembered thinking, *Who the fuck is this guy?* 'Trust me, I deserved it.'

'No, you didn't.'

'And what would you know about it?' Fin looked at him, pain throbbing across his face, and seeing the stranger properly made it so much worse. He had the kindest eyes Fin had ever seen.

'You didn't,' the stranger said again, quietly insistent.

Another outburst of screaming made the stranger look

away for a moment, and Fin took the opportunity to leave without looking back.

The front door opened at 07.38, and Fin didn't bother getting up. He had curled up at the foot of the bed to get some sleep at around four, only to wake a couple of hours later and resume position. He heard Andrew hang up his coat, take off his shoes and walk to the bedroom.

When he saw Fin sitting at the foot of the bed, he looked stricken. 'You waited up?'

His clothes were creased, like he had slept in them. Better than him *not* having slept in them, Fin supposed. He scanned Andrew's hands, his trousers, neck, then his face.

Andrew seemed to be barely breathing. 'I'm sorry I was out for longer than I said.'

'Is he okay?'

'I think he'll be okay.'

Fin nodded, back teeth clenched. There was something Andrew wanted to say, he could sense it.

Instead, Andrew took off his shirt and walked to the bathroom, and his voice was quieter than usual when he asked, 'Did you sleep at all?'

'Well, it's a Saturday.' Fin stood up and stretched, shoulders and lower back aching. 'I can always make some coffee.'

'I'm going to try and sleep for a few hours.' Andrew returned from the bathroom dabbing cream under his eyes. He continued to undress, neatly hanging his clothes and dropping his socks in the laundry bag. 'You can join me, if you want?'

Fin watched him get into bed, looked at everything he wanted looking back at him. Did he deserve it? Probably not. But people didn't get what they deserved, they got what they were willing to take.

He held Andrew's gaze, crawled down the bed and kissed him deeply. He tasted of peppermint mouthwash but his kiss was different. The way Andrew touched him was like the first time, when he was unsure, and his most recent memory was of touching someone else.

When Fin pulled back, Andrew's eyes were beseeching and swimming with shame in a way that made Fin want to put his hand over them, shut them.

Andrew said, 'I need to tell you something.'

'No!'

Fin turned away and scooted to the end of the bed. His mouth was dry and he needed water. By the time he got to the doorway he was almost running. If he got out of the room, maybe Andrew wouldn't say what he was going to say.

'Fin, wait –'

'Just because you feel like you need to say something, doesn't mean I want to hear it!'

'Nothing happened.'

It was a concession. An admission, of sorts. Saying *nothing happened* conceded that something could have. Fin had bullshitted people enough to recognize his own methods. If *nothing happened* had to be stated, then *nothing happened* was no longer assumed. He and Yun *were* something.

It was the kind of argument Andrew would respond to. But Fin looked him in the eyes and realized, either way, he had to believe him. He had to believe him, even if he didn't. Because yes, Andrew had left. But he had also come back.

Fin noticed his fists were clenched, and unclenched them. 'I'm just glad you're home.'

This was a language Andrew understood; the language of not talking about it. Fin saw him take the words on board, recognize what Fin needed him to do, and nod. The oil slick of guilt pervading his expression cleared, and he nodded with more conviction. 'I'm sorry.'

Those two words sounded more sincere. But Fin could accept them.

'Okay.'

Fin left the room, walked to the kitchen and took a bottle of water from the fridge. He ran the tap and dashed some water on his face. He told himself that if he could end up in an apartment like this, with a man like that, then he could do fucking anything. He could graduate, against all the odds. He could take this job in LA. Or he could find another one. He and Andrew could move out there, and however long he and Andrew had together it wouldn't be enough for Fin, who felt so greedy for happiness. But it would be enough for Andrew, who Fin knew would remind him that their one year or five years or ten or twenty was more happiness than most people ever get. He would grab ahold of everything he didn't deserve with both hands. He would achieve above and beyond his mother's wildest dreams for her son. He would be happy. He *would* be happy.

He took a long drink of water and returned to the bedroom. When Fin got into bed, Andrew turned to face him, and Fin pulled himself into his arms and let himself exhale with relief, or surrender.

KirstensKitchen @kirstenskitchen
From a wellness perspective, the spread of catatonia among the unhealthy should be a wakeup call for all of us to work harder to schedule MEDITATION and STILLNESS into our self-care routines

36.

Yun stared out of the train window and caught sight of the occasional house across the Hudson, embedded amongst the hills and trees. He thought he had a decent enough grasp on what it meant to be upstate, but hadn't realized quite how far away they were going to be from what he considered civilization. It got dark out here. The kind of dark you only experienced outside cities, where everyone was white and you didn't often encounter other Asians.

When he messaged Emory to tell her he was catching the Hudson train, he was surprised when she replied saying they would pick him up in Poughkeepsie. He was surprised that when he told her he loved her, she told him she loved him too. But then Emory was a good person, and he shouldn't have been surprised by any of that.

By a force of habit, going back to childhood, he asked himself what part of the movie this was. The movie of his life. It made for a romantic image: catching a train, leaving the city, heading towards someone who – he hoped, against all the fucking odds – still loved him. His musical instruments were already there. He should feel hope, some excitement for what came next. Better to be on a train than somewhere worse.

The main problem with his life-as-a-movie theory was that it wasn't easy to apply to other people who weren't the protagonists of his reality. What happened to everyone else?

To Rose, Michelle, to Lara, to Mike's parents, Rose's family, to so many other families. It wouldn't make much sense for movies to end in the way theirs had, slow and devoid of closure, throwing the people left behind into a messier and more confusing grief. Too cruel and too chaotic for narrative structure.

What Yun really wanted was to experience the flash-forward in the middle of a comedy drama, or the writing over a black screen at the end of a movie based on a true story. He wanted the part where an omniscient producer assured him that everything did in fact turn out okay, for everybody. And even if it didn't, well, at least you didn't have to experience it. You just had to read it.

He said as much to Andrew that night, or maybe it had been that morning. Some parts stood out clearer in his memory than others. No, it was definitely the morning. Before Andrew left and right after he told Yun he should go upstate. Both of them sitting on the couch, empty plates on the coffee table.

Yun said, 'I wish life came with, like, an inbuilt highlights reel.'

'A trailer?'

'No, a highlights reel, at the end. But you get to see it halfway through, for morale.'

'I'm not sure I'd like that. I think I'd lose motivation if I knew everything that was going to happen, if everything was predestined and inevitable.'

'I don't even care about *doing* any of it, I just wanna know. It wouldn't even matter if I didn't get to live it, as long as I knew everything turned out fine in the end.'

*

Yun didn't want to fall asleep, but he was so tired he had no choice in the matter.

'I did think of you,' Andrew said.

'Hm?'

'You said I never thought of you. I thought of you.'

Yun didn't open his eyes, but he smiled. Smiling was the last thing he remembered. When he woke up, the room was brighter and his head pounding. Andrew was asleep, still leaning against the headboard, and it hurt to swallow. Yun tried to sit up and the bed beneath him seemed to move.

He struggled up as quietly as he could and staggered to the bathroom to retch and heave until his stomach was empty. Then he turned on the shower. Before stepping under, he went to get some water and a painkiller and found Andrew awake, checking the time on his phone.

'Don't look at me,' Yun exclaimed, hiding his face. 'I feel like shit.'

Andrew looked uncharacteristically dishevelled. 'I'll go to the bodega and see if they have eggs.'

Yun stopped gulping water for a moment, embarrassed. 'You really don't have to. You didn't even have to stay over.'

Andrew ignored the second statement and said, 'They're twenty-four-hours, aren't they? I'll make you something to eat and then I'll go.'

Unable to argue, Yun went back to the bathroom and stripped out of his clothes, which stank of alcohol-sweat. He began counting down the seconds until the pain in his head, shoulder, chest and arm lessened, then melted away. With a lax smile of relief, he turned the water to cold and blasted away what remained of his hangover.

Shaking excess water out of his hair, he tied a towel

around his waist by leaning his hip strategically against the wall, and picked up his clothes by hooking them with his feet. He could smell food as he crossed to the bedroom and pulled on some boxers.

It was six thirty and he didn't have any messages from Emory. He should apologize. This was one of the few scenarios in which he was certain he should, and he should do it first. He *would* do it first, today, in a few hours, after he had time to think, about everything.

Andrew was stir-frying some tomato eggs, drawn from lack of sleep. He didn't look up when Yun walked in, taking the pan off the heat and turning the stove off. 'Do you feel any better?'

'Okay, I guess.' Less than an hour after the first pill of the day, Yun felt fantastic, but didn't want to admit to that. 'There's instant coffee if you want it.'

'Do you have any real coffee?'

'No, sorry. I know I've always disappointed you in that area.' Yun realized Andrew was looking at him. Really looking at him. He glanced down at his bare torso and ran a hand through his still-wet hair. 'What?'

'Do you remember much about what happened last night?'

Yun had to avert his eyes. It made him self-conscious, being looked at like this. The hairs on the backs of his arms stood up. 'I was in pretty bad shape but . . . I remember it, yeah.'

'I didn't realize it was like that for you, back then.'

'It was . . .' Yun wasn't sure what he was about to say. *It was fine? It was nothing?* There was nothing he could say now that would explain away what he'd said last night. He shook his head, at a loss, then realized leaving the sentence at 'It was' was simply an agreement.

Andrew walked around the counter and before Yun could come to terms with what was about to happen he was gathered close. His heart was in his throat, Andrew's face buried in his neck and one arm around his waist, avoiding his left arm and shoulder. They stood like that for so long they were breathing as one, like Andrew was somehow breathing for him.

Yun could feel the featherlight passage of a drop of water running down his temple, cut off as Andrew rested his forehead against it and inhaled deeply. He closed his eyes, leaning into it. The warm breath on his skin, the fingers stroking through his hair, his whole body murmuring with a slow, dulcet sensation.

He wanted something too large and all-encompassing to articulate, and even if he had known what he wanted, he didn't know how to ask. How do you ask someone if you can go back? Asking if you could both go back was too much to ask of anybody, certainly too much to ask of someone who was moving forward. He could ask for anything but more time, to go back and right that misstep.

Turning to look Andrew in the eyes, he found himself looking at the corner of his mouth instead.

'I'm sorry,' Yun said, for always being one step in front or one step behind.

Andrew touched the side of his face, fingertips lingering as if mapping the pieces of a precious object he had inadvertently broken beyond repair, then let him go with careful hands. He shut his eyes for a moment, confirming something, or forging a mental path ahead, and Yun knew what he was going to say a fraction of a second before he said it.

'I love Fin.'

'I know.'

'It doesn't mean I don't . . .'

'I know.'

Yun went to put on a shirt and they sat down to eat. Andrew drank a small cup of instant coffee and complained. Yun drank his and didn't think it was that bitter. Or maybe he just had a taste for bitter things. Andrew said something about Fin looking for jobs in LA, and Yun couldn't help laughing because the idea of Andrew moving there – to a city Yun was certain he'd hate – before him was preposterous. And the idea of him not coming back was too excruciating to touch.

'What about your job?' Yun asked.

'I hate my job.' Andrew laughed, as if the freedom of unthinking honesty still came as a surprise to him. 'I love the students, I hate my job.'

When Andrew's car was a few minutes away, Yun smiled suddenly.

'What?'

'The best song about the end of the world is "The End of the World" sung by Karen Carpenter,' he said, tears springing to his eyes, because it was so much easier to say than goodbye. 'I changed my mind.'

'Wow.' Andrew gave it some thought before his face lit up, and just as quickly became sad. 'You're right.'

He messaged Derrick to say goodbye, who joked that they needed an emergency signal in case Yun found himself in a *Get Out* situation. In that scenario, Derrick would apparently get a crew together to drive up and rescue him.

He scrolled through social media and followed the new viral prank sensation of people pretending to be catatonic to scare their partners, family, room-mates. The girl who started it had over eight million views, and was invited on someone's talk show.

They would be arriving in Poughkeepsie in twenty minutes.

For the first time in a long while, watching the river, Yun let himself flash-forward into a vision of the future. *A* future, anyway. The one which started with a viral video, a performance online – maybe something he composed one-handed, people *love* that shit – and turned into a collaboration, an album or hit single, then another. Or more likely writing for others, moving to LA, starting the day with coke, finishing with weed, fucking around with a closeted A-lister, getting photographed with the girlfriend he would probably end up marrying; a singer of mid-level fame. Money in the bank. Not an ostentatious amount but enough to impress his parents, enough to wear a rotation of shirts and hoodies that cost more than thirty dollars each. Enjoying everyone being nice to him in the brief period he was the cool new thing.

But he wouldn't enjoy it.

Yun knew he was a bad loser, but he was a worse winner. He felt contempt for the people who loved him now, but that was nothing compared to the contempt he would feel for those who loved him only *after* he became successful. Love as flaky and temporary as a scab. He would pick at it for fun, out of spite. Where had all that love been before, when he wouldn't have wanted it but it would have *meant* something? If it couldn't be applied retroactively, he didn't want it. He didn't want anything aside from an apology from the world, and for time to somehow inexplicably move backwards. Because nothing ever got better. Wasn't that the sum of all he had learned? Was that why this imagined future felt so fundamentally dishonest?

Fifteen minutes.

The river passed by, and Yun let himself flash-forward into another future. The one that started with this train journey and led to another surgery on his shoulder, because in this future he took Andrew's money. Another train journey nine months later, back to New York so Emory could start a research job with some news corporation. Yun picking up where he left off. He and Emory married within another year due to a baby – unplanned but not life-destroying – and divorced three or four years after that. Not amicable, but able to make it work. Never quite making it, but never losing in such a way as to constitute definitive failure. He and Derrick making a decent enough living for themselves and their kids by writing library music for Universal or Sony, the soundtrack to various prestige TV shows. Emory would travel. Emory would make it; one of those journalists or news anchors everyone knew and trusted. Her own podcast or talk show. Face-on-the-side-of-a-bus make it. He never doubted she would. His shoulder would hurt sometimes, especially during the winter, but never bad enough to warrant anything stronger than paracetamol. Jarah would end up married, and he would be genuinely happy for her. Not a better future – nothing so outlandish – but enough of the same, until the oceans boiled and all the bees were dead. Maybe enough of the same, for as long as he could, was the best he could hope for. Maybe Andrew would come back from LA or wherever he went. Andrew would come back and –

The idea cut through the quick-fire images like a record scratch. He didn't really believe Andrew would come back. And coming back wasn't *going* back. Neither of them could go back.

Ten minutes.

Watching the river go by, the occasional house hundreds of yards away, thinking about how dark it would get out here, and Yun didn't imagine another future so much as let it come to him, in Kevin's voice and then in Andrew's. The details were incidental, whatever did or did not happen when Andrew was at college, the exact sequence of events at Mike and Lara's wedding, the first glimpse of the catatonia, mass psychogenic death, Kevin's dispassionate crash course in painless deaths, hitting the car, deciding whether or not to nuke his relationship in the middle of a D&J grocery store, whether or not to take the train, leave Skillman, take Andrew's money or refuse it, or however long Emory chose to stick around after his arm had healed. Because this future was so narrow and inevitable as to render everything else irrelevant and, for that reason, it was the easiest to think about.

The future in which mass psychogenic death burned out in the way all things do. The future in which people lost the will and the hope, eventually, to even die on their own terms. The future in which all he worried about was the next painkiller, 5mg to 10mg. Maybe he could push another doctor up to 20mg. Or maybe he would buy 20mg from someone else, cut with something else. Thirty days at a rehab facility Andrew paid for. Everyone telling him to go

357

home, go back to San Diego, because he was running out of people to look out for him here, running out of people like Derrick, people like Emory, who said she couldn't – wouldn't – watch him die. Getting out of rehab, going back to New York and getting straight on to heroin. Dead at thirty-two in the back seat of someone else's car from an overdose, due to a slight overestimation of his post-rehab tolerance. Accidental, or maybe not. Andrew answering the call. What a tragedy, *they* would all say. So much potential, burned out, in the way all things do.

Yun blinked and he was back on the train, in the present. He watched the river go by, took a look around the carriage. A woman reached into her bag of snacks to give her daughter a sandwich. An older couple in front, one of them falling asleep. A man in his fifties across the aisle looking at his phone.

Five minutes.

Yun curled his fingers around the handle of his case, which felt heavier than it had before. He should stand up and wait in the aisle. He would probably see Emory waiting on the platform when the train pulled in. Maybe Esther or their father would help him with his case. Maybe he would grow to like it here. He could adjust. Maybe. But he should stand up and wait in the aisle. The train was about to arrive, and all he had to do was stand up. All he had to do was stand up. All he had to do was stand up. All he had to do was –

Acknowledgements

The first iteration of this book was commissioned by the genius Katy Loftus at Viking, who has been such a champion of my work and who I missed working with on this a lot. Hermione Thompson also offered editorial notes before the book landed finally with Harriet Bourton, who showed a remarkable amount of faith in my ideas for how to edit this work, and always listened to me. I knew from the first moment I spoke to you that you fully understood this book and loved its characters as much as I did. And thank you for the rare perfect title!

I'm lucky to have some pretty damn smart and awesome friends, who read this book at various stages of its long development. Simon Underwood, who read and loved it when it was a screenplay! Aniqah Choudhri, who has read more of my work than most people. Carrie Darmanin, who dubbed it 'the most Millennial novel ever'. And Alan Greenspan, who has always been so wildly supportive at every stage of my career.

Lydia Fried and Vikki Moynes at Viking went out of their way to send such kind words and encouragement about this book at rewrite stage, and I'm so very grateful for that. Also to my copy editor, Karen Whitlock, who provided the final polish, wrestled a few wayward commas from my grasping, furious hands, and whose enthusiasm for this book and *The Last* was so touching.

Delphino Huang and Al K. Teng carried out two of the three sensitivity reads the manuscript went through. They're great readers and even greater people. Dani Moran carried out the third, and I'd like to offer my heartfelt thanks to all three of them for their valuable insights and editorial input on this project.

During the research process, Cathy Park Hong's *Minor Feelings*, Catherine Cho's *Inferno: A Memoir of Motherhood and Madness*, Ocean Vuong's *On Earth We're Briefly Gorgeous*, and *Korean Memories and Psycho-Historical Fragmentation* edited by Mikyoung Kim, really stuck with me. As did some stories from *Passions of the Cut Sleeve: The Male Homosexual Tradition in China* by Bret Hinsch. In addition, *Human Acts* by Han Kang is maybe the best and most powerful novel I have ever read, and I'd also like to thank Mò Xiāng Tóng Xiù, whose unparalleled storytelling set me upon the long and extremely fun path of learning Mandarin Chinese.

Furthermore, I'm very aware of the privilege of being able to publish a novel where half of the main cast are Asian, given that – being white – I didn't have to worry about being told the book was *too* Asian as a result, or too 'culturally niche', or enduring any of the many excuses I've heard given to authors of colour as to why an agent won't represent, or an editor won't publish, their book centring characters who look like them and reflect their own experiences.

There are so many anonymous writers online I'd like to thank by name but can't. The staggering amount of talent, creativity and dedication to the craft shared online within fanfic communities has levelled up my writing like nothing and no one else. Most importantly, these writers have allowed me to keep enjoying it. I don't know a lot of your real names but I'm so grateful to and in awe of you. Do not let any snobbish writer (pro or otherwise) tell you shit.

Writing can sometimes feel isolating. Publishing even more so. I'd like to thank the amazing Sara Collins for being there these past few years, making me feel less alone in this cool, weird, often infuriating job.

I wrote the vast majority of this book from Christmas 2020 to March 2021, during which time I was living alone during lockdown and had almost zero contact with anybody. My brilliant therapist, Helen Thomas, was an absolute godsend.

My career would not look anything like the way it does now without the insane work ethic and enormous brain of Marilia Savvides, my agent and friend. Thank you for putting up with all the phone calls, the out-of-hours messages, the *angst*, the complaining . . . Thank you for always understanding where I'm coming from. Several weeks before I started writing this novel I told you I was going to quit publishing. I'm sure I will dramatically announce I'm quitting publishing again in the future, probably just before starting or finishing another book.

I also want to thank everyone who read, enjoyed and/or has messaged me about how much they loved my last novel, *The Last*. I would stare at all of you lovingly (maybe a bit creepily) across a crowded room if I could!

The first person to read and edit absolutely everything ' write is my mum, Marianne. I love you so much! You are huge part of the reason my first drafts are so good.

Lastly, I can't even think about starting work withou' right song. The playlist for every book, every chapter, scene, is different. *Are You Happy Now* was sound' mainly by: Eric Nam, Fountains of Wayne, Adam Schlesinger, Nine Inch Nails, Wolf Alice, The Weeknd, Nujabes, Kendrick Lamar, Talib Kweli, Key, Taemin, Jonghyun, Mew, Stevie Wonder, Paul Mauriat, David Bowie, Nick Cave, New Order, Morcheeba, Woodkid, Stray Kids and Taylor Swift.